TV dramedy you can't stop watching: both serious about family and lighthearted, both packed with details but not choking on them. . . . *We're All in This Together* is about the traces we leave behind that do not evaporate, about the expansiveness of familial love and its capacity to absorb even this." — *Globe and Mail*

"[*We're All in This Together*] will satisfy all types of readers. It is fast-paced and constantly surprising, shockingly real and, at turns, both suspenseful and humorous, all delightful tools for an author to have. . . . A hilariously real look into the messiness and depths of modern families and estranged relationships. This is a chaotic family full of characters worth getting to know. . . . *We're All in This Together* won't disentangle you from its grasp until the very last page." — *Atlantic Books Today*

"Amy Jones makes me laugh. Her captivating book, the entire byzantine history of a modern family distilled into one feverish weekend, will do the same for you. A multi-voiced choir of crazy birds all singing their own tune, *We're All in This Together* makes real music." — Marina Endicott, author of *Close to Hugh*

"The complex and messy relationships that constitute family have been at the heart of literary comedy and tragedy for as long as there has been comedy and tragedy – and families. Amy Jones brings both together beautifully in *We're All In This Together*. . . . The story is so entertaining that the poignant universal truths frequently dropped by Jones don't interrupt the fast-paced turn of events but, rather, illuminate them." — *Toronto Star*

"*We're All in This Together* is a complicated layering of time shifts and perspectives, as each character takes their turn revealing their inner emotional lives and personal history." — *Metro News*

WE'RE
ALL
IN
THIS
TOGETHER

AMY JONES

McClelland & Stewart

McClelland and Stewart and colophon are registered trademarks
of McClelland & Stewart, a division of Random House of Canada Limited,
a Penguin Random House Company

Library and Archives Canada Cataloguing in Publication data
is available on request

ISBN 978-0-7710-5065-7
EBook ISBN 978-0-7710-5066-4

Cover design: Kelly Hill
Cover images: © Dorling Kindersley / Getty Images
Cast of characters (pancakes): © VectorPainter / Shutterstock.com
Typeset in Berling by M&S, Toronto
Printed and bound in the USA

This is a work of fiction. References to real people, events, establishments,
organizations, and locales are intended only to provide a sense of authenticity,
and are used fictitiously. All other characters, and all incidents and dialogue,
are drawn from the author's imagination and are not to be construed as real.

McClelland & Stewart,
a division of Penguin Random House Canada Limited,
a Penguin Random House Company
www.penguinrandomhouse.ca

1 2 3 4 5   23 22 21 20 19

For my sister, Erin Jones.
I'm sorry I told all the neighbourhood kids
you were left on our doorstep by aliens.

CHARACTER LEGEND

FINN

KATRIINA

SHAWN

WALTER

LONDON

TANYA

NICKI

KATE

ADAM

ANASTASIA

FRIDAY

His eyes remind Finn of cola – deep, caramel brown, fizz-ing with bubbles that burst at the surface. He has Prince Charles's ears and a mole on the left side of his jaw, but he is tall and lanky, the type of guy who gets a lot of "Play any basketball?" and hates it because he never played basketball, just hockey, and never as well as he wanted to. Finn knows he's married before he even crosses the bar to talk to her, all arms and legs in a suit, shimmy-ing between the sweaty after-workers in their four-beer eupho-ria leaning back precariously in their wooden chairs. Something about the way he walks, it's clear he has a back-up plan: he can go home to someone else if he really has to. Not that it matters to Finn – she just needs someone to help her make up for lost time. She has until nine the next morning, when her plane takes her home to Thunder Bay, to transform her life into something she's not acutely ashamed of.

Finn is with some co-workers from the marketing department she barely knows, four women who invite the whole company out for drinks every Friday, never thinking anyone outside of their clique is going to take them up on it. But Finn knew it was the only invitation she was going to get, and she couldn't just sit at home all night freaking out about her family and the goddamn Conqueror of Kakabeka. The marketing women are all day-to-night with their blazers slipped off to reveal sleeveless silk blouses, with fresh lipstick and powdered noses, their hair unpinned and falling around their jutting collarbones as they sip their martinis. Finn drinks her third double rum and Coke in her jeans and T-shirt, trying to remember what it was like to not work from home, to have to talk to colleagues in person and make a good impression. When she was still working at the office she had been intimidated by these marketing women and their sharp tongues and high cheekbones, their expensive shoes, their ability to hold their liquor. She tried to be like them, to exude effortless, sexy professionalism, to be brave and charming and confident. It didn't work, of course. She was still just Finn, only in nicer clothes.

She has explained to the marketing women that she has to make an emergency trip home, and when she tells them where "home" is, they vow to get her nice and wasted so she can have something to remember fondly when she's stuck in the middle of nowhere. Just from the pitying way they soften their eyes, Finn knows they are all Toronto born and bred, that they can't even conceive of a place unreachable by public transit.

"Seriously, Fiona," says one of the women, leaning across the table. It's not until she touches Finn's arm that Finn realizes she is talking to her. "Are you going to be okay up there?" Finn thinks the woman's name might be Bianca, but the others just call her B.

"It's northern Ontario, not North Korea," one of the other women says.

"Shut up, Carrie," B says. "It might as well be North Korea. Don't they have weapons of mass destruction hidden somewhere in North Bay?"

"It's actually Thunder Bay," Finn says. "Completely different bay." They all stare at her blankly. To them, "up north" means "cottage country," and anything beyond that is like another planet.

"Well, here's something that will cheer you up," Carrie says, pulling out her phone. "Have you seen that Conqueror of Kakabeka video?"

Finn feels her rum and Coke rising up in her esophagus. She swallows it down and excuses herself to go up to the bar – slipping away from the table unnoticed as the marketing women all crowd around Carrie's phone, their eyes wide with the delicious anticipation of watching a catastrophe unfold – and wedges herself onto a barstool. *Breathe*, she tells herself. *Just breathe*. And that's when he comes over, this walking distraction in a suit. She smiles at him, and he smiles back.

"Can I buy you a drink?" he asks.

"You could," she says, her hand snaking along the bar towards his arm. "Or we could just go back to my place and drink for free."

She has no idea where that comes from, but it works – it's so easy, in fact, that she can't believe she hasn't done it before. They take a cab from the bar to her house and he pays as Finn stumbles out into the humid summer night, over-tipping the driver, grinning at him with some kind of misguided sense of camaraderie, all *boys will be boys* with undertones of *please don't tell*, like the cab driver gives a fuck what they're doing.

He doesn't ask her name, but when they get to her place he stops to scrutinize her bookshelf while she searches her bathroom for a condom, which suddenly seems so intrusive, as if everything he needs to know about her is right there in front of him, catalogued and arranged in alphabetical order. As if with the right interpretive tools, her books could be parsed to reveal the complete inner workings of her psyche. As if her collection of dog-eared Agatha Christie paperbacks says it all: *Spinster. Loner. Nerd.*

She pulls him away from the bookcase and they tumble from room to room with the lights out, bumping into furniture and hurling themselves into the bedroom like they're crossing a finish

3

line. When his phone rings, he shuts it off without even checking the caller ID. Shoves it back in his pocket and moves in to kiss Finn's neck, but not before she catches a glimpse of his background image, a black lab with a Frisbee in his mouth, eyeing the camera warily. At least it's not a baby, some blond-haired cherub staring at her accusingly from the screen, maybe a mother's face hovering somewhere above. Thinking about this imaginary woman, this imaginary child, Finn seethes with resentment for how willing he is to throw all of that away for a sexual experience that was going to be, let's be honest, barely memorable for either of them.

"What's wrong?" he asks, pulling back suddenly, and Finn realizes she is clenching every muscle in her body. "I'm sorry, do you not . . ."

"It's fine," she says, forcing herself to relax, to make the required noises and facial expressions.

In bed he's like a teenaged boy, awkward and desperate, pawing at her hooks and clasps until everything pops open just by sheer force of will, finished before Finn has even started. And it's as if everything she needs to know about him is right there, as if the way he bites down on her clavicle says it all. His wife, once a long-legged sixteen-year-old, now slack-waisted and baby-weary, was his first, possibly his only; he has never cheated before because he's never been presented with the opportunity. Finn made things effortless for him, and now a part of this unremarkable man will always be hers. Unremarkable Man, like some kind of lame superhero, with the power to make you forget him the instant he walks out the door.

Unremarkable Man falls asleep immediately, and Finn gets up, puts on a pair of shorts, and sits on the front stoop with a cigarette and a glass of Malbec. She checks her phone: 5 a.m. Her flight home is in four hours. Funny, how she still considers Thunder Bay "home" after all these years away. *It's just a word*, she tells herself, *it doesn't mean anything*. But she knows that's not true. She loves words too much to believe it.

On her street, people are getting up to walk the dog, take the kids to swimming practice, head to cardio boot camp. The sky is still black, pierced with only a few of the brightest, pluckiest stars. And even though this is one of the things Finn usually loves about living in the suburbs, tonight it's like those few stars are laughing, winking their luminous and condescending plasma-filled eyes at her.

She clutches her legs tightly to her chest, tipping back the wine from the glass wedged between her knees. She doesn't light the cigarette. *Fuck you, stars*, she thinks. *Fuck you for thinking you're the only ones who can harness the power of gravity to hold yourself together. Fuck you for thinking you're so much better than me. Why don't you get off your hundreds-of-light-years-away asses and come down here and say it to my face. Why don't you come down here and watch me nucleosynthesize when I go supernova. Why don't you come down here and watch me fucking explode.*

The first call had come at ten that morning, while Finn was sitting outside with her coffee on the back steps of her townhouse, watching Max the golden retriever run around in the yard.

"Ms. Parker?" a husky female voice asked. "I'm glad I caught you at home."

Finn sighed. One of the perils of working from home is that you're *always* at home. "Who is this?" she asked.

"My name is Cassandra Coelho. I'm a reporter with Thunder Bay News. I was wondering if I could ask you some questions about your mother."

Finn felt something like an electric shock spark in her brain. "My mother? Why?"

There was the sound of paper rustling. "You *are* Serafina Parker, right? From Thunder Bay?" Cassandra Coelho paused. "Your mother is Katherine Parker? The Conqueror of Kakabeka?"

"My . . . The *what*?"

"How is she doing? Is there any word on her condition? We'd love to talk to her when she comes out of the coma."

Panic crashed over Finn as she tried to process what she was hearing. Her mother, in a coma. This much Finn could understand, the words lining up with their proper meaning, an entire library of reference points tumbling out of her mental archive. *Coma*, noun: A state of deep unconsciousness that lasts for an indefinite period, from the Greek *kōma*, meaning "deep sleep." The rest, she had no idea. She hadn't been home to Thunder Bay in over three years, hadn't spoken to her mother in probably six months, with the exception of a few brief emails, which meant months and months of blanks she couldn't fill in. It had been working for her. As long as she filled her days with the present, then the past didn't exist – she could pretend she just sprang fully formed from the earth, or just willed herself into being all on her own. But now it was cracking open, this entire potential world of things Finn didn't know. On the other side of the yard, Max chased his tail, and Finn watched him, mesmerized, as he turned around and around, her own brain spinning along with him.

"Ms. Parker?"

"No comment," Finn mumbled and hung up. There were choices to make now, courses of action to decide on – it was almost as though she could see them all, playing out in front of her like movies overlapping on a screen. She picked the only one she could handle.

Her brother, Shawn, answered on the seventh ring, out of breath and annoyed.

"What the hell is going on?" she asked.

"Oh. Finn." Shawn said her name as though he'd just remembered her existence. When was the last time she'd talked to him? Two weeks ago? Eight? "Can I call you back? It's not a good time."

Finn made a fist and jammed it into her thigh to keep from screaming. "Not a good time? I just found out my mother is in a coma from a fucking *reporter*."

"I was going to call you."

"Of course you were," said Finn. "I'm sure I was at the very top of your list of priorities."

Shawn sighed. "I just got to the hospital. I have to find someone to cover for me at the restaurant. And I still have to figure out who's going to pick up the kids." Shawn's boys were named Tommy and Petey. That way, Shawn always said, when they were grown-ups they could be Thomas and Peter. And then when they were old men, they could be Tom and Pete. Their names could be modified to fit any stage of life. Finn imagines Shawn likes this because Shawn was just Shawn, you couldn't even make a nickname out of it except for maybe Shawny, which sounded less like a person and more like a town or a piece of farm equipment.

Shawn's wife's name was Katriina. No one ever called her anything but Katriina.

"First you need to tell me what's going on," Finn said. She started pacing the yard, the too-long grass prickling her bare feet. "The reporter said something about Kakabeka Falls?"

"Yeah." In the background, she could hear a tinny voice droning over a loudspeaker, an unintelligible din that Shawn practically had to yell over. "She went over."

"She . . . went over?"

"The falls, Finn. She went over the fucking falls."

"Oh my god. When?" asked Finn, hoping to hell it wasn't two days ago, two weeks ago, two *months* ago.

"This morning."

The droning stopped. In the resulting quiet, Finn could hear her own heart firing off in her chest. "She got caught in the current?" she asked hopefully. But somewhere inside her, she knew what the answer was.

"No." Finn heard the sound of a door closing. "Kate went over the falls on purpose," Shawn said, his voice low.

And there it was. "How do you know?"

There was a long pause. "She was in a barrel," Shawn said. "One of Hamish's," he added, as if it made any difference whose barrel it was.

Finn sat back down on the step. She had a sudden, sharp memory of her mother, years ago, standing in her kitchen on Victor Street, talking about something she had seen on television. Annie Edson Taylor, that was it, a sixty-three-year-old woman who was the first person to go over Niagara Falls and survive. Finn remembered Kate sighing, gazing out the window at a far-off place in history that seemed so much prettier from a distance, saying, "I don't know. Doesn't it just seem like there's nothing left to be first at these days?"

"Finn?" said Shawn. "Are you still there?"

How would a normal person react to this news? What would someone else's daughter say? Finn took a sip of coffee and swallowed it before she realized it had gone cold. On the other side of the yard, Max was having a stand-off with a squirrel in a pine tree. She couldn't see the squirrel but she could hear it chattering away, taunting him. "Well, is she going to be okay?" Finn asked finally.

"No, she's not going to *be okay*, Finn. She's in a coma." Shawn paused. "You need to come back to Thunder Bay. You need to come home."

Finn closed her eyes. "I don't think I can."

"Why?"

"You know why."

Shawn sighed. "Come on, Finn, it's been three years. Grow up."

She wished she was on a cell phone and not the cordless, so she could pretend that the call had been dropped. Shawn still talked to her as if she were a teenager, even though he was only four years older. He wasn't even her real brother. He was just some street kid who hopped trains and sold drugs and lived in a tent in the woods behind the house where she grew up – until the day he stopped the family car from crushing Kate after she forgot to put on the emergency brake and it started rolling down the driveway towards her. After that, he started sleeping in their basement. "We could use a man around the house while your father's away," Kate had said to Finn and her twin sister, Nicki, winking at the scrawny kid with a forehead full of pimples and the ratty beginnings of a moustache, as though he could actually be mistaken for a man. "You know, someone to look after us girls." Her mother's idea of irony, Finn supposed. None of them had ever needed looking after. Not then.

"You need to look after us girls," Finn said under her breath.

"What?" Shawn said.

"Nothing." Years later, she found out that the only reason Shawn had been there to save Kate is because he was trying to steal propane from their barbecue so he could do hot knives with a blowtorch. "How's Dad taking it?" she asked.

"Walter's out on the lake with a research team. He won't be back for a couple of days." Shawn paused again. "Nicki's pretty upset, though, in case you wanted to know."

"Right," said Finn, rolling her eyes. "She still in rehab for that toe?"

"Oh my god, get over yourself, Finnie."

In the background, Finn suddenly heard Katriina, clear as her own thoughts, say, "Who's Finnie?" Katriina was from Finland – which Finn used to think of as *her* land until she met Katriina and realized it would never be anything but Katriina's land, even though Katriina has lived in Canada for most of her life. Sometimes Finn suspects Katriina just pretends to not understand what people are saying in order to seem more exotic.

"Serafina," said Shawn, muffling the phone to keep Finn from hearing Katriina's response.

Finn tucked the phone between her ear and her shoulder and walked across the yard to clip the leash to Max's collar. The back-yard was fenced, but Max, while in a particularly focused state, had been known to fly right over it. "I can't just drop everything and come back," she said to the muffled phone. "I have stuff going on."

"What stuff?" Shawn asked.

"Stuff." She had no stuff, of course. She worked from home. She didn't have a boyfriend, a sex life, or even a social life. Max wasn't even her dog – she just took care of him for her neighbour, Dave, a divorced plumber with every-second-weekend kids and a Charger up on blocks in his backyard. She didn't even have any plants to water.

"You are coming home, Finn," Shawn said. She could hear the Shawn-ness in his voice. He might as well have called her "young lady." "Kate will wake up, and she will need you. She's not doing good, Finnie."

Finn shaded her eyes, searching the tree's branches for the squirrel. She finally spotted it, halfway up, nibbling delicately on a pine cone, which it promptly hurled in Max's general direction. "Superman does *good*," Finn said. It was one of her favourite expressions, which also might explain why she had no friends.

Max took off towards the squirrel like a sprinter at the starting gun, so fast that he ripped the leash from her hands. The phone tumbled to the ground. The squirrel tore farther up the tree and bounded lightly to a power line, and then was gone. When Finn picked up the phone again, Shawn was gone, too. Max trotted over to her, tongue hanging out, unfazed by his defeat, and licked her hand.

"Mom does *well*," Finn said to him. Although even Max knew it wasn't true.

She led Max into her townhouse instead of taking him back over to Dave's, and because she didn't know what else to do, she decided to try to get some work done. Finn was a technical writer, writing warning labels for small appliances made by a division of some multinational conglomerate called UniTech. They sent her the raw data and she translated them into plain English, something that people like her neighbour Dave or her sister, Nicki, would be able to understand. Well, Dave, anyway. The people at UniTech barely knew her name – most of the time they just referred to her as "the warning girl" – something she is sure her family has been calling her behind her back for years. But before she could even open a document, the phone rang again.

"Ms. Parker," a man said. "This is Lance Goodman from CityTV. Would you be interested in talking to someone on camera about the Conqueror of Kakabeka?" Finn hung up and then unplugged her phone. After three more voicemails were left on her cell, she turned that off, too.

She stared blankly at her computer screen for half an hour before realizing she was not going to get any work done. And so she opened her email. The only message in her inbox was from a co-worker whose emails were almost exclusively forwards of stupid jokes, "inspirational" quotes, chain letters, and panicked warnings about lottery scams and chloroform-wielding rapists in parking garages. Finn was about to delete the email when she noticed that the subject line, buried beside a long line of FW:FW:FW:, read "The Conqueror of Kakabeka: MUST WATCH!"

Oh god, she thought. *No. I can't.* And yet her finger travelled over the touchpad, scrolled past the lines of addresses to find a small blue link buried at the bottom. *Don't do this. You don't want to do this.* Slowly, she brought the cursor over the link and clicked.

She immediately recognized Kakabeka Falls, the "Niagara of the North" and one of northwestern Ontario's most recognizable landmarks. The video was shot from the first viewing platform, where she had stood countless times, posing for family photos with the water crashing over the precipice behind them. The video panned across the top of the falls, and in the background she could hear the oohs and aahs of tourists. Suddenly the camera jerked back towards the centre. "What's that?" a voice asked.

The camera zoomed in, and Finn could clearly see a barrel hurtling down the river towards the edge of the falls. She could also see a face peering over the rim. Her mother's face. Then the barrel dropped off the edge, crashed with a loud bang against something jutting out from the centre of the falls, flipped in midair, and disappeared into the frothy pool below.

"Holy shit," the voice said. "That was a lady in a motherfucking barrel!"

When Finn and Nicki were young, their mother used to tell them the story of Green Mantle, an Ojibwe princess who saved her father's tribe from certain destruction by leading their Sioux attackers down the Kaministiquia River and over Kakabeka Falls to their deaths, including her own. If you look closely enough, Kate would say, you can see the image of Green Mantle in the mist at the bottom of the falls. From then on, every time they visited the falls, the girls would climb down to the lowest platform built into the escarpment and stare hard into the mist, waiting for Green Mantle to appear. It never happened, but they waited anyway, until their father started complaining their parking pass was about to expire, or Kate's camera ran out of film. Why couldn't they see her? Finn wondered. What were they being punished for? Did they not believe hard enough? Were they not true-hearted enough? The failure of magic can be tough on little girls.

Now, watching her mother's own epic plunge, Finn couldn't help but think of Green Mantle. Thankfully Kate, unlike Green Mantle, did not die. According to the news reports, her barrel – white oak with a steel rim, which Finn knew was used by her brother-in-law, Hamish, to make bootleg whisky in the back shed – was carried on the Kaministiquia River to the precipice of the falls, then plunged forty catastrophic metres over the edge. The barrel hit the shale cliff face halfway down the falls with a sound like a gunshot, then flipped into the air before disappearing into the mist gathered in the gorge, carved twenty thousand years

12

ago into the Precambrian Shield by meltwater from the last glacial maximum. The barrel stayed submerged for another twenty metres before bobbing to the surface of the Kam and beaching itself on the western bank.

The rescue team called the coroner. Radio stations cut into Rush and Nickelback to report the death of a woman at Kakabeka Falls. No one was making a joke of it yet, but they would – it's natural selection, they said, modern-day Darwinism, where the stupid will fail to survive. But in the end it was Kate who had the last laugh – Kate with her two broken ribs, a fractured pelvis, two chipped front teeth, a ripped-off pinky nail, and a severe concussion. The barrel, the reports said, was actually what saved her life – hitting the rock face directly on one of the steel rings, which kept it from shattering, then trapping her in an air bubble when it flipped over, which saved her from drowning. No one could figure out how she didn't get pulled down into the whirlpool. A one-in-a-million chance. Survival of the blind-luckiest. The giant pain in Darwin's ass, smiling meekly on the homepage of the local news site, waving a trembling hand to the camera from the back of an ambulance before slipping into a coma on her way to the hospital.

"I'm not going home," Finn said to Max, who just stared at her. "I'm not."

Max spun around once and thumped down on the floor with a sigh, resting his chin on his paws.

She knew Max was right. If she didn't go home now, she would never be able to go home again.

The stars are still out when Finn goes back inside and pours herself another glass of wine. She can hear Unremarkable Man in the bathroom, coughing – probably throwing up. She hopes that he will just leave, maybe sneak out the back door so she doesn't ever have to talk to him again. Against her better judgment, she turns

13

on the television, and as if she were the punchline of some great cosmic joke, the screen resolves into a photo of her mother. Finn immediately recognizes it as one taken at Shawn and Katriina's wedding, Kate's eyes focused on something beyond the camera, a dreamy expression on her face, her lips painted fuchsia, her grey curls pinned back with a huge white flower. At first Finn thinks she must be imagining it, too much wine and not enough sleep, a preoccupied subconscious. *How did they get that picture?*

Then Unremarkable Man is behind her, wiping at his mouth and saying, "Ohmygod, have you seen that video? That lady in the barrel?" and she knows that it is real. Of course he has seen it; everyone has seen it – 450,000 YouTube views in one day. Jokes in all the late-night monologues, links posted on Facebook walls, an amusing story to end the local evening news. Over and over again, endless video loops of the initial plunge, the loud bounce, the flip into the air. Drop, bang, flip. It's funny now – she lived, so everyone can laugh about it. And now everyone knows who she is.

"Yes, I've seen it," Finn says, shrugging his hand off her shoulder.

"Wait," he says, leaning forward and squinting towards the television. "Is that . . . *you?*"

Finn goes cold. There she is – it's clearly her, no getting around it. The round face and red-apple cheeks, the wide lips, the deep-set eyes, grey like an angry ocean, the strawberry-blond (although uncharacteristically over-styled and over-highlighted) hair: it's Finn, giving an on-air interview. Except that it's not Finn. It's Nicki, a parallel-universe, white-trash, reality-TV version of Finn, with her spray-on tan rubbing off on the edge of her white tube top, giant pink sunglasses pushed back on her head. It has been three years since Finn has seen Nicki, but she looks exactly like Finn expects her to. Even through the wobbly television image, she can tell that Nicki has aged in the very same ways she has, a thought she finds supremely disturbing, as if she can't even grow older on her own without Nicki being seven and a half minutes behind her. Finn can't hear what Nicki's saying, but she can tell she's upset, one hand moving spastically through the air as if she's trying to shoo away a fly.

"Whoa, you have a twin," says Unremarkable Man. And even though Finn knows he doesn't mean it literally – it's just one of those things people say when they wear the same pair of shoes or do their hair the same way, as if they had any idea what being a twin really meant – as soon as he says it, she can feel her lips start to prickle, her throat close over. It's as if hearing the word *twin* is enough to send her into anaphylactic shock, as if her body is actually physically allergic to the thought of having to share its nuclear DNA with another living organism just because its progenitor cells decided to fucking split during a blastocyst collapse.

If this were a movie, she would offer to pay Unremarkable Man to go home to Thunder Bay with her and pretend to be her fiancé, and then somewhere along the way, they would really fall in love. But this is not a movie, thank god. She slams her wine glass down on the coffee table. "Get out," she says. Unremarkable Man just stands there, blinking at her, so she stomps into the bedroom, grabs his shoes and his belt and his wallet and throws them at him, and then closes the bedroom door.

She stares at the doorknob, daring him to come in, but after a few minutes she hears the front door open and close. She lets out a deep breath. Then she climbs onto the bed with her laptop and wraps herself in the sweaty sheets, searching through news sites until she finds it: footage of Nicki standing in front of the hospital, screaming at the camera like she's on crack, giving the television station's censor a heart attack. "Why the bleep are you still bleeping here? She's just a bleeping crazy old lady who did a stupid, bleeped-up thing and you guys are talking about it like it's the biggest bleeping news story since . . . since bleeping ever, and if you think I'm going to just stand here and cry for your bleeping cameras like some kind of bleeping baby, then you're bleeping crazier than she is. Now get the bleep away from me before I call the bleeping cops."

Finn stares at the screen until Nicki's face fades away. *Welcome home, Finn!*

She closes her laptop and lies back on the bed, staring at the ceiling. She can still smell Unremarkable Man's ridiculous frat-boy cologne hanging in the air. It will probably still be there when she gets back from Thunder Bay, just like the bed will be unmade, like her dirty dishes, she suddenly remembers, will still be piled in her sink. *If* she gets back. The stuff she has going on is not what's keeping her here, in this nondescript suburb, in her nondescript townhouse with its plain white walls and straight-from-the-showroom furniture – 9-piece living room, 5-piece bedroom, without any personality or history, just the way she wanted it. No, the stuff she has going on is keeping her away.

Finn is good at writing warnings because she is good at anticipating the ridiculously stupid things people will do. This toaster? People will stick knives in it. This popcorn popper? They'll leave the lid off. This slow cooker? Well, sure, why wouldn't they put the electric base in the dishwasher? They'll try to blow-dry their hair in the bathtub, they'll think it's totally fine to take the protective grate off the front of that oscillating fan. Finn is good at warnings because, when it comes to basic common sense, she expects the absolute least of people. And she expects the least of people because of growing up with bleeping Nicki.

The last time Finn saw anyone in her family was just after Nicki and Hamish's wedding, which in itself was some kind of strange, unexplained scientific phenomenon, like the Kuiper Cliff or tetraneutrons. For one thing, they had only known each other for six weeks.

Nicki had been driving down Broadway in her beat-up Civic, talking on her cell phone and trying to apply a coat of lip gloss, when she ran a cyclist right off the road. Finn had been in the passenger seat, praying she would die a swift and merciful death.

"Watch where you're fucking going!" Nicki shouted through the window as she drove away, while Finn watched the cyclist in the rear-view mirror as he scrambled around in his ridiculous neon spandex picking up his belongings, now thoroughly strewn across someone's front yard.

Later, drunk at Scuttlebutts after a night of tequila shooters with some of her ugly friends from hairdressing school, Nicki made out on the dance floor with a gorgeous twenty-year-old kid with a Scottish accent and a bad case of road rash who she vaguely understood was spending part of his gap year cycling across Canada. Finn, roped into being DD once again, watched the whole thing unfold from their corner table, where she was nursing a rum and Coke and wondering, not for the first time, why all the guys liked Nicki so much. *I have a master's degree*, Finn thought. *I've been to Japan, for fuck's sake.*

"Did you get in a fight or something?" she heard Nicki ask the kid, legs wrapped around his waist, her fingers running along his scuffed-up jaw while the lights flashed and R. Kelly played in the background, some random girl puking on the dance floor behind them.

"Nah, some clatty bint with her head up her arse tried to drive me off the road on me bike."

Nicki just stared at him. "I have no idea what you just said, but it sounded adorable."

It wasn't until the next morning, when Finn picked them up from the hotel in Nicki's car and Hamish recognized the Civic – the Minnie Mouse figurine hanging from the rear-view mirror, the dented bumper – that he put it all together. But by then it was too late. He had already proposed to Nicki in what Finn can only assume was a complete drunken stupor, although Nicki had sworn up and down on the phone that they were "basically sober" and just "retardedly in love."

Finn doesn't know if Hamish knew then that Nicki was ten years older than him, or that she had four children with three different fathers, but she's quite certain that on some level he must have known that his marrying Nicki was actually one of the twelve prophecies of Nostradamus predicting the end of the world. Still, ever true to his word, six weeks later young Hamish stood up in his kilt and ghillies on the wooden landing beneath the Visitors Centre at Fort William Historical Park in front of almost 150 people and vowed to love Finn's twin sister until the heavens rained down fire and the streets flowed with the boiling blood of innocents and the earth opened up and swallowed all of mankind – or at least that's what it sounded like to Finn.

Although Finn was sure an annulment was imminent before sunrise, Nicki and Hamish seemed maddeningly happy. They had a family dinner the next night, and the newly married couple sat at the table with their hands on each other's thighs, making out between courses while the kids all made barfing noises. Later, they gathered round the computer and looked at pictures from their pre-wedding trip to Winnipeg, Nicki sitting on Hamish's lap. "Clearly I stopped at the right place," Hamish said in this heart-breakingly optimistic little voice, showing them photos of trees and rocks and trees and rocks and then that flat, endless prairie as soon as you cross the border into Manitoba, before moving on to photos from the wedding, their father in a suit that he hadn't worn since the sixties, their mother with flowers in her hair, Nicki and Hamish watching the sunset over the Kam from the back deck.

"It's beautiful," Kate said, her eyes not on the pictures but on the chocolate curls of her new son-in-law.

"God's country," Hamish said, his fingers tracing a pattern on the inside of Nicki's arm.

God's country. Finn didn't have the heart to tell him about the Rocky Mountains, Saskatchewan sunsets, the Pacific Ocean. Better to let him believe the lie he had been telling himself about where he had ended up, the great city of Thunder Bay. Let him believe that the Sleeping Giant is magic, that the basin of Lake Superior is lined with fucking gold, and that everything west of here is shite. Let him believe he had found the most beautiful woman to grace the annals of history, that Scuttlebutts was some kind of enchanted fairy-tale castle, and he had become the luckiest man in all seven kingdoms the moment that Nicki had put her pink-lipsticked mouth on his ear on that grimy dance floor and told him she loved this song so much and oh my god did he want to go buy her a Jäger Bomb because she could really use, like, a jolt of something, you know.

It was better that way. It was none of her business. It was better to let it go.

Except she got drunk, and she couldn't just let it go. So after dinner she took her new brother-in-law out onto the back deck and by the light of a gorgeous harvest moon reflecting off the river that seemed frustratingly determined to disprove her point, she told him that he had, in fact, picked the exact worst place in the entire country to stop.

"There are trees in Vancouver you can drive your car through," she vaguely remembers telling him. "It's green there all year round, and they have beaches, and sushi, and the best weed." She was obsessed, suddenly, with Vancouver, even though she had never been there herself. She just wanted him to understand that there was something else out there, something so much better than this.

"It cannae be green all year," he said, not meeting her eyes.

"And the beaches are right in the city, and they go on for miles," she said. "You'd have to see it yourself to believe it."

Was she not supposed to love her sister? To watch out for her best interests? To try to protect her from heartbreak, from sorrow, from all the terrible things the world has in store for her, instead of leading those same terrible things straight to her doorstep? Was she not the responsible one, the one with the head on her shoulders? Was she not the goddamned Warning Girl? Well, fuck it. Fuck all those things. After a bottle and a half of wine, Finn wasn't sure Nicki deserved her protection. She certainly didn't deserve Hamish. No, Nicki didn't deserve anything except a helping of the same abject goddamn *misery* she had caused Finn when she slept with Dallas.

"Go," Finn whispered to Hamish. "Be free." She leaned in to give him a kiss on the forehead, a chaste, fairy-godmother blessing – but he moved his head and the kiss landed on his lips. His eyes merged into one big eye in the middle of his forehead, frightened and confused. Neither of them moved for a moment, until he pulled away and Finn staggered forward, sloshing some red wine out of her glass and onto her shirt.

"Whoops," she said, swallowing hard, all of a sudden overwhelmed by how disturbingly not sorry she was.

And Hamish, the little prick, he just backed away, looking at her like she was crazy, and while Finn went to the kitchen to try to get the wine stain out, Hamish went to the living room to report to Nicki everything she had said and done. And then in a flash of light and heat there was Nicki coming at her with the fireplace poker, which, based on the searing burn she managed to leave on Finn's neck, she had clearly been in the middle of using. Finn still remembers the feeling of her skin sizzling beneath the iron before Hamish and Shawn managed to pull Nicki off her, screaming and spitting, her face purple with rage.

Finn sank to the floor, her hand on her neck. "She's trying to kill me! You guys saw that, right? She's actually trying to murder me!"

"Fuck you, you stupid bitch!" Nicki yelled, articulate as always, and then she kicked her leg out and jammed her big toe against the kitchen table, howled in pain and fell back against Hamish as though she had just been punched in the face, and promptly passed out in his arms.

"Nicki, love, say something!" said Hamish.

Pain shot up Finn's neck as she moved to a chair to sit down. She could see everyone now crowded in the doorway, her mother and father, Katriina, all the kids. No one said anything. Shawn and Hamish lowered Nicki to the floor.

A long silence followed. "What did you do, Finn?" Kate asked finally.

"What did *I* do?" Finn stared at her mother in disbelief. "What did *I* do? She fucking *branded me*!"

Katriina's hands went over Petey's ears. Nicki let out a moan.

"But *why*, Finn?" Kate asked. "Why would she do that?"

"I don't know!"

Hamish stood up, wiping his hands on his jeans. "She tried to kiss me," he said. "Now stop standing there like a shower of eejits and help me get my wife to the hospital!"

Great, thought Finn, rubbing her neck. *He fits right in.*

Then Nicki miraculously came to, opening her eyes and rolling her head back and forth on the floor. "You just can't fucking stand to see me happy, can you?" she said. Her head lolled to one side as she glowered at Finn – angry, yes, but also a little bit smug.

"Why do *you* get to be happy?" Finn asked. She held Nicki's gaze for a few seconds until Nicki broke away, grabbing her toe and moaning again.

Later, after Nicki was rushed off to the emergency room, leaving Finn at Victor Street to Google "how to treat a burn" on her laptop, Kate came into the sunroom, where Finn had retreated for the night, too drunk to drive back to her apartment. The sunroom was, as usual, hot and stuffy, and through the open blinds Finn could still see that stupid harvest moon, taunting her with its breathtaking fucking magnificence.

"Hamish called," Kate said. "Your sister's toe is broken, but the doctor said there's nothing they can really do about it. She just has to let it heal on its own."

"Will it leave a scar?" Finn asked, without looking up. "You know, like the giant one I'm going to have on the side of my neck from this burn?"

"No, honey, it won't," Kate said, her voice small and sad. "But maybe what happened with your brother-in-law, maybe that will leave a scar."

"Yeah, I'm sure," Finn said. She waited for Kate to leave, but she just stood there, running her hand along the doorframe.

"Things . . . they've been hard for Nicki, you know," Kate said.

"Oh, I know," said Finn. "You've told me a million times." *What you've never told me is that you know how hard things have been for me.* That, and a thousand other things that Finn needed to hear – things she knew her mother would never say to her. And still, Finn raised her eyes expectantly, willing her mother to say something, *anything*, to acknowledge the pain she was in.

Instead, Kate sighed, turned around, and walked away, and Finn felt her insides coil with frustration. She opened a new window on her laptop and Googled "Apartments Toronto." The next morning, before anyone else was awake, she got up, drove back to her apartment, threw some clothes in a bag, and, without a word to anyone, she left. She just left.

Yes. She expects the absolute least of people. Including herself.

Finn stares out the window the entire flight, too anxious to sleep. Which is why when they land in Thunder Bay and she emerges through the doors into the arrivals area, it takes her a few moments, blinking in the light of the terminal like an idiot, before she realizes what is going on. She's hungover and unshowered, all fuzzy-slippered teeth and tangled hair, yoga pants and a holey sweater – not at all how she imagined her triumphant return to the north. The prodigal daughter is not supposed to have split ends and coffee breath. Around her, people are hugging, shaking hands, laughing, smiling – one woman even gets flowers – but no one from the Parker family has bothered to show up.

Finn's bag is one of the last ones off the plane, sad and lonely on the carousel. She drags it through the airport, wheels locking and tangling with the revolving door, and then out onto the sidewalk into the furnace-heat of a northwestern Ontario summer. She is struck breathless. There it is, all of it: Mount McKay, the highway, the big sky, the stench of the paper mill. The men in camo jackets and the girls in pyjama pants, everyone driving trucks or Mustangs, blaring bad radio through open windows. The Native kids on their bikes, doing tricks in the parking lot, rubber skidding against pavement. The rumble of the trains scaring the deer off the tracks. The unrelenting wind blowing from the west. The constant pull of the lake to the east. The overwhelming vastness of the boreal forest, that feeling she had almost forgotten, as if you have been set down in the middle of nowhere, a floating city in an infinite wilderness. And Finn wants to cry because it's been three years, and nothing has changed and everything has changed. It's all still here, still the same. And even if she never left the airport parking lot, she could still tell people she experienced Thunder Bay and it would be true. It's all right in front of her.

All except her family, of course. Who the hell knows where *they* are.

TWO

E xactly two hours after her mother-in-law goes over Kakabeka Falls in a barrel, Katriina Parker has a miscarriage. She would never suggest the two incidents are related, but she also doesn't believe in coincidences. It had been an uneventful Friday morning, spent sitting at her desk updating the MLS listing for the Paulsson place and trying to figure out what she is going to make for supper that night and whether Shawn will be finished at the restaurant in time to pick Tommy up from tae kwon do or if she will have to end her open house early. And then the phone rings and Shawn is calling from the hospital and Kate is in a coma and no one can pick anyone up from anywhere. *Did Kate finish mending Petey's soccer uniform or will I have to do that too now?* Katriina wonders, before realizing what a horrible thought that is. She pulls back the elastic band she wears like a bracelet, snapping it against her wrist, the sting reverberating through her body, briefly quieting her anxiety.

"I just can't understand it," Shawn says on the phone, his voice shaky, defeated. "Did she ever say anything to you?"

Katriina suddenly has a memory of Kate standing in the kitchen at Victor Street three weeks earlier. She was washing dishes, her hands plunged in the sink, her grey curls pulled back from her face with a band that looked like it had been made out of an old athletic sock. "Did you know that Bobby Leach, one of the first men to go over Niagara Falls in a barrel, later died of gangrene contracted after he fractured his leg slipping on an orange peel?"

"Where did you learn that?" Katriina had asked, a dishtowel in her hand, her attention half focused on the boys in the front yard, making their way a little too high up in a tree.

Kate slopped water over a plate, soaking the sleeve of her hoodie, though she didn't appear to notice. "Any of us could die at any time," she said. "But how many of us could say we went over a waterfall in a barrel?"

Now, Katriina scratches her fingernails lightly across her forearm. "No, not that I can think of."

After she hangs up, she snaps the elastic against her wrist again. Why hadn't she said anything earlier? What if she had been able to stop this? "Be a better daughter-in-law," she whispers into the monitor of her laptop while staring at the reflection of her own lean, pale face layered over the only slightly Photoshopped picture of the Paulsson place. "Be a better daughter-in-law," she says again.

A few minutes later, she is getting ready to leave for the hospital when her stomach cramps. She runs to the bathroom, locks the door, and vomits in the sink. She doesn't even bother to check for the blood between her legs – she knows it is there. When she comes out of the washroom, Krista Shepherd is standing by the door with her arms crossed. Krista with her perfect highlights and throaty laugh and one-hundred-percent sales record, a vulture who waits for other agents to fail so that she can pick their bones clean.

"Feeling okay, Katriina?" Krista asks.

"Perfect," says Katriina, raising her hand to her mouth, hoping she hadn't missed cleaning any traces of vomit.

"Oh, good." Krista taps her bright red gel nails against the back of her iPhone. "Wouldn't want you to get sick with month-end coming up." Her teeth are so white they are actually glowing, ethereally, like ghost teeth.

Katriina feels like she might vomit again. As she leaves the office and walks out to her car, she pulls the band on her wrist. "Be a better liar," she whispers.

Katriina cancels her open house and arranges for her sister, Hanna, to pick Petey up from soccer and Tommy from tae kwon do. At the hospital, she stops in at the gift shop and buys a card and a potted plant. The front of the card says, "Hear you're under the weather" and has a picture of a bunny holding an umbrella. She signs it with a pen she borrows from the salesclerk. *Lots of love, Shawn, Katriina, Tommy, Petey.* The way she signs every card, as though people won't be able to tell that all the names have been written by one person.

She takes the back elevators to the eighth-floor trauma ward, as Shawn instructed, managing to avoid the throng of reporters gathered at the hospital's entrance. When the doors open, she sees Shawn standing by the nurses' station, talking on his cell phone. He looks up as she walks down the hall towards him and raises a finger, telling her to wait. "Oh my god, get over yourself, Vinnie."

"Who's Vinnie?" Katriina asks, putting her hand on his back. She assumes it's someone at Kahvila, the restaurant that Shawn manages for her father, maybe a new waiter or busboy. But Shawn just stares at her like she's crazy, and she realizes too late that he's actually said "Finnie."

"Serafina," he says, pressing the phone against his chest.

"Oh," says Katriina, dropping her hand from Shawn's back. "How nice that you called her." It has been months since Shawn has talked to Finn, as far as Katriina knows. But it makes sense that he would call her to tell her about her mother. He is a good brother, he wants her to know, Katriina assures herself. Even if Finn doesn't actually care.

"*She* called *me*," Shawn says. He puts the phone back to his ear. "What stuff?"

Katriina moves down the hall to wait out the conversation, staring at the fire escape route map on the wall next to the stairwell. It's not that she doesn't like Finn. It's just that whenever Shawn wants to take Katriina down a peg, he brings up his sister. Not on purpose, of course. But if Katriina is ever apprehensive about trying something new, there is always the story about how Finn moved to a new city where she didn't know anyone on her own; if Katriina worries about what the neighbours will think of their overgrown hedge, there is that time Finn told her neighbour to go fuck himself because she caught him looking in her window while she was changing. In Shawn's mind, Finn is the brave one, the one who does what she wants, who stands up for herself – unlike Katriina, so submissive, so appeasing, so bland. He would never say these things to her, of course, but she knows he thinks them.

"Babe," Shawn says when he hangs up the phone. "Thank god you're here." He kisses her on the forehead. It's a distracted kiss, something he does by rote. Then he sees the plant in her hand. "What is that?"

"A ficus, maybe?" says Katriina. "I just thought it would be nice. For Kate's room."

Shawn sighs deeply, the way he does when he wants to make it clear to everyone around him that he is carrying the weight of the world. "She's in a coma. I'm not sure she needs a houseplant. And what's this, a card?"

"Yes. I bought your mother a card. Because that's what people do when people they love are in the hospital. They buy cards to show they care."

"Okay, great," Shawn says and walks down the hall. Before Katriina follows him, she places the ficus plant on the counter of the nurses' station, tucked off to the side where she hopes it won't be in the way. They'll appreciate it more anyway. She doesn't know what she was thinking. Kate has never had much of a green thumb.

Outside Kate's room Katriina pauses, takes a deep breath, and positions her hand over her elastic. Aside from the births of her sons she has not spent any time in hospitals, and she is unsure what to expect – machines all over the place, things beeping and whirring, and people rushing around. But she is surprised to discover there is nothing of the sort. Kate is in the bed with a quilt pulled up to her chin, her head slightly turned to one side. A cosmetics bag on the side table tells Katriina that Nicki has, thankfully, already been by. Kate is hooked up to a heart monitor and an IV, but you could almost believe she is just having a nap if not for Shawn, who pats down his mother's hair and wipes a line of drool from the corner of her mouth so carefully that Katriina can hardly bear it.

She snaps the elastic once, lightly enough so that Shawn won't be able to hear it, and wonders at which point a good wife would tell her husband that she has miscarried for the third time in a row.

The first time Katriina had a miscarriage, she was shopping at Old Navy. She had been trying to pick out a new shirt for Shawn, unable to decide between the short-sleeve blue-and-green plaid or the short-sleeve blue-and-yellow plaid, when pain shot through her abdomen, as if her organs were being clamped into a vise. She put both shirts back on the rack and walked between the tables of graphic T-shirts and two-dollar flip-flops, bent slightly forward, muscles clenched, vision blurring as she made her way to the bathroom.

In the stall she sat down on the toilet and unclenched, the rush of blood and tissue coming as almost a relief. She pulled out her cell phone and texted Hanna. "How long do miscarriages last?" The store closed in four hours. Would anyone come in searching for her? She thought about the little blond fitting-room girl, Marcia or Marta or Marika, who had asked Katriina her name when she went in to try on a pair of jeans and written "Catrina" on the whiteboard on the door. Katriina wondered whether it was her job to check the bathroom at the end of the night, whether she was meeting her boyfriend after work – maybe she was kind of bored with the relationship, all he ever wanted to do was order pizza and play *Call of Duty* – and if, distracted by her thoughts, she would just flick off the bathroom light without paying much attention to the closed stall door, without noticing a pair of sneakers mashed up against the base of the toilet. Maybe Katriina could stay in the store all night, curl up in a pair of fleece pyjama bottoms, go to sleep in a pile of clearance hoodies. Maybe she wouldn't have to ever leave, maybe she would never have to tell Shawn about any of this.

"Will probably seem like forever," Hanna texted back a minute later. "Are you in the Old Navy bathroom?" No one knew Katriina like Hanna, in this case her pathological need in times of stress to buy vast amounts of cheap, poorly made clothing. She heard a flush in the next stall and with her head resting between her knees watched a pair of brown ballet flats walk out the door without visiting the sink.

Her phone beeped again. "Buy wine. Go home." Katriina balled up some tissue paper, stuck it in her crotch, and stood up. She tried not to look down, but of course she did, and was overwhelmed with a horrifying urge to scoop out the contents and take them home with her in her purse. But she was almost equally appalled by the thought of leaving it all there.

When she told Shawn about the miscarriage, that night after Tommy and Petey went to bed, he was so kind to her, such a perfect husband. He poured her a glass of wine, he brought her a heating pad, he rubbed her feet while telling her that it was fine, it was normal, these things happen all the time. It wasn't her fault. Just a minor setback. They would try again. They watched a late-night talk show together – Katriina can't remember which one – and Shawn kept glancing over at her during all the funny bits, to see if she was laughing, the way he used to back in high school when they first started dating. Making sure that they thought the same things were funny. Making sure she was having a good time.

Katriina's second miscarriage came six months later, a few hours after she had found out she was the number one sales representative at Blue Sky Real Estate in the Superior North Region for the first quarter of 2011. They were celebrating, everyone sitting in the backyard at her parents' place, Katriina and Shawn and Hanna and one of Hanna's boyfriends, the kids chasing a soccer ball. They hadn't yet told her parents that she was pregnant, and sitting there in a lawn chair with a virgin mai tai in her hand, she suddenly knew she wasn't pregnant anymore. She turned to Shawn, who was standing in front of the barbecue flipping hamburgers for the kids and searing steaks for the adults, a grimy white apron hanging loose over his wide chest.

"Hey, Shawn," she said, tipping forward in the chair, pressing her legs together as if she were trying to fuse them into one. He raised one eyebrow at her. The words "I need help" heavy and awkward in her mouth, a handful of marbles stuffed into her cheeks. "How are the steaks coming?" was all she could manage.

His eyebrow collapsed back down. "I told you, they have to be medium-well," he said. When she had been pregnant first with Tommy and then with Petey, Shawn had barely understood any of the risks – it was all fun, talking to her belly, playing with her suddenly massive breasts – but now it was as if he had turned into a walking medical dictionary. When Katriina had requested her steak rare, he just shook his head, as though she wasn't taking their future seriously enough. As if she wasn't doing her best.

Shawn has told Katriina about his past. She knows about the drugs, and the stealing, and the fighting. She knows about the trains, how he would hop on empty railway cars, chugging back and forth across the country, sleeping in the woods or breaking into homes along the tracks and trading the things he stole for food, sometimes staying in abandoned buildings in the city with other street kids. About his real family, Katriina knows next to nothing. She knows he lost his mother when he was very young, too young to remember her as anything more than a black eye and a hunched back on her hands and knees cleaning broken glass from the kitchen floor. She knows his father worked too much and showed his affection first with an open palm, later with a fist; that he remarried a woman half his age who did something to Shawn that he still won't tell her about. She knows he had been on the run for close to three years before coming to live with the Parkers.

She prefers to picture Shawn during his train-hopping days like a hobo in a cartoon, playing a harmonica in overalls and a floppy hat, a bright red bandana tied into a bindle and balanced on his shoulder. Once, when they had been dating for a few months, Katriina asked him if he had ever been scared of wild animals, and he just shook his head and turned away, and she realized that what he had seen on the street was far more terrifying than anything he could have encountered in the bush. His entire life had been fight or flight. Since then she had tried to keep him safe, keep the bad things away from him as much as she could. But telling him about the second miscarriage felt like opening the door to a new kind of animal, something that he couldn't fight or fly from, something that was impossible to understand because it made no sense – the person he loved breaking his heart over and over again, denying him the thing he wanted the most.

"It's fine, it's normal, these things happen all the time. It's not your fault," he had told her again, repeating those same words as he held her in their bed that night. But later, after he fell asleep, she wondered: wasn't it?

◆ ◆ ◆

Under ordinary circumstances, Katriina would have been the one to take charge – set up camp at Kate and Walter's house on Victor Street, bake casseroles, field calls from friends and family, do laundry, help Nicki keep all the kids under control. But today she just doesn't have the energy. Instead, when she leaves the hospital a few hours later, she stops in at the Paulsson place, pulling into the driveway and sitting in her car with the air conditioning blasting. Eventually she gets out, walks up the overgrown pathway, and lets herself inside.

The Paulsson place has been on the market for over a year, ever since that winter morning when Margaret Paulsson went into her twelve-year-old daughter Claudia's bedroom to wake her up for school and found her hanging from a leather belt attached to the ceiling fan. Had Katriina known this, she never would have signed on to sell the house. Thunder Bay was a small city, and the neighbourhood of Westfort was even smaller. Everyone knew what had happened to Claudia Paulsson. The house was unsellable.

Katriina has heard all the theories – Claudia had been cyberbullied, a buzzword people can recognize from all the afternoon talk shows, or there was some kind of abuse going on in the home. But Katriina has met Margaret Paulsson, a single mother and school librarian with a pixie cut and wire-framed glasses who is barely taller than Petey, and she just can't picture it. But people will surprise you.

As she walks down the hallway and into the kitchen, Katriina tries to imagine what it must have been like for Margaret Paulsson. She tries to replicate the pain, thinks about finding one of her own sons, her husband, her sister, dead in front of her. But it is just a facsimile of pain – it is a drawing, or a television version of a person with a broken heart.

Her phone rings in her pocket. "Where are you?" Hanna asks when she picks up, before she even has a chance to say anything. "Your kids are driving me bananas."

"I just had a couple of things to finish up at work," Katriina says. She runs her hands along the kitchen counter, feeling the smooth surface, wondering how many sandwiches had been made there, how much milk had been spilled. "I'll be there shortly."

"Tommy claims you promised they could order pizza."

"Tommy has a startling aversion to the truth." But pizza, she realizes, is the only thing she has energy for. She sees it coming: she will become one of those mothers who is just too tired for anything more than takeout and television. She will marshmallow out into stretch pants and bras from a box. Shawn will leave her for one of the young Finnish waitresses at Kahvila who will bear him seven more children, and Katriina will grow old alone surrounded by several yapping terriers and the crushing weight of her own inadequacies.

After she gets off the phone with Hanna, she sits cross-legged on the floor in the empty kitchen. The whole house smells of cleaning liquid, of plastic and bleach. There are none of the human smells of a lived-in house, no rotting food or garbage or dirty laundry, no air fresheners or soup on the stove or sweaty gym bags or kitty litter. There is no outside noise from open windows, no dust floating through the air. Every time she walks through the house, Katriina has the impression that the air has not moved since the last time she was there, that she is the only one to disrupt the house's stillness. Though she knows it's irrational, she senses that the house prefers this, that it clenches up whenever she walks in, bracing for the impending chaos of her presence, resentful and sulking until she leaves.

As she is sitting there, imagining morning breakfast conversations and midnight snacks, she hears it. A low moan, the sound an injured animal would make. Katriina goes to the window and peers out into the backyard, where she can see nothing but a breeze swaying through the trees. She flicks on the kitchen light and stands motionless in the doorway, leaning forward, as though

33

this will somehow help her hear more clearly. She hears the cry again, feral and anguished, coming from upstairs. Katriina tiptoes through the hallway, avoiding the spots on the floor that she knows to be creaky, hoping that she can be stealthy enough not to frighten whatever wild animal she is sure must be trapped up there. The loneliness of an unlived-in house, with no one to shelter – eventually, out of sheer need to fulfill its purpose, it will lower its defences and let in the wild things: squirrels in the rafters, mice behind the baseboards, birds roosting in the eaves.

Katriina follows the sound until she is at the threshold to Claudia's room. Standing there, she imagines Margaret Paulsson standing in that exact spot before the door opens. Katriina has become mildly obsessed with thinking about those seconds, and the ones after, about how easily a life can be split in two. Margaret Paulsson reaches for the door handle as a normal woman, a woman with a normal life. Then that door opens, maybe creaking on its hinges, a long, mellow sunbeam stretching out from the window across the floor, a shadow swinging through it like the pendulum of a clock. Katriina imagines the destruction of that normal life as more of an unravelling – pieces of the old Margaret Paulsson slowly crumbling away with every agonizing heartbeat between the moment she sees and the moment she understands. To an outsider it would seem quick, but in reality it would take a terrible, breathless eternity.

Katriina opens the door. It is not the first time she has been in this room, of course – she has led dozens of potential buyers through, pointing out the light in the room, the depth of the closet, all that space. The furniture has been removed, but there it is, the faint girl smell, of baby powder and something earthier, more bodily – blood and sweat. The room is perfectly square, with a street-facing window on the far wall set into an alcove with a built-in bench underneath it. Gauzy curtains dangle limply from a rod. The fan has been taken down, leaving a discoloured circle in the centre of the ceiling. Katriina shivers. It's as though the window has been left open and the wind has ripped through the room, although the curtains remain resolutely still.

"Hello?" she calls into the void.

The sound is coming from the closet, she is sure of it. She feels around in her purse for some kind of weapon, but she has nothing, not even a can of bear spray or a hunting knife, what kind of northern girl is she? She does have her keys, which she holds in her fist as she slowly stalks across the room, before yanking open the closet door and thrusting her keys into the space with one hand while holding the other over her eyes.

Nothing. There is nothing in there, of course. Her hands shake. *Stupid, stupid.* She leans back against the door, breathing heavily, and snaps the elastic hard against her wrist. When her breathing doesn't slow, she digs her fingernails into her opposite arm, pressing to the point of pain, then pressing past it, and as she scrapes her nails across her skin she can see the marks become freckled with blood. Her breathing immediately begins to even out. She tries again, in a fresh spot, and feels the panic begin to subside. She stands there, waiting for her heart rate to drop, for the world to return to normal again, and thinks about how it was just like her to be so undone by someone else's tragedy when she was standing in the middle of her own.

THREE

At any given point, Shawn Parker's life has only ever been about one singular thing. When he was younger, right up until the day he met Kate, it was basic survival. And then it was Kate, even though it took him some time to figure that out. And now, it is pancakes. Every day, pancakes. And not just any pancakes, but *Finnish* pancakes. And not just any Finnish pancakes, but world-famous Kahvila Finnish pancakes, the first stop for tourists and food bloggers and college students home on break, and the one thing, other than hockey players and high murder rates, that Thunder Bay is famous for. Yes, Shawn's entire life is flat, golden, paper-thin pancakes, stacked on a plate.

He supposes it's about Katriina and the boys, too, but somewhere along the line they got conflated with the pancakes.

Shawn knows everything there is to know about Finnish pancakes, and he's not even Finnish. "It's time," was what Nik Saarinen had said to Shawn that evening after closing twenty years ago, back when Shawn was only a line cook at Kahvila, just out of high school and with no plans for the future other than buying a case of beer for the weekend and having sex with Nik's oldest daughter. "It's important that you understand the history that has gone into this recipe," Nik added solemnly as he led Shawn into the kitchen and showed him his secret pancake recipe, the one he had brought with him from Finland when he and his wife, Lilja, were young and broke and full of dreams, with a three-year-old child and another on the way, and nothing more than a pancake recipe in their back pocket.

Shawn nodded, out of a desire to keep his job and his girlfriend, trying to pay attention as Nik talked about his great-great-grandmother and how hard it had been for her to find eggs. Looking back, Shawn thinks that what Nik *should* have told him was not that the recipe had a past but that it had a future. And its future was with Shawn till death do they part, forever and ever, amen.

Eggs, milk, salt, sugar, flour, butter. He's allowed to divulge that much of Nik's secret recipe. "Anything more and I'd have to kill you," he always jokes. He can't even eat them anymore. It's like tasting his own death.

Despite this, it is still in the Kahvila kitchen where he feels most like himself – in the zone and focused only on the incoming tickets, the mixing, the pouring, the flipping, the rhythm of it all, not thinking about anything except the next table, the next ticket. And so even though his assistant manager, Dawn, is covering the dinner shift for him, he drives to Kahvila after he leaves the hospital. He knows he should want to be with his family, and he will. He can't wait to see the boys, to pick them both up in his arms at once and turn them upside down and shake everything out of them, and he can't wait to crawl into bed next to his wife and sleep with her cool back against his chest. But first, he needs to get his head straight. He needs to make pancakes.

Even if Walter wasn't away on one of his week-long guiding trips and out of cell phone range, it still would have fallen to Shawn to take charge, Shawn to field the first calls from reporters, Shawn to tell the twins what happened, Shawn to spend the afternoon talking to doctors, asking the right questions, signing the forms. It was Shawn who had to do all this with terror weighing down in his gut like a bowling ball, from the horrible moment that morning when he was woken from a rare sleep-in by a phone call from a police officer – "Am I speaking with Shawn Parker? Son of Katherine Parker?" – and he had been sure, he was *sure* that Kate was dead.

"You need to look out for us girls," Kate had told him the day she met him, and he had. He *had*. At least, he wanted to believe that he had.

The dinner rush is already starting when Shawn gets to the restaurant at four. Kahvila closes early, and its customers like to eat early, although there are a couple of tables of Lakehead University students who Shawn is pretty sure are having their first hungover meal of the day. Behind the cash register, refilling the napkin dispensers, is Dawn, a fifty-two-year-old grandmother who has been working at Kahvila since before her first daughter was born, and whose husband has been on disability for even longer than that. She can eat more pancakes than anyone Shawn has ever seen, and can handily drink him under the table.

"Natalie called in sick," she says immediately.

"Again?"

Dawn finishes the last dispenser and spins it around on the counter, lining it up next to the others. "Artie said he saw her at Crocks last night drunk out of her skull."

Shawn sighs. "We have to fire her."

"Ha ha. *We?*"

There are a lot of things Shawn likes about the restaurant, despite what he says most days. He likes its location, at Bay and Algoma – an area sometimes known as Little Finland – near his favourite coffee shop and his favourite bar and two blocks away from his house. He likes that, after more than thirty-five years in business, the place runs like a well-oiled machine. He likes the customers, and how much they like the food. He knows Kahvila is a bit cheesy, but he has been working there for over twenty years, and in that time he has seen people who used to come in as kids now coming in with kids of their own. He likes his staff, for the most part, especially the lifers like Dawn. He does not, however, like firing people.

"Let's see when she's in again," Shawn says, coming around the counter and pulling out the clipboard holding the staff schedule. "Someone must need more hours on here."

"Jean-Marc's girlfriend is pregnant," Dawn offers, scooping the dispensers up in her arms. "He'll work any hours he can get."

"Okay, I'll take care of it."

"Oh, and you have a phone message." With her elbow, Dawn pushes a piece of paper towards him. "Someone named Cassandra Coelho?"

That fucking reporter. Shawn crumples up the paper, throws it into the trash. "Thanks," he says.

Dawn puts the dispensers back down with a crash. "God, I'm so sorry," she says, wiping her hands on her apron. "I'm an idiot. How's your mom?"

"Fine. And you're not an idiot." He doesn't want to talk about Kate, but it was stupid of him to expect that he could get away with not talking about her, especially with Dawn. Has she seen the video? he wonders. Has everyone at the restaurant seen it? "She's in a coma, actually. But the doctors say she could come out at any time."

"That's good," says Dawn. She studies him carefully. "Was it an accident, then?"

Shawn readjusts the papers on the clipboard, avoiding her gaze. "I don't know, Dawn. I didn't get to talk to her."

"Oh." When it becomes clear that he isn't going to say anything else, Dawn picks the napkin dispensers up again and carries them out into the dining room. Shawn knows what she was waiting to hear – the same thing that all the reporters want to know, the one thing that Shawn doesn't have an answer for.

It's not the who, what, when, or how that people care about. It's the *why*.

A few weeks earlier, Shawn was offered another job. He had gone out for drinks with his buddy Alex from high school, home from Ottawa for his niece's graduation. "You need to stop wasting your life in that tourist trap," Alex had said, after probably one Heineken too many, and then added, "Come work for me." At the time, Shawn laughed it off, but Alex's offer rattled around in his head for the next few days, until finally he realized he needed to talk to someone about it, to put it out there in the world, to see it reflected back in someone else's eyes. He needed someone to tell him he was crazy, that he had another kid on the way, a family to consider, a duty to Nik.

And so he went to talk to Kate. It was the first time he had been alone with her in what seemed like months, all their time together usually boxed in by Nicki and her kids, or Katriina and their kids, or some unholy mixture of the two. Is that why he hadn't noticed before the hollowness of her face, the strange fidgeting habit she had developed for a woman who had always been so collected, her vacant expression as she sat down at the kitchen table across from him? Had his everyday routine of work and kids and marriage and everything else taken up so much of his mind that he hadn't seen what was happening right in front of his face? Or *had* he noticed and chosen to ignore it? How could he have let this happen?

"My darling, I am so happy to see you," she said, reaching for his hand, and Shawn felt a renewed pang of guilt. Just a cup of coffee, that was all it would have taken. It would have been so easy to make the time.

He tried to smile. "I'm happy to see you, too, Mom," he said, hoping that she would understand how much he meant it. But her eyes never moved from the middle distance, and her hand flitted away from his as though she had forgotten it was there.

He supposes he had wanted it to be like the old days, when he used to sit at the kitchen table watching Kate while she made coffee for the two of them, slipping a small shot of whisky into their mugs even though he wasn't old enough to drink. Telling him all kinds of insane things, like he was the smartest, most amazing boy she had ever met and he could do anything he wanted if he put his mind to it. It was because of Kate that he had first asked out Katriina, who was a grade ahead of him in school and an honour roll student, captain of the girls' volleyball team, and head of the student council. She was beautiful but had never had a boyfriend, not only because she was self-possessed in a way that was utterly terrifying to most of the boys – including Shawn – but because she never expressed any interest in dating, rebuffing all offers of book-carrying, of lunches bought in the caf, of rides home from school. Still, after the pressure of living with "you have to look after us girls," it was exhilarating to imagine being with someone who could take care of herself, thank you very much.

"Why would she want to date me?" Shawn can remember whining.

"A better question to ask yourself," Kate replied, "would be why would *you* want to date *her*? You're the catch here, Shawny. Don't ever forget that." It was ridiculous, really, the amount of faith Kate had in him. It almost made him believe that he wasn't actually a dirtbag. Almost. In retrospect, that was probably what he had really wanted that day when he went to visit Kate: not someone who would tell him he was crazy, but someone who would tell him he wasn't.

This time, there was no coffee and whisky, just weak tea with milk. "I got offered another job," Shawn said, taking a sip of the greyish water.

"That's great!" said Kate, pushing her teacup around by the handle with her index finger. "At another restaurant?"

"No. It's a marketing position at a tech firm. Something completely different."

"Well," said Kate, the spinning growing faster. "That sounds exciting!"

Shawn took a deep breath. "The thing is, it's in Ottawa." He leaned back in his seat, bracing for her reaction.

"Oh." Kate was quiet, the only sound in the room the spinning teacup. "Oh dear," she said finally. "What's Ottawa? It sounds familiar."

"It's . . . a city?" Shawn said. "Ottawa?" Kate blinked. "Nicki and the girls went there last year to see One Direction."

"Oh, *Ottawa*," Kate said. "Of course, the city. How silly of me." The teacup suddenly tipped onto its side and the table flooded with liquid. Shawn jumped up and grabbed the roll of paper towels, while Kate just sat there, watching the tea drip to the floor.

Who could he talk to about this? Not Walter, certainly. And not Nicki, either – her default when it came to anything to do with Kate was complete and utter denial. He knew he *should* want to talk to Katriina, but no matter how that scenario played out in his head, it always ended in a fight. So that night, while Katriina was in the shower, Shawn called Finn.

"There's something going on with Kate," he said, keeping one eye on the bathroom door.

"There's always something going on with Mom," Finn said.

In the background, he could hear the click of a keyboard, Finn only half paying attention to him, as usual. *I'm the only one in the family who ever even calls you*, he screamed in his head. *The least you could do is get off your stupid laptop.*

Shawn closed his eyes and tried to picture Finn's house, sterile and sparse, piles of books everywhere and not much else. Was it weird that no one in the family had ever seen it? Was that their fault or Finn's? Nicki could hold a grudge forever, and Kate always seemed uninterested in Finn's life in Toronto, but even still, wasn't it strange that no one ever suggested visiting her? He had assumed that she wouldn't want them there anyway – she'd been so determined to leave everything in Thunder Bay behind, including her family. But what if he was wrong? What if she had just been waiting for someone to make the suggestion, to reach out to her across the distance and extend an olive branch? If anyone was going to do it, it should have been him. Another thing that got lost in the shuffle of work, kids, marriage.

"This is different," Shawn continued. "This is . . . She's not herself."

Finn sighed. "You need to spend less time worrying about Kate and more time worrying about your own family."

"Kate *is* my family, Finn. She didn't even know what Ottawa was."

"Lots of people don't really know where Ottawa is."

"No, Finn, she didn't know *what* it was. Like, I said, 'I got a job offer in Ottawa' and she said, 'What's an Ottawa?'"

The typing stopped. "You got a job offer in Ottawa?"

"No," said Shawn. *Shit.* He hadn't meant to say it. Or had he? "Well, yes. But that's not the point."

"What's the job?" Finn asked.

"It's nothing."

"It doesn't sound like nothing."

"I told you it's nothing."

"No, what's going on with Mom is *nothing*," Finn said, her voice growing faint. "Getting offered a job in Ottawa is *something*. But whatever. Those pancakes aren't going to flip themselves, I guess."

"A self-flipping pancake. That's something I need to invent." He paused, waiting for Finn to laugh. But she was already gone.

The next time he talked to Finn was when he told her Kate had gone over Kakabeka Falls in a barrel. And even still she had been reluctant to come home. Maybe rightly so – he is probably the only one who is going to be happy to see her. And even part of him wishes she had decided not to come. Not because he doesn't love her, or because he doesn't want to see her, or even because he is worried about dealing with the inevitable twin drama. Twin drama he can handle. But the truth is, Finn's life scares him – reminds him of something he thought he had given up, brings up a deep ache in his stomach, makes him restless in a way that he knows he does not have the luxury to be. Because Finn's life reflects his own fears of what a life outside Thunder Bay would mean. It would mean losing the Parkers. And that isn't something he can afford to lose.

Shawn hasn't told anyone else about the job offer. Not even Katriina. There's no reason to – he's not considering it, not for real. Kahvila wouldn't work without him, anyway. He's been there so long he's part of the recipe now: eggs, milk, salt, sugar, flour, butter, Shawn. But lately, when he's in the kitchen elbow-deep in batter, or sitting in his office at night after everyone else has gone, he looks around and he thinks, *Yes, it could work*. Even Finnish pancakes would go on without him.

Katriina or Hanna could have easily run Kahvila, but Nik is old school – Shawn remains the closest thing to a son he would ever have. And back then, Shawn didn't exactly have what one would refer to as prospects. For all of Kate's encouragement, he had missed too much school while he was on the rails. He was working maintenance for the city when Nik offered him a job on the line, as a favour to Katriina. At the time, it seemed to him the best thing he could ever hope for.

"You can do anything you want!" Kate had told him, but Shawn didn't know what he wanted. He only knew he wanted Katriina. It was only later – only now, really – that it even occurred to him he could want something more. If this were a movie, he would realize this and then whisk his family off to have great adventures in the city. But this is not a movie. In real life you just realize things and nothing changes.

In the kitchen he washes his hands and pulls on his apron, tells Jean-Marc he can go home if he wants. "We might have some more hours for you coming up, if you're interested," Shawn says, lifting the lid on the giant pot of *mojakka* and giving it a stir. The lack of tension in the room tells him that none of the kitchen staff have seen the video yet, thank god. "I hear you got a little one on the way," he adds, trying his best to act normal and be his jovial boss-self.

Jean-Marc gives Shawn that grin of the first-time expectant father – stoked, sheepish, and scared as hell. "Thanks, man," he says. "Things are getting a little tight."

"I hear you," says Shawn. Then: "We've got another one on the way, too." It just slips out before he can stop himself. *Stupid.* They haven't even told Katriina's parents yet.

"Hey, congrats!" Jean-Marc says. "Three kids, man. That's crazy."

"Yeah." Dawn shows up in the window with a ticket, and Shawn grabs it from her. Three orders of pancakes, one with bacon, two with sausage, and three orders of strawberries and whipped cream. "Just, uh, don't say anything to anyone, okay? We're trying to keep it on the down low."

"Of course, man, sure." Jean-Marc wipes his hands on his apron. "You sure you don't want me to stick around?"

"No, that's fine," says Shawn. He's already working on another batch of batter. Later, he knows he will have to go back to the hospital, face the reporters again, look at Kate's motionless body without breaking down. But for now, there is just eggs, milk, salt, sugar, flour, butter. Over and over, until the end of time.

FOUR

The morning that Kate takes the barrel over Kakabeka Falls, Walter wakes up and knows something is wrong. It had rained the previous evening, though the researchers he is guiding on Caribou Island – three men and a woman from Arizona State University who wear head-to-toe Gore-Tex and apparently don't mind sleeping in the rain – had happily zipped themselves into their high-tech tents for the night. But sick of the damp, Walter had dragged his soggy self out of the woods during the night and holed up in the cabin of the *Serafina* with a mug of hot chocolate and an Agatha Christie novel until he fell back asleep on one of the narrow benches. That's where he is when his eyes fly open at eight with a panicked start, overwhelmed by the need to go home.

Walter doesn't normally get feelings about things – that's Kate's department. But the dread sticks with him all that day, until finally he can no longer ignore the vague ache sitting low in his stomach. "I'm going into Nipigon to pick up some more fresh water and firewood," he tells the researchers, even though they have plenty of both. As he readies the boat for the trip, he tries to calm himself by running through the names and positions of the eighty-eight constellations, the way he used to do when he was a child. *Andromeda, Antlia, Apus, Aquarius*, making it all the way to Gemini before he starts to think about the twins – could something have happened to one of them, or to one of Nicki's children? – and then the house, one of the other boats, his truck, the dog. Anything to keep his mind occupied, to keep at bay this nagging worry that is likely nothing. Anything to chase away this feeling of helplessness, of being too far away.

Anything to keep from thinking about Kate.

Walter almost lost Kate on four separate occasions. There may have been other times, too, but Walter doesn't want to know about them. Loving Kate has been a nebulous thing, like trying to catch vapour in your hand. Even before the falls, before the grandkids, before Shawn, before Serafina and Veronica even, there were moments when he was quite sure Kate had never actually looked him directly in the eye. There are still moments, now, when Walter can't understand why she married him, why she finally decided to be with him, although sometimes it seems as if she is still trying to make up her mind.

Although he can't remember a time when he didn't love her, Walter has been almost losing Kate since the beginning of their lives. They grew up on adjoining farms in the Slate River Valley; her father kept cows and pigs, and his father grew potatoes and corn, and the two would often trade meat for vegetables when the summer turned into fall. Walter's memories of the farm are hazy – it was his older brother's birthright, and Walter had never thought there was much point in showing any interest. But even now he can still recall the sound of the wind rustling the cornstalks, the night's silence in the expansive land around him, the rhythmic pulse of the creek that ran between the Parker and Babiak farms underscoring the clear, melodic voice of Katie Babiak calling to him from the other side. The creek would freeze in winter, solid enough to walk over, and dip so low in the summer that you could easily skip across it. But in the spring, when the water was high, Walter was afraid to cross the creek, and he would stand on one side and wait for Kate, who was utterly fearless, to leap across at the narrowest point, her rain boots squelching into the mud on the bank as she landed.

"Waiting Walter," Kate called him, as in "I'm crossing the creek to be with my Waiting Walter." There were worse things she could have called him then, things that Walter called himself in his darkest moments. He supposes he is glad that she didn't, although who knows what she really thought behind those sparkling eyes and bright smile?

He and Kate would wait for the school bus together, although the schoolhouse was just down the road, and if the weather was nice they would walk. Sometimes on the way Kate would question him about a book they were meant to have read for class, or ask him to go over a history lesson that she should have studied the night before. It wasn't that Kate wasn't smart. "She doesn't apply herself" – that's what his mother used to say, as if she were a piece of adhesive tape that was meant to be stuck to some particular piece of homework, or maybe to the idea of work in general. Kate always thought she was being sneaky and subtle when she quizzed him, but in everything she did Kate was always about as subtle as a freight train.

"So when was the Battle of the Plains of Abraham again?" she asked him one morning, kicking a pine cone with the toe of her Mary Janes.

"September 13, 1759," Walter replied.

"And it was part of the . . . Seven Years' War?"

"Yes."

"And who were the generals again? I forget."

"Oh, you forget, do you?"

"Yes, I do! I forget."

"Well, you'd better start remembering. We have a test today."

"Maybe you could just . . . remind me?"

And of course Walter did. He always did. He would do anything Kate wanted because back then he believed that to deny Kate anything was to hurt her, and he couldn't stand to see her hurt. "Wolfe and Montcalm," he told her. "If you remember anything about the Battle of the Plains of Abraham, remember Wolfe and Montcalm."

"Montcalm. Montcaaaaalm. Hmm." She brought her hand up to her face, pushing back a piece of hair that had freed itself from her braid. "I'll remember that one because it's fun to say."

"So is Wolfe. Wooooolfe."

"Nice try."

"You'll remember. Wolfe. Like the animal. Arooooo!" He tilted his head back, howling to the sky. Kate skipped ahead, ignoring him.

Kate was right – she did forget Wolfe. But weeks later, when the snow had just started to fall and they had lugged out their winter boots, still dusty from sitting in cellars all summer, she remembered. Their grade seven class had planned a pre-Christmas trip to Chippewa Park, where they were going to go on a sleigh ride and tobogganing, and then throw maple syrup on the freshly fallen snow. Walter was surprised to discover that Kate did not share his excitement.

"Don't you want to see Lake Superior?" he asked as they left the schoolhouse, trailing behind the other kids in their class as they rushed towards the bus. Despite how close they lived to it, neither of them had ever been to the lake. Still, it loomed large in Walter's imagination, overwhelming him as he tried to picture that much water at once. It was like trying to picture the Milky Way, or the distance between Thunder Bay and Antarctica. Or, he supposed, the way he felt about Kate. He didn't have a frame of reference for it, or a way to make it manageable in his mind.

But Kate had never had a problem with the infinite. "It's just water," she said, climbing on to the bus. "And this trip is still school, only outside."

"But the outside part will make the school part fun."

"Or the school part will make the outside part boring." She slid into one of the last pair of seats available, right behind the bus driver. Walter sat down beside her. The outside of her right leg pressed against the outside of his left as she leaned into him, whispering so the driver wouldn't hear. "But maybe we can avoid some of the school part."

So when they got to Chippewa, while the rest of the class went off to identify rabbit tracks in the snow, Walter and Kate slipped away. As they made their way down to the shoreline, Walter watched the snowflakes melt on Kate's eyelashes under the brim of the red woollen hat that her mother had made to match her red woollen coat, although she hated wearing it because it made her ears itch. She was talking about Christmas, which was always the only thing on her mind from the first snowfall onward. That year, she was hoping for a bike, but was probably not going to get one, since the Babiak farm had lost three cows in the fall and her father needed some kind of expensive dental work. Still, she talked about careering down Candy Mountain and over a series of jumps. "Imagine," she said, turning around to walk backwards in front of him. "It would be like flying." Walter, who was only hoping for his father to not be drunk for Christmas, kept his head down as she talked, concentrating on the outline of the soles of his shoes biting into the snow cover.

When he raised his head to look at her again, suddenly all he saw was water: Lake Superior, rising up beyond the frozen crust built up on the edge of the sand, stretching towards the horizon, vast and bright with a delicate sheen of ice. Walter temporarily forgot how to breathe. For the rest of his life he would never forget the first time he saw the lake – with Kate standing in front of it in her red woollen hat, with the snow on her skin, the sparkle of the ice floes suspended around her head like a halo.

"What?" said Kate, turning away from him to skip off towards the shoreline, oblivious to the monumental significance of the moment.

"The lake," Walter managed to squeak.

"Yeah, it's a lot of water!"

Walter sat down on an overturned tree, trying to catch his breath. He gazed out across the lake towards the darkened silhouette of the Sleeping Giant against the grey sky. They had learned about the Sleeping Giant in school – how someone once thought the series of mesas and stills projecting out from the lake sixteen miles across the Thunder Bay harbour at the end of the Sibley Peninsula resembled a man lying on his back. Mr. Mulligan had told them that, according to Ojibwe legend, the man was actually the trickster spirit Nanabozho, who turned to stone in the lake when the secret location of the silver mine at Silver Islet was discovered by the white man. Walter had only ever seen pictures of the Sleeping Giant, and had been embarrassed to admit that he couldn't see the man that the rock was supposed to resemble. All he saw was, well, a rock. Now, he squinted towards the horizon and tried to unfocus his eyes, tried to make himself see what others saw. But it was still just a rock.

"I still can't see it," he said. "What's wrong with me?"

"The lake?" asked Kate.

"No, the Sleeping Giant."

Kate cocked her head, eyeing him curiously. "Do you need glasses? It's right there." She gestured out into the lake.

"No, silly," he said, kicking snow at her. "I mean, I can't see the man. It just looks like a rock."

"Oh, well." Kate sat next to him and turned his body to face the left side of the formation. "There's his head," she said, pointing. "See? And his neck. He has a little Adam's apple."

"Where?" asked Walter. He liked the feeling of Kate's hands on his shoulders. "That's just a lump."

"That's what an Adam's apple *is*, dummy." Kate poked at his neck through his scarf. "A little lump."

"Well, in that case, I guess *you're* an Adam's apple, too," Walter said. "My little lump."

Kate sighed and jumped to her feet. "I'm not the one who can't see the Giant's head," she said, running for the shoreline. At the edge of the ice she stopped, tracing her hand through the sky. "See? Right there!" Walter shook his head. Kate took a tentative step out on the ice, then another, and another. "Right there!" she said again, waving her arms emphatically.

"I see it," Walter said, anxiety fluttering through his stomach. "I see it, okay?"

"Liar," said Kate, sliding backwards across the ice. "Who's the lump now?"

Walter stood up, crossing to the shoreline. "You're crazy!" he yelled. "You'll fall through!"

She took another step backwards, away from him. Her body bisected the outline of the Giant, a bright red beacon in the middle of all that grey. She jumped up and down, once, twice, then shrugged as if she had just proven something. "Are you just going to stand there, my Waiting Walter?" she asked, reaching out her hand to him. "Or are you going to come out here with me?"

Walter put one foot on the edge of the ice, and then pulled it back. He could hear the laughter of his classmates far behind him, and he wished he and Kate were there with them, where they'd be safe and he wouldn't have to choose between being Waiting Walter and being out on the ice with Kate. "Come back," he called, "and I won't make fun of you for not knowing who fought in the Battle of the Plains of Abraham anymore."

"I *know* who fought in it. It was Montcalm!"

"Montcalm and who?" Walter called. "Come back here and I'll tell you!"

"I *know* it!" yelled Kate. She fixed her gaze on him. Walter could feel it all the way across the ice, generating a vibration that built up in his veins. Then she turned her back to him, facing the Giant, and jumped a third time, his heart leaping up and down with her. "It was Wooooooolfe!" she yelled at the Giant. "Arooooooo!" She howled out over the lake, the icy air vibrating with the church-bell ring of her voice. Walter laughed, shoved his hands in his pockets, threw his head back, and began howling along with her, his own voice mingling with hers. When he stopped howling and looked back down to the lake, Kate was gone.

Walter stared, his brain moving at an alarmingly sluggish pace. That tiny puddle of darkness couldn't *really* be a hole in the ice, it was too small for a body, *surely*. There had been no crack, no splash, no sound at all. Kate hadn't even let out a breath, a gasp. Walter would have heard it. He knew he would have.

She must be behind him, playing a prank, sneaking around him while his eyes were closed in his howl, setting up to scare him. She had to be there, but he couldn't make himself turn around. Because if she wasn't behind him, it meant she was still out there. And if that was true . . . *I just need a few seconds*, he thought. *I just need to figure out what to do.* And yet there he was, as immovable as the Giant, his body turning to rock.

A pair of red arms appeared through the hole, followed by a little red hat bobbing above the ice. Like a goddamned lump, Walter stood and watched his best friend claw her way out of the frozen lake, heave herself onto the ice, and inch her way on her belly towards land, her eyes dark, terrified. Then, as if he'd just been waiting for her to make up her mind to come join him, he reached out for her and pulled her onto the shore.

Walter doesn't know how he got Mr. Mulligan's attention. He doesn't remember everyone running to the shore, all their classmates shedding their own coats and hats to wrap around Kate, or the trip to the hospital, or going home afterward still not knowing if she would live or die. He doesn't recall the long bouts of pneumonia, the weeks that Kate was confined to her room; he doesn't even really remember her coming back to school, or what she was like after, the ways in which she had changed. He only knows what Kate has since told him about that time – how she had nightmares about the darkness she saw beneath the ice, how she couldn't sleep properly for months – and that he never saw her jump the creek again.

Walter's only memory is of Kate's face as she lay there on the beach, white and waxy and ethereal, and thinking that she was dead, that she had died beneath the ice and it was a ghost he had seen emerge from the lake. Kate was gone and it was his fault. Waiting Walter had finally waited too long.

On the boat ride into Nipigon, Walter finishes naming the constellations, ending with one of his favourites, Vulpecula – once Vulpecula et Anser, or "The Little Fox with the Goose," until astronomers separated them. He can remember Kate being sad about that when he described it to her. "But what happened to the goose?" she had asked. "How could he just disappear?"

"Well, there's a star in the new Vulpecula constellation called Anser. So he didn't disappear – it was more like he was consumed." Walter shook his head. "Poor goose. Eaten by his closest friend."

"Poor *fox*," Kate said. "He couldn't help it." She tilted her head back, looking up at the sky. "He was only doing what nature intended him to do."

When he gets to Sal's General Store, Walter browses through racks of fishing lures, debating whether to call home, trying to convince himself he is just being paranoid. At the other end of the store, a group of locals are gathered around the counter, watching the television perched on the shelf. "Hey, Walter, this shit is crazy, come check it out," Sal calls over to him. Walter makes his way across the store, slowly, his feet heavy in his workboots. There is part of him that knows what is about to happen, but he raises his eyes anyway, adjusting to the faintly snowy picture just in time to see it.

Drop, bang, flip. The barrel, and his heart.

Then, in spite of himself, he allows himself to think about Kate. He thinks about the past few years of their marriage, the lies they have told themselves, pretending that everything is all right. How when he comes home from his guiding trips now, there is a brief moment when her eyes flash with confusion, until she shakes her head and says, "Walter," answering a question that she understands she can't say out loud. How he is such a goddamned coward, running away instead of staying, instead of dealing with what is right there in front of him.

"Pretty crazy, eh?" says Sal. "You hadn't seen it before?"

Unable to speak, Walter merely shakes his head. But the truth is, he *has* seen it. He has been seeing it – or some version of it – his entire life.

FIVE

Finn sits in the back of a cab, watching the familiar sights fly by the window on the short ride from the airport to Victor Street – a tree missing here, a new house there, a bigger sign at the Tiki Hut, the street sign for Victor Street hanging at a forty-five-degree angle, a new mailbox at the end of the long driveway. The stand of red pines in the front yard, the blue Civic parked on the grass, next to her father's truck and her mother's Volvo and Katriina's SUV. Bruno, the Parkers' ancient, arthritic husky, sits up on two of his three legs and barks half-heartedly as the cab pulls up to the house.

She pays the driver and stands on the lawn for a few moments, scratching Bruno's head and staring at the front door, willing herself to climb up the steps and open it. If this were a movie, a montage of front-porch-related scenes would flash through her mind, with sentimental music playing in the background. Her first kiss, at fourteen, with Ben Stickney, that set off the sensor light and scared the crap out of both of them. That afternoon she spent playing cards and drinking beer on the steps with Shawn, when he told her he was getting married. Her father dressed as a scarecrow on Halloween to frighten the trick-or-treaters. Tying her niece

London's roller skates before carrying her over the gravel driveway to the paved road. But this is not a movie, and so Finn thinks only of that morning three years ago when she left, quietly closing the door behind her, not looking back.

If you ask Finn's father, he will tell you their house was the first one built along the Kaministiquia River back in the 1860s, when the land was opened for settlement, before the construction of the CPR and the Neebing rail yards, when the actual fort in Fort William was just beginning to fade into obsolescence. The house is set back nearly fifty metres from the road, and the land stretches another hundred metres back to the Kam – a generous property, even by semi-rural Vickers Heights standards. Her father's story is that the man he bought the house from—an Italian immigrant named Vittorio—was actually the one who built it. But Kate would respond, "We bought the house in 1973, Walter. Do you really think the man who pinched my bum while showing us the bathroom was 120 years old?"

Finn puts her hand on the doorknob, takes a deep breath, and turns it. The smell hits her immediately, that distinct Victor Street smell. Dryer sheets and roast chicken, Nicki used to call it, although Finn always thought it was more hair product and wet dog. She has to plough through piles of shoes to get the door open wide enough to let her suitcase through, which is nothing new – the hall closet had never been big enough, hats and mittens and skates and umbrellas forever spilling out into the foyer. Finn gives up, leaves her suitcase on top of the pile, and steps through the entryway into the kitchen. *Please don't let anyone be home.*

Nicki and Katriina are sitting at the wooden table with mugs of acrid-smelling coffee. *Figures*, thinks Finn. *The exact wrong combination of people.* Katriina is dressed in her real estate agent finest: a blouse and pencil skirt, her blond hair pulled back severely into a flawless ponytail. Nicki is flipping through a magazine, and she doesn't look up when Finn comes in.

"Oh, hi," says Nicki. "You made it."

Katriina glances at Nicki as if they are the ones who are sisters now, as if they are the ones who share the same thoughts.

"Yup," Finn says, slipping out of her flip-flops. Part of her wants to yell at Nicki for not meeting her at the airport, but a more rational part just wants to get out of there as quickly as possible.

Katriina pulls herself together and stands up. "Serafina," she says. "So good to see you." She gives Finn an awkward hug, arms outstretched, her body as far away from Finn's as it can possibly be. Finn's arms stay at her sides. She can feel her back muscles tensing under Katriina's bony fingers.

"You, too," says Finn. *Now get the hell off me.*

Katriina pulls away. "Excuse me," she says. "I've got to get the kids to Hanna's." And then she is gone, dismissing Finn like a mosquito that landed on her arm.

Nicki finally raises her head when Finn sits down at the table across from her, but her eyes remain unfocused, as though she's concentrating on something just past Finn's head. She has never liked looking at Finn. Finn imagines how surreal their tableau would seem to a stranger, some kind of horrifying before-and-after makeover shot from a terrible reality-TV show – Finn with her rat's-nest hair and last night's red wine staining the inside of her lips, Nicki with her platform wedges and Bumpit, her face spackled with makeup at eleven in the morning on a Saturday, wearing lipstick several shades lighter than her lip liner that makes Finn want to grab her and wipe it all off with the back of her hand.

The moment is broken by Nicki crossing her arms. As Finn watches her toss her head to the side, she knows exactly the impulse that caused it to move there and understands Nicki's movements so intrinsically that they might as well be fired off from her own synapses. She is chewing gum, some kind of strawberry-scented sugar bomb that they used to love as kids. A tiny hot-pink flap of it peeks out of the corner of her mouth as she chews. Finn's stomach heaves.

"How's Mom?" Finn asks.

"Why the fuck do you care?" Nicki shoots back. She blows a bubble, pops it.

WARNING: PROVOKING ANGRY TWIN MAY CAUSE BODILY HARM. "Because she's my mom and I love her," says Finn as evenly as possible. She's not going to let Nicki bait her, not this early. She pulls out her cell phone and scrolls through her old messages even though she has no new texts. Anything to avoid eye contact with Nicki.

Nicki plays with a piece of her over-processed hair, makes a little "pssht" noise with her lips. "That's debatable."

"I'm here, aren't I?"

"What do you want, a medal?" Pink bubble gum fumes waft from her mouth. "Finn Parker: World's Greatest Daughter."

Nicki Parker: World's Biggest Pain in the Ass. But Finn is trying to make an effort, so she keeps her mouth shut. When she turns off her phone and raises her head, Nicki has left the room, the scent of strawberries lingering in the air behind her.

After a minute, Finn gets up and begins to move through the house, which folds her into its body as though she never left. It's all so much smaller than she remembers, so familiar but unfamiliar, like rereading a beloved childhood book as an adult. The stairs creaking in all the same spots they used to, the railing wiggling at the fourth post as usual as she leans against it. Yellowing plants in the hallway, ugly oil paintings on the walls, framed school pictures gathering dust on every surface. All the things that are supposed to be there, a movie set for a Typical Canadian Family. It could be anyone's house, anyone's family living here. But it's not. It's hers.

In her parents' room, Finn finds her three nieces watching a documentary about sharks on the Discovery Channel. They don't hear her come in – the television is loud and London is worked up about something, her hands whipping through the air, her cherry heart of a mouth pouting between breaths, her Parker-grey eyes wide and earnest as she stares at the TV while her twin sisters sit face to face, painting each other's toenails.

"They estimate that, like, up to a hundred million sharks are killed by people every year, due to commercial and recreational fishing," London says. She pauses, pulling on a pink braid she has woven into her long black hair. "Compare that with the 4.3 humans that sharks kill every year. That's, like, twenty-five million times the killing, you know?"

"Uh-huh," say Milan and Vienna simultaneously, concentrating on their toes. The three of them seem so grown up it makes Finn ache with remorse. When she last saw them, three years ago, the twins were still playing with their identical American Girl dolls, and London was obsessed with the Disney Channel.

London, Vienna, Milan. And Ross. Nicki has never been to London, Vienna, or Milan, although she did go camping in Rossport in high school – drunken, hormone-fuelled weekends to which Finn was never invited. Nicki had been planning a trip to Europe when she finished high school, and kept a map on her bedroom wall with pins stuck in all the cities she wanted to visit. Then she found out she was pregnant, by either the Native kid who sold her a voltage adapter at Future Shop or the one who sold her smokes out at the reserve. She still hadn't made it off the continent a year and a half later when, on a twenty-first-birthday trip to Minneapolis with some of her old cheerleading friends, she met a Nigerian engineering student working as a waiter at the Tony Roma's in Mall of America whose name she couldn't remember past "there might have been an *M* in it." Nine months later, she had twin girls delivered by C-section while Finn sat at home studying for her literary theory final. The last time Finn was home Nicki still had that map on the wall, although Finn assumes the pins are now just potential future baby names.

Finn has always called her nieces by their first initials to avoid her own embarrassment: L, V, and M. They don't seem to mind – they call her Aunt F, as though her name were a curse word. Her nephew, Finn doesn't call anything at all, if she can help it. Most of the time she can't even bear to look at him.

"Did you know that some commercial shark fishermen will just, like, catch the shark, cut off their fins, and then totally just fucking throw away the rest of the body?"

"Nice language, L," Finn says.

London's eyes flick towards the doorway and then just as quickly back to the TV. "Hi, Aunt F," she says. Finn isn't exactly surprised by her dismissiveness – according to Shawn, London was pretty upset when Finn left. Still, she's surprised at how much it stings.

But Milan and Vienna both jump up to hug her, shouting, "Aunt F, Aunt F!" They're thirteen, just on the cusp of adolescence, and unlike London, who is sixteen and apparently knows everything, they still have their moments of being adorable. They are also clearly still inseparable, judging by their identical T-shirts and barrettes, their matching lopsided smiles, their stereo chatter – something that causes Finn tiny pangs of jealousy whenever she's around them. There was a time, believe it or not, when Nicki and Finn were like that – safe within their own twin world, not so much reading each other's mind as simply having the same thoughts.

"Hey, you little brats," says London, "you spilled nail polish on the duvet!" A blue sparkly stain spreads across the pink and white bedspread. She picks up the overturned bottle, pinching it delicately between two fingers. "This stuff is so gross," she says. "Do you know how many chemicals must be in that?"

"Like as many as in your hair dye?" Milan says.

"It's not *dye*, it's *henna*," says London. "It's *all natural*."

"It's ugly. And it stinks," says Milan.

"Yeah," says Vienna. "It really stinks, Aunt F. Like garbage."

London grabs a pink hoodie off the bed and begins to mop up the spilled nail polish.

"That's my hoodie!" Milan screeches. "You bitch!" She runs out of the room.

"Bitch!" Vienna echoes, ripping the hoodie out of London's hand and following after Milan.

London wipes a bit of nail polish off her hand onto the duvet and turns back to the television as though nothing has happened. "I was just telling the girls about these sharks? In Mexico? Where they keep them in tanks and put muzzles on them so that they can't bite anyone? And the people tease them and get them all worked up so they go into a frenzy and then they ride them like bulls? It's, like, *so horrible*. You probably don't even know anything about it."

"That's not a real thing, L," Finn says.

London juts her chin forward. "It is, Aunt F. I saw it on the internet."

"Not everything you see on the internet is real," Finn says, sitting down on the edge of the bed. "Or on TV, for that matter. Or in newspapers. Or . . ." London stares at her like she has a horn growing out of the middle of her forehead. "Never mind."

London flings herself back on the pillow in a huff. "You don't know everything, Aunt F."

Finn is not going to argue with that. "Who's that guy?" she asks instead, gesturing towards the television, where an attractive man in a wetsuit is talking to the camera from a boat.

"Adam Pelley," London murmurs. "He's a marine biologist who works at the Monterey aquarium. He rescues sharks and films documentaries about them to counteract the negative shark stereotypes perpetrated by the mainstream media."

"He's cute."

"He's a genius," says London. "Not that it's anything you would appreciate." The look in her eyes is pure disdain, and while Finn would like to believe that it's all just passed down from Nicki, deep down she knows that she brought this on herself. All those nights that London spent at Finn's apartment when she needed to get away from her mom and her sisters, the late-night trips to Safeway for gummi bears, the secrets whispered once the lights went out – Finn took all that away when she left without any explanation, without even so much as a goodbye. London hasn't talked to her since, and Finn knows she deserves whatever London dishes out to her now.

London watches Adam Pelley with her arms curled around a pillow, clutching it to her chest with the same expression on her face that Finn used to get watching Backstreet Boys videos. Since when did teenaged girls start crushing on scientists instead of pop stars? Finn heard something from Shawn a few months ago about London getting in trouble for something – shoplifting? The details are fuzzy in Finn's mind, but seeing her niece now, innocently chewing on her hair while fixated on her famous crush, it is so hard to believe. For the first time since she left, Finn feels a rush of real regret. *I could have been important to someone.*

"So how have things been here?" Finn asks, as though this pathetic attempt at caring could possibly make up for the past three years.

"Do you know what will happen to the ecosystem if sharks go extinct? They're, like, apex predators, so it will screw up the entire food chain."

WARNING: THE FRONTAL CORTEX IS STILL DEVELOPING IN THE BRAIN OF AN ADOLESCENT. ADJUST YOUR EXPECTATIONS ACCORDINGLY. If London wants to talk about sharks, they will talk about sharks. "So how do we stop it?" Finn asks.

London eyes her warily. "Well, if you really want to help, you can sign this petition? Against shark finning? It's what I was talk-ing about when they kill the shark and then just cut off the fin, just for some dumb soup. It's barbaric."

"I can do that," says Finn. *Surely, I can do that.*

"Okay, I'll get you the link," London says, pulling out her phone.

Finn settles back against the pillows, cautiously hopeful about this wobbly first step towards regaining London's trust. Then she turns her head and there in the doorway is Ross – chubby, blond, balloon-headed Ross, dressed in a pair of babyish overalls that make him look like a toddler instead of an eight-year-old – staring at her with one finger tunnelling into his nose. He doesn't say anything, he just watches them. London keeps talking, but Finn can't concentrate on what she's saying. She can feel her heart contract in her chest, squeezing out some kind of emotion that she can't yet identify. All she knows is she is staring at Ross, but she can only see Dallas.

"Get out of here, weirdo!" London yells, chucking a pillow at her brother, which hits him in the knee and drops to the floor. He glances down at it, glances back at Finn, and walks away. London says something else, but Finn can't hear her over the noise in her head.

Dallas. Her own city-named boy. Dallas the artist, or writer, or filmmaker, depending on the day; Dallas the baristo most days. Dallas the dreamer, the idealist, the early riser, the maker of eggs Benedict with homemade hollandaise, the drawer of maps on ceilings, the poetry whisperer. Dallas the lazy stoner, the jamband apologist, the staunchly bearded. Dallas, the only man Finn had ever slept with, until last night. Finn met Dallas during their first year of university. He was the cool guy, she was the nerd, and when they fell in love it finally seemed like she could have something all her own. Still, in the eight years they were together, he had never actually given her anything other than acute anxiety. "I'll write a play for you, Finn," he told her. Then he knocked up her twin sister instead. But whatever. It's basically the same thing, right?

After Finn found out that Dallas had slept with Nicki, he brought her a coffee. A venti white mocha, no whip. So she lied: he *had* given her something.

"A coffee?" she asked. "You fuck my sister and then bring me a *coffee*?" She was standing in the doorway of their apartment, bags packed, ready to move back home – back with the sister he'd fucked, as if everything wasn't already twisted enough. But she had nowhere else to go.

"It was really confusing," was all he said. "She just looked so much like you." Eight long years, disintegrating into the muddy cocktail of Finn and Nicki's shared genetic code.

Immediately after Nicki found out she was pregnant, Dallas skipped town. Finn heard through her friend Alyssa that he had moved to one of those crunchy-granola islands off the coast of B.C. Not that this was surprising to anyone. After all, Nicki already had three daughters – by then seven and four and four – three beautiful, spoiled, toffee-skinned girls parading in full princess regalia around the house, stuffing marshmallows in the mailbox, feeding Silly Putty to Bruno, and making peanut butter in the kitchen by scattering nuts all over the floor and roller-skating over them, even though their grandfather is allergic. Their mother's girls, all three of them.

Finn spent two months at Victor Street dodging those princesses – and their angry pregnant mother – before she'd had enough and took her newly acquired master's degree in English to Japan to teach ESL. When she came back the next summer, with a fat bank account and the prerequisite collection of photographs of monasteries and cherry blossoms and neon signs, her moral superiority was unimpeachable, her pretentiousness off the charts.

"Hairdressing school?" she said to Nicki. "Well, sure. I guess that makes sense *for you*." As though travelling to the other side of the world to mope around her tiny apartment eating noodles and watching Japanese TV somehow proved that Finn was winning their unspoken war over who was having a better life. She kept her supposed victory wrapped tightly around her at night, when she could hear her infant nephew crying in the next room, could hear his mother cooing at him as she rocked him back to sleep. Even though Finn had never held him, never even looked in his eyes, still he haunted her – a glimpse of the back of his head or the scent of baby powder in the air momentarily stopping her breath.

Nicki managed to graduate by the time Ross was four months old, and set up a salon in their parents' garage, cutting the hair of all the women in the neighbourhood with one hand while jiggling Ross in the other, telling everyone about how she was going to raise him to be a real man, unlike his no-good daddy. By then, Finn had moved in with Alyssa and gone back to her job at the bookstore. She found a new bar to hang out at, new television shows to watch at night, new things to hate about living in Thunder Bay. Nothing had changed from when she lived with Dallas, except everything had. Because now Finn was alone.

Finn liked to tell people that by age twenty-six, Nicki had made four lives and destroyed one. Of course, Finn was always careful to stress that she meant it had been Nicki's own life she had destroyed. And yet.

"Did you know that sharks will grieve when they lose a member of their family?" London says. "Adam Pelley says that if people just got to know these things, they wouldn't want to hunt them anymore."

"Who's Adam Pelley?" asks Finn.

London glares at her with what she can only assume is thousands of years of evolutionary hatred passed down from her teenaged girl ancestors. Then, summoning all the power of her undeveloped frontal cortex, she screams, punches Finn in the shoulder, and runs out of the room.

Finn knows she should follow her and apologize, but she's just so tired. Instead, she closes her eyes and crosses her arms over her chest, sinking into the bed, imagining herself being surrounded by sharks as she drifts off to sleep.

SIX

S aturday morning, Katriina takes Tommy and Petey over to Victor Street early to help Nicki get breakfast ready for the family. It's not that Katriina particularly likes Nicki, but they are thrown together in that way that family often is, and she has learned to love her. And she doesn't ever worry about Shawn's relationship with Nicki. Nicki and Shawn are close, but they don't have that same bond that he and Finn do – no inside jokes, no shared favourite books, no secret phone conversations while Katriina is in the shower. Or maybe it's just that there's nothing mysterious about Nicki. Either way, with Finn on her way to Thunder Bay, Nicki is clearly on edge – considering what happened the last time the twins saw each other, Katriina can't blame her – so Katriina tries to remain cheery as she stirs scrambled eggs for Ross and flips pancakes for everyone else.

"This is your husband's fault, you know," Nicki says. "He was the one who told her in the first place." Nicki has been ranting about Finn for the better part of an hour, and Katriina has been trying to pay attention, she has. The same way she tried to pay attention to her sister the night before when she had gone to pick up the kids, Hanna telling her about the art exhibit she had seen on the weekend, the new pub opening up on the waterfront; the same way she tried to pay attention to Shawn when he came home from the restaurant and told her about the young cook he was going to have to fire. But it's like watching television on mute – their mouths are moving, but nothing is coming out. So she nods her head and makes the appropriate noises because this is what she has learned to do.

"Katriina?" says Nicki.

Katriina tries to bring herself into focus and takes hold of the pancake pan. Another thing she's able to do by rote: pour, turn, flip. She did grow up in a Finnish pancake house after all; she should be able to do this in her sleep. But Nicki is still staring at her questioningly, so she looks down and sees the pancake is burning. It has been one pancake this whole time, burning itself right into the pan.

"Sorry," she mumbles, scraping the charred remnants from the bottom of the pan into the garbage. For a minute she considers telling Nicki about the miscarriage, but decides against it. Nicki is too preoccupied – with the impending Finn situation, with her mother, with her kids, with everything. Besides, Nicki shouldn't know before Shawn, it's just not right.

"Mom!" she hears one of her boys scream from the living room. "Mom! Ross won't let me play with his Legos."

"Ross, stop being such a little brat!" Nicki yells.

"It's probably one of my boys' fault," Katriina says. Her head starts to throb, a tiny flash of light pulsing behind her right eyeball. "They're probably just being grabby." She finishes scraping the pan and runs it under the tap. "You have lots of toys!" she calls, forcing cheerfulness. She feels the elastic band digging into her arm and fights the urge to snap it.

"Mom! He's stuffing the Legos in his pants so we can't play with them!"

"Ross, that's gross!" Nicki says.

Suddenly there is a scream from the other room, and Ross comes running into the kitchen crying, his face indented with Lego markings, little round pockmarks in his delicate skin. Katriina runs into the other room, grabs the nearest boy, and smacks him across the bum. Then all the kids are crying, and Katriina is yelling Finnish curse words that she didn't even know she remembered, and when it's over she locks herself in Nicki's bathroom and stares at herself in the mirror as she snaps the elastic over and over again – *be a better mother, be a better mother, be a better mother* – until her wrist has gone completely numb.

Katriina knows that the main reason Shawn wants to have another baby is because he thinks it will save their marriage. It's not that she and Shawn don't love each other, or even that they fight, or have resentments; there is no cheating or lying or drinking or abuse. It's just that after all this time together they seem to have nothing left to say. When they were first married, all they did was talk: late into the night the way new couples do, over food and wine or while trying to watch a movie, lying in bed after sex, playing each other their favourite songs. They didn't have much in common then – at least, not in the way she had had with the other guys she dated before, all good Finnish boys whose parents were friends with her parents, who worked as busboys at Kahvila on weekends after hockey practice and still spent Sunday afternoons with their *mummus* making *pulla*. What Katriina and Shawn loved then was the sound of their own voices, the radiant glow of their own beautiful goddamned hearts. Then they loved Tommy and Petey when they came along, one year after the other, right at a time when that glow was starting to dim – they loved being new parents, loved the attention it brought them from both their families, how it gave them something to concentrate on other than each other.

But now that Tommy and Petey are older and starting to have their own lives, their own interests, Katriina is beginning to realize how rarely she and Shawn see each other most days. One of them always comes home late, either Shawn from the restaurant or Katriina from an open house, and then he is up at the crack of dawn to oversee breakfast service, or she is rushing out to meet with a potential client, leaving them to text each other during the day about where the kids are, who is going to pick them up, what they are going to have for dinner, whether they need anything at Shoppers Drug Mart, who they will call to fix the driveway. On the odd occasions when they do run into each other – in the bathroom in the morning while brushing their teeth, or collapsed on the couch for a quick glass of wine before going up to bed – they speak awkwardly, politely, as though they are strangers. Katriina can't even remember the last time Shawn kissed her on the mouth instead of on the forehead as he is running out the door. When they have sex, it's like a chore being completed, and only then because they've decided it is time to try for a third child, so they will have something to talk about again, so they will have something novel to interrupt the monotony of their everyday lives.

Ironically, what has happened to Kate could be a good thing for them. That morning, Shawn had pressed snooze on the alarm and wrapped his arms around her, pressing his face into the back of her neck and pretending to bite her; later, he sat on the edge of the bathtub while she put on her makeup and told her about going back to the hospital to see Kate the night before, about how aggressive the reporters were getting.

"There was this one reporter, Cassandra something, from Thunder Bay News. She told the nurses she was Kate's niece and just walked right into her room. If I hadn't been there, no one would have even known," he said, rubbing his hands over his face. "Apparently there are clips of Kate all over the internet. People are posting them on fucking Facebook."

"Oh dear," said Katriina, flicking her powder brush over the tip of her nose. She knew the clips were out there, of course – unless you lived under a rock, you knew about the Conqueror of Kakabeka – but she couldn't bring herself to watch them. One of her co-workers had even emailed it to her – *Take a look at this lady – crazy!!!!* – not realizing the crazy lady was Katriina's mother-in-law. She had deleted it without watching.

"I just don't understand it," Shawn said, stretching his legs out in front of him. "Why would she do this? What could have possibly been going through her head?"

Katriina swept her mascara brush over her eyelashes, trying to keep her hand steady. "But how many of us could say we went over a waterfall in a barrel?" she heard Kate say in her head. Earlier, she had considered telling Shawn about this conversation but had convinced herself it wouldn't make any difference, that it wouldn't make him feel any better. Now, she realized deep down that she didn't want to tell him because she knew it wouldn't make *her* feel any better.

The silent seconds ticked by. *Say something*, she thought. *Anything.* "I'm sure she'll be able to tell us soon, Shawn. I'm sure there's a reasonable explanation." As soon as she said it, she knew it was the wrong thing, the wrong combination of letters and words. She concentrated on her own reflection in the mirror, avoiding Shawn's eyes, afraid of the contempt she was sure she would find there. And just when she was about to say something else, to try to make it better, she felt the mascara brush stab against her eye and she dropped it into the sink, squeezing her eye shut as oily black tears spilled out over her cheeks.

Through her one open eye she saw Shawn reach out and put a roll of toilet paper on the counter and walk out of the bathroom. She blotted at her face with the tissue, trying to fix her mistake, but later, in her car, she checked in the mirror and saw the faint black streaks across her cheeks, lingering evidence of her failure.

———

As they are finishing breakfast, Shawn calls Katriina from the restaurant. "Where are you?" he asks. "I'm stuck at work for a bit."

"Victor Street." With her free hand she starts stacking dirty dishes on the table. The three girls are upstairs watching television and the three boys are in the backyard, and Nicki is sitting at the kitchen table, reading a magazine. All while Katriina cleans up. "Just having breakfast with Nicki and the kids," she says brightly.

"Wait, Nicki's there?" Shawn asks. "She was supposed to pick up Finn at the airport forty-five minutes ago!"

Katriina takes a breath. "Nicki," she says, pulling the phone away from her ear. "Shawn says you were supposed to pick Finn up at the airport."

Nicki stabs at a piece of pancake with her fork, then sticks it in her mouth. "No I wasn't," she says through her chewing. "Shawn was going to do it."

"Nicki says you were supposed to do it."

"How was I supposed to do it?" Shawn yells. "I'm at *fucking work*!"

Katriina pulls the phone away from her ear again. "Shawn says he's at work."

"I'm at work, too."

"You're eating pancakes."

Nicki holds up a magazine, the front of which reads *Hair Today*. "It's research," she says, shrugging.

With the phone pinned between her neck and her shoulder, Katriina snatches up the stack of plates and deposits them in the sink a little too forcefully, wondering how she keeps getting caught up in the dramas of a family that isn't even hers. She thinks about her own family, about Hanna and their parents and all their small, easily contained lives. If there are problems, they keep them to themselves. There is none of this leaving people at airports or screaming obscenities into cell phones. No riding barrels over waterfalls.

"She's not going," Katriina says into the phone. "Sorry."

Shawn sighs. "Can you go, then?"

"Me?" Katriina says, raising her brows at Nicki. Nicki rolls her eyes. "I . . . I'll have to see if my car's still here . . . Hamish might have borrowed it . . ."

As she steps to the window, pretending to check for her car that she knows is there, she sees a cab pull up into the driveway and Finn get out. "Oh, she's here," Katriina says.

"Lucky you," Shawn says.

Finn comes into the house with her eyes blazing, her head a halo of frizzy hair. She is perfectly dishevelled, as if she has just taken the red-eye from Paris after partying all night with rock stars or something. Even after all these years, Katriina is still startled by how identical Finn and Nicki really are, although now she notices that Finn appears years younger – her skin smooth and unwrinkled, her body lean in the places where Nicki's has grown flabby. Do either of them notice? she wonders. Or do they just see themselves when they look at each other?

"Oh, hi," says Nicki. "You made it."

"Yup," Finn says, slipping out of her flip-flops. The air vibrates with things unsaid. Katriina can feel it – it's as if Nicki and Finn are having a conversation that only they can hear.

"Hello, Serafina," Katriina says, trying to break the tension. "It's so good to see you." She reaches out to hug her, feeling awkward and gangly and all angles as she tries to manoeuvre her arms around Finn's small frame.

"You, too," says Finn, flinching.

Katriina could swear that Finn and Nicki's eyes meet behind her back. Katriina pulls away quickly, her cheeks starting to burn. "Excuse me," she mumbles. "I've got to get the kids to Hanna's." She slips out of the kitchen and through to the backyard before anyone can say anything else, two sets of identical eyes following her as she leaves.

Finn might think she is the outsider in her family, but she is still more of a Parker than Katriina ever will be.

◆ ◆ ◆

On the best of days, Katriina's life is a messy chaos of travelling between houses – her own, Hanna's, her parents', Victor Street, the Paulsson place, and any other house she is trying to sell. She finds herself, more often than she would like, making tea in someone else's kitchen, forced to make do with someone else's choice of milk. This afternoon it is almond milk at Hanna's place, where she drops off the kids before her next showing, because Hanna has decided she is lactose-intolerant. As if any Scandinavian was ever unable to eat cheese.

"Did you see her?" Hanna asks as they sit at her sleek granite-topped island. Hanna owns a clothing store downtown and lives next door in the closest thing to a hipster loft that you could possibly find in Thunder Bay, an industrial space that has been converted into studios. She is all about the downtown north core, that two-block radius of stores and restaurants that can make you feel like you're in a real city until you realize you have walked the entire length of the neighbourhood in less than a minute. Still, if you never left that two-block radius, if you lived and worked and partied there, you might be able to forget where you are. Katriina knows this is what Hanna is trying to do.

"Yeah," says Katriina, embarrassed that for a minute she is unsure which "her" Hanna might be talking about. "Last night. She is still in a coma."

Hanna shakes her head. "I still can't believe it," she says. "The clip's been on all the news stations. They're calling her the Conqueror of Kakabeka."

Katriina takes a sip of her coffee. For her, what's happened with Kate has been such a private thing, it is a jolt every time someone mentions it – she has a hard time believing that the world is having a reaction to something that she herself hasn't really had the time to react to yet. "Yeah," she says. "It's a weird thing."

"What's wrong?" Hanna asks immediately. Secrets have never really been possible between the Saarinen sisters. From their parents, yes, boyfriends, even husbands, yes, but never from each other.

Katriina gazes down into her coffee, organically roasted and fairly traded, she assumes. "I lost the baby," she says. "Again."

Hanna shrugs. "It's not a big deal."

"Not a big deal?" Katriina swishes her coffee around in her cup, focusing on the whirling liquid. "How can you say that? It's like my uterus is broken."

"If that were true, you wouldn't have *them*," Hanna says, nodding to the frosted glass balcony doors, through which they can see the wavy outline of Tommy and Petey. The boys love going to Hanna's place. They love her hardwood floors, the balcony overlooking the harbour, the nine hundred channels on her high-def TV. It's strange, seeing her outdoor-loving boys – who will no doubt grow up as northern as they come, as northern as their dad and their granddad, who will fish and hunt and drink beer, who will drive quad runners in the summer and snow machines in the winter and trucks year-round – sitting on rattan deck chairs, sipping some kind of artisan root beer, and taking pictures of the Sleeping Giant with their iPhones. They turn into different creatures here, city boys, and sometimes Katriina can see little glimpses into alternate futures for them. It never lasts, though – five minutes at home and they will be devising new ways to maim each other with household objects, new things to drive their BMX bikes over.

It's not that she doesn't love Tommy and Petey. She does. It's just that everything with them is so physical, so immediate, so loud. So Shawn. Part of the reason she agreed to try again was to give her own genetic material one more chance to fight its way to the top, to see if she could produce a child who people might recognize as her own.

"Maybe they broke me," Katriina says.

Hanna lowers her coffee mug. "It seems to me that you're more worried about your body not performing the way you think it should than you are about having or not having another baby."

"Maybe," says Katriina. The whirlpool in her coffee is still spinning, and she has a strange, irrational urge to be inside it, to surrender herself to the void. Maybe she is beginning to understand what drew her mother-in-law to that waterfall.

Later that afternoon, Katriina is showing a young couple from Winnipeg around the Paulsson house when she hears a sudden, sharp wail coming from above them, a keen so profound that she has to stop and hold on to the doorframe as she is discussing the possibility of fitting an eight-person table plus a buffet in the dining room.

"I'm so sorry," she says to the couple. "I can't even explain that."

"You're explaining it fine, I just don't see it," says the woman, who is called Irene or Aileen, Katriina isn't sure.

"Excuse me?" says Katriina, holding a hand over her right ear to try to block out the noise. She hasn't even said anything yet about how the sound might be from a passing train, or a neighbour's cat that has been trapped in the rafters.

"There's just not enough space over here," Irene/Aileen says. "The hutch is at least a foot and a half deep. There wouldn't be any room to push your chair out from the table."

"I don't know," her husband says, whose name Katriina remembers because it is actually Shawn, even though he is small and wiry and bald, nothing like a Shawn should be. "I mean, once you had it in here, you'd see it's not as big as you think it is."

"I've heard that one before," Irene/Aileen says. It is a joke without mirth. In the midst of this, Katriina realizes they can't hear the wailing, which has pitched up an octave, into a range that feels like it is burning holes through both her eardrums.

"Let me show you the kitchen," she says, a little too loudly. Irene/Aileen and Shawn both give her a strange look but follow her out of the possibly-too-small dining room, their hands linked together in solidarity. The wail is now a scream, and as Katriina explains that the cupboards are brand new, only two years old, she can barely hear her own voice. All she can think is, *How can they not hear this?*, immediately followed by *Maybe I'm having a stroke.* She blinks, testing her vision. Her tongue feels normal. She can clench and unclench her left fist. She has no idea if these things are actual stroke warnings or not, but for a moment it takes her mind off the noise. She smiles brightly, opens cupboard doors, talks about the school in the neighbourhood. It doesn't matter; she knows they are not going to buy the house. They could sense the tragedy as soon as they walked in, the heavy, burdened feeling in the walls, the heartache in the floors.

"The longer a house stands empty, the lonelier it gets," Katriina's boss, Paula, is fond of saying. Paula, who once suggested stashing crystals around the Paulsson place in order to "heal its spirit." Katriina took the crystals, worried that if she didn't, Paula would suggest something even more drastic, like a séance or an exorcism. But she left them in her car – at the very least, she might not have to worry about that slow leak in her right front tire. Paula was right about one thing – the longer a house was up for sale, the harder it was to sell, regardless of the market or the location or the upgrades or anything. It was as though the house lost confidence the more it was rejected, which led to even more rejection. Or not the house, Katriina supposes. The person trying to sell the house.

After Irene/Aileen and Shawn leave, Katriina leans against the front door, breathing in deeply. The wailing has stopped. She goes upstairs, checking all the rooms for stray raccoons, for hidden smoke alarms, but can find nothing. Nothing but a silent house, waiting to be occupied.

"Claudia?" she whispers into the silence.

She is going crazy. She must be going crazy. She reaches for her elastic, but it's not there. She has a flash to it sitting in a pool of water on the edge of the sink at Victor Street, where she took it off to rub Polysporin on the scratches. With increasing panic, she searches the medicine cabinet in the bathroom, the floor of the closet in Claudia's room, the junk drawer in the kitchen, anywhere there might be a stray elastic band.

In the end, all she finds is some garbage bag twist-ties and a pad of yellow Post-it notes in a kitchen drawer. She digs a pen out of her purse and writes on the top Post-it. *Be a better* . . .

But there are too many things to cover, too many aspects of her life that she has let slide. She sticks the note to the inside of the cupboard door. Then she changes her mind and crosses out the "a": *Be better.* Just be better.

SEVEN

It is Saturday morning before Walter is able to head back to Thunder Bay. He tells the researchers he has a family emergency and arranges for another local guide to pick them up and take them back to Nipigon. They nod, barely looking up from their work. It doesn't matter to them. All that matters is the research.

I was once like you, Walter thinks, watching them unload the last of the supplies from the *Serafina*. Needing to catalogue, report, and document everything, to find connections and understand the delicate balance between nature and man. To change the world. But he learned long ago that the more he documented, the less he understood, and the fight to change the world was actually carried out in a series of committee meetings in which people argued over the wording of how to publicly refer to the destruction of nature. Should this be an alert or a warning? How many beneficial use impairments do we need to qualify as an area of concern? How do you define the delisting criteria? If you asked Walter, all of Lake Superior should be an area of concern, but no one ever asked Walter. They just took his data and filed it away, filtered it through report after report until he gave up following the trail. Now, he sees Lake Superior as a cancer patient who has been deemed ineligible for chemo. He just wants to be with it as much as he can in the time it has left.

"Lady Superior," Kate called the lake, half-jokingly, in the early days of their marriage – his royal mistress, occupying his thoughts when they should have been on his family. God, he hasn't thought about that for years, the way she would tease him about finding secret stones stashed in his pockets, the smell of lake water on his collar. She still wouldn't go near it, the water that tried to drag her down, her nemesis, stealing everything from her in small increments – including her husband.

Her nemesis, his passion. Today, at least, he has three more hours to spend with Lady Superior as he makes his way across, back to Thunder Bay harbour and up the Kam, then back to Kate. He wonders what she would think about him coming back for her now, after all those times he didn't. The kids never understood why he was always away from home, on the boats from April until November, then heading out to man the ice huts as soon as the ice was thick enough, trekking out across the region to set them up and maintain them for the weekend fishermen with their souped-up snow machines and their coolers of beer. But Kate knew, she always knew. What kept him out here, and what kept him away.

Walter and Kate remained friends through high school. He became studious and surprisingly athletic, which seemed to cancel each other out in the hierarchy of popularity, rendering him somewhere in the middle. Kate grew beautiful and rebellious, which kept her hovering around the fringes. Walter suspected that most people were a little intimidated by her. After the incident at Chippewa Park, when the pieces of the Kate he knew slowly started fitting back together like a jigsaw puzzle, there was a new edge to her, a new destructiveness that kept others at a distance.

"I know it's crazy," she told him one night after the two of them had snuck into the hayloft of the old Babiak cow barn to drink her father's brandy, "but I feel like God has forgotten about me. Like I was supposed to die that day, and no one up there ever bothered to double check that I had."

"That *is* crazy," said Walter, who wasn't even sure he believed in God. He sat down against a bale, the scratchy hay digging through the back of his shirt, and breathed in that sweet, musty smell. "Anyway, it's not like you're invincible."

"I'm not?" Kate asked before taking another gulp. Then, with the bottle still in her hand, she climbed up to the loft door, precariously close to the edge. Walter's body tensed, but he didn't say anything. He was getting tired of always being the one to call her back.

"You think you're so brave," said Walter. He crossed the loft and reached up for the bottle. A shock of electricity surged through him as their fingers touched, and he jerked his hand away.

Kate smiled coyly. "Scared of that little spark between us, are you?"

She leaned down and kissed him, her mouth sweet with the taste of brandy. Walter let his lips linger on hers, and then forced himself to pull away. Of course Kate knew that Walter was in love with her. It had never been much of a secret. And this was not the first time they had shared kisses in the hayloft – or the Parker woodshed, for that matter, or the front seat of Walter's truck on the days when he drove her home from school. But he also knew that he was not the only one she was taking to the back of the barn, or getting rides home with. And he had promised himself he wouldn't be one of many. Not anymore.

"What's wrong?" Kate asked, running her finger along his collar.

Walter shrugged her off. "Nothing."

"It doesn't seem like nothing."

"It just seems like you have that spark with a lot of people." Walter could hear the humiliating whine in his voice, like a petulant child who finds someone else playing in his sandbox.

"You're so uptight, Walter," she said. "You need to stop taking everything so seriously."

"Maybe you need to start taking some things *more* seriously."

"Like you?"

"Like *us*."

Kate took a final swig from the brandy bottle and tossed it into the hay. "Oh, I am *very serious* about us," she said, turning to look out the opening across the farm. She was so beautiful, standing there in the loft door, her hair a tangle of curls backlit by the mellow evening sun. *Maybe I'm going about this all wrong*, Walter thought. She was a free spirit. She did what she wanted, and she didn't care what other people thought. Neither should he.

"Marry me," he said, feeling his face grow hot with adrenaline.

Kate laughed, turning back to face him. "Well of course I'm going to marry you."

"You are?"

"Yeah. I mean, eventually. When I'm ready to get married and settle down."

"When will that be?"

"I don't know. Sometime. You don't want us to turn out like our parents, do you?"

Walter thought of his own parents – civil enough to each other but sleeping in their separate beds, avoiding each other in the morning, arguing about who paid the mortgage or swept the floor – and concluded it would take a crazy turn of events to turn him and Kate into them. "I don't see what that has to do with anything," he said.

"Just wait for me," she said. "My Waiting Walter." She held her arms out to the sides, closed her eyes, and let herself drop backwards. Walter let out a screech and ran to the edge, only to see Kate lying on top of a pile of hay bales in the back of her father's pickup, laughing hysterically.

"What is wrong with you?" Walter yelled.

"See, I told you," she said. "Invincible."

And so Walter waited. They graduated high school, and Walter began a biology degree at Lakehead University while Kate went to work at a seamstress shop in Westfort. Walter had just assumed that she would work there until he graduated and then they would get married. But one afternoon two years after that day in the hayloft, while they were sharing a plate of fries at the Coney Island, Kate squirted a puddle of ketchup onto the plate and said, "Oh. You know that girl Martha Jane, from the dress shop? We're going to Europe together."

Everything in the restaurant went silent – the voices of the other diners, the hum of the milk fridge, the waitress counting change behind the counter, the sizzle of the fryer through the kitchen window. All Walter could hear was his own pulse thrumming in his ears. "Europe?" he said, his voice resounding like a megaphone in his head. "What are you going to do in Europe?"

The sound in the room returned, like a record player speeding up.

"We're not going to *do* anything," Kate said, sipping her Coke. "We're just going to experience things. Life. We're going to experience life."

Walter watched the brown bubbles travelling up her straw, trying to think of something to say. "But isn't it dangerous?" he asked finally. "Two girls on their own?"

"Walter, it's 1969. Girls can do whatever they want."

"I'm not saying they can't." Walter picked up a fry, dragging it back and forth through the ketchup smear. It had been eight years since he had watched Kate disappear through a hole in the ice at her feet. Now he felt as though he was the one who was disappearing. "I'm just saying, is it the best idea?"

"The best idea either of us have ever had." But her eyes were wandering and her leg shook under the table, and she had begun to chew on the end of her straw. Maybe she was having doubts. Maybe there was still a chance he could change her mind.

"You know, European men are a lot more aggressive than Canadian men. They'll see you two as targets."

"Targets for what?" Kate asked, finally focusing her eyes and staring at him so hard that Walter felt himself shrinking into the booth.

"Nothing."

"No, please, tell me," she said. "What will we be targets for?" When Walter didn't say anything, she leaned forward provocatively, one slender finger resting against her bottom lip. "Are you talking about . . . sex?" she said, her voice barely above a whisper.

"Kate . . ." he said in what he hoped was his best warning voice.

"Walter . . ." she said, mimicking his tone.

"Kate," he said again, softer. They locked eyes. He could feel her daring him to look away, but he held her gaze, determined not to be the one to break eye contact. Not this time. She straightened her back, jutting her chin forward, a hint of a smile on her lips. Then he felt her foot touching his leg under the table, travelling up along his calf. He jerked his leg away. Kate went back to her Coke, sipping demurely through her straw, hair falling over her shoulders and onto the greasy tabletop.

"You need to relax," she said. "You're such a prude."

"I am not."

"I bet you haven't even had it yet." She picked up a fry. "You know. *Sex.*"

"Like you have."

"Sure I have," she said. "It's no big deal." She slid the fry into her mouth while Walter's world swiftly came crashing down around him.

"With who?" he finally managed to whisper.

"Billy Hamilton. In the woods behind the Texaco on Highway 61." Saying it as though they had done nothing more intimate than talk about the weather. "It's pretty great. You should try it."

Walter wanted to scream. He felt his insides coil with frustration, for all the things that he was unable to say and unable to do, for being so immobile, so weak, for wanting what was apparently the wrong kind of life. Kate just watched him, as if she knew what he was thinking – a trait that he had often attributed to her, even though he knew now that it clearly wasn't true, that there was no goddamn way she could possibly know him at all.

Enough is enough, he thought.

Two nights later, Walter went to a party out at Oliver Lake, where a bunch of guys from the track team were slinging back beer and skinny-dipping with some girls from the cheerleading squad. Walter ended up having sex with Frances Halliday in the front seat of his truck, their bodies still wet from the river, cold and clammy and sticking together in all the wrong ways. When it was over, Walter drove her home to Riverdale, and they bounced along the dirt road in silence. Walter hoped that Frances had used him in the same way that he had used her, that there was someone else on her mind while her hands were on his body, but when she turned around and smiled shyly at him as she skipped up the front steps of her house, he knew that there hadn't been.

The next day, Kate came tearing up the driveway at the Parker farm in her little red MGB, her blond hair waving behind her like a flag as the car flew in and out of the potholes. Walter was outside changing the oil on his truck, his smile fading as she got closer and he could see the anger on her face. "Frances Halliday?" she yelled before she even stopped the car. "Frances goddamn Halliday?" She slammed the car into park and jumped out, standing in the driveway a few feet away from him as though she couldn't physically come any closer, as though her anger was a force field keeping everything hurtful away.

Walter felt his whole body take the impact of that anger, and he recoiled in surprise, blood rushing to his head, adrenaline spiking in his extremities. He took a deep breath and forced himself to turn away from Kate, sticking his head back underneath the hood of his truck. "Billy Hamilton," he said calmly, his voice echoing through the engine. "Todd Westin. Joe Leonetti. Paul Wachowski. Jimmy Medina." The names tumbled out. *Well, who cares?* he thought. *She doesn't have any right.* His hands were shaking and his vision was blurry – he was so upset that he couldn't tell what anything was, or remember what anything was called, so he just felt around blindly, pretending to tighten the thingamajig, fiddle with the whatsamabob, waiting for Kate to respond. He could hear her behind him, breathing hard, could feel the tension and anger radiating from her, and for a moment he wondered if she would slam the hood down on his head. A part of him actually hoped she would.

Instead, she went back to her car, and Walter raised his head just in time to see her drive away, her blond curls flying out behind her. He didn't see her again for over a year. A year without a single word from her, with nothing but the image of her driving away burned into the back of his eyelids, haunting him every night as he fell asleep. Until one brilliant spring morning when he opened the door of his apartment and there was Kate, in a long white cotton dress and wild roses in her hair. She looked thinner than she had when she left, and her hair was darker, her skin a bit more sallow. But in her eyes was a light, a spark of the little Katie Babiak who had jumped the creek every spring, all energy and fireworks and joy.

"Walter Parker," she said. "Will you marry me?"

And for once, Walter didn't wait. Not a single heartbeat.

Walter knows that if someone were to look back at the story of his life with Kate, it would seem as though the climax came early, and everything else was a long, drawn-out denouement. After the morning Kate showed up at his apartment, the next forty years seemed uneventful. Not to say that there weren't adventures, that there weren't hardships – the business, the twins, Shawn, the grandkids, illnesses, loss – but none of that had been exclusively the story of them, the narrative of their relationship. Kate's early-morning proposal was their kiss on top of the Empire State Building, it was their "Love is never having to say you're sorry."

He had almost convinced himself that it didn't matter if he ever saw her again. He had just graduated from Lakehead with a bachelor of science degree, but what really interested him was the new field of ecology, specifically studying contamination from pulp and paper effluent in Lake Superior and how it affected wildlife populations.

"I hope you haven't found someone else," Kate had said that morning at his door. But Walter had – not some*one*, but some*thing*. The lake. It was a gradual thing: a walk along the shoreline, a quick paddle, his feet buried in the black sand at Mission Island, or working his way over the rocks at Tee Harbour, transfixed by the shape of the shoreline, the clatter of stones being pulled back and pushed in by the pulse of the waves. The constant pressing ache in his chest whenever he was near – and then, whenever he was far, which prompted his move from his parents' farm in the Slate River Valley to Port Arthur, to a nondescript apartment building on the hill with drafty windows, too-small closets, and stained carpets, just so in in the morning he could gaze out those drafty windows and see the lake, covered with ice in winter and teeming with ships in summer, and the Sleeping Giant, still only a pile of rocks on the horizon.

The lake had tried to take Kate. In Walter's mind, it had wanted her as much as he had – he could hardly blame it for that. And the more time he spent with the lake, the more protective he felt. He was certain that he was meant to make serving Lake Superior his life's goal. To thank it for giving Kate back. But there had to be room in his life for a lake *and* a wife, surely.

Kate and Walter were married at city hall and bought the house on Victor Street. In 1976, he quit his job and bought the *Miss Penelope*, an old fishing trawler that he remodelled with a canopy and bench seats and converted into the first of his tour boats. For years he ran Superior Tours right out of the woodshed he built at the back of the property, at the edge of the Kaministiquia River. Back then, he only went up and down the river and sometimes into Thunder Bay Harbour. It wasn't until after his daughters were born that he bought the *Serafina* and the *Veronica*, twin cabin cruisers as identical as the twin girls he named them after, and started chugging people out to Sibley, and then later on overnights up the North Shore to the Black Bay Peninsula, St. Ignace Island, even all the way to Neys. When the business expanded to include the ice huts, he moved his office from the woodshed to a storefront on Cumberland, near the expanding marina, but he still kept his boats docked along the Kam.

Kate made dresses, raised the babies, stayed strangely quiet about her years in Europe – which was fine with Walter, he didn't want to know, not really. With Kate, he had learned, there were some things that were safer left unsaid.

It is early afternoon by the time Walter docks the *Serafina* in back of Victor Street, and the river is so still – deferential, even. *It's okay*, he whispers in his head. *It's not your fault.*

He grabs his spare set of truck keys from the garden shed and drives straight to the hospital. They will know he's back when they see the *Serafina*, but for now he wants to go see Kate, alone. In the lobby by the gift shop he sees a young reporter standing with a microphone in front of a man holding a camera. Walter gets a sinking feeling in his stomach as he realizes she is talking about Kate. "Sources close to the woman, who media are now referring to as the Conqueror of Kakabeka, report that there is no change in her condition. We will keep you updated on the situation as it progresses. Reporting live from Thunder Bay General Hospital, Cassandra Coelho for Thunder Bay News."

The Conqueror of Kakabeka. Well, Kate would like that. He wonders if he should just ask this Cassandra Coelho person to update him on Kate's condition, since she seems to know so much about what's going on. Maybe she could tell him why the hell she did it. Tell him what he has to do to make things right.

Walter has to show ID at the nurses' station to get into Kate's room. "It's for her security. You understand," the young nurse informs him. She is small and blond and wearing a pair of pink scrubs, her girlishness belying her authority. She refuses to even look at Walter until he shows her his boating licence.

"It's all I have with me," he says.

She studies the picture, then raises her head. "You're the husband."

"Yes." For some reason Walter feels like he should apologize for this. The nurse leads him down the hall, Walter following along like a child trying to keep up with his mother. She pushes open a door and gestures inside. Walter steps across the threshold tentatively, as though he's entering another dimension.

"Dr. Penfield will be along shortly if there's anything you want to ask him," the nurse says, shutting the door behind her.

Finally, Walter is alone with Kate. She is lying on her back, her head turned slightly towards the window. Her face is puffy and bruised, and her hair is matted against the pillow. He tries to remember the last time they were alone together like this, no children or grandchildren demanding their attention. It must have been months.

"Hi, Katie," Walter says. She doesn't move. He walks over to the side of the bed and takes her hand, immediately thinking back to all the other times he has done this in a hospital: the birth of the twins, her mastectomy, her broken leg. And now this, whatever *this* is. Unexpectedly, he feels tears sliding down his cheeks. Where was he? When she was going over the falls, when she was alone with the twins, when she fell through the ice. *Where the goddamn hell was he?*

"I'm here now, okay, Katie?" he says. He can't stop the tears, so he just stands there with her hand in his, saying over and over again, "It's okay. I'm here. I'm here."

He wants her to know, even if he's not sure it matters anymore.

EIGHT

Things Katriina hates herself for thinking: how, with Kate in the hospital, the logistics of her life have gotten monumentally harder; how she has been back and forth across town more in the past twenty-four hours than she has in the past month. Not that she would complain about it, even as she heads back across town yet again, trucking the boys from Hanna's place to the grocery store to pick up steaks and salad greens before returning to Victor Street for Finn's big welcome-home dinner that Nicki has unexpectedly insisted they have.

They arrive at Victor Street at the same time as Shawn, who kisses her cheek and hands her a tray of brownies he has brought from Kahvila. "I'll unload the groceries," he says, maybe as a way of apologizing for walking out on her in the bathroom that morning, but who knows – her reading of Shawn has been a little off in the past few days.

As she makes her way towards the house, she is surprised to find Walter standing on the front lawn next to the garden shed, seemingly inspecting something on the ground. "Walter?" she says, crossing the driveway.

He straightens up, scratching his head under his Tilley hat. "Oh, hello, Katriina." He eyes the tray of brownies. "You're baking now, I see."

Even though she and Walter have never had a conversation that lasted more than five minutes, Katriina has always thought of him as something of a kindred spirit, someone who values focus, industriousness, decorum. Once, when she and Shawn were first married, she snuck away during a family dinner to the shed that was then Walter's office. She had told herself it was to get some work done, but really she just needed a break from the Parkers. She found Walter studying a map rolled out across the floor.

"I'm sorry, I didn't mean to interrupt you," she'd said.

But Walter just gestured towards the desk. "Have a seat," he said without lifting his eyes from the map. They have been meeting up there ever since, even after the woodshed was converted into Hamish's distillery – silently smiling and nodding and carrying on their work. She likes to think those evenings mean as much to Walter as they do to her, even though they have never said anything about it to each other.

Now, Katriina smiles, looking down at the brownies. "They're from Kahvila. You know I'm a terrible baker."

Walter peers at the brownies through the cellophane, then touches her wrist. His eyes lock with hers. "You look tired," he says. "I hope you're taking care of yourself."

The words hit her straight in the stomach. For one sickening second she wonders if the sleeves of her sweater have rolled up, if he can see the scars. She furtively tries to adjust them, rubbing her arms against her sides while balancing the tray. "Of course," she says. "Why would you ask that?"

Before Walter can respond, Tommy and Petey run up to them, jumping on him like puppies.

"Hey there, little monsters," he says.

Katriina bites her lip, harder than she means to. *Just let it go.*

"It's nice that you're here," she says brightly. "I thought you didn't get back until tomorrow night."

With the back of his hand, Walter rubs at his left eye. For a moment he reminds her of a little kid, confused and scared. "Well, I saw Kate on the news," he says. "I figured it was the kind of thing I should come back early for."

Katriina feels her face turning red. While she stands there wishing the ground would open up and swallow her, Shawn comes up behind her and nods at Walter.

"Have you been to see her?" he asks.

Walter returns the nod. "Just got back," he says, bending down to the ground and running his hand through the grass. Tommy and Petey both bend down next to him, examining the ground as if they know what they are looking at. It's uncanny, Katriina thinks. The way they mimic him. You'd never guess that they weren't related at all.

"How is she?" she asks.

Walter shrugs. "The same, I guess." He grabs a handful of brownish grass and rips it up, opening his palm to show the boys. "Pythium blight," he says. "Poor water drainage." Overturning his hand, he lets the grass blow away.

"Are you coming inside?" Shawn asks. "We've got steaks."

"Lawn's not going to de-thatch itself," Walter says.

"Well, no," says Shawn, "but you've got to eat, right?" He grabs the nearest boy, Tommy, and pulls him towards the house in a headlock, the grocery bags falling to the ground. Petey runs after them, egging on his father as he rubs his knuckles into Tommy's head.

Katriina sighs. It's like Shawn has something to prove every time he's around Walter, like he needs to show him what a great father he is, how much fun he is, how much the boys love him. It's moments like this, when they're around his family, that her love for Shawn is the strongest – she suddenly feels so fiercely protective of him, as though she can make up for everything else that has gone wrong in his life.

Or at least she can pick up the groceries he's dropped. If she doesn't, who will?

Sometimes Katriina wonders if her life is made up of just a few choreographies that she plays out over and over again. For tonight's performance of *In the Kitchen with Nicki*, while Nicki prepares the marinade for the steaks, Katriina makes spaghetti and meat-balls for the kids, none of whom will eat a steak except for Ross. It sounds complicated, but the spaghetti is from a box, the sauce from a jar, the meatballs from the freezer. The girls sit at the table, all three of them with their phones out; Hamish and Shawn have the boys out in the backyard playing soccer; Walter is presumably still out de-thatching the lawn. There has been no sign of Finn yet. Nicki tells Katriina she has been asleep all afternoon.

"Fucking lazy bitch," Nicki says, spinning the top of the pepper grinder wildly.

With her eyes still on her phone, London makes a face. "Ugh, have some class, Mom."

"Oh, what? You and your aunt are best friends now, huh? You've forgotten how she just left without even saying goodbye to you?"

"*No*," says London. "I just think you need to get over yourself."

Katriina, slicing a loaf of French bread at the counter, holds her breath, waiting for the explosion.

But Nicki just laughs. "Well, I'm not the only one," she says, flicking the side of London's head. London bats her hand away, her eyes still on her phone, but she is smiling.

Nothing about Nicki and London's relationship makes any sense to Katriina, but maybe it's just a mother-daughter thing. If this one is a girl, Katriina won't know what to do with her.

Damn it. An unexpected surge of grief overwhelms her as she realizes her mistake, a howl boiling up in her lungs. She tries to swallow it down, but she feels herself choking, unable to breathe. Out of sheer panic, she glides the knife across the top of her finger. Immediately her airway opens, and she sucks a quick, hot breath through her teeth. "Ouch," she says loudly, dropping the knife.

"Holy shit, Katriina," Nicki says. "Be careful."

At that moment, Finn appears in the doorway. "Sorry, guys," she says, rubbing her hands over her face. "It was an early flight."

The cut on her finger now blooming with blood, Katriina abruptly crosses to the sink and turns the water on, watching the blood diluting as it runs down the drain. Behind her, she hears Shawn's voice say, "Finnie." She turns around just in time to see him wrapping her in a hug.

Finn presses her forehead into his shoulder. "Hi," she says.

Katriina turns off the tap and reaches for the paper towel, trying to pull off a piece with one hand while holding the other up in the air to keep the blood from dripping, trying not to watch Shawn and Finn's oddly intimate embrace. She will never get used to the way Shawn is around Finn. Maybe if she was his real sister she would feel differently, but Finn was already ten before he came into her life. Still, she sees that he has that same inherent understanding of Finn that Katriina does with Hanna, that knowing without having to speak, the raised eyebrow, the twitch of the lip. He will never know Katriina the way he knows Finn. It doesn't make Katriina jealous – it doesn't. But unless you're related to her, you're not supposed to have that sort of bond with a woman other than your wife.

Of course, Shawn would say he *is* related to her. And Katriina wouldn't argue because she is not a horrible person. Still.

Shawn pulls back from Finn, holding her by her shoulders, then he smooths down the top of her hair and shakes his head. "Your hair looks like shit," he says.

"Yeah, well, you got fat," Finn says, poking him in the stomach. "I thought you started lifting weights?"

Katriina rips off a paper towel, smiling to herself at the thought of Shawn lifting weights. Maybe Finn doesn't know Shawn as well as she thinks she does. But then she sees Shawn push back the sleeve of his T-shirt, flexing his bicep.

"I'm crushing it. See?"

Finn touches his arm and makes her lips into a little round *o*. "Crush harder," she says, rolling her eyes.

"Hey, it's only been four weeks. Give me a break."

Katriina jerks around so abruptly that the paper towel roll falls to the floor, unravelling in a long white ribbon before stopping at Finn's and Shawn's feet. "Whoops," she says. Everyone turns to look at her. A bright coin of blood shimmers on the counter beneath her upturned finger; another spreads across her new dress just about her navel. She picks up the roll and with one hand starts to awkwardly wind the paper towel back around it, waiting for someone to come over and help her. But no one does.

Later, when everyone moves into the dining room, they all stop and stare at Kate's empty chair. "You take it, Finn," Walter says eventually, waving his hand dismissively. "No point in getting all sentimental about it." Finn sits down reluctantly, and suddenly Katriina can see how much she resembles Kate, in a way that Nicki never has. Something about her eyes, the way they seem so far away. Nicki might be difficult to handle at the best of times, but at least she was always *present*.

Katriina knows the evening's seating arrangement is like a game of Jenga: one piece out of place and the whole thing comes tumbling down. So she steers Nicki and Hamish to the other end of the table, leaving a buffer of kids between them and Finn. Katriina, her finger wrapped in a paper towel secured with duct tape, seats herself between Tommy and Petey, making sure they don't gang up on Ross, who sits quietly next to Nicki, watching her cut up his steak for him. Walter sits on one side of Finn, Shawn on the other. Just like Katriina knew they would. As they settle in to their plates of food, Finn passes Shawn the bottle of HP Sauce and he dumps a little pool on his plate, leaving Katriina to wonder since when has Shawn liked HP Sauce? It seems like today she is finding out all kinds of new things about her husband.

Across the table from Katriina, Milan and Vienna are trading meatballs according to some obscure, predetermined shape system. London, who is a vegetarian of course, watches them with a look of disgust. "So sick," she says. "I can't even believe you're touching those, let alone eating them." But Milan and Vienna ignore her, lost in their own private twin world.

"Be quiet, London," Nicki says, pushing Ross's plate back towards him. "You don't hear us complaining about your gross-looking kwin-noa."

"It's actually pronounced keen-wah," Finn says, dishing some salad onto her plate.

"Whatever you say, Finn," Nicki says, sawing violently through her steak. "Everyone knows you're the smart one."

"Come on now, Nick," says Hamish. He puts his hand on her arm. "Don't murder the meat, for chrissake."

Shrugging off his hand, Nicki leans forward and stares at Finn. From across the room Katriina can feel her vibrating with anticipation, like a jungle cat preparing to pounce. "Hey, Finn," Nicki says. "I've been wondering. How did Thunder Bay News get that photo of Mom?"

Finn snorts in disbelief. "You think I gave the media a picture of Mom?"

"Finn wouldn't do that, Nicki," says Shawn. Coming to Finn's rescue, of course.

"She was the only one taking pictures at your wedding."

Katriina looks up from her plate, startled. She hasn't seen the picture, but knowing that it was taken at her wedding suddenly makes it seem personal, as though someone was deliberately trying to put a black mark on a happy memory. *Who else could it have been but Finn?* A swell of anger rises up in her chest.

"Mom was taking pictures, too," says Shawn.

"Not of herself, dummy," says Nicki.

Finn slams her wine glass on the table and leans forward as well, mirroring Nicki. "How could I have given it to them when I didn't even know what had happened?" she asks. "You know, *because no one bothered to tell me.*"

Nicki shrugs. "We didn't expect you'd care."

"Girls," says Walter, his brow furrowing deeply. "This isn't productive."

How can they be so self-centred? thinks Katriina. *Can't they see their father is in pain?*

"Anyway, I just assumed it was from your Facebook," Finn says. "You've got all kinds of crap on there."

"There are no pictures of Mom on my Facebook."

"Sure." Finn holds her wine glass out to Shawn, who is pouring some for Walter. "I'll have a little more," she says.

"Yeah, great, have more wine," says Nicki.

"Thanks, I think I will," says Finn.

"You might as well get completely hammered. Nothing bad ever happens when Finn Parker gets drunk."

"At least then it won't hurt as much when you stab me in the back."

"Oh, that's funny. *I* stabbed *you* in the back."

"That's enough," says Walter abruptly.

Leaning over her plate, Nicki impales a piece of steak on her fork and shoves it in her mouth, grinning at Finn from across the table. Finn rips open a roll and begins buttering it while Nicki continues to stare her down, chewing her steak menacingly. Everyone is silent. Katriina concentrates on cutting her own steak, which is well done, of course, charred so badly she can barely get her knife through it. At least she can feel the peaceful throbbing of her finger beneath the paper towel.

"Can I have some wine?" London asks.

"No," says Nicki, between chews. "You don't want to become a drunk like your aunt." Walter glares at her. "What?" she says.

"Nana always let me have wine."

Nicki shakes her head. "Well, Nana also thinks it's a good idea to take whisky barrels over waterfalls. So, you know, not a great example, babe."

They all keep their eyes down on their plates, except Nicki, who gazes straight ahead, a tiny smile on her lips as she chews. This is Nicki's element, thinks Katriina. She could sit here and screw with us all night.

But London is fuming. "Like you even know what Nana thinks," she mumbles.

"What was that?" says Nicki.

"Like you even fucking know what Nana thinks!" London yells.

Katriina feels the collective intake of breath around the table. Milan and Vienna cover their ears, and Ross slides off his chair and crawls under the table – their coping mechanisms for dealing with London's temper. She has always had a soft spot for London – she remembers what it was like to be a teenaged girl, volatile and con-fused. Still, she presses down on her finger and prays for London to let it go.

"No one knows what she thinks," Nicki says, unfazed. "She has just about as many brain cells as a wad of chewing gum."

"That's not true!" London looks like she is about to cry. "You all think she's crazy because she doesn't play by your stupid rules. But did you ever think you're the ones who are crazy for being so, like, rule-oriented to begin with?" She swipes her fork through the air, narrowly missing the wine bottle.

"Hey, L, watch out," says Finn, reaching out and gently push-ing her arm away from the bottle.

London turns to Finn, her face dark. She snatches her arm away from Finn's hand. "Don't touch me!"

Finn raises her hands in a gesture of surrender. "Holy crap, chill out," she says.

"Shut up, Aunt F, you don't even live here! Stop acting like you give a shit about us! And get the fuck out of Nana's chair!" London pushes back her own chair so violently it topples over, skidding into the wall behind her. She gives it a little kick as she stomps out of the room.

No one says anything. Hamish makes a move to go after her, but Nicki glares at him and he sits back down. After a minute, Walter gets up and picks up London's chair, setting it back into place. Ross crawls out from under the table and into his mother's lap. Utensils clash against plates, teeth meet teeth. Katriina concentrates on chewing her steak, trying to figure out how to break the silence.

Shawn beats her to it. "Well," he says. He takes a sip of wine. "I know it's been a terrible couple of days for everyone. I think we could all use some good news."

Katriina feels a knife slice through her chest, hot and sharp and nothing like the relief of the knife in her finger. *No*, she silently pleads, over and over again. *No, no, no. Oh please no.*

"We're having another baby!"

No, no, no, no, no. Katriina smiles weakly as ten sets of eyes turn to stare at her. She resists the urge to run out of the room. "It's true," she says, shrugging in what she hopes is a blithe sort of way. "Eight weeks now." She can't even bring herself to look at Shawn, can't bear to see his goofy grin, eyes wide, radiating hopefulness.

This is the moment he wants the most, she realizes. *At least I can give him this.*

"Oh, great," says Petey loudly. "It better not be a girl." The table erupts in laughter. Her darling Petey, the little comedian, unknowingly saving her once again. Everyone starts talking at once, congratulating her, patting Shawn on the back, teasing Petey about having tea parties with his new sister. Amidst the activity, she sees Finn turn to Shawn.

"I guess this means you're not moving to Ottawa," she says.

Katriina feels her heart explode like a bomb in her chest, the words *moving to Ottawa* like shrapnel ricocheting through her body. *Moving to Ottawa. Moving to Ottawa.* She excuses herself and goes to the bathroom, where she spends the rest of the dinner meticulously prodding at her wounded finger with a pair of tweezers, trying to figure out how to breathe again.

After dinner, Shawn tells Katriina he wants to go to the hospital to see Kate. "I'll come with you," she says, even though it is getting late and she is tired and she will have to go to the office tomorrow, even though it is a Sunday, because there is month-end and there is Krista Shepherd and there is everything and nothing all at once. There is her life collapsing while Kate is lying in a coma. She just wants a moment with Shawn, away from the rest of the family. Just one moment, to be with her husband, to remind herself that they are a team, that they are in this together.

"We forgot to get milk," Shawn says as they pull out of the driveway. He already has his tablet open on his lap, scrolling through emails. All of his earlier joviality is gone. Katriina wonders if it was even real, or just a show for his family.

"Okay," she says. "Can I have the Safeway card?"

"You have it," says Shawn. "I gave it to you when you were buying the steaks."

"I gave it back to you."

"No, you didn't."

"Yes, I did." She might not have. She doesn't know why she's pushing, though sometimes she wonders if these mundane details are the only things they have left to talk about. At the next red light, she gives Shawn a pointed look, and he pulls out his wallet, flinging it across the dash.

"Go ahead, check," he says. "It's not there."

"Forget it," says Katriina, manoeuvring the SUV out onto the highway. "You're right. You're always right."

"What's that supposed to mean?"

"Nothing."

"Clearly it means something."

"It means nothing, Shawn, okay?"

"Right," he says. He turns back to his tablet. "Nothing."

Katriina squeezes her hands on the steering wheel. "Fine, you want to know what it means? It means since when did you start liking HP Sauce on your steak? And since when did you start lifting weights?"

"What?" She can feel him looking at her, but she keeps her eyes focused on the car in front of her. "What the hell are you talking about?"

"Lifting weights, Shawn. Why didn't you tell me you started lifting weights?"

"I don't know, I didn't tell anybody."

"You told Finn."

Shawn exhales loudly. "Oh," he says. "Of course. This is about Finn."

"This is not about Finn!" She turns towards him. "This is about you!"

"Watch out!" Shawn yells, bracing himself against the dashboard. She turns back to the road to see the car in front of her is no longer moving. She slams on the brakes, stopping just inches before hitting it. As she sits there, trying to catch her breath, she sees a deer and a fawn bound across the road. Her eyes fill with tears, but she quickly blinks them away.

"What's in Ottawa?" she asks.

Shawn doesn't say anything. The car in front of them starts up again, and Katriina eases her foot onto the accelerator. She wonders if he is going to answer her, or if he is just going to pretend he doesn't know what she's talking about. "A job offer," he says finally. "At Alex's company. But it wasn't serious. If it was serious, I would have told you."

"Right," says Katrina. "But since it wasn't serious, you told Finn."

"It just came up while we were talking about something else!"

"Something else you didn't tell me?"

"Jesus, Katriina!" Shawn leans his head back against the seat and shuts his eyes.

Right, I guess this conversation is over. She resists the urge to slam on the brakes again, sending him flying into the dash. They drive the rest of the way in silence.

When they get to the hospital, there are still a few reporters standing outside the doors. They try to slip by unnoticed, but one of them, a beautiful young woman with long brown hair and overly made-up eyes, recognizes them and extends a microphone towards them as they cross the lobby. "Excuse me, you're relatives of Katherine Parker, aren't you? Do you have time to answer a few questions?"

"Get out of my way," Shawn says, pushing aside the microphone.

"I'm sorry," Katriina says automatically, then cringes as Shawn glares at her. She feels under her sleeve for the elastic.

When they get to the eighth floor, Shawn goes to talk to one of the doctors, and Katriina goes into Kate's room and sits in the chair next to her bed. Kate's breathing is shallow, noisy, but her face is peaceful. Her hair is matted, and Katriina leans over, prising apart the knotted strands with her fingers before smoothing it down with her palm. She is startled by how warm Kate is. She holds her hand to Kate's forehead, realizing as she does that Kate is not running a temperature, she is simply alive where Katriina had assumed she would be cold, lifeless.

As Katriina draws her hand away, she can feel Shawn in the doorway, watching her. "I lost the baby," she says, without looking up.

When she finally does look up, Shawn is gone. She collapses against Kate in the bed, willing her to wake up, to reach out to Katriina, to tell her something about Shawn that only a mother would know. But there is no comfort there, just an unrelenting heartbeat. Katriina can't stand it anymore – the panic gnawing at her insides, the desperate need for distraction – and so she dumps the contents of her purse onto the bed, pawing through the pile until she finds a nail file, which she cleanly and swiftly stabs into her thigh. The relief is immediate, followed by a guilt so crippling that she shoves everything haphazardly back into her purse and bolts from the room without looking back.

NINE

I f London could be any kind of animal it would be a shark, even though most people don't really think of fish as animals, like all those dumb girls at school who claim they are vegetarians but still chow down on fish sticks in the caf when it's the daily special. London would like to be a nurse shark or a whale shark, one that is friendly and doesn't eat a lot of meat, one that's sort of an underdog that just goes about its business of being awesome while great whites go around hogging all the attention. Her second choice would be a seal because they seem so relaxed all the time, having fun with their seal friends in the ocean and not worrying about much of anything. Third would probably be a wolf or a cougar maybe, something that lives on land and stalks and kills its prey like a real badass. Although in real life London is a vegetarian, she understands the importance of the food chain and respects an animal that has to kill its own food, as opposed to, say, just eating a poor little innocent pig that lives in a tiny pen and has never even seen the outside. It's like the true wild animal is really man.

Most girls in her class would probably say they would want to be a horse. London doesn't have anything against horses except that being super into horses is kind of *vanilla* for a real animal lover. Anyone can like horses. It's like saying your favourite food is a cheeseburger or your favourite music is anything except for country; it's easy, it doesn't take any imagination at all. No, on her hierarchy of animals she would want to be, a horse is pretty far down on the list.

London likes wild animals, and she likes the ones from the ocean best, even though she has never even seen the ocean, thanks to her stupid parents who never take her anywhere. But she has read every book about the ocean she can take out from the library, from guides to marine animals to novels about fishermen. She also has a pirated collection of underwater documentaries and a DVD of *The Little Mermaid* that Hamish bought her because he was trying to bond with her or something, and that her mom makes her keep even though it has nothing to do with the real ocean. London is also a member of the aquarium at Mall of America in Minneapolis, even though her mom hasn't taken her there for two years. But when they do go, while the twins and Ross ride the stupid rides and her mother shops for bras at Victoria's Secret, London sits outside the shark tank and watches the sharks for hours, trying to block out the screaming kids and the moms with strollers and the dads with cameras and just be *one* with the sharks. Then when they leave, the twins pinch their noses and complain that she smells like fish and Hamish sings "Under the Sea" to her in that dumb Sebastian the crab accent and London sulks for the rest of the trip because obviously no one in her family takes her seriously at all.

London often suspects she was born into the wrong family, like God or whatever had her lined up for another family – parents who were marine biologists maybe, or oceanographers, who would have taught her how to scuba dive and taken vacations to exotic locations where they would shoot video of coral reefs and schools of dolphins. Then Nicki got randomly knocked up and screwed up London's true destiny. Like some kind of cosmic joke, here she is, an ocean girl living on the biggest lake in North America, a body of water that looks like an ocean and sometimes sounds like an ocean but is totally *not* an ocean. People are always so excited about dumb old Lake Superior, but there is nothing really interesting down there except maybe bass or pickerel. London knows this because she has checked, going out on the lake with Papa on his coffee cruises or snorkelling methodically along the shore searching for something, anything, to make it worth living next to. But there's nothing, just sticks and rocks and leeches and everyone splashing around like idiots, floating on blow-up tubes or spraying each other with water guns.

The only person in Thunder Bay who even sort of understands London is her grandmother, and now she is in a stupid coma, and so London has no one.

◆ ◆ ◆

PONYO: I don't think I can come.

SHARKBOY: Fuck. Are you sure? Have you asked everyone?

PONYO: Yes!

PONYO: Well, no. I guess there's my aunt. She's visiting from down south.

SHARKBOY: You need to ask her.

PONYO: I don't know, I don't think she'll go for it. I kind of yelled at her at dinner tonight.

SHARKBOY: What happened?

PONYO: I don't even remember.

PONYO: I was so mad.

PONYO: I told her to go fuck herself or something.

SHARKBOY: LOL, that's my girl.

PONYO: She used to be cool, you know? But now she only cares about herself.

SHARKBOY: She's scared of living, just like the rest of them.

PONYO: That's what I thought, too!

PONYO: Promise me we won't be that lame when we get that old.

SHARKBOY: We'll never get that old.

◆ ◆ ◆

Adam Pelley, marine biologist, television celebrity, philanthropist and ecologist and world-famous adventurer, is London's boyfriend. It still seems so hard to believe. It's as if the stars fell right out of the sky and into her front yard or something, as if the laws of nature had been broken. One minute she's just a regular teenager writing algebra tests and fighting with her sisters, and the next she's online talking to someone whose television show she adores and watches every week without fail. And then that person is telling her that he loves her. He wants to be with her and have her join him in his mission to save the world's oceans. Suddenly, instead of writing algebra tests, she is getting ready to begin her life's work alongside the man she loves.

Adam. Even his name is cute. Has anyone ever heard of an ugly Adam? She is pretty sure there is no such thing. There aren't even any boys in her school named Adam. They all have dumb names like Hunter or Jayden or Cody, names that in a few years are going to start sounding really dumb when they have to wear suits and go to work or whatever. Like, as if there would ever be a Prime Minister Cody, ha ha. London isn't super happy about her own name, but at least there's a reason for it: it's a real place that her mother was supposed to go to before she got pregnant. And even though London knows she must have been sad about it at first, her mom always tells her that in the end she got the better London.

You might not be able to tell from television, but Adam is kind and gentle and not at all like you might imagine a celebrity to be. Plus he's only twenty-five. That's just nine years older than London is, so it's not like it's a crime or anything, she's pretty sure. London knows much more about Adam than just what people know from television. She knows that he loves animals as much as she does, and that he had trouble in school when he was younger because he spent all his time volunteering at the local animal shelter and at the aquarium, because he knew what his true calling in life was from a young age. She knows that he grew up poor in the slums of Los Angeles, with just his mom and his younger sister, and that he felt like he had to be the man of the house, which put a lot of pressure on him. She knows that when he got older he worked really hard in school and earned a scholarship to the University of California, because he wanted to do something bigger with his life than just sit around on a Saturday night and get wasted with his friends, did she know what he meant?

Of course she knew what he meant. It's like he read her journal or something. It's like he knows her life. That's why they are so close, even though they have never met. That's why she knows they are meant to be together. Adam is her *spirit guide*. He knows her soul, he gets that she sometimes feels like an alien in her family, that she wants to do something bigger with her life, too.

The day before her grandmother went over Kakabeka Falls in a barrel, she was going to drive London to Duluth, Minnesota, three hours south of Thunder Bay. In retrospect, London supposes it might look like she was taking advantage of her grandmother, but London would never do that. Never. She loves Nana so much. Even though London had pretty much been avoiding her since the Around the Track incident – which was pretty embarrassing for London, the way it just gave everyone one more thing to make fun of her for – she really had thought that Nana understood what she was going through and wanted to help her. And London knew her grandmother had been depressed lately, so maybe helping her granddaughter would give her some kind of renewed purpose in life? And it would be *life-affirming*, London thought, for Nana to go on one last adventure, something that she could remember the way she remembered her wedding day or any of the other big events that had happened in her life. (London couldn't think of any right then, but she was sure there must be a few.) There wasn't much that Nana remembered these days, but London was pretty sure that taking her to Duluth would be one of them.

And it wasn't like it was premeditated or anything. London and her grandmother had been at the grocery store, shopping for ingredients for the bake sale that London was organizing to help raise money for the World Wildlife Fund at the community centre the next weekend. She was telling Nana about how she had wanted to hold the bake sale at school a few months earlier, but then Anastasia Peters and a few of the other suck-up student council girls complained that it would compete with their bake sale to raise money for some kind of stupid dance, and the vice-principal said they had priority because it was *school-related*, even though their brownies were super gross and probably just from a package and everyone liked London's cookies so much better.

"I'm so proud of you, baby," Nana had said. "You're really trying to change the world. And you will."

London shook her head. "I don't know. It's just a dumb bake sale. There are people out there who are doing actual, real important work, you know?" And suddenly she was spilling it all, telling Nana about Duluth and Adam and the bull shark that he was going to try to rescue. The next thing London knew, they were driving down Highway 61 towards the border.

"This is going to be fun," Nana had said. "We're going to meet a real live celebrity!"

"Yeah," said London. "And we're going to help him rescue a shark. Remember? That's the important part."

"Oh dear. What's a shark?" Nana asked. "It sounds familiar."

They were just past Loch Lomond when London remembered they didn't have their passports, so they drove back to Victor Street and London made her grandmother stay in the car while she went to get them. While she was home she decided to pack some extra clothes for herself, and for Nana, and maybe some snacks, too? At the last minute she went into the drawer next to the fridge and grabbed an envelope of American money that her mother kept hidden under the phone book, just in case.

And then London turned around and Nana was standing in the doorway. "London, dear," she said. "Where are you going with all that stuff?"

"Uh, Duluth?" London said.

Nana nodded. "Okay, then. Have fun!"

And so London had to explain everything again, and Nana said the same things that she had said before. She agreed that they definitely should go to Duluth as soon as possible, but they should wait until tomorrow morning because the weather that night was going to be bad. London was annoyed, but she knew she shouldn't push it or else Nana might change her mind or tell someone, and then it would be all over.

The next morning, London watched out her bedroom window as her grandmother lugged a whisky barrel into the back of Papa's truck and drove off. *Of course she fucking forgot, she's a fucking nutcase*, she thought then, sitting back down at her desk. Now that she knows what happened, she wishes that she had had some nicer thought about Nana instead.

◆ ◆ ◆

SHARKBOY: Did you ask her yet?
PONYO: No, she's not here right now, surprise surprise.
PONYO: I'll ask her tomorrow. But I'm nervous!
PONYO: She probably hates me.

SHARKBOY: Don't be nervous. Who cares what she thinks.

SHARKBOY: You just need to get here, I can take care of
everything after that.

PONYO: I'll figure it out.

SHARKBOY: You'd better!

SHARKBOY: I don't know how much longer I can go on without you.

PONYO: Whatever.

SHARKBOY: It's true.

PONYO: WHATEVER!

SHARKBOY: You're cute.

◆ ◆ ◆

London and Adam met in a chat room on the Monterey aquarium
website. There's this webcam set up in the shark tank, and you
can log in and watch the sharks and talk to the other people who
are watching the sharks, too. There's a bunch of regulars. London
supposes she is a regular, since she's on it all the time. She doesn't
always talk to people, but she likes to have the live stream in the
background when she's doing homework or writing her petition
emails to stop animal testing or regulate zoos. She even used to
watch the shark cam sometimes at school, although she had to stop
once Anastasia Peters found out and started calling her Chum,
like the gross fish guts fishermen use to lure sharks, and then of
course all the other girls in her class started calling her that, too.
All the girls London goes to school with are bitches.

One day, when London was still grounded after the whole
getting arrested thing, she got a private message in the chat room
from a user she had never seen before.

SHARKBOY: Are you a mermaid?
PONYO: Huh?

SHARKBOY: Your name. Isn't that from a movie about a
   mermaid?
PONYO: Yeah.
PONYO: How do you know that? No one knows that.
SHARKBOY: I like movies.
SHARKBOY: So are you?
PONYO: What?
SHARKBOY: A mermaid!
PONYO: No, I'm just a regular girl.
SHARKBOY: You don't seem like just a regular girl.
PONYO: Shut up and leave me alone.

She ignored him after that because she assumed he was making fun of her, which was her default thought whenever anyone talked to her, no matter what they said, because it was usually true. But then as soon as she logged on the next night, he started talking to her again.

SHARKBOY: Hey, regular girl.
PONYO: Go away, I'm busy.
SHARKBOY: Busy watching sharks swim around?
PONYO: No. Homework.
SHARKBOY: You are not. You're probably reading National
   Geographic or something.
PONYO: If you must know, I'm researching aquariums in
   Canada. I want to work at one someday.
SHARKBOY: I work at an aquarium.
PONYO: You do not.
SHARKBOY: Yes, I do! I work at this aquarium.
PONYO: You work at the Monterey aquarium?
PONYO: Doing what?
SHARKBOY: Research, mostly.
SHARKBOY: And I look after the sharks.

PONYO: So you're like an old man?
SHARKBOY: I'm 25!
PONYO: Like I said.
SHARKBOY: So I guess you're some kind of little kid then.
PONYO: I'm 16!
SHARKBOY: Like I said.

He wasn't online the next day, or the day after that, and London found herself wondering where he was. He was annoying, but at least he was kind of interesting, not like those other people on the chat room who just kept wanting to talk about their kids or their cats.

On the third day, she was at school when she saw him sign on a couple of minutes after she did. She felt her stomach do a little jump, which made her angry, like who was he to talk to her and then disappear for a few days and make her care?

SHARKBOY: So what's your favourite kind of shark?
PONYO: I don't have one. That's like a mom saying which one
    of her kids is her favourite.
SHARKBOY: My mom would say my sister. No question.
PONYO: See, even your mom doesn't like you.

She stopped chatting with him after that, even though he kept sending her stupid smiley faces. She was sure that he must be a creepy old guy because who other than creepy old guys used generic smiley faces? Finally, after a few days, she got fed up.

PONYO: Stop sending me those stupid smiley faces!
PONYO: They just make you look desperate.
SHARKBOY: Are you ever going to talk to me?
PONYO: I am talking to you.
SHARKBOY: You know what I mean.

118

SHARKBOY: Really TALK to me.

PONYO: Why should I?

PONYO: I don't even know you.

SHARKBOY: The only way to get to know me is to talk to me.

PONYO: Why do you care so much?

SHARKBOY: I think you're interesting.

SHARKBOY: You ARE interesting.

PONYO: Okay. I'll tell you one thing.

SHARKBOY: What's your name?

PONYO: Ponyo.

SHARKBOY: Your real name.

PONYO: It is my real name. I'm Ponyo. I was taken from the sea.

SHARKBOY: Not true. Ponyo went from the sea willingly.

SHARKBOY: I think you'd rather go back to the sea.

SHARKBOY: You're like a reverse-Ponyo.

SHARKBOY: You're not a mermaid who wants to be a girl, you're a girl who wants to be a mermaid.

PONYO: Whatever.

PONYO: If you already know so much about me, why do you even need me to talk to you?

SHARKBOY: I don't know everything about you. I don't know your name.

SHARKBOY: You there?

PONYO: London. My name's London.

SHARKBOY: Adam.

PONYO: Your name's Adam and you work at the Monterey aquarium?

PONYO: LOL

SHARKBOY: What's so funny?

PONYO: And you look after the sharks?

SHARKBOY: Yup.

PONYO: As if you're Adam Pelley.

SHARKBOY: . . .
SHARKBOY: How did you know that?
PONYO: AS IF YOU'RE ADAM PELLEY.

It was so funny to think back at how mean she'd been to him, when now it was like she couldn't even remember her life without him. After all, what were the odds that she would meet her soul mate so early in her life, when so many other people had to wait so long, until they were like thirty or whatever? And then, when he told her he was going to be in Duluth, which was only three hours away, to shoot that Discovery Channel special, it was like the planets had aligned and given them an opportunity to be together. London was not going to waste it, no matter what she had to do to get there.

TEN

After dinner, Finn gets up from the table and goes to the living room. Her father is watching the baseball game. The Jays, of course. Finn had been worried about seeing her father – seeing the ways in which he had grown smaller, weaker – but if anything he seems healthier, more robust. Aside from a little more grey in his dark brown hair, it's like he hasn't aged at all. Finn hopes he isn't disappointed in the way she looks. Suddenly she wishes she had taken better care of herself – visited the dentist more often, gone to the gym. She wants him to know she can take care of herself. She wants him to know that she is doing all right.

Walter smiles at her as she sits down, pats her hand. "I'm happy you're here, Serafina." Her father is the only one who still calls her Serafina, the only one who can say it in a way that makes her feel like he's actually talking to her and not someone else.

"Me, too," says Finn. In the kitchen she can hear Katriina and Nicki doing the dishes. She knows that she should go in there and help, but she can't bring herself to face them – Nicki with her snide remarks, Katriina with her happy baby glow. It makes Finn ill just thinking about it.

Walter leans forward in his seat to reach for a brownie on the coffee table. "You can come out on the coffee cruise with me tomorrow morning, if you'd like," he says before taking a bite. Finn cringes involuntarily. Every Sunday morning from April until November, Walter runs a tour of the Thunder Bay harbour, where he serves coffee and pastries from Kahvila. If he's out of town, one of his employees will run it, but when he's home he never misses it. When Finn was a teenager her parents used the tour as punishment: come home too late on a Saturday night and you had to work the coffee cruise on Sunday morning. Finn hopes that her father isn't trying to punish her for something now.

Shawn comes through the back door and sits down next to her. "Sounds like you're in trouble, Finn." From the yard, she can hear the kids screaming, but no one seems worried. She wonders how parents can tell the happy screams from the dangerous ones. "Planning on breaking curfew tonight?"

Finn yawns and leans back against him. "Right. I'm lucky if I can stay up past ten these days."

They watch the baseball game in silence. Finn tries to remember the last time she and Shawn and her father were in a room together, just the three of them. Before she moved out, certainly. On the rare occasions they were all back at Victor Street, Walter tended to avoid her and Shawn. Or maybe it was the other way around, Finn isn't sure. But being together now feels oddly natural, as though they are survivors of a war heading back to the battleground together to survey the damage. There is a sense of solidarity. Or maybe Finn is just imagining it, desperate as she always has been for some kind of connection with her father. She glances up at Shawn to see if he feels it, too, but his face is unreadable, his eyes staring straight ahead at the television.

When the game goes to commercial, Walter flips the channel to the local news. Finn has forgotten how bad it is – the graphics that haven't been updated since the 1980s, the theme music that sounds like it was composed on a toy synthesizer. The reporter is talking about a group of concerned citizens who have been protesting a potential wind farm on the Nor'Wester Mountains. That's another thing Finn had forgotten about Thunder Bay: there is always a group of concerned citizens. This is why no shit ever gets done. A group of concerned citizens protesting is probably the reason the local news hasn't changed its graphics in thirty years.

The camera goes back to the anchor. "Coming up after the break, Cassandra Coelho will update us on the local Thunder Bay woman who made history yesterday at a local landmark. We'll have more on the Conqueror of Kakabeka, next on Thunder Bay News."

Walter sighs and flicks back to the game. "I can't even enjoy the news anymore."

"That reporter called me yesterday," Finn says. "At home in Mississauga."

"She called me, too," Shawn says. "At the restaurant."

Walter stares at the television, unblinking. "Unbelievable."

"I wonder how she found us," says Shawn.

"The Facebook?" Walter says.

Finn smiles. Her father, social media guru. "Maybe," she says. "I didn't talk to her, though." It's suddenly important to Finn that her father knows this.

"Talk to who?" Nicki asks, coming into the room and plunking herself down in the armchair.

"Cassandra Coelho," says Finn. "The reporter."

"Oh yeah, that bitch," says Nicki. "She can rot in hell before she gets anything from me."

Walter, Finn, and Shawn all nod. The four of them sit there, staring at the baseball game, united in their hatred of a woman who is just doing her job. But they *are* united, for what is probably the first time ever. It would give Finn the warm fuzzies if she wasn't sure it was all going to come crashing down around them in the next five minutes.

123

In reality, it takes less than one minute for things to go from fuzzy to potentially homicidal: the amount of time it takes for Hamish to walk through the living room carrying an armful of empties for the recycling bin, and Finn thoughtlessly asking him if he needs any help.

"What the hell?" Nicki says. "Katriina and me are out in the kitchen slaving away over the dishes, but you ask *him* if *he* needs help?"

"Katriina and I," Finn says before she can stop herself.

"Shut the fuck up!" says Nicki. "What is wrong with you?"

"Nicki!" Shawn says, glaring at her. Walter stares straight ahead, suddenly very interested in the batting average of the Jays' star hitter.

"I'm fine," says Hamish, adjusting his grip on the bottles. "I just need someone to get the door."

"I'll do it," says Finn, standing.

"He said get the *door*, not stick your *tongue* down his throat."

Nobody moves. Finn can feel a lump form in her throat. "You know what, Nicki," she says. "That's not fair."

"You should have stayed in Mississauga where you belong," says Nicki.

Blinking back tears, Finn goes over and with a flourish holds the back door open for Hamish. He walks through hesitantly. Then she steps outside after him, slamming the door. "Give me your keys," she says as he dumps the empties into the bin.

"I only have Nicki's," he says.

Of course. "Well, give me those." He hands them over reluctantly, standing as far away from her as possible, as though she's going to attack him or something. So she reaches out and grabs his face and plants a wet one on his mouth.

As she gets into Nicki's car, Finn starts to think: *Shit. Maybe that was the wrong way to handle things.* But there's nothing she can do about it now.

———

Finn knows she should go to the hospital, but instead her instincts take her all the way through town to Barkley's, the sports bar where her old roommate Alyssa works as a bartender. As she drives she tries to keep her eyes on the road, to not look around and see the ways in which Thunder Bay has changed, although she already knows that, at least in this neighbourhood, the change has come in the form of decay. All the businesses around Barkley's – other than a pawn shop and a deli that processes freshly shot deer into sausages and pepperettes – have closed down since she was last here, including their favourite old diner, a hardware store, a bakery, and an appliance repair shop.

At least Barkley's is still there. In a place like Thunder Bay, people will always need to drink. And Alyssa is still there, too, god help her. Alyssa: blond, gorgeous, hopeless, working behind the bar in a Leafs T-shirt and a ponytail, pouring two-dollar draft for the toothless barflies since high school, when her mother got sick and her father got laid off from the mill. Finn watches her through the window, suddenly nervous about going in because it occurs to her that Alyssa might be kind of pissed at her. The last time Finn spoke to her was from a payphone in Wawa, on her way to Toronto, swearing up and down that she wouldn't be gone long.

Finn opens the door, bracing herself for a confrontation of some sort. But when Alyssa sees her, she simply raises an eyebrow and motions to a stool. That's it – no fireworks, no drama. And that's when Finn remembers why she loves Alyssa so much. She is stoic as a goddamned rock.

Alyssa doesn't ask what Finn is doing back in Thunder Bay. She doesn't have to. The TVs in the bar are all showing the waterfall footage. "I'm guessing you need a shot of something," she says.

"Anything," Finn says, sitting down next to a long-haired white guy wearing a jacket from the 1995 World Nordic Games. Gasp, thunk, splash, her mother goes over the falls.

Alyssa quickly changes the channel to baseball, then pours Finn a shot of Jack Daniel's and a beer. "How's your mom?"

"Still in a coma," Finn says. "I mean, as far as I've heard."

Alyssa nods. "I ran into her last week at the grocery store. She said that she and your dad were thinking about taking a trip to Minneapolis. It didn't sound like, you know, she wanted to . . . It sounded like she was making plans for the future, that's all."

Finn takes a long drink of beer. What if Kate had never meant to make it out of that river? The thought is just too much for her to handle. "Yeah, well," she says. "Hey. I'm sorry for . . . you know. Leaving like that."

Alyssa waves her off. "Why would you be sorry? You don't owe me anything." She gives a little half smile. "Except maybe a couple months' rent." When she comes out from behind the bar to clear some beer bottles, Finn realizes her stomach is the size of France.

"You're pregnant?" Finn asks, immediately thinking, *Oh god, please let her actually be pregnant.*

"Seven months."

It seems like a weird, clichéd question to ask, but she has no other choice: "Who's the father?"

Alyssa laughs. "Come on, you can't be that far behind." She motions to a booth in the corner, where Eric, Barkley's owner, sits talking on his cell phone, the table in front of him littered with papers and empty beer bottles. Finn shivers. She and Alyssa used to make fun of Eric, call him Mr. Hands, for obvious reasons. Looking back at all of that now, it seems painfully clear that it was Alyssa's destiny to be impregnated by her skeevy, hard-luck boss. Watching Alyssa resting the drink tray on her stomach as she helps him straighten up his papers, Finn wonders if maybe Alyssa didn't actually get it right, keeping things uncomplicated, within reach. Then Eric winks at Finn with his scuzzy little beady eye and she scratches that thought.

126

"Congrats," she says when Alyssa gets back, with all the sincerity she can muster.

Alyssa waves her off again. "It's not like I ran a marathon. Anyone can get knocked up." She puts the tray back down on the bar. "But I'm guessing you're not here to catch up with me."

"Hey, Lyss," the white guy next to Finn slurs. "Can I get another Canadian?"

"You can wait till I'm finished talking, Marv." She leans her elbows on the bar, and close up Finn can see how tired she is. Her eyes still sparkle, though, with a hint of the old Alyssa, the one who used to dance around in her underwear to Britney Spears, help Finn steal gum from the Tiki Hut. "He's in the pool room."

"Who's in the pool room?"

Alyssa raises her eyebrows. "Dallas," she says slowly. "Isn't that who you're here to see?"

Finn feels her insides drop to the floor. "Dallas? Dallas is here?"

"Dallas Vaughn's always here," Marv says. "He's here like it's his *job*."

"No one asked you, Marv," says Alyssa. She turns back to Finn. "You didn't know he was here?" She has that concerned-head-tilt thing going on – no one knows what a mess Dallas made of Finn better than Alyssa. *But I am not that person anymore*, Finn tells herself. *I am an adult with a life outside of Thunder Bay, in a real city with real bars where they don't make you pay up front for your drinks. I have a house and a car and a lawnmower that I sometimes even actually use to mow the lawn. Hell, I even own not one but two sets of matching royal blue Egyptian cotton sheets. The world is my motherfucking oyster. There is no way I'm going to let Dallas take that away from me.*

She shouldn't be surprised that Dallas didn't stay out in B.C. – his parents are here, and so is his whole giant Polish family, who all treated him like he was the second coming of Christ. Why wouldn't he come back? Finn wonders if Nicki knows. If he's seen

Ross. "It's fine, Lyss," Finn says. "Like I give a shit about Dallas Vaughn. It's not like I haven't been with anyone else in the past, what, eight years?" *I made sure of that last night.*

"Hey, Dallas!" Marv hollers. "There's a chick here to see you."

"Go home, Marv," Alyssa yells back, waving the bar cloth towards the door. Finn covers her ears, but she can still hear the footsteps approaching behind her. She has the childish desire to shut her eyes and make loud noises until he goes away, wishing like hell that she had changed out of her yoga pants. You always imagine how reunions with ex-lovers will go, how you will be beautiful and happy and have your shit together, and they will be the ones broken apart. You're not supposed to smell like the last time you bathed was a month ago. You're not supposed to look like your mother just went over a waterfall in a whisky barrel.

Finn takes a deep breath, fixing her face into what she hopes is a casually sexy expression. She spins the barstool around. And someone punches her right in the nose.

Next thing Finn knows she's lying on a rotting couch in the back room of Barkley's, her head throbbing. Alyssa is sitting beside her on a stack of empty beer cases, her fingers drumming against her stomach. "Wow," she says. "Who knew you'd go down like that?"

Finn touches her nose, then breathes in sharply. "Is it broken?"

Alyssa laughs. "Man, southern Ontario has made you soft," she says, handing Finn an ice pack wrapped in a bar rag. "Have you forgotten how to take a punch?"

Finn's vision is kind of blurry. "I'm not used to being hit by guys," she says. She presses the ice pack to her nose and flinches.

"That wasn't a guy," Alyssa says. "That was Tanya."

"Tanya?" Finn tries to think back: the spin on the stool, a fist coming towards her, the flicker of a moment in between. It was a nondescript fist, neither overly masculine nor feminine. "It was Dallas," she says. "Dallas hit me."

Alyssa laughs again. "Dallas would never hit anyone. He's too much of a pussy. It was Tanya."

Finn closes her eyes again and sees the hazy features of an extremely pissed-off woman. "Native chick, short black hair, straight bangs, glasses?"

"Yup. She's Dallas's girlfriend." Alyssa smiles. "I guess she's heard about you."

Finn sits up slowly and then immediately feels dizzy so she puts her head between her knees. Of course Dallas has a girlfriend. Dallas cannot live without a girlfriend. And while she's remembering this, she's also remembering that he has a giant mole above his left nipple, that he always says "film" instead of "movie," that he fucked her twin sister. She is remembering that all the trouble in her life has always originated with Dallas Vaughn.

WARNING: DO NOT UNDER ANY CIRCUMSTANCES LET DALLAS VAUGHN BACK INTO YOUR LIFE. PERIOD.

"Do you want some water or something?" Alyssa asks.

Finn stands up, wobbling. "Maybe another shot," she says. Alyssa shrugs, unimpressed. She thinks Finn has lost the northern part of herself. Maybe she's right.

They walk back into the bar and Finn slides back onto her stool, rests her head in her hands as she gingerly dabs the ice pack against her face.

"Hey!" she hears someone shout. Tanya is standing by the door, her jacket hanging from one arm. "Stand up, bitch."

"Eric!" Alyssa calls across the bar, where the father of her child is trying to fish a quarter out from behind the jukebox with the handle of a broom. "I thought I told you to get rid of her."

"Shut up, Alyssa!" Tanya yells. "I'll hit you, skank, I don't even care that you're pregnant."

"Bring it!" Alyssa yells back, coming out from behind the bar with her game face on. Finn stands up, looking around for some kind of weapon she can defend herself with. But Tanya's not coming for Finn now, she's coming for Alyssa, and Alyssa stands her ground, hands out like she's going to rip those glasses off of Tanya's face and shove them down her throat.

Just as Alyssa makes a run for Tanya, the bathroom door opens and Marv comes out, wiping his hands on his jacket. "Hey, hold up, little lady," he says to Alyssa, grabbing her by the arms and pulling her into him. Eric lets out a roar, cracking the broom handle across Marv's back. Marv howls and lets Alyssa go, stumbling forward. Eric hits him again with half of the broom handle, and Marv whips around and swings blindly, hitting Eric in the leg. Alyssa kicks Marv in the shin and then loses her balance, falling onto her butt on the disgusting Barkley's floor.

Finn sees Tanya drop her jacket and make her way towards Alyssa, so she kicks over a barstool right into her path and watches her trip and fall, skidding head-first past Alyssa and knocking into Eric, who falls on top of Marv. Then everyone is in a loud pile on the floor and Finn doesn't know what to do. She throws a twenty down on the bar and grabs her keys, but just as she's about to leave she spots him standing there in the doorway to the pool room. Dallas.

He doesn't look any older, which is infuriating. She wants him to be pudgy, or gaunt, or bald; she wants him to be lacking something. But there he is, hustling pool at the bar after work as though he's still twenty-five and his main goal in life is to save up enough money to spend the summer following Phish on tour in a beat-up camper van.

Their eyes meet for a moment, but instead of thinking what an absolute dick he is and how he's just standing there passively watching this fight happen, all she can think is how much she misses him. Then it occurs to her that she is just standing there and watching, too.

Maybe we did deserve each other.

Dallas turns around and goes back into the pool room, and she feels some kind of spell being broken. "I should go home," she says to no one in particular. What she means is her real home, her front stoop, her living room with the soft white lighting, her bed with the Egyptian cotton sheets, Max, quiet, space, familiar night skies. But she knows that, at least for tonight, she will have to settle for Victor Street.

Finn drives around for hours, not knowing where to go. She stops at McDonald's on Cumberland and gets a milkshake and a cheeseburger, then eats it parked at the marina watching the kids in the skatepark, the old people walking their dogs, the gulls shitting on the statues. Then she drives to County Park to buy a bottle of bourbon at an LCBO where no one will recognize her, bringing it back to the same McDonald's and drinking half of it while sitting in a stall, listening to two drunk teenaged girls talk about whether or not they are technically still virgins if they let a guy come in their mouth. When the girls leave she orders another cheeseburger, which she eats in the car in the parking lot in thirty seconds, stuffing the wrapper into Nicki's glove compartment. Then, because nothing else she's done tonight makes any sense in the slightest, she goes back into the restaurant and orders a third cheeseburger. The kid behind the counter doesn't miss a beat.

"Are you sure you want just one?" he asks as he punches up her order.

"Just give me the cheeseburger," Finn says.

When she's finished, she drives to the hospital. It's late, and the only remnant of the earlier media circus is a lone cameraman perched on a bench outside the gift shop, staring at his phone. He doesn't even notice as Finn slinks past him, trying to make herself as inconspicuous as possible. Visiting hours are over, but no one stops her as she wanders, somewhat drunk, down the hall to her mother's room. Once inside, she keeps her eyes fixed on the wall somewhere between the bed and the ceiling. "Hi, Mom," she says, focusing intently on a spot of chipped paint. "I'm home."

It's not until she crosses the room and is next to the bed that Finn finally allows herself to look at her mother. Her hair is now completely grey where once there were merely silvery threads woven through her blond curls. Tentatively, Finn leans down and kisses Kate's cheek, feeling how waxy her skin has become, how dry her hand is when she holds it. It's as though she's aged thirty years since Finn last saw her. There is no warning label for aging, nothing to prepare you for how much smaller and frailer everything is going to appear when you come home. Though if her mother were awake, she might think the same thing about Finn – that her lovely daughter is now on the cusp of decay. Although Finn is sure the fact that she hasn't washed her face in two days isn't helping.

For some reason, she finds herself remembering how, when she was a teenager, she and Kate used to sit in the kitchen at Victor Street and play Scrabble while Nicki was out with her friends. Kate would always try to play fake words and then make up all these ridiculous definitions for them. Finn can still remember some of them, as though she and Kate had invented a new language only they could speak. *Buloc. Terriot. Jitch. Sluba.*

"Sluba? What the heck is a sluba?"

"It's an acronym. Like scuba but bigger."

"Bigger?"

"Yeah. Instead of self-contained underwater breathing apparatus, it's a super-large underwater breathing apparatus."

"*You're* a super-large underwater breathing apparatus."

"Did you just call me a sluba? Because I didn't tell you its other definition. In some countries, calling someone that can get your fingers chopped off."

But just as quickly Finn hears Kate say, *Things have been hard for Nicki.*

Even after all those Saturday nights. Kate had been there; she couldn't say she didn't know about Finn's loneliness. Her isolation.

132

Finn had never fit in anywhere, except in that kitchen. And then suddenly, for reasons she could never understand, she didn't fit in there either anymore.

"What happened, Mom?" she asks.

She's not sure if she means with the waterfall or with the two of them. Most people would say the waterfall was the bigger mystery, but Finn knows which of the two questions will keep her up at night.

It's after midnight when Finn pulls back into the driveway on Victor Street. She's disappointed to see that the kitchen light is still on, even though the rest of the house is dark. She parks Nicki's car on the lawn and leaves her keys in the ignition. Her feet make no sound as she walks across the lawn, her hands on the railing as she climbs up the front steps, giving the finger to the stars as she goes.

Nicki is sitting at the kitchen table with a mug of tea, reading another hairstyle magazine. "I wasn't sure you were coming back," she says. She doesn't look up, just keeps flipping the pages, although Finn can tell she's not really paying attention to any of the pictures.

"Sorry I took your car."

Nicki reaches the end of the magazine and flips it over. She starts pulling at a dead cuticle. Nicki's nails have always been the worst. "I wasn't worried about the car," she says.

"You were worried about me?"

She makes a little clicking noise with her tongue. "No," she says. "Of course not." She puts the end of the cuticle in her mouth and starts to pull. "What happened to your face?"

"I got punched."

"Ha," says Nicki. She spits a piece of dead skin out of her mouth.

Finn sits down at the table opposite her. The house is so quiet, but it's a different kind of quiet than she's used to. It's the quiet that six sleeping people make, the house heaving with their breath, the air vibrating with their fluttering eyelids. "Did you know that Dallas is back in town?" she asks.

Nicki stops chewing and holds her body motionless, her eyes unblinking. Finn has never seen her sit so still. "No," she says after several seconds. "Is he the one who punched you?"

"No. That was his girlfriend."

"Oh." Nicki sticks her finger back in her mouth.

Finn has to stop herself from warning Nicki about how much dangerous bacteria there is on a human hand. All their lives she has been warning Nicki about the perils of everything, from not flossing to texting while driving to marrying a man she has only known for six weeks, none of which Nicki has ever heeded. So what's the point?

They sit together for a few minutes, there at the kitchen table, not speaking. Nicki flicks at the edge of her magazine. Then, wiping her nail on the front of her shirt, she gets up and opens the fridge. "There's some leftover spaghetti if you want it. Just don't expect me to heat it up for you or anything."

"Thanks."

Nicki keeps staring into the open fridge, as though the meaning of life is hiding there behind the carton of almost-expired milk. "Is she pretty?" she asks, her back still to Finn.

Finn thinks about it. "Yeah," she says, finally. "But she can't throw a punch."

"You can't, either."

"That's true."

More silence. The cold air from the open fridge reaches Finn, a welcoming sensation in the stifling heat of the kitchen. She doesn't know how she's going to get to sleep tonight, buried beneath piles of blankets in the stuffy sunroom, the morning sunrise beating through the windows, turning it into an oven. But her old room has twin girls sleeping in it these days, sharing wordless secrets across the gap between their beds. She wonders if this abundance is what her parents were hoping for when they bought a four-bedroom house – full of kids and grandkids, Parkers spilling out of every room, beautiful chaos between the walls, happy messes covering the floor.

"Nicki?" she says. "Did Mom ever talk to you about . . . wanting to –"

"Are you asking me if Mom tried to kill herself?" Nicki says into the fridge.

"I guess, yeah. It's just, I mean . . ." Finn is having trouble finding the words. Or maybe she just can't bring herself to ask questions she doesn't want to know the answers to. "Why else would she do something like this?"

"I don't know. Because she's Mom? Because that's what she does?"

"It's *not*, though." Finn pauses. "Is it?"

Nicki slams the fridge door. "I have to work tomorrow." She finally turns to Finn, and Finn can see the worry on her face. She doesn't have to read her mind because they're having the exact same thoughts. *It's what she does now.* The problem is, neither of them knows why.

"Thanks for waiting up," Finn says, but Nicki is already halfway down the hallway, her fuzzy leopard-print slippers scuffing along the floor.

ELEVEN

6 a.m.

Katriina wakes up and she is alone.

The room is dark, and she can hear the ticking of her watch, a metronome that she unconsciously has timed her breath to match. She rolls onto her back and stares at the ceiling. Normally it would be starting to get light by now, but this morning is grey and dark, and she can hear rain pelting against the bedroom window. No one has turned on the air conditioner, and she can feel matted, sweaty strands of hair sticking to the back of her neck, the sheets damp as she frees one leg from her nest and kicks it up over the top. She feels oddly buoyant without Shawn's weight beside her, drawing the mattress down.

Shawn's side of the bed is still neatly made, in contrast to its usual chaotic mess – pillows askew, fitted sheet coming undone at the corner, duvet kicked down to the foot of the bed. He didn't come home last night. She lets the thought roll around in her head for a few minutes, unencumbered by meaning. *Is he having an affair?* But she casts the thought aside – he would never give her the satisfaction. Maybe he spent the night at Victor Street, or at the restaurant, or at the hospital. All of those places, apparently, are preferable to coming home and spending the night with his wife.

Katriina wonders if she can stay in bed forever, if she could be one of those people who has a nervous breakdown. As if on cue, she hears Petey's footsteps padding down the hallway towards the bathroom. She knows it is Petey – he is the early riser, the first one up in the morning, happily munching on cereal in front of the television before his brother climbs out of bed a few hours later, grumpy and bedraggled. Katriina's mother claims this is because Petey was born in the morning and Tommy was born in the evening, but really it's just the only time of day Petey can get any peace from his older brother. Katriina understands this – it is why, most mornings, she is awake before Shawn. Of course, now that he is gone, she wishes he were here, that they could linger in bed together for one more minute, one more hour, one more morning; that she could feel his presence, boisterous and all-encompassing even in sleep, his breath filling the room with each exhale, depleting it with each inhale. She hated that when he was here. She would like that back now.

She sits up abruptly, swings her feet onto the floor. She's acting like an idiot. They had a stupid fight, that's all. He has only been gone one night, just one night, blowing off steam. It's not like their marriage is over. It's not like he's never coming back. Besides, she does not have the luxury of being able to have a nervous breakdown. She has children to care for and houses to sell, she has month-end and a mother-in-law in the hospital and a body to re-prime for pregnancy. She has things to do. She doesn't have time to be depressed.

8 a.m.

"I want Froot Loops," says Tommy.

"You can't have Froot Loops today, bud, we're all out. Have Cheerios."

"Ugh. I hate Cheerios. They're like fake Froot Loops."

"Like the anti–Froot Loop!" Petey chimes in.

"Like evil twin Froot Loops!"

"Like ghost Froot Loops!"

"Like zombie Froot Loops!"

"You like zombies, bud."

"Yeah, but not for breakfast. Come on."

"Yeah, Mom, come on."

The table is littered with breakfast detritus and her kids are still in pyjamas. Katriina pours herself a second cup of coffee – she usually allows herself only one cup at home, but she has made a whole pot out of habit because Shawn drinks coffee like it's the end of the world, and now she feels bad about letting it go to waste. Her plan had been to hit the gym before going into the office, but Tommy and Petey had derailed that by insisting on finishing the stupid cartoon they were watching, and even though Katriina had been excited to get an early start on the day, she isn't going to be that mother who won't let her sons watch cartoons on Sunday morning. Now they are dragging their heels at breakfast, and seemingly making a new mess as quickly as she can clean up the last one.

"Well, maybe your grandma and grandpa have Froot Loops," she says, even though she knows that her parents will have nothing in the way of cereal except All-Bran. She would rather leave Tommy and Petey almost anywhere other than with her parents, who have never really known what to do with children, not even when Hanna and Katriina were young. But Katriina feels like she has blown much of the goodwill she had stored with Hanna, and she doesn't want to go to Victor Street for fear of running into Shawn.

"Can you pack me a lunch for Grandma and Grandpa's?" Tommy asks. "I don't want to eat their weird shit."

"Tommy!" Katriina says.

"Weird stuff," he says, blushing. "I don't want to eat their weird stuff."

"I don't want to eat their weird shit either," Petey says. Tommy laughs, rocking back in his chair, and then he is falling backwards, holding on to the tablecloth to try to pull himself back up, and before Katriina can even move, he is lying on the floor with the entire contents of the breakfast table on top of him, silverware clanging to the ground, glasses shattering, the sugar bowl spraying everywhere, Cheerios floating by on rivulets of milk like life rafts, converging with little streams of orange juice to make one big curdling puddle. Petey laughs, but Tommy starts to cry. Katriina leans her head against the cupboard and closes her eyes.

10 a.m.

Once the boys are dressed and their backpacks filled with granola bars and fruit and every Nintendo DS game they own, Katriina herds them out the door. The floor is now spotless, although everything from broken glasses and intact plates to the butter dish and the tablecloth has been stuffed into a garbage bag and left in the middle of the kitchen. Tommy has a cut on the back of his shin from the smashed sugar bowl that he won't stop complaining about, even though Katriina has cleaned it and applied Polysporin and covered it with a Band-Aid that has robots all over it. He probably should have stitches, but Katriina isn't going to be that mother who takes her kid to emerg the second they get a hangnail.

At her parents' house, her mother tries to make her sit down at the kitchen table and have a coffee. "I'm running late, Mom," she says, dropping the boys' backpacks on the floor in the hall.

"Katriina, honey, just relax for a moment," her mother says. "You look like you haven't slept in a week." Her mother is, as usual, dressed in an oversized wool sweater and thick wool tights even though it is the middle of summer. Inside the house, the air conditioner is cranked to walk-in-freezer temperatures. Katriina feels like she is trapped in the frozen food aisle at the grocery store, but Tommy and Petey don't seem to notice. They run through the house in search of their *ukki*, who they know will pick them up and shout at them and wrestle them to the ground – which, as Katriina understands it, is really the main ability that eight- and ten-year-old boys value in a fellow human being. That, and feeding them junk food. Give her children a Happy Meal and they will love you for life.

"I'll grab something on the way in," Katriina says. "I've got a ton of work to do today."

Her mother shakes her head. "It's Sunday, for crying out loud." Sunday has always been sacrosanct in the Saarinen house, which is why Kahvila has always been closed on Sunday, regardless of the massive amounts of business Shawn has repeatedly told her father they could be doing. "It's ludicrous to close a pancake house on Sunday," Shawn had said, and he was right, of course, although Katriina has noticed that over the years he didn't seem to mind having Sundays off to take the boys fishing, or snowboarding, or mountain biking. Today, she tells her parents that Shawn is playing golf, which is one of the few officially sanctioned Saarinen Sunday events.

"The world doesn't stop on Sunday just because you do," Katriina says, more snappishly than she means to, and she instantly regrets her words. "I'm sorry," she says, digging her fingernails into her palms. *Be a better daughter. Be a better daughter.*

"It's okay, honey," her mother says. "Go sell some houses or something."

On her way out the door, her phone rings. "I got your text," Hanna says. "What's going on?"

Katriina glances back, but her mother has already shut the door – heaven forbid any of the cool air escapes outside. "Shawn didn't come home last night."

"Oh."

There is a long silence on the other end of the line. Katriina gets into her car and turns the key in the ignition. The radio kicks in, playing AC/DC's "TNT." She turns the volume down, then waits, her hands on the steering wheel, the phone tucked in between her ear and her shoulder. "Are you still there, Hanna?"

"He's here."

"What?"

"Shawn's here. He's sleeping on my couch."

There are a million places where Katriina has imagined Shawn to be, and none of them are at Hanna's place, asleep on her couch. "What the fuck, Hanna," she says, banging her head back against the headrest.

"I'm so sorry, hon. He asked me not to call you. I didn't think you'd be so worried."

"You didn't think I'd be worried about my husband not coming home?" Katriina tries to steady her breath. She reaches for her elastic and snaps, hard, before she can say anything more. She tries to recall the times she has seen Hanna and Shawn together, how they acted with one another, whether they touched each other on the elbow, on the shoulder, on the inside of the wrist, all those places along the arm that are safe, those places you can touch and it doesn't mean anything until it means everything. "Did you sleep with him?"

"Katriina! Of course not."

Of course not. They are both too good for that. "Sorry," she says. "I guess I'm just confused."

"He showed up after the bar closed. He was drunk, and he didn't want to go home." There is another pause. "He's worried about you."

"Oh he is, is he?"

"Yeah. Hang on." There is a muffled sound, and Katriina realizes she must be talking to Shawn. She resists the urge to scream,

144

to bite the steering wheel, to slam her hand through the windshield. Instead, she yanks the elastic over and over again.

"Hanna," she says. "Hanna." But her sister doesn't answer, so she hangs up and backs out of the driveway. Her breath is ragged and uneven, and her wrist thrums with pain, but she ignores it all and turns the volume back up as she pulls out into the street, determined to keep this day under control.

10:30 a.m.

There is no one else at the office when Katriina gets in, which is surprising for any Sunday, let alone month-end. In the quiet of the empty room she sits in her cubicle and stares at her blank computer screen for fifteen minutes before she shakes herself into action. *Forget about it*, she tells herself. *It's a new day, a clean slate. It's time to get a move on, to get things done, to hit the ground running.* She fires up her computer, flips through some paperwork. She feels more productive already. Time to make some coffee.

In the break room Katriina has taken the coffee off the shelf and filled the carafe with water before she realizes that Krista Shepherd is standing in the doorway, watching her.

"Good morning, Katriina. You're here bright and early!" She checks her watch. "Well, sort of."

Katriina has the urge to leave the coffee where it is and go back to her desk. Instead she smiles, just as sweetly and naturally as if she were smiling at her children, all the while imagining how satisfying it would feel to punch Krista in the face. The ability to do this is what makes her a good real estate agent. "You betcha," she says.

Krista holds her hand out in front of her, examining her flawless gel nails. "It's such a bitch having to come in on Sunday, isn't it?" she says. "I mean, you could be at home all cuddled up in bed having breakfast with your husband right now, am I right?"

145

She knows! How could she know? She can't know. She doesn't know. "We do what we have to do," Katriina says. She shoves the basket back into the coffee maker and jabs the On button, then turns around and leans against the counter next to Krista. They smile at each other.

"Yes," says Krista. "Indeed we do."

"Indeed we do," echoes Katriina.

They stand there in silence. Behind them, the coffee maker gurgles and belches, spitting liquid out into the carafe. Katriina can hear movement outside the break room, the office coming to life. So much for her morning of solitude.

"So," Krista says suddenly, smiling wider. "How's the Paulsson house?"

Katriina feels a sick kind of churning in her stomach. "Great," she says. "Just great."

Krista crosses her legs in front of her, delicately, at the ankles. Katriina looks at those legs and imagines that Krista must do a lot of hot yoga. "I really admire you, you know?" Krista says. "That house must be a nightmare. But you just charged ahead courageously, throwing caution to the wind, and said, 'I'll take it,' dead kid and all."

Dead kid and all. The room begins to spin. "You know what?" Katriina says. "I think I'll just come back in a bit for that coffee." As she bolts from the break room, she can feel Krista's Cheshire-cat smile beaming out behind her.

11:30 a.m.

Katriina stares at her computer screen. She had gotten as far as opening up the accounting software and bringing up her numbers before paralysis set in. Now, she feels all of her already waning optimism seep out of her slowly, as through a tiny hole in an air mattress. After a while the numbers don't even make sense – they might as well have been entered into her spreadsheet by a baby mashing her fists on a keyboard. When she senses Paula, her boss, standing in front of her, she forces herself to pull her eyes away from the screen.

"Katriina," Paula says. "Are you okay? You don't look so great." Her brow knits together under a straight-cut fringe of mahogany-coloured bangs. She is wearing a long black skirt and a gauzy printed kimono-type thing that hangs below her knees and falls open in front to reveal several heavy necklaces dangling over her ample chest. Just thinking about it makes Katriina start to sweat.

"I'm fine, just a little tired," Katriina says, trying to appear like she is fine, just a little tired.

Paula picks up the mug at her desk. "You're not drinking coffee, are you? That will just make it worse, you know."

She smiles meekly at Paula. "You think so?" *Tell that to ninety-nine percent of Canada.*

Paula grabs Katriina's arm, her wrists jangling with bangles. "Come with me," she says. "I'll make you a tea that will fix you right up."

In Paula's office, Katriina sits in an armchair upholstered in a dark green velvety material while Paula plugs in her kettle. It's a chair that encourages false comfort, to make the person sitting in it relaxed enough to buy. Paula may seem like a flake, but Katriina knows that you don't become as successful in this business as Paula has been by being flaky. Underneath all that earth mother stuff, Paula is shrewd. Not that she doesn't like Paula – she does – but she would still like to get out of her office as quickly as possible.

"There," says Paula, placing a thick pottery mug in front of her. "Siberian ginseng tea. It will boost your immune system and make you more mentally alert."

Katriina takes a sip. It tastes like dirty socks. "Thanks," she says.

Paula perches on the arm of the couch opposite the armchair and studies Katriina's face. "You know I'm here for you, right, Katriina?"

"Of course," says Katriina. "You've always been a great friend and mentor." She takes another sip of the tea. "I've just got a lot on my plate right now."

"Do you want to talk about it?" Paula asks. "Sometimes just being able to verbalize our stress and anxiety can help relieve some of the pain."

"No, that's okay."

With both hands Paula takes the mug from Katriina and sets it on the table, then grasps both of Katriina's hands in hers. "I heard about your mother-in-law," she says, her voice barely above a whisper. She closes her eyes. "Something like that . . . I just can't even imagine what your family must be going through."

Katriina's breath catches in her throat. She hasn't thought about Kate once since she opened her eyes this morning. Her body starts to tremble, and she can feel the blood racing through her veins, as though they are too close to the surface, about to break through. All she wants to do is rip her hands away from Paula and pull on her elastic. Instead, she bites down hard on the inside of her cheek and seconds later feels the soothing warmth of the blood spilling into her mouth, the metallic, tinny taste coating her tongue. She swallows. "Thank you, Paula," she says with as much sincerity as she can call up. "It has been difficult."

"I've been meditating on something," Paula says, letting go of Katriina's hands. "I think we should transfer the Paulsson house to Krista. It's the only house on your roster. You need some time off to be with your family."

"No!" Katriina jumps to her feet. "Paula, you can't." *Krista Shepherd can't have that house. Krista Shepherd can't have Claudia.*

Paula stands up and wraps her arms around Katriina, hugging her close. "Oh, Katriina. Always so passionate." She draws away, holding her by the shoulders and staring into her eyes in what

Katriina assumes is meant to be a meaningful way. "This is why your clients love you. Because you will work for them through thick and thin. Because you take care of them. But let me ask you this. Who is taking care of Katriina?"

Katriina jams her tongue into the wound on her cheek, and a fresh pain bursts inside her head. She removes her tongue. "I think I take care of myself just fine."

"Just let us take the Paulsson house off your hands –"

"I sold the Paulsson house." The words come out before she can stop them.

"You did?" Paula's face breaks into a broad smile. "That's wonderful! Who did you sell it to? Why didn't you tell me?"

"They, uh, just agreed this morning. I still have to finalize it. It was an anonymous buyer. A developer, I think. Yeah, a developer."

Paula claps her hands in front of her like a little kid. "Hooray for you!" Her enthusiasm, Katriina realizes, is genuine. The house was probably almost as much of a burden to her as it was to Katriina. She claps her own hands weakly. Paula grabs her by the shoulders and spins her around, pushing her towards the door. "What are you waiting for, go finalize that sucker!"

"Okay," says Katriina, feeling vaguely like she is going to throw up. She looks back at Paula, who pumps her fist in the air.

Seated again at her cubicle, Katriina puts her head down on her desk and closes her eyes. Beneath her desk, she picks away idly at her elastic, but she doesn't even really feel like pulling it. She needs something bigger. A bigger punishment. With her head still on her desk, she reaches into her top drawer and pulls out her stapler. Then calmly, as though it is something she does every day, she staples the webbing in between her thumb and index finger, first on her right hand, then on her left. *Be a better businesswoman.* Then she picks up the phone and calls Fred, her mortgage specialist at the credit union to whom she filters business on a regular basis, and tells him she is going to buy a house.

TWELVE

Shawn wakes up to the sound of a train going by. He is so hungover and confused that for a moment he loses twenty-five years and he's right back on the rails, trying to sleep amidst the shunting and the clanging and the squealing, the cold breath of fear on his neck. Then the smell of coffee leaps him forward, those twenty-five years rushing back, carrying him along right up to the present. Well, almost. He still doesn't know where he is.

"I got you a coffee," a voice says. It sounds like Katriina, but also not Katriina – lower, huskier, more laid-back. He keeps his eyes closed, knowing that when he opens them he is going to have to deal with whoever it is. Although even as he's lying there he realizes it's Hanna. He is on Hanna's couch, in Hanna's loft. He opens one eye and sees a white paper cup with a brown plastic lid sitting on a coffee table in front of him. Moving as few muscles as possible, he reaches for the cup and brings it to his lips.

"Ouch," he says, putting the cup back on the coffee table.

"Your tongue or your head?" Hanna asks. The loft is open concept, and from the couch Shawn can tell she is in the kitchen, although he still can't focus enough to see her as more than a flicker of movement out of the corner of his eye. He shifts onto his back and feels the sharp edge of something digging into his neck. He reaches behind him and extracts a TV remote from under his head.

"If it's my head, it's because I slept on this all night," he says, flinging it across the couch.

"Right," says Hanna. "Nothing to do with the distillery you drank last night." He can hear her voice moving closer. Shawn tries to recall the last time he was at Hanna's place. It might have been years ago.

He rolls over to face her. She is sitting on an overstuffed brown armchair, holding a paper cup like the one in front of him, licking the foam off the top of some kind of espresso drink. Her hair is pulled into a messy braid that hangs over one shoulder, and she is wearing cut-offs and a loose tank top with a picture of a beagle wearing sunglasses on it. Shawn is frequently disturbed by how much she looks like Katriina – a younger, blonder, hippie-chick Katriina – but right now he finds it comforting. It's like being with his wife without having to actually be with his wife.

"What time is it?" he asks.

"Ten," she says. "Katriina's been texting me. She thinks you've run off with the daughter of an oil tycoon and are making a new life for yourself in South America."

With considerable effort, Shawn props himself up to a sitting position and tries for the coffee again, this time removing the lid and blowing on it before taking a sip. The coffee is rich and dark and bitter. It might be the best thing he has ever tasted. "I'm guessing you didn't make this," he says.

"Who has time to make their own coffee? It's from the bakery downstairs. There are some muffins in the kitchen, too, if you want them."

Shawn shakes his head, taking another sip of coffee. "I want a bottle of Advil and seven more hours' sleep," he says. "Did you tell her I'm here?"

"No. Should I?"

"I guess so." He tries to think of where his Jeep might be. Then he remembers that he left it at Victor Street the night before, that Katriina had driven him to the hospital to see Kate. And suddenly he remembers everything. He jerks upright, and coffee sloshes onto his chest. "Shit," he says.

"Are you okay?" asks Hanna.

Shawn stares at the coffee stain on his T-shirt. "Katriina lost the baby."

"I know."

"Of course you do." Shawn thinks back to the day that Katriina told him she was pregnant again. Tommy and Petey had spent the night at Hanna's, and he and Katriina went out for dinner at a real, grown-up restaurant, not a pancake in sight. The next morning when Hanna dropped off the boys, the first thing out of her mouth was, "So did you tell him?" That's when Shawn realized that there was never going to be anything about his wife that he would know before her sister did. It was a strange thing for Shawn to have to deal with – he was used to sisters who hated each other.

Hanna eyes him and picks up her phone, presumably dialling Katriina. "I got your text," Hanna says after a minute. "What's going on?" She gets up and wanders over towards the kitchen, her phone pressed to her ear.

Shawn leans his head against the back of the couch, staring at the ceiling and zoning Hanna out. Despite his raging hangover, all the anger and sadness from last night is still there, buried somewhere under the pain of his throbbing head. He doesn't know how he's going to go back to his life, back to the kids and the restaurant and his marriage. He doesn't know how he can just pretend nothing has happened.

From the kitchen, he hears Hanna suck in her breath. "Katriina! Of course not."

"Did she ask you if we slept together?" Shawn calls across the space.

Hanna waves her hand spastically at him. "He showed up after the bar closed. He was drunk, and he didn't want to go home."

"Hanna, answer me! Did she really ask if we slept together?"

"He's worried about you."

"Hanna!"

"Hang on." She presses the phone into her shoulder. "*What, Shawn? Did you think that wouldn't be the first thing that crossed her mind?*"

Shawn wants to say yes. He wants to say that he has a marriage built on trust, and that his wife knows him to be a deeply loyal person with a strong sense of morality, but lying on his sister-in-law's couch, hungover after a bender, he knows that these are things he can no longer lay claim to. So he just drinks his coffee and says nothing.

What am I going to tell Jean-Marc? This was the only thought Shawn had after Katriina told him about the miscarriage. Not *What am I going to tell my family* – the family who, just hours ago, he had announced her pregnancy to – but *What am I going to tell my employee who I barely know?* Jean-Marc had been so happy for him, so happy to have someone to commiserate with about the anticipation and worry of impending fatherhood. Now Shawn was going to have to face the awkward attempt at sympathy, the whole *I'm sorry, man* thing.

He knows Katriina is hurting, too, but he's still upset with her for not telling him sooner. And there is a part of him that can't help but wonder if she's not secretly relieved it happened. After all, he was the one who wanted another baby in the first place, for reasons he can't even remember anymore – just that they tried, and failed, and now must keep trying until they succeed. Because Parkers don't give up. Kate had taught him that.

If this were a movie, Kate would have woken up last night. Shawn would have come back into her room after his brief but humiliating breakdown in the hospital bathroom and she would have opened her eyes and told him everything was going to be okay. She would have told him something poignant about accepting the things we cannot change, or about everything happening for a reason, or about how we can't always get what we want, but she would have said it better than that. She would have said it like she was the first person to ever say it, and it would be the exact thing that Shawn needed to hear.

If this were a movie, Kate would always say, and then instead of being sad about life not being a movie, she would just go ahead and make it like one. *If this were a movie, you would come and live with us*, she'd told him that morning almost twenty-five years ago, sitting at the kitchen table, feeding Shawn toast and homemade strawberry jam – the first time he'd ever tasted real strawberries. *If this were a movie, I'd give you a future, I'd love you like a son.* Maybe she hadn't actually said that part, but it's what Shawn heard. She said it and then she did it. Because why *can't* life be like the movies? Why do those perfect, heartbreaking moments only exist in some screenwriter's imagination?

At the time, becoming a Parker was a scam. Another method of survival. That morning, twenty-five years ago, Shawn had looked into Kate's eyes and taken her for a sucker, and with the taste of those strawberries on his tongue he told her an avalanche of lies. He told her his parents were dead, for one thing. He told her he didn't have a record. He told her he had just been walking by when her car started rolling back towards her. He even gave her a fake last name. Some of these things came out, later, but she never knew who he was before he was a Parker. And it didn't matter – he liked to think that he had always been a Parker, he just hadn't known it yet.

"If this were a movie, you would come live with us," she said.

"Well maybe I could stay, for just a few days," he said, wiping the crumbs from his face with the back of his hand.

"Sure," said Kate. "Let's say a few days." There was a moment of understanding between them – he didn't know why, but it was also a tactical move for Kate. They weren't going to rat each other out. They were in this together.

Shawn slept under the Parker roof, he ate Parker food, he watched Parker television. He enrolled in school and got rides there in the Parker car. He spent his weekends in the Parker back-yard playing Star Wars with the Parker twins. It was the best deal on the planet. He pretended to be a Parker, and in return, he got a free ride. And Kate, what did she get? Shawn is still not sure if he knows. He thinks he may have an idea – some unspoken struggle that seemed to go down between Kate and Walter when he was home, sideways glances, sentences left unfinished, clipped tones at the dinner table – but they never talked about it. If this were a movie, she would have told him last week, before the falls. She would have released her secret to him in some final, poignant speech instead of asking him whether Petey still wore a size four shoe.

Whatever it was, it let them live in a peaceful balance, each of them getting what they thought they needed. Shawn had set up a nice little drug-dealing business at his new high school, and was gradually inventorying things he was going to steal from Victor Street when he finally took off. He planned to stay a month, tops, and then head out West, hook up with some buddies in Vancouver who had a squat somewhere, knew all the best panhandling spots. Every day he could hear the train running by the house, and every day he told himself, "Tomorrow, tomorrow." A month turned into three, and then six. Before he knew it, he had been playing Parker for an entire year. He had clean clothes and a haircut done by a real barber. He owned his own stick of deodorant. When he was hungry, he could just open the fridge and eat. There was always a kid around who wanted to play with him, or cuddle up on the couch. He started to sleep with both eyes closed.

Still, leaving was always at the forefront of his mind. Leaving, and planning his next score. His next move. Maybe he was just expecting it to all fall apart, but he couldn't stand the thought of staying still, of letting himself get too comfortable. That was what killed you in the end. Not the things you did, but the things you didn't do.

Then one afternoon, he came home from school and found Kate in her bedroom, sitting cross-legged on her unmade bed, eyes closed, one hand on her chest. He paused in front of her doorway. Her eyes were still closed, but somehow she knew he was there.

"Does cancer have a sound?" she asked.

"What?"

"A sound. When all those abnormal cells are growing, do they make some kind of noise?" She opened her eyes and looked at him. "I swear I can hear it. It's like a whistle."

"You have cancer?" Shawn backed away a step. Then took a step forward. Then back. It was like a dance. He was fifteen – moving towards adulthood, moving away from it. At that point, moving away from it, mostly.

"I have *something*," said Kate. "Abnormal cells are destroying my healthy cells."

"That sounds like cancer," said Shawn. He felt himself growing angry. Kate was such a good person, and he was still at an age when he felt life should be fair.

"So it *does* have a sound," said Kate. "Maybe it's more like a hum."

She was like a three-year-old trying to understand it. The rudimentary details of disease. *Does it move? Is it alive? Does it feel?* Shawn didn't know, so they looked it up in the old *Encyclopaedia Britannica* on the shelf in the living room. Their research just led to more questions. *What is a cell? What makes a cell abnormal? How does it kill you?* So many things you think you understand until it is inside of you, and then you realize you don't even know the basics.

Kate kept reading and reading. Walter wasn't due back from his guiding trip for another four days, so Shawn made dinner for the twins. It was only Hamburger Helper, cheeseburger macaroni, but it was the first meal he had ever made by himself and he didn't screw it up. Nicki ate two bowls and told him he should be on *That's Incredible!* for being the only teenager who could actually do something useful. After the twins went to bed, Shawn made Kate some tea and put a shot of whisky in it.

"Do you want to watch TV?" he asked.

"All right," said Kate. They watched *Murder, She Wrote* and Jessica Fletcher solved another mystery in Cabot Cove. Shawn took the next day off school and went to the oncologist with Kate. He talked with the doctor about her options. He pocketed some brochures to take home and read later. He asked questions. He learned what the word *mastectomy* meant. He held Kate's hand for the first time. At home, he put her to bed even though it was only three in the afternoon. An hour later, he went out to meet the twins at the school bus. He told them that Kate wasn't feeling well. He made more Hamburger Helper, beef stroganoff. He made a salad. He even made milkshakes for dessert.

He made the decision to stop stepping back. He made the decision to stay still.

But this is not a movie, and last night Kate didn't wake up. So to distract himself from thoughts of Katriina and the baby, Shawn went out and got completely shitfaced with some of the kitchen staff from Kahvila at some dive bar that he used to frequent before he was married, until he realized that getting drunk with his employees was probably a really bad idea – maybe his last lucid thought of the evening. He remembers stumbling up to one of those new bars on Red River, where a live band was playing and no one paid any attention to him as he sat down at a table in a corner, his head in his hands. He asked the waitress for a bottle of water and a shot of Johnnie Walker, but somehow she ended up bringing him a beer instead, so he nursed it while he watched the band play, a wall of sound that washed over him and blocked out everything else, including his own sorry thoughts.

He also remembers – suddenly, sharply, like a kick in the ribs – what happened when the band stopped playing. The woman at the next table, ordering another drink. That voice, low and sexy, that he would know anywhere. Cutting clean through him like a taut piece of wire.

"Hey," he said. The woman ignored him. "Hey," he said again, louder. "Cassandra Coelho."

She turned, flashing him an on-air smile. "Nice to see you," she said.

"Cassandra Coelho." He stood up, pushing back his chair, which clattered to the floor. Heads turned. "You better stop fucking with my family, Cassandra Coelho." He had meant to sound intimidating, a little like Liam Neeson, maybe, in control, authoritative. Thinking back on it now, he knows how he really sounded: drunk, crazy.

"Hey, I'm just here with my friends," she said. "We're all just trying to have a good time, okay?" She turned away from him, flipping her long hair over her shoulder and leaning into her group, all women around the same age as her, too young to think of Shawn as anything but a creepy old man. Her friends all laughed, and Shawn felt his face go red with rage – they were laughing at him, he was sure of it. The son of the Conqueror of Kakabeka. Harassing them at the bar. He grabbed the back of Cassandra's chair and ripped it away from the table with her still in it, spinning her around to face him, surprised at how light it was. She gave a little squeal and stared at him, stunned.

"Leave my family alone," he said. "Stop calling, stop coming by the hospital, stop talking about us on air. Just stop. Stop."

Recognition dawned in her eyes, and she gave a little half smile that terrified Shawn right down to the bottom of his heart. She opened her mouth to say something, but before she could, Shawn felt himself get pulled backwards by the collar by a very strong man with very bad breath – a bouncer who twisted Shawn's arm behind him and propelled him through the bar and out the door. Shawn stumbled forward and fell, his knees skidding across the sidewalk.

"You stay the fuck away from her, and this bar," the bouncer said before slamming the door.

Shawn stood up, stretching his arm forward and back to make sure his shoulder wasn't dislocated, and through the front window he could see Cassandra watching him intently, memorizing every last detail of the scene for future reference, locking it away in her brain for safekeeping until she needed it for her next newscast on the preposterous Parker family.

After that, things get hazy again. Shawn remembers trying to get a cab. He remembers bumming a cigarette from someone outside a different bar. He doesn't remember getting to Hanna's, or anything else after that.

"You cried a little bit," Hanna says matter-of-factly. "You didn't want to talk about it, so I just left you on the couch." She is getting ready to go to the store – inventory, she claims, but Shawn is sure she just wants to get away from him. "Do you want to take a shower or anything?"

"No," says Shawn. He feels drained, defeated, unsure what he should do. "I just want to go home."

THIRTEEN

Like she does every morning, the first thing Finn does on Sunday morning is check her work email, but nothing new has come in. So instead of jumping into warning mode, she wanders down to the river with her cup of coffee and heads out onto the dock. The grass is wet from an early-morning rain, but the sun is peeking out from behind the clouds, and Finn can tell it's going to be one of those humid northwestern Ontario summer days, the air hot and heavy and still. Crouching down at the end of the dock, she dips her hand into the water, feeling the current pulling eastward, albeit weakly. She wishes she could take off all her clothes and jump in, like she and Nicki used to do as kids – floating downstream on inner tubes tethered together and getting their father to tow them back upriver behind the *Miss Penelope*. Instead, she slips off her shoes and sits down with her legs dangling over the edge. The river is so low that her feet barely graze the surface of the water, but it's enough for now.

Although the *Miss Penelope* is not in its usual spot in the river behind the house, the *Serafina* and the *Veronica* are docked, rustling against each other in the current. Those stupid boats. Her father has always treated them as some kind of stand-ins for his daughters, like they were less whiny, more lake-faring avatars of Nicki and Finn. "Boats," he would say, looking at them with a mixture of sadness and bafflement, "come with instruction manuals." In some ways, Finn supposes that she and her father are very alike – wanting everything to be quantified, compartmentalized, laid out step by step. Including people.

Earlier that morning, he had shown up at her door the way he used to when she was a teenager, making loon calls to wake her up, his hands cupped around his mouth, while Finn had lain there with her eyes squeezed shut, pretending to be asleep.

"Finn?" he had said, opening the sunroom door. "Are you awake? Do you want to come on the coffee cruise?"

She groaned. "*Oh my god*, Dad, it's seven in the morning," she said, rolling over.

"Yup, the best time of day."

"Seven a.m. shouldn't even *be* a time of day." She knew she sounded like a bratty teenager, but she couldn't help it. Being back home was making her regress to adolescence.

Walter took a step towards her, peering into her face. "Are you okay? What happened to your nose?"

Finn reached up and touched her face, the night's events tumbling back into her memory. "Nothing," she said, an auto-pilot response left over from a childhood full of her father's interrogations. "I'm fine."

"You don't look fine. It looks like it might be broken." He made a small move towards her, and she recoiled, pulling the blankets tighter around her chin.

"I said I'm fine. I just want to go back to sleep."

Walter hesitated. "Okay then," he said finally, his shoulders sagging.

WARNING: ASSUMING YOUR DAUGHTER HAS GROWN UP TO BE AN ACTUAL ADULT MAY LEAD TO EXTREME DISAPPOINTMENT.

Beyond the dock, the Kaministiquia River winds away from the edge of their property and curls around a corner, making its way past the mill and out to the lake. As kids they were allowed near the river only during deep summer, when the water was low; the rest of the time it was unsafe, a seething force waiting to carry them away or pull them down. She had known kids in the neighbourhood who had fallen through the ice, heading out too early, too impatient for hockey. She vaguely remembers one kid dying upriver at the public boat launch, there one minute and through the ice the next, leaving nothing but a black hole. But even in the deepest freezes – when snow machines regularly patrolled up and down the river, their loud buzzing like angry bees echoing off the riverbanks – her parents were so adamant. They were never allowed on the ice.

Then there were the spring swells, the years when the water would rise so high that it would pick things up from the banks: giant tree stumps, people's deck chairs and inflatable boats, a picnic table or a garbage can from Fort William Historical Park – all rushing along on the surface to the lake, and after that, who knows? Maybe they washed up on the shore in Duluth or Sault Ste. Marie, or were carried through the locks and down the Gulf of St. Lawrence and out into the Atlantic Ocean. All rivers flow to the sea, isn't that what people say? Maybe somewhere on some beach in Ireland there is an oar from one of their neighbours' canoes, or a flip-flop that someone forgot to bring in from their dock. But once it was on the river, it didn't matter where it went – it was just gone. That was what the river did. It made things disappear.

Except Kate. Was that why she had decided to go over the falls? The Kam just outside her door, taunting her with its quick escape route? The thought startles Finn. All those years, smiling in the kitchen window and waving as the school bus pulled up to the driveway, playing the happy housewife. Had her mother secretly yearned to wash up on some beach in Ireland? Had she dreamed about finding out what lay beyond the river, the same way Finn had?

"Aunt F?"

She turns around to find London standing behind her. She's wearing a pair of cotton Hello Kitty pyjama pants and holds her laptop under one dark, slender arm. On her face is a pair of thick-framed glasses. Since when did London wear glasses? Why didn't she know London wore glasses?

"Hey, L," she says. "Want to sit down?"

She creeps over almost shyly, with none of yesterday's teen-aged bluster. Maybe she's feeling contrite about her blow-up, or maybe, in that foggy swirl of wildly fluctuating serotonin and dopamine levels that is the brain of a teenaged girl, she has just completely forgotten about it. But no matter how bratty London gets, Finn can never really be angry at her, given what she knows about her life: mainly, that her parents are crazy, and that she can't even rely on her siblings to be on her team. Finn has been there.

London sits down on the dock and Finn is surprised to see that her feet are completely submerged in the river, her legs at least three inches longer than Finn's.

"What happened to your face?" London asks, peering intently at Finn's nose.

"Oh," Finn says, touching her bruise. She decides there's no point in lying about it. "Someone punched me last night at Barkley's. A girl. Who I don't even know. She just punched me."

"Oh, cool," says London.

It's pretty apparent that she isn't listening, or just doesn't care. Finn tries to remember what it was like to be a teenager, to be that self-absorbed.

"Um, Aunt F?" she says again, pushing her glasses up on her nose with her finger. "Can I show you something?"

She flips open her laptop. Finn assumes she's just going to show her some funny pictures of her friends on Facebook, or maybe an email she got from a boy that she's unable to decipher. Something aunt-appropriate and easy for Finn to deal with at ten o'clock on a Sunday morning. But instead, she opens up a link to a news site from Minnesota and plays a video. A pretty young reporter comes on the screen.

"Most people think that, living on a lake, they don't have to worry about sharks," the reporter says, her face sombre. "But for one North Shore family, their worst nightmare came true."

The camera jumps to an obese woman with dyed red hair, standing in front of a rocky shoreline. "My son and I were fishing in my boat when all of a sudden I looked out across the water and saw a shark fin sticking up in the waves," she says. "At first I thought it must be some kid with one of those novelty fins attached to his head, but then it got closer and I could see that it was a real shark."

The camera cuts back to the reporter's face. "They're called lake sharks," the reporter continues, "and they are, indeed, very real. Scientists say that the shark the Larabys saw was likely a bull shark that had lost its way and travelled up the Mississippi River through the canals and made its way to the north shore of Lake Superior. Bull sharks have adapted to live in fresh water, and in South America they have been known to reside in rivers and lakes for indefinite amounts of time, although in these colder northern waters, it's unlikely the shark will survive more than a few weeks. Before the Larabys' sighting, sharks had been spotted as far north as Lake Michigan. This is the first known sighting of a shark in Lake Superior, although it doesn't necessarily mean that it is the first shark to visit us here, or the only one. Bull sharks are notoriously aggressive and should be avoided at all costs."

Of course the next cut is to the most redneck fisherman they could find saying, "I don't care how angry it is, we're going to hunt it down and kill it."

When Finn turns to face her, there are tears in London's eyes. "They're not really going to kill it, sweetie," Finn says, pulling her feet up out of the water. "They're just talking shit for the camera."

"How do you know they're not?" London asks. "That poor shark is just, like, lost. He just wants to get back home, to his family and the ocean. He didn't do anything wrong. He didn't even hurt that family!" She's completely in tears now. "What if they do kill it, Aunt F? How could we go on living as, like, a society?"

"It would be tough. But what can you do?"

London runs a finger along the top of her laptop. "Remember Adam Pelley? The marine biologist I was telling you about yesterday? He's in Duluth right now," she says. "He's trying to rescue the shark before anyone else gets to it."

"That's good. See, there's nothing to worry about. Your marine biologist is on the case."

London blushes and casts her eyes down at her hands resting on the keyboard. "He needs volunteers to come help him. I really want to go. But I have no way to get there." She raises her eyes, widening them behind her glasses. "Maybe you could take me, Aunt F?"

"To Duluth?" Finn says, trying to decipher the expression on London's face. *Is she seriously trying to use puppy-dog eyes on me?* "It's not really a great time right now, L, with your grandmother in the hospital and everything."

"Oh, come on. It would be so fun. It would be, like, aunt–niece bonding time. You know, since you've been gone so long and everything."

Ouch. It would seem that in three years, sweet little L has turned into a master manipulator. Finn glances down at London's feet dragging in the water. "L, why don't you pull your feet up, honey?"

London stares at Finn, her eyes hardening. "You're scared of it, aren't you? Everyone's so scared of everything!"

The news video finishes and jumps to the next clip. "A Thunder Bay woman made international headlines this week as she attempted to go over Kakabeka Falls in a whisky barrel." The photo of Kate flashes on the screen.

Finn grabs the top of London's laptop and slams it shut. "We don't need to see that," she says. "No one needs to see that."

London kicks at the water, sniffling. "Nana wasn't afraid."

"No, but there's a reason for that," Finn says. "She wasn't thinking straight. Or else she would have been scared."

"You know what I think?" London says. "I think that she's the only one who's thinking straight. I think it's the rest of you who are all broken, hiding in your big houses with your cushy jobs and your retirement savings and your, like, first world *privilege*." She says that last word almost proudly, as if it's something she has been waiting to use in conversation. "Have you forgotten how to care about something, Aunt F? When did your soul die?"

It's all Finn can do not to laugh, but her soul is not quite that dead. "I care about what's important," Finn says. "I care about you."

"If you cared about me, you'd take me to Duluth."

"I can't do that, honey."

In what Finn now recognizes is a pattern of violence followed by storming off, London lets out a frustrated scream, then jumps to her feet, kicking Finn's empty coffee mug into the river, where it slowly sinks into the depths. Then she runs back up to the house. Finn stares down into the river, imagining the mug getting hooked on the fin of a bull shark and travelling back down the Mississippi to the Gulf of Mexico, finally free of the Parker tyranny of bad coffee and weak tea.

After a mind-numbing hour of Americanizing the manuals for UniTech's new line of microwaves – changing "colour" to "color" and questioning her life choices – Finn gets bored and logs onto Facebook. Ever since dinner, she has been thinking about that photo of her mother and has come to the conclusion that it must have been taken from Nicki's Facebook page – neither of her parents are on Facebook, and both Shawn's and Finn's pages are private.

Shawn and Katriina's wedding was eleven years ago, in the dark days before social media, but Nicki could have easily uploaded some old photos as well. Finn isn't friends with Nicki, so all the photos are new to her. Scrolling through Nicki's albums is like seeing a time lapse of her kids growing up – birthdays, Christmases, vacations, graduations, what must be thousands of photos of Nicki and Hamish's wedding. Finn finds it all hard to look at – she knows that everything always appears so much better online than it actually is in real life, but everyone is just so damn *happy*. And she missed it all.

There are a few non-family photos as well, all of which seem to involve large groups of heavily made-up women, a lot of cleavage, and brightly coloured drinks in dark bars. Nothing from Shawn and Katriina's wedding, nothing from any other earlier family functions that would have included Kate. There are no photos of her mother at all, Finn realizes, as she scans row after row of thumbnails, searching for someone resembling her mother. She supposes she shouldn't be surprised. Even when they were kids, Kate was always the one behind the camera, snapping away at every opportunity, telling them to smile, waving off the occasional offer to have her own photo taken.

"No one wants to look at this face when they can look at your beautiful faces," she used to say when they were little. Later, she'd say nothing at all, just laugh as though the thought of someone taking her photo was absurd. What happened to all those photos Kate took? Does her mother ever look at them anymore, or are they just sitting in a box somewhere, fading a little more with each passing year?

The phone rings, startling Finn out of her thoughts.

"Oh, Finn," Nicki says when she answers. "You're home."

"Uh, yeah," Finn says, stretching the phone cord to peek out to the garage, where Nicki should be, cutting hair and plucking the eyebrows of all the Vickers Heights royalty. "Aren't you?"

"Hamish's truck broke down on the way to meet a client," she says. Hamish claims he has a "business" and calls his customers "clients," but what he really does is buy crap at police auctions or on eBay, puts a coat of paint on it, and then sells it to dumb rich people for a huge markup. He also sells bootlegged whisky on the side, but they are not supposed to talk about that. "I had to pick him up and take him to Terrace Bay."

"So, you're, what, three hours away?" Finn asks, trying to remember where Terrace Bay is. One of those tiny towns along the North Shore, fighting for survival as the pulp and paper industry collapses and the trains stop coming through. It would be depressing if she ever actually thought about it.

"Yeah. Is London there?"

Finn peers out the window and sees that London's bike is still there. "I think so. I saw her this morning, but I'm not sure where she is."

"Shit," says Nicki. Finn hears her take a deep breath. "Can you keep an eye on Ross?"

"Uh, keep an eye on Ross?" Finn repeats dumbly.

"You don't have to do anything, just make sure he doesn't eat anything weird or fall in the toilet."

Finn wraps the phone cord around her finger. "Fall in the toilet?"

"Finn!" Nicki shouts. "Stop repeating everything I say! Can you look after him or not? He's probably just in the basement with his Legos."

"Okay," Finn says reluctantly. Look after Ross. Sure. That should be fine. No problem. She hangs up and goes searching for the little eight-year-old walking reminder of betrayal.

Ross is, as Nicki said he would be, playing with Lego. The structure he's building is a catastrophe of epic proportions: a multicoloured monstrosity of a tower that might fall over at any moment. "Hey," Finn says. "What are you doing?"

"Building," he says. He sticks another piece of Lego onto the top of the tower, which is nearly as tall as he is. It doesn't even seem possible that one person could physically have that much Lego. They must be experiencing Lego shortages in other parts of the world in order to accommodate Ross's unwieldy design. "What happened to your nose?"

"Uh, I got into a fight," Finn says.

"Oh." Ross just stares at her.

"Wow," she says, crouching down next to him. "How long have you been working on this?"

"I dunno. Since last summer?" He goes over to a pile of Lego and starts sorting through it, searching for the next perfect piece. He must be moving slower than most contractors if this is as far as he's gotten in a year. But Finn can tell he's picky. He obviously has a plan, even if it's a monumentally screwed-up one.

"Want some help?" she asks.

He eyes her warily. "Why are you talking to me?"

"What do you mean?"

"You never talk to me. You just talk to my sisters."

It had never occurred to Finn that he would notice. "Well," she says. "I'm sorry about that. I just don't know much about what to say to boys."

He runs his hands through the pile of Lego. "Mom says it's because of my dad. She says you don't like me because of him."

Really, Nicki? "Well, she's wrong," Finn says. "Of course I like you. You're my nephew." *You should have been my son.* The words explode in her head, and for a moment the room starts to spin.

"And you're my aunt," Ross says. "I guess I like you, too."

Finn watches him for a few minutes with the Lego, trying to figure out his system. She picks up a long green piece, but he shakes his head. "Have you ever met your dad?" she asks him.

"No. Mom says he lives far away, and that he's a bad word that I'm not allowed to say."

"That's not entirely true." She doesn't know why she feels the need to defend Dallas all of a sudden. "He's a nice person. And he likes to make things, just like you do." *Liked*, she thinks. She doesn't know anything about Dallas now: what he likes, what he doesn't, if he still writes plays, if he ever wrote one for Tanya. She touches her nose. It's tender, but not broken. She can't even punch right. Dallas deserves better.

"What does he make?" Ross asks.

"Well . . ." Finn thinks for a minute. "He was a great cook. He could make anything in the kitchen, even if you didn't have many ingredients." That wasn't exactly true: Dallas could cook, but he needed to have the very best of everything, the perfect setup, all the right tools, or else he would just have a complete meltdown and you'd end up having to order pizza. "He was a perfectionist," she says.

"I don't know what that means," says Ross.

"It means he wanted everything to turn out perfect. Just like your tower."

"My tower isn't perfect. It's ugly."

"Then why do you keep building it?"

"I don't know," he says. "I just can't stop until it's finished."

Now Finn remembers why she never talked to Ross before. There's so much of this conversation that is Dallas: the bluntness, the oddball logic. "Then that means you're a perfectionist, too." She can't speak after that, so they just sit together in the basement in silence, sorting through Lego. Although Ross looks like he would be an oaf, boorish and clumsy, with his wide face and high forehead, his torso too big for his stubby arms and legs, there is actually a strange and eerie grace to his movements. She watches his chubby, precise fingers flitting over the plastic blocks, the economy of his movements, each muscle isolated, like a dancer. Unlike his sisters' narrow, grey Parker eyes, his are all Vaughn, watery-blue and innocent, and will likely stay that way even after the innocence becomes just a facade, a shtick – those eyes will get him off the hook for the rest of his life.

Weeks after Dallas and Finn broke up and she moved back into Victor Street, he came by the house in the middle of the night, throwing pebbles at her window like a smitten cartoon character. He was drunk and sad and full of beautiful words and apologies. He said he had wanted to hold a boom box under her window, but it had run out of batteries. Finn let him in, cringing as he put his foot right down on the creaky step, and led him to her room, where he cried and she cried and then they made out and then they stopped and then they fought and cried some more and he played a song for her on his iPod and then they had sex. Immediately afterward, it was like a veil had lifted from his face, and where before Finn had seen a complex mix of emotions that he was simultaneously trying to express to and hide from her, now she saw only regret.

"Finn," he said.

"No."

"This was a mistake."

It occurred to Finn, then, that it wasn't Nicki who broke them up. Dallas had been gone long before he ever slept with her. This thought was the only thing that saved Finn, the only thing that let her come home and look her twin sister in the eye, that kept some semblance of her relationship with Nicki alive.

A few days later, she found Nicki sitting on the bathroom floor with one of those pregnancy test sticks in her hand. "No," said Finn. "Please tell me this is a fucking nightmare."

"It's a fucking nightmare," said Nicki, her voice dangerously low. Finn slammed the door. After all those years, she had finally found something she had in common with her twin sister, something beyond shared DNA. She and Nicki had both been fucked over by Dallas Vaughn.

Now Finn is crying, hot tears falling down her face and breaking dark and wet on the rug like little splatters of blood. Ross sees her cry but doesn't say anything – with three teenaged sisters and Nicki as his mom, he is probably used to seeing women cry for no reason, exploding with emotion as incomprehensible to themselves as it is to their dumbfounded little brother. Finn feels a stab of pity for Ross.

Resolutely, she wipes her eyes, watching Ross as he steadily builds his Lego tower, placing a piece, removing it, pressing it to his lips thoughtfully, then putting it back where it was, then removing the piece once more.

"Come on," Finn says. "Let's go."

Ross puts down the Lego piece. "Where are we going?" he asks.

Finn takes his hand, hot and clammy and soft. "To meet your father."

FOURTEEN

Sunday afternoon, London decides to borrow Nana's car to take into town. She feels kind of weird about it, especially since she only has her learner's permit, but it's not like the cops are really going to stop her, and as long as Nana's in the hospital she's not going to be driving, so what's the point of just letting it sit there? As she gets into the Volvo, she promises herself she'll stop by the hospital later. It's true what she told Aunt F – she hasn't visited Nana yet, mostly because she's been busy trying to figure out how she's going to get to Duluth, but also because she doesn't know what she's going to say to her. What do you say to a person who's in a coma? Can they even hear you? Or do they just, like, pick up on your vibes? London doesn't know, and it's not like anyone is going to explain it to her. No one will tell her anything about what is going on. Her mother just slams stuff around the kitchen and Hamish hides in the shed, just like usual. She has barely even seen Uncle Shawn, and Aunt Katriina kind of scares her. And Aunt F, well, she used to be cool, London supposes. But then she left. *So fuck her,* she thinks as she turns the key in the ignition. London might as well not even *have* a family. She might as well be an orphan.

Angrily, she throws the Volvo into reverse and smashes into something behind her. "Shit!" she says, slamming her hands on the wheel. She looks in the rear-view mirror and sees the back end of the Volvo embedded into the side of Uncle Shawn's Jeep. She puts the car in drive and lurches forward. The Volvo seems unscathed, so she makes a split-second decision and before anyone comes out to see what the noise was, she drives away.

At the bus station she waits in line behind a strung-out couple arguing about whether there is caffeine in Mountain Dew. "I can't drink it if there's caffeine in it," the woman says as she absently twirls a cigarette in her fingers. "It's bad for the baby."

"There's no fucking caffeine in it," the man says. "Just drink it. You need to stay hydrated."

"What does that even mean?"

"Hydrated. Like with water and shit."

"That's not water, it's Mountain Dew."

"Same thing."

London finally makes it up to the counter. The bored ticket lady, who is probably around Nana's age, has crunchy dyed blond curls and glasses with pink frames, and is wearing a T-shirt with a photograph of a kitten screen-printed on the front. She has her head bent over a piece of paper and is studying it intently while she chews her gum with her mouth open. London tries not to gag as she watches her, but other people's saliva is just, like, so gross.

"How much is a one-way ticket to Duluth?" London asks.

"Eighty," she says, without looking up.

London fumbles in her purse and counts out a wad of damp fives and tens. That would take up basically all of her savings. She hoped Adam wasn't joking when he said he could take care of everything once she got there. "Um, what time does it leave?"

"Noon."

London glances at the clock. It's two thirty. Crap. Another day wasted. "Um, I guess . . . can I buy a ticket for tomorrow, then?"

she says, smoothing the money out along the counter, more to calm her shaking hands than anything else.

The ticket lady finally raises her head. She eyes London up and down, slowly chomping on her gum. "How old are you?"

"Eighteen," says London.

"Let me see your ID."

"Sixteen."

"Uh-huh," says the ticket lady. She bows her head back over her paper, and London can now see that it is covered with concentric circles, the ink so deeply etched that the paper is ripped in some places.

"But I'm a mature sixteen," says London.

"Sorry," the ticket lady says, not sounding sorry at all. "Bring along a parent or guardian and then we can talk."

"I don't have a parent or guardian," says London, stuffing the money back in her purse angrily. "I'm an orphan. I'm just trying to find my way in this mad, mad world."

"Aren't we all," the ticket lady says. "Next, please!"

The universe is against her. London knows this is what all teenagers always say, but in her case, it's actually true. The universe has never been more against anyone than it is against her at this moment. She might as well just go home and lock herself in her room for the rest of eternity. She might as well have gone over Kakabeka Falls herself.

London is outside the bus station searching for her car keys in her purse when a bright red Mustang convertible pulls into the parking spot next to her. London doesn't have to see the personalized licence plate to know that it's Anastasia Peters, with her brain-dead boyfriend, Andy, in the passenger seat. Raggedy Ann and Raggedy Andy, London calls them – not to their faces of course. She has too much invested in her own face. She doesn't have any secret nicknames for their two creepy androgynous sidekicks, Ryan and Dylan, who are sitting in the back, dressed in black and nearly indistinguishable from each other.

"Heeeeey, London," Anastasia says. She is also dressed all in black with a black and white headband in her black hair, and is simultaneously smoking a cigarette and drinking pop out of one of those ginormous McDonald's cups that London is pretty sure is illegal in parts of the world. "What's up, buttercup?" Anastasia's voice is throaty and low, and if she keeps smoking the way she does it will probably turn into one of those gross old lady voices before she's even twenty.

London takes out her keys and positions them in her hand like a weapon. "What are you doing, stalking me?"

"We were just in the neighbourhood and we saw your Nana's car." Anastasia pauses, sucking back some pop from the straw. "That *is* the same car I saw her driving around the track at school, right? Looks a little banged up. I hope she didn't get in an accident."

Around the track. Nana swore to London afterward that she wasn't crazy – she just wanted to see "what it would be like to be a race car driver." But it didn't matter what her intentions were. Intentions mean nothing to teenaged girls.

"What do you want, Anastasia?" she asks.

"We thought maybe you'd want to go to Merla Mae with us and get some ice cream?" She finishes her cigarette and flicks it to the ground. "Or do they not give out food stamps for that?"

"Ha ha, good one, a poverty joke." London leans against her car and crosses her arms. She's not afraid of Anastasia, even though most people are. Not really. "Why don't you go drown yourself in your swimming pool, you classist bitch."

"Sounds like someone misses being invited over for pool parties," Dylan says.

"She was never invited to any pool parties," Anastasia says. "Not any good ones, anyway."

"None of them were good ones," says London. It's a lame dig, but it's all she's got.

Anastasia lights another cigarette and hoists herself up in her seat until she is sitting on the top. She swings her bare legs in front of her and rests her high-heeled feet on the steering wheel. "What are you doing at the bus station, anyway?"

"None of your fucking business."

"You're not running away from home, are you? I'm not going to turn on the news tomorrow and see your missing person report?" She leans over to flick some stray ash off the toe of her shoe. "That would be tragic. I'd have to testify that I saw you here and I didn't even try to stop you."

If Anastasia Peters were an animal, she would be a black mamba snake – highly aggressive, very fast, and prone to attacking without provocation. Anastasia is one of those girls who knows how to game you. She games teachers into believing she's a good student, she games her parents into thinking she is a good daughter, she games her friends' parents into thinking she is someone they want their kids to hang around with. But she is a criminal, plain and simple. Her father runs a construction firm that everyone knows is connected to the Mob, so maybe it runs in the family, maybe it's, like, embedded in her genetic code. London has seen Anastasia blackmail people; has seen her commit assault, fraud, theft, and vandalism; has seen her perjure herself on the stand, possess with intent to sell, and impersonate a police officer, even.

Anastasia gamed London for years. She pretended to be her friend, linking arms with her in the hallway, letting her eat lunch at her table, inviting her to her house after school to hang out in her enormous rec room and play *Guitar Hero* and eat nachos. She made London trust her – and then she got London arrested. London and Anastasia have known each other since kindergarten, but it wasn't until a few months ago that London discovered who she truly was. That's a long game. The longest game in the universe, maybe.

"Fuck off and die, Anastasia" London says, getting into her Nana's car. As she drives away, the last thing she sees is Anastasia's arm above her head, waving goodbye.

◆ ◆ ◆

PONYO: It didn't work.

PONYO: They wouldn't let me buy a ticket cause I'm only 16.

SHARKBOY: That's bullshit.

PONYO: I know.

PONYO: I don't know what else to do.

SHARKBOY: I still don't get why your grandma can't take you.

SHARKBOY: I thought you said she was excited about the idea?

PONYO: She just can't.

SHARKBOY: Did something happen?

PONYO: No.

PONYO: I don't want to talk about it.

SHARKBOY: London, if we're going to be together there can't be any secrets between us.

SHARKBOY: Don't you trust me?

SHARKBOY: London?

PONYO: Yes, I trust you.

SHARKBOY: Well?

PONYO: You promise you won't tell anyone?

SHARKBOY: Of course not.

SHARKBOY: Besides, who would I tell?

PONYO: https://www.youtube.com/watch?v=HffbME_B7JGGHSTN

◆ ◆ ◆

A few months ago, London saw a cougar. She was walking Bruno along the high side of the Kam River and suddenly this thing came out of the trees and sat down and began licking its paw and London looked at it and thought, "That's a big cat." A second later she thought, "Oh," and crossed the street to turn around and head home. Then the cougar crossed the street, too, and Bruno started whining and London walked very fast until she was back at Victor Street.

"I just saw a cougar," she told her mother.

"No, you didn't," her mother said. She was busy doing something else, like she always was. London went and found Hamish, who was in the backyard testing samples of his whisky, which he made in these big barrels in the woodshed.

"I just saw a cougar," she said.

"Rawr," Hamish said, tipping some amber liquid into a beaker. "What was she wearing?"

"Gross," said London. Inside, her sisters were playing with Ross, trying to get him to eat disgusting things off the floor, like a Cheerio they found under a cushion or a rotten raisin they found behind the TV. But she didn't even want to talk to them. They were young and stupid and only talked to each other. If Uncle Shawn was there, she would have told him, and maybe he would have told her a story about a time when he lived in the woods and he wrestled a cougar for a sandwich or something like that, Uncle Shawn had all these really great stories. But Uncle Shawn wasn't there. And Papa was away, like Papa always was. She even thought about texting Aunt F, but she was probably super busy with her awesome new life in Toronto and wouldn't care about something so stupid as seeing a cougar in dumb boring Thunder Bay. So London went into Nana's room.

London had been avoiding her grandmother ever since the Around the Track incident. Besides, Nana was just so different now, like she couldn't always focus her eyes on you anymore, or maybe her mind was just far away. London missed the old Nana, who knew secret things about the world, like why there was a trap door in the basement or what would have happened if London had been born a boy. But everyone else was busy, or stupid, and so London went and found her grandmother, who was in bed already, doing a crossword on a little folding table that opened over her lap, a cup of tea on the nightstand, a Magic Bag hanging around her neck.

"Nana, I saw a cougar!"

"Oh, dear," Nana said, wrinkling her forehead. "What's a cougar? It sounds familiar."

"I can show you," said London. She came back with her laptop and sat beside her grandmother on her bed and they read about cougars together on Wikipedia. They read about how cougars are more closely related to house cats than actual lions, about how they are stalk-and-ambush hunters, about how they have been excessively hunted and are practically extinct in the eastern part of North America.

"It says that there are only 850 cougars left in all of Ontario," Nana said, frowning. "That's not very many."

"Poor cougars," London said, trying not to cry even though reading about the cougar was incredibly sad.

"It also says that they are reclusive and usually avoid people." Nana ran her finger over the picture on the screen. "I'd say you were very lucky indeed to have seen one of these beautiful creatures."

London, who up to that point was just relieved to not have been *eaten* by one of those beautiful creatures, looked at her grandmother and wondered if maybe she was actually still secretly super wise and it was just that no one understood her.

Now whenever London thinks about her grandmother, she tries to remember that moment: a still point in the chaos of their lives, when she knew without a doubt that her grandmother was her grandmother, and she didn't feel quite so alone in the world.

PONYO: Did you watch the video?
PONYO: Adam? Did you watch it?
PONYO: Adam, are you still there?
PONYO: Adam?
PONYO: . . .

FIFTEEN

1 p.m.

It's surprising how little time these things can take when you know what you're doing. By one o'clock, after just a couple of signatures on a few pieces of paper, Katriina is the proud new owner of a probably haunted house.

She just needs a little more time, she tells herself. She knows she can sell it, maybe on the national market, to someone just moving to the area, someone who doesn't know the history, someone who would think they were getting a really sweet deal. All it would take was a few cleverly worded write-ups. She can do it. She's not the number one sales representative in the Superior North Region for nothing. Besides, it's not unheard of for real estate agents to buy a house they are trying to sell. It's probably a little more unheard of for them to lie about it, but she had no choice. She tries to imagine what would happen if Krista Shepherd finds out about what she has done – it would be like an animal exposing its belly or its throat, leaving itself open to attack. She doesn't even want to think about what would happen if Shawn finds out. But she also can't imagine Shawn spending the night at Hanna's, so there's that, too. *It's a business decision*, she tells herself, sitting in her SUV in the parking lot of the bank, both hands on the steering wheel, breathing deeply. *I'm a business-woman. It's a business decision.*

She drives to the house. Her house. She puts the key in her lock and walks into her hallway, taking off her shoes and leaving them on her floor. She pads silently into her kitchen, where she stands over her sink, looking out her window into her yard. For a moment, she pictures another life, a life where she lives in this house, where she does dishes at night in this sink looking out over that yard with those trees and that fence, that one branch dipping down low into her field of vision, that one fencepost bent at an odd angle. She imagines a quiet morning spent in the breakfast nook eating toast and reading the paper, evenings curled up on a small, plush sofa watching hospital dramas on television, or reading a book by the fire, cool, clean floors that don't leave your feet sticky, a compost bin full of orange peels, egg shells, and tea bags. Long, hot baths followed by freshly laundered sheets. Another life, contained. A life alone.

She slides down to the floor. *It's too much.* It's not as though she has just gone out and bought a purse, or even a car. This is next-level nervous-breakdown stuff. A house is something with mean-ing, something you build your life around, not something you just buy on a whim. You don't just go out and get a new life because you feel like your old life is failing. *But it's not another life*, she reminds herself. *It's just a business decision.* Still, she can't shake this strange feeling she has, as though she has walked into a film about someone else's life and she's trying to remember her lines.

Her throat begins to constrict, her breathing coming in gasps, but she can't even gather enough energy to pull her elastic or to dig through her purse for something sharp. Instead, she opens her hand and drives her palm into her forehead, smashing the back of her head into the cupboard behind her. The impact leaves her ears ringing, the reverberation echoing through her skull, making her nose itch and her teeth hum against the inside of her mouth. When she closes her eyes, she can see strange patterns of light dancing across her eyelids. But she instantly feels better, more focused. She is a businesswoman, and she will approach this like a businesswoman. Assess problems, find solutions, achieve success.

She opens all the cupboard doors and then closes them, checking for creaks, for loose hinges. She opens that window over the sink and feels a breeze sweep in, warm and smelling of cut grass, of tree sap, of childhood. Westfort really is a lovely neighbourhood, so charming and friendly, so close to nature, with all its little green spaces, Mount McKay watching over everything. All those prospective buyers really didn't know what they were missing.

She plugs in the refrigerator, hears it hum to life, and imagines the things she will buy to put in it. No string cheese or squeezable yogurt, no four-litre jugs of milk, no warped Tupperware containers full of leftovers. White wine. Smoked gouda. Dark chocolate. These are things potential buyers would want to see, things that would make them picture their lives in this house as being just a little bit better than their lives are now. A vase of tulips. A colourful shower curtain. A papasan chair.

"Hey, Claudia," she says suddenly, without thinking. "How would you like a papasan chair?" The sound of her own voice startles her in the quiet of the house, and she can hear it rippling through the empty rooms. It makes her happy to think about Claudia, her little ghost daughter, following her silently from room to room, frozen in time at age twelve, quietly watching Katriina as she goes through the motions of making a home, even if it's not real, even if it's all just for show.

Humming to herself, Katriina digs out the Post-it pad she found the day before and starts to make a list.

Katriina had forgotten how fun it is to furnish a house. Her own house, the one she lives in with Shawn and Tommy and Petey, was furnished almost exclusively with wedding presents – smaller items chosen from Katriina's carefully curated gift registry; larger ones purchased by Katriina herself with the money given to her by her parents. Walter and Kate had offered to buy them a couch, but Katriina had politely declined, knowing that they couldn't possibly afford the couch she wanted, and not wanting to put anyone in an awkward position. It's not that she didn't appreciate the homey comfort of Victor Street, it just wasn't something she wanted for her own home. Even before the wedding, she spent months poring over home decor magazines, trying to figure out her and Shawn's style personality, trying to put together the perfect collection of things to adorn their new lives together. She would never admit this to anyone, but she can't recall anything she has done since that has made her quite as happy.

At The Brick she feels like a newlywed again, choosing bedroom sets and small appliances as though she is arranging a set for a magazine shoot. This time, she doesn't need months of prep time – she has years' worth of scrutinizing other people's houses, picking out all the things she would have done differently. For the Paulsson house – *her* house – in cozy, quaint Westfort, she has decided to go simple country chic, with a lot of whitewashed wood, cotton fabric in lavender and cornflower blue. Everything fresh and clean, and likely to stay that way with no sticky-fingered kids around, no hurricane of a husband. She buys everything off the floor, so she won't have to wait – she wants everything as soon as possible, so that she can embark on her new marketing campaign right away.

"The only thing we can deliver today is the couch." The salesman, Jeff, is a young guy, early twenties, with over-styled hair and an awkward-fitting suit who has probably been selling furniture for as long as Katriina has owned the Paulsson house. He has been sweating profusely the entire time he has been helping her, probably from the adrenaline of what is likely the sale of a lifetime. She knows that feeling, the euphoria of impending greatness, the near-paralyzing fear of making that one wrong move that will screw it all up. "We can get everything else to you by Wednesday," he says, spitting the words out as quickly as he can, hurling them at her and then stepping back – if this is the wrong move, he wants to get it over with.

"That's fine," Katriina says amiably. She likes Jeff, she wants him to succeed in life. She wishes there were some small bit of wisdom she could pass on to him now, but she can't come up with anything that doesn't sound trite. *Follow your dreams! Never give up! Always do your best!* Jeff deserves better than that. Jeff deserves to be inspired, to be motivated, to be *uplifted*. "Hey, you know, a famous person once said that success is getting up just one more time than you fall."

"Okay, good, great," says Jeff, running his hand through his hair. "So what's the address again?"

On the way out of the store, Katriina's phone rings. Shawn. She lets it go to voice mail the first and the second time, the ring tone clanging insistently on the passenger seat as she drives away from the store. She finally answers it the third time, pulling her car over to the side of the expressway and putting it in park.

"Where are you?" he asks before she can even say hello. "Where are the boys?" He sounds impatient, tired. She remembers that he is probably hungover, and so she vows to be gentle with him, to not make things worse.

"They're at my parents'," she says. "Are you still at Hanna's?" She feels mildly pleased at her tone – she sounds as though none of this is a big deal. A transport truck whizzes by, shaking the car. Katriina puts her hand against the door to brace herself. *None of this is a big deal*, she thinks. *It's just a normal Sunday afternoon.*

186

"No, I'm at the house. Why are they at your parents'? And what the fuck happened to the kitchen?"

Katriina takes a deep breath. She wishes she had just left Shawn a note instead of having to go through all of this. Notes are so much easier, you can say what you have to say all at once without the other person interjecting, and you never have to worry about your tone being misinterpreted. Now, she tries to keep her tone as neutral as possible. "I'm sure we both have a lot of questions," she says. "I just have to catch up on some work, and then maybe we can talk about all this later?"

"You make it sound like we just need to discuss changes to our retirement plan."

"I had a rough morning, Shawn, that's all."

"You always have a rough morning. Every morning is a rough morning for you."

"I'm doing the best I can." She stares out the window, trying to keep herself in check, mesmerized by the cars racing by her window, so many of them, one after another. Where are they all going? she wonders. How can there be so many people with somewhere to go right at this exact minute? It's Sunday, for Christ's sake. It's supposed to be a day of rest.

"Katriina, what are we doing?"

"I don't know, baby." She can picture Shawn in their kitchen, leaning against the counter, his hand on the back of his neck, head hanging low. "This is stupid. We shouldn't be fighting, not now, not with everything else going on."

"No, that's not what I mean." His voice is hoarse. "I mean . . . us. This marriage."

Katriina feels all the air leave her lungs. "Excuse me?" she manages to whisper.

There is a long silence on the other end. She tries to catch her breath, but the air just won't come back. Fragments of thought stagger through her mind, but she can't grab on to any of them. She can hear Shawn's breath on the other end. It's like they are teetering on the edge of something, waiting for the slightest breeze to push them into the chasm.

"Nothing," says Shawn. "I don't know. Nothing."

Everything is going to be okay, Katriina reassures herself, forming the words with her mouth without making the sounds.

4:30 p.m.

Katriina lies on her new couch in the middle of her new living room, where she has been stationed since it was delivered an hour ago, and where she plans to stay indefinitely. The couch is dark blue corduroy, plush and overstuffed, still stiff around the edges where no children have repeatedly slid off to retrieve a toy, no husband has leaned his forearms against tree-trunk legs hinged in a wide V while watching the football game. The rest of the house is still empty of furniture, and lying here Katriina has the sensation that she is floating on a raft in the middle of a vast ocean, drifting lazily under a ceiling of stars. She stares up, unblinking, and feels the walls recede away from her, the room opening up into a dark expanse as wide and endless as she imagines the hole in her heart must be. With one pale hand she begins drawing a long, looping spiral on the inside of her calf with a box cutter, focusing all her energy on her task. She watches the blood ooze out onto the dark fabric of the couch, no longer caring about the stain, the scar, the questions. There will be no more questions. Not anymore.

As she cuts, she wonders if Claudia is watching, her little ghost daughter. Wonders if she thinks that Katriina is a coward, letting the life drain out of her too slowly, year after year, drop of blood by drop of blood, ache by bright and shiny ache, instead of having the guts to just get it over with.

SIXTEEN

After the morning coffee cruise, Walter ties up the *Miss Penelope* at the marina and sits on the upper deck, watching the kids at the splash pad, their harried parents trying to avoid getting wet. He knows he should go back to Victor Street, but he can't bring himself to leave just yet. He hadn't realized how difficult it would be with Kate not there, how empty the house would seem even when it was full of people. When Kate isn't there, the family isn't a family – it's just a group of people who happen to be related. Kate is the one who holds everything together. She is the one who makes everyone else make sense.

He still has one more load of dishes to wash, but that can wait, too. It has been taking more out of him doing everything himself lately. When she was younger, London would occasionally join him, but the novelty wore off for her around the same age it had worn off for Finn and Nicki. And Walter knows better than to suggest using the coffee cruise as punishment, the way he did with them. He had thought, back then, that it would be one of those things that they appreciated when they were older, but remembering the expression on Finn's face when he had gone into the sunroom to wake her up, he realizes that it is still a burden, the way spending time with him is still a burden. And while he knows he was a fool for expecting something more, he is surprised to discover how much it hurts. Walter would never admit it to anyone, but it broke his heart that neither of his girls showed any interest in being out on the lake. He knows that children need to forge their own path in the world, and he would never want to impede them in that. He had just hoped that one of them would have wanted to follow in his footsteps. That was all.

"Let me guess, she's not going," Nicki had said when he ran into her in the kitchen on his way out. She was already dressed for work, her hair and makeup done, standing waiting by the toaster. He wondered, not for the first time, if his manic daughter ever slept.

"She had a long day yesterday," Walter said, pulling a carton of orange juice from the fridge and pouring himself a glass. "She deserves some rest."

Nicki snorted. "Yeah, right." Her toast popped up, and she pinched it by the edge and flicked it onto a plate. "Poor little overworked Finnie."

Walter took a sip of his orange juice. "Maybe you'd like to come with me?"

"Oh, come on, Dad," she said, scraping a hard chunk of butter violently over the toast. "You know I don't have time to go *boating*." She stuck the toast in her mouth and strode out the front door, leaving a trail of crumbs behind her.

Walter sighed. Just like when they were teenagers, each girl had used different tactics to get out of the coffee cruise. Nicki would throw tantrums, stomping around the house in a little black cloud of anger that grew blacker the closer the time came to leave and the more she realized she was not going to get out of it. But once on the boat, she would be cheerful, joking with the regulars, doing what needed to be done. Nicki is a hard worker – not many people give her credit for that. She didn't mind getting her hands dirty, no matter how much she whined about it. Finn, on the other hand, was the exact opposite. She would never complain about getting pulled out of bed, but once she was on the boat she would drag her feet, scowl at the customers, and hide out in the cabin reading a book when she was supposed to be serving coffee or washing dishes. It was as though she thought the entire thing was a huge waste of time, that she was destined for a life more extraordinary than this city – or her family – could give her. Walter had hoped she would grow out of it, that if she just spent enough time on the lake, or in the bush, or in the mountains, she would realize how lucky she was to live in a place surrounded by such an abundance of natural beauty. But in Finn's eyes, Thunder Bay was nothing but a boring, cultureless, working-class city full of backward, camo-wearing, gun-toting rednecks with bad haircuts and terrible taste in beer.

Walter has always loved Finn, just – heaven help him – not as much as he loves Nicki. He would never tell anyone that, of course. But there is too much of Kate in Finn, too much of that dangerous restlessness and unpredictability, the desire for some-thing bigger, for something more, that drives her to push away everyone who loves her. When she told him and Kate that she was moving to Japan, he had been happy for her – she would be away from Thunder Bay and all the myriad things she hated about it – and when she came back, he had almost been disappointed. "I thought you might meet a nice Japanese man and we'd all have to sit on the floor and eat rice at your wedding," he'd joked one night at dinner, prompting a rant about how racist he was and how backward everyone here was, how clueless and provincial. After that, Walter found himself watching everything he said around her, trying to avoid setting her off again.

Years later, when Finn finally did leave for good, she had already pushed everyone in the family away so much that it took almost a week for any of them to notice she was gone. One evening, Kate came into their bedroom with a confused expression on her face. "I just called Finn's apartment, and she doesn't live there anymore."

Walter sighed. "That's ridiculous." He was already in bed, engrossed in a *Maclean's* article about Canadian troops in Kandahar. "You must have gotten mixed up."

"No, I talked to her roommate. What's her name? Amanda?"

"Alyssa?"

Kate didn't say anything. When Walter finally glanced up, she was crying. "Katie, I'm sure everything is fine. You probably misheard her. Finn wouldn't move without telling us."

Shaking her head, Kate reached for a Kleenex on the bedside table. "No. She's gone." There was something in her eyes that made Walter's breath catch, something he had seen only a few times before – a deep clarity, a knowing that went deeper than anything Walter could understand. And seeing that, he suddenly knew too. Finn really was gone. Just like that, without a word to anyone, propelled away from Thunder Bay not by a desire to be somewhere else but by a desire to be anywhere but here.

Yes, there is so much of Kate in Finn, but there is so much of Walter, too. And the older he gets, the more he wonders if *that* is the part of Finn that he really finds difficult to love.

As Walter is untying the boat and preparing to head home, a man in khakis and a Hawaiian shirt he doesn't recognize comes up to him.

"Walter," he says. "James Buhler. We went to high school together."

"Of course." Walter reaches out his hand. "How are you, James." He doesn't remember James, not really. But then, he hasn't really thought about anyone from high school since high school.

James grins. "I knew, I just knew you were going to end up marrying Katie Babiak."

"Oh," says Walter. "Yes, well."

"I was just saying to Joan yesterday – my wife, Joan, you remember her. She used to be Joan Fairweather?"

"Oh, sure," Walter lied.

"I was just saying to Joan, when we saw that picture on the news, 'Now doesn't that look like Katie Babiak all grown up?' And she said, 'Jimmy, that reporter said her name was Katherine Parker.' And that's when, I don't know, it just clicked."

"Nice to see you again, James," Walter says, tossing the line up onto the deck of the *Miss Penelope* and jumping up after it. He starts the boat and angles it out of the marina. When he turns back, he can see James Buhler still standing there, waving at him, a big dumb grin on his face as he snaps a photo with his smart-phone. He and Joan are going to have a lot to talk about at dinner tonight, Walter thinks as he pulls away from the dock. He hopes they can really bask in it; he hopes the excitement of Walter's life falling apart reinvigorates their marriage.

Walter knows the twins believe he wasn't around much when they were growing up, but when they were very small, he was around all the time. Because it was hard for Walter to be without projects, he would spend the winter months in the backyard, constructing things for them from snow. One year he made an igloo castle, complete with a turret for each twin, with an ice slide down the back that Nicki once got her tongue stuck to. Another year, he made a snow maze that one of the neighbour's kids actually got lost in. He didn't have a lot to offer his daughters, except for what he could teach them about the outdoors, what he could make for them from nature. That turned out to be not enough – for them, or for Kate, he supposes.

Kate hadn't wanted to have children, at least not at first. "Let's just let it be you and me," she said. "We should be enough for each other."

"You are enough for me," Walter said. *But I might not be enough for you.* The thought had plagued him ever since Kate's proposal. He felt a mild but persistent terror every time she drove away to the grocery store or to visit her parents – all he could see was her driving away from him in her MGB that afternoon so many years ago – and every time he thought, *She's not coming back.* But she would come back for a baby. He was sure she would.

It was a self-fulfilling prophecy. The more Walter talked about having kids, the more distant Kate became, until one day he came home from work and she was gone. He felt her absence as soon as he walked in the door, and knew it was different this time, that she was not at the grocery store, or at her parents'. He sat in the kitchen at Victor Street until dawn, staring at the snow falling outside the window, not moving, barely able to breathe from the ache in his chest. At seven the next morning he saw headlights piercing the pre-dawn dark, fat flakes illuminated in the beams. Walter watched Kate get out of the car and walk towards the house, and then open the door to the kitchen. He reached out his hand to her and suddenly had a vision of her that day at Chippewa, climbing out of the ice and making her way towards him. For a split second he saw that same haunted look on her face, and it was as if she had crawled out of an abyss all over again.

Then in a flash the look was gone, and her face lit up with a smile. "I'm pregnant," she told him, and Walter hugged her, and laughed, and hugged her again, all the hours spent staring out the window forgotten. But not that look. He never forgot that look.

The twins were born, and for almost a decade things were as close to normal as Walter could hope for. When Kate was around the girls she seemed content, but he could never fully shake the feeling that she was merely acting – playing the role of the good mother, the perfect wife, while pushing the real Kate further and further down. The real Kate: the one who drank brandy in hay-lofts, who proposed on doorsteps, who didn't care what anyone else thought of her. *But I love that Kate*, Walter wanted to yell. Was it his fault? Had he led her to believe that this was what he wanted? *Was* this really what he wanted, after all?

Still, he could see glimpses of the real Kate when she was with Nicki and Finn – out in the yard climbing trees or catching bugs, coming home from tobogganing, running the wrong way up the escalator – until she saw Walter and fixed the mask back on her face. "Welcome home, darling," she would say, kissing his cheek, then retreat to the kitchen to get supper started, her body closed off like a treacherous road.

It got to the point where it hurt him too much to come home, to see the change in her. So he just stopped coming home as often. The truth was, he may have been wrong about there being room in his life for the lake and a wife. In the scope of things that he could understand, that he felt he could love unconditionally, the lake won every time. At the very least, if he wasn't there, he couldn't screw it up. If he wasn't there, she still had to be.

For a while, it seemed Walter was right. Ten years went by without an incident. And then one day he came home from a two-week guiding trip and Kate disappeared for two days.

Walter was strangely calm as he went through the list of people they knew, calling them to ask if they had seen his wife, reassuring the girls that their mother was just off visiting a sick relative. It wasn't just that he had been through this before. Waiting for Kate was now part of his muscle memory – something he could do on automatic pilot, without having to think about it too much. It was always best if he didn't think about it too much.

He was calm, too, when she eventually came home. "We missed you," was all he said.

Walter had hoped that Kate's disappearance had been a momentary lapse in judgment. But deep down, he knew better. Over the next few months, her reckless behaviour started to escalate in alarming ways. Whenever Walter was home, she would disappear, sometimes for a few hours, sometimes overnight, once for an entire weekend. She never gave him any explanation, and feeling guilty about his own absences, he never felt he was in a position to ask. Once, he came back from a trip to discover that she had bought a motorcycle; another time she had bought a pet snake. That time, Walter had to put his foot down. There was no way he was going to live with a snake.

One evening, Kate was brought home by the police, who had found her standing in her bathing suit on the side of the James Street Swing Bridge with a rope tied around her feet. "I wasn't trying to kill myself, I was trying to bungee jump," she said later, her hands wrapped around a mug of tea.

"What the hell is that?" asked Walter, pacing through their kitchen, trying to keep his anger under control.

Kate shrugged. "You jump off of a bridge with your feet tied to it. I saw it on *That's Incredible!* They filmed the first American woman bungee jumping off the Golden Gate Bridge. I thought maybe I could be the first Canadian woman."

"But . . . why?" It was the only word he could think of. Over and over again in his head: why, why, why? "Are you bored? Do you want to go back to school? Get a job?"

"Don't be silly," she said. "I have the girls to take care of."

"Then why?"

"Why not?" said Kate. "It looked like fun." She took a sip of her tea. "Walter, I know it's dangerous. I'm not an idiot. I just needed, I don't know." She put the mug down, and it made a solid clunk against the wood. A good, heavy, comforting sound. "I needed something."

Walter sat down across from her. "I know I haven't been around much," he began. But Kate's eyes had lost focus, and she leaned back in her chair, licking her lips.

"It's okay, Walter," she said, and he felt the words sink into his skin like a salve. "Everything is okay."

Maybe it *was* okay. Maybe he was making too big of a deal out of it. It was a bit of fun – she just took it too far. He wanted her to be happy. The only thing he had ever wanted was for her to be happy. But he was beginning to believe it wasn't possible.

"You can't just go jumping off bridges. Those girls need you."

"I could die at any minute, Walter. I don't have to jump off a bridge for that to happen." Something dark descended on Walter. *I feel like God has forgotten about me*, he heard her saying. *Like I was supposed to die that day, and no one up there ever bothered to double check that I had.*

"Promise me, Kate," he said, taking her hand. "Promise me you won't do anything to unnecessarily risk your life."

She stared past him, out the kitchen window. "I promise." But her voice sounded far away, and Walter was never really sure that she meant it. A promise from Kate, he had learned, was like the promise of summer: it would arrive sometime, but you never knew for sure when, or what form it would take.

Weeks went by, and Walter let his guard down. Maybe the worst was over. Then one day he came home from a government research trip to find a stranger sleeping in the guest room.

"Who is that upstairs?" Walter asked Kate, who was in the kitchen preparing a pot roast. The meat sat on the counter, bleeding into a bed of paper towels while she chopped potatoes.

"Oh, that's Shawn," she said. "He lives here now." She put the knife down and scooped the potatoes into the pot, and then moved on to decimating an onion. Kate could chop onions without shedding a tear. Walter had always thought it was magic, but now, watching her, he wondered if instead it pointed to some kind of basic human deficiency.

"Kate, what the hell is going on?"

She began chopping faster. "Shawn needs a home," she said. "We have a home with an extra bedroom. It's simple math, really."

"Get rid of him," Walter said. Kate kept chopping. Walter put

197

his hand across the top of the knife. He could feel the sting in his own eyes, the tears forming.

Kate stopped moving, still staring down at the half-chopped onion. "If he goes," she said, her voice low, "then I go, too." And in that one sentence, Walter heard a lifetime of unspoken ultimatums suddenly solidifying in the space between them, all of his deepest fears made real.

For a moment, neither of them moved. Then Kate shrugged his hand off hers and resumed chopping. Walter walked out of the house and grabbed his bike out of the shed, knowing that it was the only method of transportation he could trust himself on. If he had taken his truck or the boat, there was no guarantee that he would have come back.

When he did come back, hours later, everyone was sitting around the dining room table having dinner. The stranger, Shawn, sat in Walter's seat, shovelling pot roast into his mouth, seemingly swallowing without even chewing. He reminded Walter of a stray dog with a piece of meat, eating as fast as possible in fear that someone would come along and take it from him. Later, Walter would learn that this was what Shawn was, essentially – a stray dog that Kate had rescued.

Finn beamed up at him from the table. "Hey, Daddy, did you know that Shawn is double-jointed? Do you want to see?"

Shawn put down his glass of milk and wiped his mouth. "I don't think he wants to see, Finnie."

Hearing Shawn say Finn's name jarred something loose in Walter. *That's my daughter,* he thought. *You don't say my daughter's name.* "Can I speak with you for a moment?" he said to Shawn.

"No," said Kate, delicately working her knife through a chunk of beef. "You cannot."

"Daddy, aren't you going to have dinner with us?" Nicki asked.

"No, sweetheart, I'm not," said Walter. He went into the kitchen and took his plate out of the oven and ate sitting at the kitchen table, listening to his family in the next room. For the next three days, he ate his meals alone, or stayed out in his office or working on the boats, avoiding everyone as much as possible. At night he would sneak into bed once he was sure Kate was asleep – or at least pretending to be. He knew what she was doing, and he wasn't going to have any part of it.

On the third night, he came back in from his office to find Shawn sitting at the kitchen table, eating a sandwich. The few times that Walter had seen the boy, he had never not been eating. Walter was sure that if he stayed much longer, he would surely bankrupt them on groceries alone.

"Do you want a sandwich?" Shawn asked. "I have three of them here."

Walter closed the door behind him with a sigh. "Did you just offer me some of my own food?"

"Hey, man, sorry. I just thought maybe you were hungry."

Walter was hungry. But he certainly was not going to eat one of Shawn's sandwiches. He knew he was being petty; he didn't care. Kate had no right to invite someone to live with them – to stay in their house, for chrissake! – without even consulting him. But when he opened the breadbox, he saw that Shawn had used up all the bread.

"Fine," said Walter. "I'll take one."

Shawn held the plate out to him, and he took the top sandwich. Bologna and mustard. His favourite. The kid had piled four pieces of bologna on each sandwich and squished the bread down, turning it into a solid block. But it tasted good, Walter would give him that. He took a small bite, eyeing Shawn.

"You don't trust me, do you?" Shawn said, hunching over his second sandwich.

"No," said Walter.

Shawn smiled at him and licked a dribble of mustard off the side of his hand. "That's good," he said. "You shouldn't."

Walter never forgot those words, and for the next several months, he waited for the other shoe to drop. But Shawn never did a single thing to indicate he was anything but a good, decent kid, which on many levels was more unnerving. And he slid so easily into the family, something else that bothered Walter immensely. It was as though he knew exactly where Walter was failing and filled in the holes. He took Finn to the movies, he let Nicki paint his nails, he stepped in when the two of them were fighting and made everyone laugh with a dumb joke. And when Kate was diagnosed with breast cancer, Shawn took her to all her radiation appointments and helped her recover from her surgery. Finn had an ally, Nicki had a sounding board, and Kate had a rock. Shawn was better at being a Parker than Walter was. Now when Walter came home, *he* was the stranger in the house.

Walter had chosen a side, and it turned out to be the wrong one. No matter what he did to try to make up for it, that one fact would always be true.

When Walter docks the *Miss Penelope* at Victor Street, Shawn is sitting on the back deck, drinking a beer. *A little early for that*, Walter thinks as he walks across the lawn, his arms laden with baking trays to go back to Kahvila. "Where is everyone?" he asks.

"No idea," says Shawn. "I was about to ask you." He puts the beer down and grabs the trays from Walter. "I can take these back for you."

"Thanks," says Walter.

"Want to join me?" Shawn asks. He nudges a blue cooler with his toe. "Left over from last night's debacle."

Walter shakes his head. "It wasn't as bad as all that," he says. "No violence was perpetrated."

"No, I suppose we can be thankful for that. Are you heading to the hospital later?"

"On my way there now."

"Can I get a ride over with you? My car's wrecked, and Mom's car's not here."

Mom. Even after all these years, Walter can't get used to that. Ridiculous, he knows. "Sure," he says. Shawn drinks back the rest of his beer and they head into the house, each carrying half of the pile of trays. It has occurred to Walter that if he had been less of a near-sighted jerk, Shawn might have been interested in taking over Superior Tours. He has a good head for business; it wouldn't have mattered if it was pancakes or boats. But what could Walter do about it now? Nik Saarinen had probably been a better father to Shawn than Walter ever had, anyway.

When they get into the kitchen, Walter looks out through the window and sees that Kate's car is, indeed, gone. As is his truck. And Nicki's car, and Hamish's truck. "Well, that's not going to work," Walter says. He goes over to the Jeep and sees that the entire right fender is smashed in. "What happened here?"

"I have no idea," says Shawn. "I just got here and found it like that." He pulls out his cell phone. "Should I call us a cab?"

"Sure," says Walter, hesitantly. Something about this seems off. The math doesn't add up. Three other drivers. Four cars missing. Could one have been stolen? No. There has to be another explanation. But he puts it out of his mind. Shawn hangs up with the cab company, and they stand awkwardly on the front porch, trying to think of things to say to each other.

"Congratulations, by the way," Walter says after a minute. "It's going to be fun to have a little one around here again."

Shawn leans against the porch railing, picking at some peeling paint. "There's not going to be a little one," he says flatly, avoiding Walter's eyes. "Katriina had another miscarriage."

Ahh, shit, Walter thinks, immediately followed by *Why are you telling me?* "I'm so sorry," he says, unable to think of anything else. Shawn's body is curled forward, his muscles clenched so tightly that Walter can feel the tension from across the porch. He wishes that he hadn't brought it up, had let Nicki or Finn tell him later. Anything to avoid this precise moment. When Shawn does look at him, there is a desperation in his eyes that Walter has never seen before, not even during his first months at Victor Street when he was still basically feral, waiting for things to fall apart at any moment, with Kate the only thing standing between him and life back on the rails. And then suddenly Walter knows exactly why Shawn is telling him – because he can't tell Kate.

Walter touches Shawn's shoulder, and a sudden jolt travels through his hand and up his arm as he realizes Shawn is shaking. *Oh god, is he crying?* But it is just Shawn's leg bouncing against the railing. Walter wonders if he should hug him, but decides against it. "It will all be okay," he says. It's not much, but it's all he has.

"Thanks," says Shawn. He stares out into the yard.

Walter keeps his hand on Shawn's shoulder until the cab pulls into the driveway and the driver honks the horn. Even after he takes his hand away, the quivering reverberates in his palm, all that pain and confusion and frustration transferring from Shawn's body to Walter's. *From son to father.* But the moment has passed, and it's too late to say it.

All he can do is hope that Shawn was able to feel it, too.

SEVENTEEN

With Ross strapped into the passenger seat beside her, Finn drives her father's truck to Barkley's. It's the only place she can think of to look for Dallas. The bar is empty, except for Marv sitting on a stool nursing a Crystal and a fat lip, and Alyssa behind the bar taking inventory with a clipboard tucked under her arm, a purplish bruise spreading across her cheek, two bands of medical tape wrapped around the middle and index fingers of her left hand. She puts the clipboard down when she sees Finn and Ross, staring at them for a moment, her eyes narrowing.

"Well, hey there," she says finally, coming out from behind the bar and putting her hands on her hips. "Who's this little guy?"

"This is Ross," says Finn, pushing him forward. She doesn't know if Ross performs well with strangers. She has a feeling he doesn't.

"Hey, Ross," says Alyssa. "Very nice to meet you." She shakes his hand, as if she is meeting a foreign dignitary instead of an eight-year-old boy. "Would you like a glass of chocolate milk? You can sit right up here at the bar and drink it if you want."

"Okay," says Ross, climbing up onto the stool unassisted.

"Since when does Barkley's serve chocolate milk?" Finn asks.

"Since the bartender got pregnant and started craving it 24/7," Alyssa says. She pours the chocolate milk into a draft glass and slides it down the bar to Ross like it's a bottle of Bud. Then she gets another glass and starts pouring a beer for Finn, even though she hasn't asked for one. Marv shifts in his seat, his synthetic track pants rustling against the vinyl of the barstool. "Don't even think about it, Marv," Alyssa says, her eyes still on her pour. "If you talk to him, I'll rip your head off."

"I wasn't going to," says Marv, lowering his head over his bottle. Finn can see a goose egg growing on his head beneath his thinning hair. She wonders if anyone actually knows who wounded whom.

Ross sits on the stool and sips his chocolate milk, and Alyssa motions Finn over to a table. She hands her the draft, takes a seat, and studies Finn's nose. "How's your face?" she asks.

Finn brings her hand to it self-consciously. "Okay," she says. "How's yours?" Close up, Finn can see that the area around Alyssa's eye is caked with makeup, and the purple is actually a lot deeper than it appears.

"What the fuck do you think you're doing?" Alyssa says, motioning to Ross. "That's Ross, right? Like, *Ross* Ross? Your nephew Ross?"

"Yeah," says Finn. "We're just hanging out. You know, aunt and nephew stuff." She runs her hands over the surface of the table, where ROBIN LOVES TROY is carved into the wood in huge, sharp letters, underneath which is a smaller etching that says FUCK THE POLICE. Are the two related? Are Robin and Troy some kind of Bonnie and Clyde deal, all crime and sex and adrenaline? Are they still together, running from the law? Probably not. That kind of intensity can't be sustained for long – it either fizzles out or kills you.

"Dallas isn't here," Alyssa says.

Finn digs the tip of her finger into the grooves of the P in POLICE. "Do you know where I can find him?" She doesn't meet Alyssa's eyes.

"Finn."

"What?"

"I just . . . I don't think you want to get in the middle of all this." Alyssa places her hands on her belly and leans back in the chair. "I mean, this kid . . . look at him." They both turn to where Ross is sitting on the barstool, his lips closed over the straw in his chocolate milk, feet dangling over the edge, staring intently at Marv, who has his head turned away from Ross at an unnatural angle, one arm curving around his beer.

"Because he's basically exactly what my and Dallas's son would have looked like?"

"No," says Alyssa. "I mean, he's just a baby."

"I'm not trying to make anything weird happen, Lyss. I promise. I just want Dallas to see him."

"Does Nicki know about this?"

Finn laughs, taking a drink of her beer. "What do you think?"

"I think you're playing a very dangerous game." Alyssa readjusts herself in her seat, reaching around to pull her T-shirt down over the small of her back. The first time Finn met her, on the third day of high school, she was all blond hair and braces and attitude, standing against the wall in gym class, as opposed to the idea of physical fitness as a school subject as Finn was. She was the first real friend of her own that Finn ever had, not someone who just tolerated her because they were friends with Nicki, or because they *wanted* to be friends with Nicki. Back then, Finn was the one who got Alyssa through math tests and history essays and science projects. Finn had been good at navigating school, but as it turns out, Alyssa is better at navigating life. It has taken Finn a long time to understand there is a difference.

Finn puts down her glass. "I won't even tell Ross who he is," she says, not mentioning that Ross already knows that they're on their way to see his father. It doesn't matter – to Ross, his father could be anyone. He probably assumes Marv is his father, Finn realizes with a shudder, watching Ross watch Marv. "Come on, Lyss. Where can I find him?"

Alyssa sighs. "He's back working at Desi's."

Finn almost laughs. "Seriously?"

"Yeah. But I don't think he'll be there now. He got pretty drunk last night after you left. He's probably still in bed." She rolls her eyes skyward, as if she can't even believe she's going to say what she's about to say. "He left his ID here to claim the pool table and he forgot to pick it up. I guess you could take it, if you want." She gets up from the table and walks behind the bar, procuring the card from the lost and found. She holds it out for Finn and her whole face is a warning. But Finn takes it anyway. Sometimes, even the Warning Girl needs to live on the edge a little.

If this were a movie, then Nicki would die, and Dallas and Finn would be thrown back together to raise her children. It's a terrible thing to fantasize about, and obviously not something that Finn actually wants to happen, but she lets herself imagine it for a few moments before she reminds herself that the man she is fantasizing about raising her sister's children with is still working at the same coffee shop he did in high school. Is there a Desi's equivalent on the island where he ran off to? she wonders. Did he father any more children out there? Is there an army of mini-Dallases running around B.C.? Did he really even leave at all, or did he just hide out in his parents' basement for eight years, waiting for the Parkers to forget about him?

Dallas's apartment is only a few blocks from Barkley's, over a Chinese restaurant that doubles as a government cheque-cashing facility. The door to the upstairs apartments is nestled between the entrance to the restaurant and a vacant storefront. A strung-out woman with two missing front teeth sits on the stoop, blocking their way. Despite the heat, she is dressed in a heavy camo jacket and pink fleece pants. "Hey, little man," she says to Ross as they squeeze past her to get in the door. "Don't suppose your mom has any smokes on her?"

"She's not my mom," Ross says.

"Oh come on," the woman calls after them as they head up the stairs. "You two look exactly alike."

Finn knocks on the door of apartment 212 and waits, fidgeting with a loose thread on the hem on her T-shirt, smoothing out a piece of hair that has come free from her ponytail. Ross stands perfectly still, staring at the wall. The hallway is stifling, and Finn can feel herself suffocating just imagining the apartment – old and stuffy, with no air conditioning or windows that catch any kind of a cross breeze. She smooths her hair down again. *Dallas*, she thinks. *Dallas. Dallas. Dallas.*

But when the door opens, it's not Dallas standing there. It's Tanya. Finn has a flash of Tanya's fist flying towards her face the night before. This is the second time she expected Dallas and got Tanya instead. The air has grown hotter around her, suffocating, just like she imagined.

"It's you," says Tanya. Finn half expects her to punch her again, but then she realizes Tanya is looking at Ross.

"It's me," Ross confirms confidently. He smiles. It is him, this he knows for sure.

Finn wishes she could say the same thing about herself.

EIGHTEEN

The woman at the door is not the woman Tanya expects. She just looks like her. But the boy, the boy she knows. The woman is an imposter, but the boy is real.

"It's you," she says to the boy, and the boy gazes up at her.

"It's me," he says, because he knows who he is. He is just himself, nobody's son. He doesn't have a shadow to live in. No legacy to tie himself to. His mother's, maybe. But with boys, it's always the father anyway.

She opens the door to invite them inside. The woman glares at her as they enter, probably wondering if Tanya is going to hit her again. Tanya wonders that, too. Not that she wants to, but you never know. Circumstances could change. This woman is a Parker, so she is Tanya's natural enemy.

Tanya regrets punching the woman. She doesn't usually drink. It causes too much chaos in her body, too much confusion. It's too easy to lose herself, her mind spiralling out of control, her small, dark thoughts becoming monstrous and wild. Plus she has seen the way it can take over someone's life. Her mother. Her brothers. Even Dallas. Sometimes, though, it's just easier to drink. People won't stare at you, ask you questions. Assume you are going to judge them. Tanya tries not to judge anyone. Except herself.

Last night, Dallas wanted to go out. And because Tanya was worried about him, she went out with him. He had shown her the video of the woman in the barrel crashing over the waterfall, then surviving, waving to the news cameras from the back of the ambulance. She knows about those Parkers, understands things about them that even Dallas doesn't. Understands the landscape of the world and where they stand in it, and where he stands in relation to them. How he shifts when they shift. He doesn't see it, but she does. She knows how he feels about them, how on some level he is always thinking about a Parker. Sometimes it's hard for her to know so much. So yeah, she drank. And she got angry, thinking about how much time she spent thinking about Dallas, and how little time he spent thinking about her. And so she hit the woman. It wasn't fair.

This Parker is beautiful, like the other one, with long waves of strawberry-blond hair, skin pale and luminous. Tanya doesn't even want to look at her. The three of them stand awkwardly just inside the door, the woman staring at Tanya, Tanya staring at the boy, the boy staring into space. No one says anything, which feels wrong in this kind of social situation.

"Well, come sit down," she says, leading them into the apartment.

The woman scans the room, and Tanya does too, trying to see it the way that she must see it. Used furniture. Cracks in the walls. The wrong kind of floor. Dirty. Broken. Poor. Tanya shuffles some books into a neat little pile on the table, straightens a pillow on the armchair, kicks a dirty sock under the couch. She doesn't know why she cares – this is Dallas's apartment, not hers, although she is here most of the time. And they *are* poor. Dallas works at a coffee shop and Tanya goes to school, and while her tuition is paid for, she gives most of her monthly allowance to her brothers, who all have families of their own. Still, it might be nice to have some flowers, or some art on the walls.

"I'm looking for Dallas," the woman says. "Is he here?"

"You're the twin," Tanya says, studying the woman's face. Her nose doesn't appear to be broken, which is good. She does have a bruise underneath her eye, which is bad. People will wonder how she got it. "Hit by some drunk Indian," she'll say. "Can you believe it?" And they will shake their heads and roll their eyes: *What else is new.*

"I'm Finn," the woman says, rubbing the back of her neck with one hand.

Of course. To Tanya, Finn is the Other One, but Finn thinks of herself as the only one. "Dallas isn't here," Tanya says.

"Oh," says Finn. She is wearing jeans and a blue T-shirt – not one of those nice T-shirts that women wear, soft and scoop-necked and fitted to their bodies, but a plain, shapeless man's T-shirt with *Superior Tours* screen-printed onto it.

"I like your shirt," Tanya says.

"Oh," Finn says again. "It's my dad's. I didn't pack very well." Her tone is defensive, as though Tanya is making fun of her. But Tanya does like the T-shirt. She's not trying too hard, and so Tanya can tell that she is actually pretty. Not like her sister, who does try too hard and ends up looking ugly.

"Would you like something to drink?" Tanya is being polite to make up for the bruise under Finn's eye, but she really does want them to stay. It's for research purposes, she tells herself. Nothing more. She has never seen a Parker this close. Except for the boy, of course, but he is half Vaughn, so it's not quite the same thing.

"Maybe some water," Finn says. "It's pretty warm in here." As Tanya goes into the kitchen, it occurs to her that maybe Finn is doing her own research. She lived with Dallas for seven years, three months, and four days. Even though he cheated on her with her sister, she must still be curious to see what his life is like now.

Compare it against her own, see who is winning. As Tanya runs the water, she has to stop herself from turning around to see what Finn is doing: looking under seat covers, peeking in the bedroom, shuffling through the mail. What if she already knew that Dallas wasn't going to be home? What if this was her plan all along?

Finn and Dallas met in a philosophy class at Lakehead University. Tanya and Dallas met at the grocery store a year ago. Finn is the same age as Dallas. Tanya is eight years younger, almost a different generation. Dallas has told her he liked Finn's independence, and her smile. He likes Tanya's intensity, and her butt. Finn was there for Dallas when his younger brother died in that boating accident. Tanya has never even met Dallas's parents. Still, she and Finn have more in common than they might imagine.

Tanya returns to the living room with two glasses of water. When she hands one to the boy his hands are surprisingly cold, considering the temperature in the apartment. He carries the glass over to the couch with both hands and sits down, drinks it with big gulps.

"He was thirsty," Tanya says, handing the other glass to Finn.

"He had something to drink on the way here," Finn says. Defensively, again. Tanya doesn't blame her. She would be defensive around herself, too.

They sit down at the small table where Tanya and Dallas eat their meals. It is covered in books and papers that belong to Dallas. The books all have titles like *Online Poker Secrets* and *Winning Strategies from Internet Pros.* So far he has broken even, which as far as Tanya is concerned is as good as he can ever hope to do. It saddens her to come home from school and see him sitting there on his laptop in front of the television, in the same position she left him in, his eyes bloodshot from too much screen time, watching his money go up and up and then down while the Home and Garden Network plays renovation shows in the background. Does Finn assume the books are hers? Tanya wonders, having grown used to people making assumptions about her. But as Finn picks up one of the books, she flips through the pages and smiles.

"If this kind of thing had been around when we were together," she says, before adding, "Sorry," as if worried she has offended Tanya by talking about her relationship with Dallas.

Tanya wants to clear the awkwardness, to reassure her that she already knows all about their relationship. "What was he like when you were together?" she asks. "Before he cheated on you with your sister?"

Finn clears her throat. "Do you know where he is? I really need to talk to him."

"You brought the boy to see him," Tanya says. "You want him to meet his son." The thought hadn't occurred to her before. She had assumed that Finn and her nephew had just been in the neighbourhood. She realizes now how silly this sounds, how naive. Everyone has an ulterior motive. She should know this by now.

"Ross," Finn says. "His name is Ross."

Hearing his name, Ross raises his head. He has been sitting quietly on the couch, playing with something he took out of his pocket. "My name is Ross," he says to Tanya. "Remember?"

Finn twists around in her chair at the sound of Ross's voice, her back to Tanya, and Tanya puts her finger to her lips. She hopes he remembers. Their little secret.

Tanya is good at finding things out. She might even say it is her true calling. She had found out about Ross a month into her relationship with Dallas, almost two months before he told her about him. Dallas wasn't on Facebook, but the Parker woman was. And she was prolific. Pictures of the boy, mostly. That blond hair. Then after all that effort, Dallas let the whole story come out one day over breakfast at Norma Jean's, eggs and hash browns and hey by the way I have a son. Oh, she said then. Trying to sound surprised.

Dallas has never brought up Ross again. It's like he's trying to pretend he doesn't exist. She understands – Ross is Dallas's connection to the Parkers, sure, but he is also a reminder of how Dallas lost them. "You don't want kids, do you?" he asked her once, as they were getting ready for bed.

"Of course not," she'd said, even though she wasn't sure. Still isn't sure.

"Why do you care if Dallas meets him?" Tanya asks Finn.

Finn just flips through one of the online poker books, her fingernails scratching against the edge of the paper. Finally, she puts the book down. "How old are you?" she asks. "Twenty-seven? Twenty-eight?"

"Twenty-five," says Tanya, feeling a flush of pleasure that Finn thought she was older.

"Twenty-five," Finn repeats. She begins tapping her fingers against the cover of the book. "I was twenty-five when Dallas and I broke up." The tapping reaches a crescendo, then suddenly stops. "Don't you think it's time he takes some responsibility?" Finn asks. "He's not a teenager anymore. People shouldn't just keep letting him get away with this shit." From the expression on her face – the tilt of her eyebrows, the curve of her mouth – it's clear that she thinks Tanya should be able to relate. Should recognize Dallas's failures as a man. But Tanya does not want to commiserate with a Parker twin, even if it is the Other One.

"That's not your place to decide. He's not your son."

"He's *my nephew.*"

That's when it hits her that maybe the only way to protect Dallas from the Parkers is to remind them of his failures, remind them why they should keep him out of their lives. "Dallas would be a terrible father," says Tanya.

"I don't doubt that," says Finn.

"He has no money."

"His family does. Or did he finally manage to piss off Frank and Rochelle enough for them to cut him off?"

213

Frank and Rochelle. In her head, Tanya always calls them Mr. and Mrs. Vaughn. She wonders what it would be like: So nice to finally meet you, Frank and Rochelle. I think you're really great, too, Frank and Rochelle. I'm so happy to be part of the family, Frank and Rochelle.

"So you're here for his family's money. Is that it?"

"No, of course not."

Tanya stares at Finn across the table. She tries to imagine Dallas kissing those lips, stroking that cheek, gazing into those eyes. She has pictured it in her head a million times, but now she has a frame of reference. She leans back in her chair, crossing her arms over her chest. "Then why are you here?"

Finn jerks her head, startled. "I . . . I just want Ross to meet his dad."

"No," says Tanya. "You're angry. You're here for revenge. You want Dallas to suffer."

Finn is silent for a moment. "Yeah, I do," she says finally. "I really, really want Dallas to suffer."

Tanya nods. She knows the dark pull of revenge, and has fought to keep it at bay – not just with Dallas but with her entire life. If someone hurts you, you hurt them right back, and you think it will make you feel better, but it doesn't. It just makes you angrier because not only have you been hurt but now you've also lost control.

She closes her eyes, takes a deep breath. Her life may seem small, sparse, insignificant, but it is *hers.* Just as Dallas is hers. Finn has no idea how hard Tanya has fought for everything she has. Why can't she understand that she only wants to protect the life she has made? How far she is willing to go to do that?

"It's okay," the boy says suddenly. They turn to look at him, still sitting on the couch. He is playing with a small ball, like the kind you get out of a machine at the grocery store when you put in a quarter. It is blue and sparkly and probably will bounce very high. But he isn't bouncing it – he is cradling it in his hands and

214

talking to it as if it were a pet. Then he puts it down on the coffee table and gives it a little nudge, so that it rolls away from him.

"Come here, ball," he says. "Don't run away. Come back here."

The ball rolls off the edge of the table and lands on a dirty white athletic sock that Dallas has left on the floor. Ross sits back on the couch and folds his hands in his lap, waiting for the ball to come back to him of its own free will.

A month earlier, Tanya had been walking by the house on Victor Street – something she did, now and then, when she and Dallas had had a fight. The house was too far back from the road for her to see in the windows, but she could see the yard, the cars in the front, the door to the garage where the salon was. Sometimes someone would drive by and turn into the driveway and she would stare at the back of the vehicle until the lights turned off. This time she saw the boy walking down the driveway with a three-legged husky who might have been the world's oldest dog.

"I like your dog," she said, when he reached the road. "What's his name?"

The boy eyed her warily. "I'm not supposed to talk to strangers."

"I'm not a stranger," said Tanya. "I'm a friend of your dad's."

"My new dad or my real dad?"

Tanya had not been expecting this question. She considered her options. "Your real dad," she said. She leaned down and scratched the dog on the top of his head. The dog's ear twitched.

"Bruno," Ross said.

"Dallas," Tanya said.

"No. The dog."

"Bruno." The dog lifted his head when she said his name. His eyes were cloudy with disease, but his tail wagged slowly.

"We're going for a walk," Ross said, pulling up on the leash and wrapping it around his hand. "Do you want to come?"

"Okay," said Tanya, even though she wasn't sure if a child his age should be out walking a dog by himself. Victor Street was a dead-end, on a point of land that the Kaministiquia River wrapped around like a snake. They walked in silence towards the end of the point. That way was all downhill, so it was easy, and beautiful – the Nor'Wester Mountains on the horizon, surrounded by acres and acres of boreal forest. But that meant they would be going uphill on the way back. Tanya would have preferred to start with the hard part.

Finally Ross said, "Do you want to know what my favourite constellation is?" Tanya nodded. "Draco. It means dragon. Dragons are all the guardians of ancient treasure, right? And Draco used to be the guardian of the pole star, but then the earth moved. So now it's a dragon with nothing to guard." He was quiet for a moment. "It's kind of hard to see."

"Where is it?" Tanya asked. "At nighttime, I mean."

Ross pointed up to the sky. They both stopped walking and tilted their heads back. Tanya didn't know if he was pointing at the exact location of the constellation in the sky, or just the sky in general. Maybe he thought she didn't know that was where the stars were. But it was kind of cool to picture a dragon up there.

"What's *your* favourite constellation?" Ross asked as they started walking again.

"I don't have one, I don't think. I have a favourite rock, though."

"What is it?"

"Shale," Tanya said, suddenly self-conscious. She had never told anyone about her favourite rock before. "It's a fine-grained clastic sedimentary rock formed through compaction."

"Oh," Ross said, sounding disappointed. "Does it do anything special?"

She thought about it. "Sometimes there's fossils in it."

"Cool." The dog stopped and squatted to poop on the side of the road, balancing awkwardly on two of his three legs. Ross handed Tanya the leash to hold while he pulled a roll of pink bags with little white hearts on them out of his pocket and ripped one off, then bent over and picked up the poop. "Do you want to carry this?" he asked, holding the bag out to her.

"No, thanks."

"Okay, then you can walk Bruno."

Tanya gripped the leash tightly. She had never walked a dog before. Absurdly, she found herself worrying she would drop the leash and Bruno would run away, even though that was silly; she knew how to hold on to things. She started to walk and the leash grew taut. When she looked down at Bruno, he was lying on the ground, his front legs splayed out in front of him like he had tripped on some ice. His eyes were closed.

"Maybe Bruno is tired," she said.

"He's old," Ross said. "I guess we should take him home."

They had only walked about a hundred feet. Bruno scratched at his ear but didn't get up. Tanya tugged a little on the leash and he reluctantly climbed to his feet. When they reached the drive-way, she handed the leash back to Ross, who wrapped it around his hand again.

"Thanks for coming on a walk with me," Ross said.

"You're welcome. I'm Tanya, by the way." She hadn't meant to tell Ross her name. It just wasn't good spying technique. But she felt quite sure that Ross was not going to tell anyone about their walk.

"I'm Ross."

"I know."

Ross scratched his head in a gesture that reminded her of Dallas. "Will you say hi to my dad for me?" he asked. "Dallas," he added, in case she had forgotten.

"I don't think that's a good idea," Tanya said. "He might not like that I came to see you."

Ross considered this. "You're probably right." He didn't seem upset about it at all, which hurt her heart a little.

"Maybe someday he'll come to see you, too," she said.

"No, he won't," said Ross. He stuck out his hand for her to shake. "Bye, Tanya."

She took his hand. It felt unnaturally cold for the temperature outside. "Bye, Ross."

Now, Tanya crouches down and picks up Ross's ball. When she hands it to him, they lock eyes. "Thanks for coming to visit me," she says.

"You're welcome," Ross says, taking the ball from her. He sits back on the couch and bends his finger over the ball, picking at the soft rubber with the nail of his index finger.

Tanya turns back to Finn. "None of this has anything to do with you," she tells her. "You need to let this go." She means this obsession with the boy meeting Dallas. Her anger at Dallas. Dallas.

"Of course this has to do with me," Finn says. "This is my family we're talking about." She settles into her seat. She is not going anywhere, thinks Tanya. Not until she gets what she wants. "So just tell me. Where can I find him?"

Tanya knows where Dallas is. She has known ever since that day six months ago when she found that shirt under the couch in the living room, the ugly pink one with the red lace trim. It didn't take her long to find out who it belonged to. A couple of minutes alone with his phone. A few casual questions at Desi's. A trip to the Super 8 on Memorial to confirm, sitting at a chain coffee shop across the street waiting for them to come out. Drinking hot black tea as they opened the door to their room and, without acknowledging each other, walked to their cars, drove away.

She just wanted to know. Became obsessed with knowing, convinced that once she knew, everything would be okay.

After she saw them come out of the motel, Tanya went home to Dallas's and made supper. A tuna melt and salad with Catalina dressing. Dallas had gone straight to work from the Super 8, which for some reason upset Tanya more than anything else – he couldn't even bother putting on a show for her, bringing her flowers or whatever it was guilty men were supposed to do. When he got home, it was late, but Tanya stayed up and they watched a movie together, the kind that Dallas liked, with a lot of things blowing up and a man saving the day.

She wears the pink shirt sometimes, even though it is ugly and too big for her. Dallas has never noticed.

But still. He loves her. He lets her lean against him on the couch when they watch television, her head nestled in the crook of his arm. He makes up nicknames for her. He cooks her dinner. Someday he is going to write a play for her.

And this is my family, Tanya thinks. *I need to protect it.*

And so she pulls out the only weapon she has left: Dallas's biggest failure. For the sake of the boy, she leans over and whispers in Finn's ear the secret that she has been carrying since she found that pink shirt. And for the first time, she says the name out loud. *Nicki.*

After Finn and Ross leave, Tanya takes the bus to school. She goes to the library and sets up her laptop in her carrel, then just sits there and stares at the screen. Numbers on an Excel spreadsheet, words on a page. None of it means anything to her right now. Tanya is doing her master's in geology. She started studying geology because she liked rocks. She kept studying geology because she wanted to stay in school. School is something she can handle, she understands how it works. You do the work, you get a grade, you pass or you fail. In the rest of life, from what she can tell, nobody grades you, and you just keep failing and failing.

Her thesis topic is constraints on the formation of depositional placer accumulations in coarse alluvial braided river systems. She likes that when people hear this, they stop asking her questions about her work. To most people, those words are like another language. To Tanya, they are like speaking her native tongue.

When she gets back to the apartment just after seven, Dallas is already home, cooking himself spaghetti on the one element on the stove that hasn't burned out. He has the noodles in the pot and a jar of sauce open on the counter. When the noodles are ready he will just dump the sauce in the pot and then eat it like that and call it spaghetti. At least when she makes it, she tries to throw in some real vegetables to make it healthier, carrots or tomatoes or maybe mushrooms and green peppers, but not the red ones because those are more expensive. And for what? They're just green peppers with a shiny red coat on. Tanya knows how to make the best of being poor – she grew up that way. Dallas did not. Tanya has never met Dallas's parents, but she has seen their house, seen his beautiful mother out running errands in a Canada Goose parka, which Tanya Googled so she knows how much it cost. Dallas's beautiful mother, Rochelle. Dallas might not get anything from his family now, but when he was growing up Tanya is sure that they must have given him everything.

"Hi, babe," Dallas says when she comes in the kitchen. "Want some supper?"

"I already ate," she says, which is a lie, but she doesn't think she can stomach Dallas's mushy noodles and jarred sauce. "At school."

"Always working so hard, Tannybear." He kisses her cheek, then pulls the pot of water off the stove, dumping it into a cracked plastic colander sitting in the sink. Then he dumps the noodles back into the pot and tips the jar of sauce in on top, just like she knew he would. He smiles over at her, and her insides coil with rage. He is being too nice to her, and it makes her crazy that she likes it.

I should leave him, she thinks. *I need to leave him.*

"Maybe I'll go back to Paul's tonight." Paul is Tanya's brother, who she technically lives with, sleeping on a futon in the living room of the two-bedroom house he shares with his wife and four kids and his mother-in-law, though she can't remember the last time she slept there.

"Come on," Dallas says, scratching his head. "Why would you want to do that?"

"I don't know." She can feel her voice shake. She is twenty-five. The same age that Finn was when she left Dallas. She could start over again, too. Couldn't she?

Dallas stops stirring the pasta and looks at her, his brows furrowed. Pretend, maybe. "Baby, what's wrong?" he asks. "Is it something to do with school?" He walks over and wraps his arms around her, pulling her into him. "Is there some kind of weird rock thing you're having trouble with?"

He always refers to her work as "weird rock things." It's a joke between them, something they share that no one else does. Tanya considers telling him about Finn and Ross's visit. Maybe telling him her own secrets will inspire him to tell her his.

"Depositional placer accumulations," she says instead. "I'm not getting the results I was hoping for. It's screwing with my data. I might have to reconsider my entire hypothesis." Another joke from so long ago she can't remember why it's funny anymore.

Dallas growls and bites her ear. His beard smells like spaghetti sauce. He is never going to write a play for her. But she will never leave him. She will never leave him.

NINETEEN

2003

Nicki wakes up, head throbbing, and runs to the bathroom to vomit. *Good fucking god, what have I done?* she thinks, hands shaking, head pressed against the toilet seat, feeling as though a thousand-pound weight has dropped from the sky and onto her back, keeping her pinned there. She can still taste the tequila coating the insides of her mouth, can still smell the tinny, stale-beer smell of the bar, and can definitely still hear Dallas snoring in the next room. It isn't even a dawning of sick recognition that hits her then, just a slow resigned sigh, like of course that's Dallas snoring in the next room, who else would it be? And here she is, kneeling on the bathroom floor of some seedy motel and throwing up like she's in fucking high school, for Christ's sake.

It was Jenna's birthday, or at least it had been Jenna's birthday on the previous Tuesday, but now that they were adults with jobs and kids and shit, they couldn't just go out and party any old night of the week. So they saved up their hairspray and the money from their tip jars and went out Friday night, seven of them wobbling on too-tall heels in too-tight skirts, outfits they never would have worn back in the day, pre-kids, pre-divorces, pre–credit card debt, when all they needed to be sexy was a baby tee and some strawberry-scented lip gloss. Nicki might have only been twenty-six, but stuffed into her Spanx, with her eyeliner stretched out to her temples, she felt more like forty-six. She hoped she didn't look as desperate as she felt, standing at the bar at Scuttlebutts, waving a twenty discreetly for the benefit of the bored bartender, who ignored her as if she was just some middle-aged mom with a bad haircut whose idea of a good time was two wine coolers and being in bed before ten. The whole thing made Nicki's head hurt.

As she made her way back to the table balancing a tray of tequila shots, she bumped into Dallas. Really, Dallas bumped into her, while walking backwards through the bar with his arms thrown up in the air, yelling something to one of his bros across the room who was making rude gestures with a test-tube shooter. She didn't even know it was him until they were both on the floor, dripping with tequila, lemon wedges scattered between them, the salt shaker uncapped and overturned on Dallas's chest.

"Watch where you're fucking going!" Nicki yelled, driving her heel into Dallas's side.

"Fuck, Nicki," Dallas groaned.

Nicki sat up, waving off a couple of outstretched hands from the crowd of amused onlookers. She found one shot glass that was still three-quarters full of tequila, hoisted herself up onto all fours, and crawled across the floor to Dallas, then leaned over and licked at the pile of salt on his T-shirt with a catlike flick of her tongue. Then she sat back on her heels, downed the shot, and dropped the glass onto Dallas's chest with a thud that made him curl back in on himself, salt spilling onto the floor. "You owe me thirty-seven-fifty," she said. "Plus tip."

She left him there on the floor and went to the bathroom. One side of her face was streaked black with what was left of her dramatic cat's-eye liner, and her lip was bleeding. All she could smell was tequila – it was in her hair, soaked into her shirt, dripping down her skirt, which was twisted sideways at an awkward angle. She hadn't been in a fight since before the twins were born, but she was pretty sure this was what her fight face looked like, the type of face that made other women see you as a wounded animal, something to either protect or destroy. For a moment she thought about going home, about taking a long shower, scrubbing herself down, climbing into bed with one of her girls, burying her face in their hair, trying to feel thankful for what she had. Instead she fixed her eye makeup as best she could, wiped the blood from her lips and smeared them with red lipstick from her purse, jacked up her tits in her push-up bra, and headed back into the bar.

Dallas was waiting for her outside the bathroom. As soon as she came out, he pulled up his T-shirt, glaring at her. "Look what you did," he said. "It's already fucking bruising."

"Poor baby," said Nicki. She reached out and touched the growing bruise gently, then bent her index finger and drove her knuckle into it.

Dallas slapped her hand away. "You're such a bitch," he said through gritted teeth.

"You liked it," she said. "Now buy me more tequila and I won't tell Finn that you tried to take your shirt off in front of me."

She made Dallas buy her eight more shots just to make it even, and together they slammed them back at the bar, one after another – salt, shot, lemon – like an assembly line. Then they ordered more. Later, Nicki remembered arguing about what they were going to play on the jukebox: Dallas wanting to put on Dave Matthews Band, Nicki saying he might as well just tell everyone in the bar he wanted them to kill themselves. Then something about walking to Nippers for french fries, how long it would take, and whether they would still be open when the bar closed. Something else about whether or not dogs could see in the dark. At some point she noticed that Jenna and the girls had left; she couldn't remember if they had said good-bye. At some even later point there was a decision made. A motel room. A late-night talk show on the TV. Blankets and sheets on the floor. A bad taste in her mouth, skin sticky, hair matted in the back. She doesn't even know if they had sex. She can only remember his hands on her, too rough between her legs, her surprise at the size of his dick, thinking, *Ahh, okay, Finn, now I get it.*

And now she's kneeling on the bathroom floor, head on the toilet, sifting through the broken pieces of her memory of the night before. There is too much blank space for her liking – Nicki always prefers to act drunker than she feels, not the other way around. That's not to say she wouldn't have wound up in the exact same place at the end of the night – she just might have shown a little more dignity getting here.

As she's lying there, she hears her cell phone ring in the next room. She moans and tries to lift her head. It's not even noon, too early for any of her friends to be calling. Her mom is home with the girls, she must be calling to see when Nicki is coming back. For a moment, Nicki contemplates never going home, at least not for the day, staying at the motel instead, ordering pizza and drinking beer – *ugh, no not beer,* she thinks as her stomach heaves, *chocolate milk, maybe* – smoking a couple of joints, watching bad reality TV. Dallas can even stay if he wants, she wouldn't mind the company. He isn't a bad guy, really, didn't deserve the shit she'd been giving him all these years about being a deadbeat with no ambition, about not shaving his beard or having no muscle tone or not committing to her sister. That last part is a no-brainer, the guy has cheater written right on his forehead, but it's in that invisible ink that you need a black light to see. Nicki is the black light, that's all. She is basically doing Finn a favour, even if Finn wouldn't see it that way. Not that she would ever tell Finn about this. She's not an idiot.

"Hello?" she hears Dallas say in the other room. She raises her head from the toilet.

"Hey," she says, crawling to the door. "That's my –"

"Finn? Hey, baby," Dallas says. "I had a rough night out with the guys."

Silence. Nicki sinks back against the doorframe. She can feel her heartbeat in every cell of her body, rocking her back and forth. Dallas is lying on his side in the bed, facing her, her phone pressed up against his ear. "You dumbass," she says, dropping her head into her hand.

"What are you talking about?" Dallas says into the phone. "You called *me*." He is sitting up now, his eyes darting around the room. He raises his eyebrows at Nicki. She just shakes her head. *What?* he mouths. "Finn, Finn, wait, what are you talking about?" He pauses, then pulls the phone away from his ear. "She hung up."

"That's my fucking phone, genius," Nicki says.

Dallas picks up the phone again and stares at it, uncomprehending. Then he looks back at Nicki. "She said to tell you to come home," he says, his voice strangely high. "Your mother's in the hospital."

2012

"Maybe I should go visit your mom in the hospital," Dallas says, propping himself up, his elbow digging into the dingy motel room pillow. "Pay my respects."

"She's not dead," Nicki says. "She's in a coma."

"Wrong choice of words, I guess."

"No shit," says Nicki. She pulls the blankets up around her chin. They have cranked the air conditioner to full blast, so even though it is probably thirty degrees outside, the room is freezing. The cold air was welcome thirty minutes ago when they crashed into the room, delirious and sweaty from heat and adrenaline – Nicki won't call it desire, that sounds too romance-novely, and there is nothing romantic about her relationship with Dallas – but now the sweat is cooling on her skin and everything seems like a really fucking bad idea, including the air conditioner.

Dallas picks up the remote and flicks half-heartedly through the channels. "Sunday-afternoon television sucks," he says. "Why can't motels have Netflix?"

"We're lucky this motel has a working toilet."

Dallas shakes his head. "Hey, I take you nice places." He flicks around some more and then settles on a nature documentary, something about sharks featuring an attractive host in a wetsuit. That guy London likes. Adam something. "Let's learn something, shall we?" says Dallas.

But Nicki is not in the mood for learning. "Do you have any weed?" she asks. Nicki hasn't smoked since she married Hamish, who, although he looks the part of a stoner, is resolutely straight edge. He doesn't even really drink, just a beer sometimes when he's fishing, or a taste of the whisky he's made to make sure nothing's gone wrong with the batch. But she suddenly wants to, can almost feel it burning in her lungs. And god knows she deserves it, this one little fucking thing.

"At my place," Dallas says. "But we probably don't want to go there."

Because of Tanya, Nicki thinks. The little bitch. "Never mind," she says. "I didn't really want it anyway." After this, she will have to go to the hospital, and Shawn will probably be there, and Shawn is basically a narc – he can smell weed on you ten miles away. But she feels the occasion calls for it, somehow. Dirty motel rooms and weed just seem to go together.

Normally, Nicki would have made Dallas take her somewhere a bit classier – a Super 8, at least, or a Best Western, something brand-name. Not one of these fucking no-tell Current River shitholes with names like Bay Vue and Lakeshore, even though the only bay or lake you can see is in the cheap reproduction artwork hanging in the bathroom – but everything in town is booked up for some kind of baseball tournament. They've gone to a few different places in the six months they've been doing whatever the fuck it is they're doing: hotels, friends' apartments, the back room at Desi's when it was closed, his parents' place when they went to Poland to visit their cousins. One time they went up to his friend's camp on Arrow Lake, a leisurely late-spring afternoon spent fucking and fishing and drinking beer, and Nicki came home with two medium-sized pickerel and splinters on her kneecaps from the wooden deck.

What the fuck *are* they doing? Sneaking around, lying to people, feeling disgusting ninety percent of the time. And for what? Nicki doesn't even like Dallas. If she had ever thought there was any feeling there, anything at all, it had been wiped away the instant she walked into Desi's and saw him standing behind the counter in that stupid long black apron taking people's orders as if nothing had ever happened, as if he hadn't knocked her up and then taken off for eight years. She had thrown a mug at him that day, still half-full with some mousy-haired Lakehead student's lukewarm peppermint tea. Just picked it up off the nearest table and hurled it at Dallas's head, although the mug was heavier than she thought and it ended up skidding across the counter and smashing on the floor at his feet.

"You fucking deadbeat!" she screamed, and Dallas just stood there like a drooling idiot, his mouth hanging open, until Nicki picked up a plate with the same girl's half-eaten blueberry muffin on it and heaved it at him like a Frisbee. He reached one hand up and caught the plate seconds before it came in contact with his face.

"Nicki," he said. "Holy shit." He put the plate down and climbed under the counter, grabbed her by the wrists. She struggled, but he was surprisingly strong. He put his mouth near her ear. "You can hit me if you want," he said, "but let's just do it outside, okay?"

He led her through the back and out into the alleyway behind the café. As soon as they stepped outside, he let her go. "Jesus

Christ," he said, reaching into his pocket for a pack of smokes. "Do you know how many times I've wanted to do that?"

"What, throw a mug at your head?" Nicki asked. She leaned against the wall, her whole body shaking.

"Throw a mug at *someone* at Desi's. We're all such fucking douches."

It might have just been the adrenaline, but Nicki laughed. "Give me one of those," she said, reaching for the cigarettes.

"So are you going to hit me or what?" Dallas asked. He took a drag of his smoke and opened his arms wide, a half smile on his face. The smug motherfucker. Like he knew she wasn't going to do it. "I deserve it. I know I do." *Well, duh*, Nicki thought and hauled off and punched him in the stomach. His face registered a brief look of surprise before collapsing into a cartoony "oof" as he stumbled backwards, reaching for the wall. Nicki sat down on a milk crate and smoked her cigarette.

After a minute, Dallas righted himself again.

"You okay?" she asked.

"Yeah," he said shakily, bringing the cigarette to his lips.

Nicki stood up, crushed out her butt, and punched him again.

They ended up back at his place – the only time Nicki has been there. Dallas still lived like a frat boy, his one-room apartment furnished with a yard-sale futon and tables made out of empty beer cases, takeout containers strewn across the floor. There were two walls not taken up by windows. A giant flat-screen TV was mounted on one; on the other was what looked like a promotional poster for a movie about bullfighting, but all the words were in Spanish. Without talking about it – without talking about anything – Dallas fucked her up against the wall with the bullfighting poster, so that when she turned her head she could see the unfamiliar words, the red of the cape, the horns of the bull.

"What's with the poster?" she asked him afterward, sitting on the futon, slightly stunned. All the fight had been screwed right out of her, and she felt almost quiet on the inside – even in that disgusting room, with its cracking ceiling and dirty windows, a place where she now felt she could sit, unmoving, for hours.

"Oh," Dallas said, following her gaze. "A friend brought that back from Spain. I thought for a while I might want to be a bull-fighter. But then I realized that meant I would actually have to fight bulls."

"You mean a girlfriend," said Nicki, leaning back on the futon. She had managed to pull up her jeans but her top was still somewhere in the mess on the floor. She ran her hand over her belly, feeling the stretch marks there, the little pouch of flesh that never seemed to go away no matter how many diet pills she took.

"Yeah," he said. "Her name was Sage. I lived with her on Salt Spring for a couple of years."

"That's such a stupid name," Nicki said, pounding her fist lightly against her stomach. She didn't try to hide the jealousy in her voice. She didn't care enough to hide anything from Dallas, maybe that was the appealing part about being with him. "I can't believe you dated someone with such a stupid name."

"Actually, we were married. For six months. We just got divorced last year."

Nicki let her hand drop against her stomach. "Awesome," she said. She sat up abruptly and started searching for her shirt.

"What?" said Dallas, watching curiously as she stumbled around the room, kicking takeout boxes away, throwing aside old crusty boxer shorts.

"You prick. What the fuck is wrong with you?" Her pulse sped up, and her vision blurred with a flood of rage. The worst part was, she knew she had no reason to be angry, which made her even angrier, to the point where she could barely see.

Her shirt was nowhere to be found. She grabbed her coat and zipped it up over her bra, smoothed down her hair, and gave

Dallas the double-middle-finger salute before slamming the door behind her.

Fucking *married*. Who did he think he was?

But she was the one who texted him the next weekend, and the time after that, and the time after that. She still doesn't like Dallas, but for some Christ-forsaken reason she really, really loves fucking him. She *loves* the sneaking around, lying to people, feeling disgusting ninety percent of the time. She loves that he's the last person on the planet that she *should* want to fuck. She loves that they can do it and then be dicks to each other, that they can bite and kick and scratch and then share a beer and go back to their lives. She loves that if Hamish ever found out, he would be devastated – loves that she can dangle his fragile heart over the gaping chasm of her betrayal and swing it there. She needs this, this knife's edge. She needs it to feel alive. And she won't apologize for it.

So they end up in dirty motels like this one, with her clients thinking she's sick and Hamish thinking she's working and the girls off doing their own thing and Ross with her mother – or in this case, Finn, something that Nicki is trying to push to the back of her mind. Her mother is too lost in her own world to question Nicki, but Finn is another story. Finn will read her mind like the morning paper.

"I should probably get going anyway," Nicki says. She doesn't say that Hamish will be home soon from Terrace Bay, or that Finn will be wondering where she is, or that Ross needs her to make him supper. She doesn't say any of that because these are not things that exist in their world, this afternoon, this motel room.

"No, stay," says Dallas, reaching over and cupping her breast.

Just then the television switches over to a local news promo, and that Cassandra Coelho bitch starts talking about Kate. The two of them watch in silence as Kate flies over the waterfall. Dallas shakes his head again. "Un-fucking-believable," he says. "How is she not dead?"

"I don't know." Nicki remembers the story of Princess Green Mantle plummeting over the falls to her death in order to save her tribe. At least she was doing something useful – if anyone should have survived the fall, it was her, not Kate, who went over for no good reason. "Finn thinks there's something really wrong with her. Like she would know anything about anything."

Dallas is quiet for a minute. "I saw her, you know," he says finally. "Finn, I mean."

Nicki pokes at the inner corner of her eye, chasing a non-existent eyelash. "I know," she says. "Do you think I didn't know?"

Suddenly the room feels oppressively hot, even with the air conditioner. Nicki can't breathe. She glances at Dallas, lying against the pillow, his too-long blond hair sticking up from his head at unlikely angles. He seems to be breathing just fine, but it's hard to tell. She checks her watch: it's nearly six. Four hours of her life wasted in this shithole. "I'm gonna go," she says.

"Wait," says Dallas, sitting up. "Are you okay?"

"Fuck you," she says, although she doesn't know why. It is their usual routine: fight, fuck, flee. She tells herself it's what she wants as she walks out the door.

2003

Nicki only has last night's clothes to wear. It couldn't be any worse: the Spanx digging into her bloated belly, everything else chafing against her hypersensitive hungover skin, all of it too tight and bright and perfectly wrong for pretty much anything that could happen before midnight. Dallas offers her his plaid shirt and she takes it, buttoning it up over her tube top, which is still sticky with tequila. She's still not talking to him. At least he has the sense to act sheepish about the whole thing, otherwise Nicki might have to drill him in the other side, give him a matching bruise.

"I'll tell her I found your phone at the bar," Dallas says, sitting on the edge of the bed, watching as Nicki puts on her shoes. "I took it and was going to give it back to you, but then it rang, so I answered it, thinking it might be you . . ."

Nicki stares at him, unblinking. "You really are dumb as a fucking post," she says. She wriggles her foot down into her shoe and limps towards the dresser, searching for her purse. "I don't know how Finn has put up with you for this long."

"I don't get it," Dallas says, his voice edging on a whine. He curls his feet up underneath him, arranging the blankets over his lap, pouting. He looks like a little kid who's just pissed the bed at a sleepover party. Pathetic. Nicki picks up an empty water bottle from the floor and throws it at his head.

"Just help me find my purse."

The room feels like chaos. Nicki doesn't know how they could have done so much damage in such a short period of time. Dallas eventually finds her purse shoved behind the bedside table, and she digs out her lipstick, her wallet, and her sunglasses, but can't find her keys. "Did you leave them at the bar?" Dallas keeps asking her, until she's ready to punch him. Like, why the hell would she pull out her keys at the bar? They must have fallen out of her purse somewhere in the room. Her car is still outside the bar and she'll need it for work the next day. No, she doesn't know where her spare is, who knows where their fucking spare is? They scour the room from top to bottom but her keys are not under the bed and they're not in the bathroom and they're not behind the television and they're not in the drawer with the Holy Bible. They're not even in Dallas's beat-up old Accord, which Nicki is shocked to discover they had driven to the motel, disgust rising up in her throat like bile, until finally the adrenaline or whatever the fuck it is that Nicki has been running on wears off and she runs to the bathroom to throw up again. When she comes back out, Dallas is sitting on the bed again, holding up his own keys and jingling them in his hand.

"I guess you need a lift," he says.

Nicki sighs and nods. "Fine," she says. "But you're not coming in."

It's not until they're in the car that it all sinks in: Her mom is in the hospital. She slept with Finn's boyfriend. Finn knows she slept with her boyfriend. She breathes in, searches her purse for lip gloss, and then runs it over her mouth, smacking her lips together. Moments like this are what Nicki lives and dies for. Life smashed into a pulp on the ground in front of you, split open, bleeding and convulsing. Those seconds where you can see, in stark relief, the essence of everything that is important, its bright gory beating heart, without the glaze of everyday, mundane, boring *details*.

She knows that if anyone were to examine her life, they would see a long string of mistakes: Getting knocked up at eighteen, then at twenty-one. Sleeping with her sister's boyfriend. And Finn would have so much more to add to that list. Skipping classes, failing exams, mouthing off to teachers. Getting her tongue stuck to frozen metal, climbing too high in a tree, swimming too far out in the lake. Shoplifting lip gloss from the pharmacy, stealing liquor from their parents, driving drunk. Staying in Thunder Bay. *Wanting* to stay in Thunder Bay. All the things Finn had spent years warning her about.

But Finn warning her about something only made her want to do it more. For Nicki there is no such thing as a mistake. She runs headlong into the fire, basking in the burn.

She should get Dallas to drop her off a few streets before the hospital, but she's got her heels on and it's raining, of course, great big spitwads of water pummelling the roof of the car. "Over here," she says to Dallas, pointing to the entrance of the emergency department. "Just pull up to the door. You don't have to park or anything." With three kids and two aging parents she knows these hallways as well as the hallways in her own home, knows which doors lead to which tragedies, knows what to say, who to say it to.

The entrance is covered with an awning – thank god for small mercies – and Nicki pulls Dallas's shirt tighter around her as she mentally prepares herself to get out of the car. "Well," she says. "It's been . . . fucked up."

"Yeah," says Dallas. "I hope your mom's okay."

"Yeah," says Nicki.

They both sit there staring straight ahead, listening to the rain hammering against the awning, the low buzz of the radio. Finally, when she realizes Dallas isn't going to say anything else, she gets out of the car. At the entrance, she sees Finn standing just inside the sliding glass doors, watching her. Nicki straightens her skirt, lifts her head, and saunters towards the door. But as she gets closer, she realizes it's not her that Finn is watching, it's Dallas, her eyes trained on him all puppy-dog and sad even as her sister walks towards her wearing her boyfriend's shirt over last night's dress, even as she comes through the door with a lazy half smile on her face, close enough for Finn to see the mats in her hair, the bite marks on her neck, a perfect image of freshly fucked bliss. Still Finn stares at Dallas, and when Nicki turns around she sees Dallas is staring at Finn, that they are having a conversation with just their eyes – a conversation that Nicki is locked out of.

She walks right up to Finn and cracks her gum. Finn blinks twice and finally looks at her.

"Hey," Nicki says. "What's up?"

Finn blinks a third time and then walks away.

2012

They don't talk about Ross. Ross is not a part of this, and the second he becomes a part of this, Nicki tells herself it will be over. "What's he like?" Dallas asked her once, in the alley behind Desi's where she had punched him that first time, while they were sharing a post-fuck smoke. Nicki liked watching Dallas smoke; he did this thing where he didn't even blow the smoke out, he just opened his mouth and let it waft away. She secretly thought it was sexy, even though she would never tell him that.

"Who?" she asked, taking the cigarette from him and trying to copy his exhale. It never seemed to work for her, she always ran out of patience and ended up blowing it out before it was all gone.

"My . . . Ross," Dallas answered.

Nicki narrowed her eyes at him. "He is not *your* Ross," she said flatly. "You do not have a Ross. As far as you are concerned, there is no Ross."

Now, driving away from the motel, Nicki wonders if this was a mistake. If this is the kind of thing that could screw up a kid for life. The realization hits her all at once, as she's waiting at a light on Red River Road, watching three teenaged boys in cargo shorts and hoodies sauntering across the street in front of her: Someday, Ross is going to find out about this. And he is going to be very, very pissed.

She remembers the first time she was with Dallas and how her mom ended up in the hospital. The two events will always seem linked to her, as if one somehow led to the other. That time, Kate had fallen off the roof of their house, where she had climbed up to watch the sunrise. Even now, thinking about the whole thing makes Nicki sick to her stomach. They had all been up on the roof before – it was something they just did as kids, climbed out the dormer window in the master bedroom and then inched up on their butts as far as they could go. But picturing her fifty-five-year-old mother doing it – it just seemed wrong. Since then, everything about Kate has seemed wrong, even to Nicki, who loves wrong, who embraces wrong, who fucking *lives* for wrong. But this wrong – it was different. Darker. Scarier. And beyond Kate's control.

When she gets to the hospital this time, Nicki immediately knows something isn't right. In the parking lot she sees her dad's truck, parked at a weird angle across two spaces, as though he had just abandoned it there. *Oh no.* She tries to remember how her mother had looked when she visited earlier that morning, whether or not Kate had seemed different. Nicki should have been able to tell; if anyone could, it would have been her, she was the only one who was here every day, the only one who was beside Kate the whole time, the only one of them who really gave a damn. Just because she doesn't want to sit around and cry about what is happening to Kate doesn't mean she's in denial. How can she be in denial about something that's in her face every single fucking day? The blank look in her mother's eyes when Nicki says a word she doesn't understand. Her head hung in humiliation when Nicki has to pick her up after she's gotten lost, or when she's pissed herself in the mall because she can't find the bathroom and doesn't know how to ask where it is. Nicki has spent the past eight years watching her smart, funny, badass mother slowly deteriorating into a scared, confused shell of a woman. So no, Nicki does not want to talk about *how bad things are with Mom.* She doesn't want to talk about it because she has to fucking *live* it every day.

Ignoring the microphones shoved in her face, Nicki rushes into the hospital, paces in the elevator until it reaches the eighth floor, races down the hall to Kate's room.

Shawn is standing outside the door. "Nicki," he says, grabbing for her arm as she tries to push past him. "Wait."

"Don't fucking touch me!" she says a little too loud. A nurse at the station looks up from her computer and starts down the hall towards them.

"Nick, she's gone," Shawn says.

"Oh god." Nicki feels her knees start to buckle. "No, no, she can't be." The world is spinning. "Oh god, oh god."

Shawn reaches out to steady her, holding her by her arms. "Nicki, look at me. She's not dead. She's *gone.* Like disappeared gone."

It takes Nicki a couple of moments to process the words. "What the hell, Shawn," she says under her breath, eyeing the nurse, who has stopped ten feet away, watching them. "What is wrong with you?" She wrenches her arms away from him and goes into Kate's room. The bed is empty, rumpled, as though Kate had just gotten up to go to the bathroom. Walter stands by the window with his back to the door, and in the chair next to the bed is Finn, with Ross on her lap. "Vroom vroom," Ross says, playing with a wooden tongue depressor, flying it through the air like an airplane before crashing it into the side of Finn's head. "Boom. Crash."

"Ross, baby," Nicki says. She goes over to him, pets his head like he's a kitten. His too-long blond hair sticking up at unlikely angles. "What are you doing? Did Aunt Finn bring you here?"

"Hi, Mom," Ross says, enthralled with his airplane, which has miraculously recovered from the crash and is now circling Nicki's arm.

"Hi, Nicki," says Finn.

Finn is staring her down, but she refuses to acknowledge her. She is still recovering from thinking her mother was dead, she doesn't need to deal with her judgmental twin making her feel even worse. She turns to Shawn instead. "What happened?" she asks. "Where is she?"

"She must have woken up and then left," says Shawn. He rubs his hand over his face, then shakes his head. "There was only about twenty minutes between the last time someone checked on her and when Finn and Ross got here and found her missing. The hospital is looking into it now."

"They're looking into it? They lost a patient, Shawn. They should be doing a little more than just looking into it."

Shawn sighs. "They're doing everything they can, Nicki. Seriously."

"Nana's gone," Ross says. He throws his airplane onto the bed, as if to make a point.

"We'll find her," Finn says, giving his arm a squeeze. She smiles. Nicki could choke her, she really could. The world starts to spin again, and she sits down on the bed, gripping the edges as if she were about to fall off.

"Are you okay?" Shawn asks. "I can get Katriina to go look after the twins tonight, if you want to stay here for a bit. And I called Hamish, he just left Terrace Bay, he should be here in a couple of hours." Nicki feels Finn flinch, but she doesn't say anything. Shawn puts his hand on her shoulder. "Do you want some water or something? You look like shit."

"You said shit, Uncle Shawn," Ross says.

"I'm fine," says Nicki. But she's not fine at all. She is tired. She lies back on the bed and stares at the ceiling, trying to imagine a place that is as far away from here as possible. Then in her mind she takes Finn and puts her there instead.

TWENTY

The trip to Europe had been Martha Jane's idea. Kate would have been perfectly happy staying home in Fort William and dancing with the Bombardier boys on Saturday nights, but Martha Jane said they needed to have an adventure before they settled down. "We're only twenty," she reminded Kate. "We have our whole lives to be boring housewives. At least we should see the world first."

Kate couldn't imagine what there was to see. Paris, Venice, Rome, Barcelona – they were all just cities, with buildings and roads and cars and people, the same as home. The only difference was they didn't speak English, although sometimes on Fridays if you went down to the Prosvita on Simpson Street for perogies and cabbage rolls, you might think the same thing of Fort William. She kept asking Martha Jane: what river could be more melancholy than the Kam? What mountain could be more majestic than Mount McKay? There couldn't be falls greater than Kakabeka, and there most certainly was no lake bigger than Lake Superior. That was just a scientific fact.

Martha Jane came from a family of seven girls, of which she was the second youngest. Had she been the youngest, perhaps she would have felt differently about the world. Her baby sister, Rosie, was everyone's little doll, her dresses always immaculate, her hair always perfectly plaited by six devoted sets of hands. Martha Jane had experienced the euphoria of this particular adoration for exactly five years before Rosie came along, so she knew what she was missing. Kate was an only child, a late-in-life surprise to two mostly uninterested parents. She had few friends, and since the incident at Chippewa she had even pushed Walter away, for reasons she didn't understand herself. Kate and Martha Jane saw themselves as two lone wolves who didn't need anyone to help them through life. It seemed natural that they would have been drawn to each other when they met at the seamstress shop where they both worked. And although Kate was hesitant at first, it seemed natural, too, that they would embark on this adventure together.

The journey to England was an adventure in itself. Martha Jane was terrified of flying, so they took a CN train to Halifax, then crossed the Atlantic on a Cunard steamer that Martha Jane's cousin captained, securing them passage for free. The North Atlantic, it turned out, was not a friendly sea, especially in February, and Martha Jane spent most of the voyage seasick in her cabin. But Kate roamed the open decks, feeling the icy spray on her face and staring out at the roiling black waves as they crashed against the massive steel hull of the ship. By the time they reached England, she felt as though her entire body was caked in salt, a casing that she cracked out of like a shell as she stepped off the gangway and onto dry land.

In London, they spent two rainy days at Miss Featherton's Guest House in Earls Court and visiting the regular touristy sights – Buckingham Palace, Big Ben, Trafalgar Square – all of which confirmed Kate's theory that cities were cities wherever you went. Then they took a rattling, musty-smelling bus to the coast, where they spent two more rainy days holed up in a drafty cottage in Clacton-on-Sea. The cottage had a thatched roof and a beautiful garden path lined with heather and pennyroyal that led away from the cottage to the beach, which Kate only ever saw through the foggy windows while she and Martha Jane played cards and drank tea in the stuffy drawing room. Even inside the cottage, with its fussy lace curtains and uncomfortable horsehair furniture, the rain crept into her bones. If on the ship she had felt her skin was encrusted with salt, she now felt perpetually waterlogged, her fingertips bloated and puckered with a dampness that never seemed to dissipate.

On the bus back to London, Martha Jane met a young musician with startling blue eyes and shiny black hair lacquered into place. His name was Colin, and he wore a leather jacket and smoked French cigarettes and claimed he had once played with the Beatles. When they got back to London, Martha Jane elected not to return to the guest house with Kate and instead left with Colin for Blackpool, which he told her was even better than Liverpool. Kate can still see them walking away from her at the bus station, their hands tucked into each other's back pockets, Martha Jane's long blond braid swinging like a horse's tail against her back. Kate never heard from Martha Jane again.

The thing that Kate doesn't understand is how she can remember the name of Martha Jane's youngest sister and the sheen of the styling product in Colin's hair, and yet at this moment she cannot for the life of her remember the name of the beautiful girl who is sitting next to her in the passenger seat as they drive down the highway. She knows the girl is her granddaughter, of course, but she's not sure which of her daughters is the girl's mother – the one who stayed, obviously, not the one who left, but which name goes with which daughter? Kate was there for the granddaughter's birth – it was Halloween, she is sure because she can remember having to drive through a crowd of children who had come to do that thing they do on Halloween where they ask for candy, little ghosts and clowns and kitty cats peering in the windows of the car while her labouring daughter screamed in the back seat. They used to have so many children in their neighbourhood, hundreds of them, so many that they would run out of candy and have to turn off the lights so no one would know they were home. Now they are lucky if they have two or three children come around. All the children have grown up and left their parents behind to grow old in the houses they grew up in.

But this girl, this daughter of Kate's daughter (the one who stayed), this girl who was born on Halloween – and her name *will* come to Kate, these things, the really important ones, they never disappear for long – is sitting beside Kate and they are driving somewhere, but at this point she can't remember where. She knows that they have recently talked to someone. A gas station attendant? A store clerk? Someone who asked them that very thing, in fact, and at the time Kate knew where they were going. The girl did most of the talking anyway. Kate just smiled and nodded and handed over the book with her picture in it.

Of course. They are in that south country. They must be on their way to pick up a package at Ryden's, or to get pizza at Sven and Ole's in the town with two words in the name. They can't be going to the place where you make bets – the girl is too young for that – but they are there to have fun, or they are there to do something important. Kate shifts slightly in her seat, causing a sudden pain to sear through her gut. She cries out, gripping the steering wheel tighter.

"Nana, are you okay?" the girl asks.

Kate can see the concern on her face, and so she searches for words to reassure her. "Yes, sweetheart, of course," she says. "Just my arthritis." Either this is actually something she has, or it is a word the girl has heard before, because she settles back against the seat, her eyes cast down on her phone.

The pain seems strange, but not inconceivable. These days, Kate is used to her body hurting and not understanding why. But where they are going – the more Kate thinks about it, the more her mind gets jumbled. They can't possibly be going to the package place because they have been driving for too long, and they might even be past the two-word town. They are on a stretch of road that she doesn't recognize. Kate tries to visualize all of her inner power and energy flowing into her brain, the way Dr. Whatshername at the clinic told her to. She tries to relax and think of word associations – *girl, tree, road, car, girl, branch, Halloween* – but the space next to each word is blank. She focuses on the last thing she remembers thinking about: Martha Jane and London. Why London? The British flag, the Royal Wedding, tea, the Beatles, Colin and his leather jacket. Is her name Elizabeth? Are they on their way to see a music show? It's no use. No matter what she does, the path behind her is a complete blank, her footprints erased as soon as they fall, her thoughts thought and then evaporating into the air.

"Nana," the girl says. "Are you sure you don't want me to drive for a bit?"

Kate gazes at her for as long as she dares take her eyes off the driving path. Can the girl possibly be old enough to drive? Kate can still see her baby face the day her mother brought her home from the doctor place, the two of them equally scared and helpless. The jack-o'-lanterns were starting to decay on the porch, the leaves already gone from the leaf-things, the wind blowing them around the yard. They put the girl in the same room her mother and aunt had been in as babies, still decorated as a nursery, Walter ever hopeful that another baby might come and live in it. And now, one had: Kate's daughter's daughter – one seeing it for the first time, the other seeing it as though for the first time. "What's with these balloons on the wall?" Kate's daughter is asking. "Why is this door blue?" The baby's hands are making fists next to her face in the crib, which is not good enough, Kate's daughter announces, but for now it will have to do.

Now the baby has purple and pink streaks in her hair. Why did her mother let her do that? She always had such beautiful hair, shiny and straight and jet black, like her father, Kate supposes. Not much of her mother in her looks, although they have the same temperament. The same incessant need for attention, the same volatile temper when she didn't get it. Kate can remember how, as a child, the girl's mother would follow her twin sister around, begging her to play, flying into a rage when it became clear her sister preferred to be left alone. One time she bit her sister's shoulder, another time she threw her typewriter out the window, where it shattered against the trunk of one of the red pines growing next to the house. As she grew older, she got in trouble – partying, mostly, promiscuity, breaking curfew, even getting arrested, once, for public indecency of all things – coming out of it all relatively unscathed. Until she got pregnant. The kind of trouble you can't come out of unscathed.

All this acting out, and for whose benefit? Kate wonders. *Did we not give her enough love? Has she passed on this longing to her own daughter through her blood and bone, or through her words and actions?* The other two, this one's sisters, they have each other, and Kate is sure their young brother will know loneliness unlike anything any of them can imagine. But this one – she is still only a child, yet she has already been arrested. Where will this legacy take her? Where is it taking them now?

For the first few weeks after she brought her baby home, Kate's daughter sunk into a deep depression. She refused to even look at her child, at her perfect dark eyes, her full baby lips. Kate couldn't be sure if it was because looking at her reminded her daughter of the father, who she claimed not to know how to find, or if there was another kind of sadness working its way through her heart. Walter was still angry at her for getting pregnant to begin with, and her twin sister had moved in with that boy and was preoccupied with the business of being in love, so during these times Kate cared for

245

the baby herself. She fed her from a bottle she carefully heated on the stove, sang lullabies to her in the still-mediocre nursery, and walked with her through the fields down to the river, naming all the trees and animals along the way – an ability she took so much for granted then. When it got too cold to go outside, they sat on the floor in the living room and watched *Sesame Street* in front of the old television set and read books about barnyard animals and construction equipment and talking vegetables. And still, Kate's daughter lay on her bed in her room, staring at the wall. Every time the baby cried, she simply pulled the pillow over her head to drown out the noise.

Her daughter's post-partum depression seemed to lift only when she got pregnant again. Kate is not in any position to judge her children on their sexuality, but she could never understand how, in this day and age, she could let it happen again. When her girls had turned sixteen, Kate made them both appointments with a gynecologist. She didn't want them to grow up the way she did, not knowing anything about how their bodies worked. They refused to let her go with them, or even go together, so Kate has no idea what took place at those appointments, but it wasn't too long after that she found condoms in the girl's mother's room, lying out on her dresser in plain sight. Looking back, Kate can only assume that she planted them there so Kate would think she was having safe sex. Either way, it's not that she wasn't prepared or informed. When she got pregnant the first time, Kate thought maybe she had just made a mistake, an error in judgment. It can happen to anyone, even someone who is prepared and informed. When, two years later, she got pregnant again, there was no doubt in Kate's mind: she had done it on purpose.

The second pregnancy, the twins – whose names have escaped Kate now – they changed something in her daughter. Where with her first baby she had been angry and depressed, pushing everyone away, with the twins she was invigorated. Well, she would have had to be, with two of them – Kate remembers what that was like, the endless feedings, the always growing pile of laundry. It's as though some basic survival instinct kicked in, as though her body got itself together and decided that it either had to find the energy to do this or it was going to die. So her daughter found the energy for two, maybe embedded somewhere in her twin DNA, who knows. Whatever happened, it left her first-born on the sidelines with her grandmother, both of them looking in.

Not that Kate and her granddaughter didn't have fun. They spent a lot of time reading, and baking in the kitchen. Kate taught her how to ride a bike and how to use a camera. In the summer they played in the yard, collecting wildflowers and drying them in between the pages of the things you read; in the winter they built snow forts in the yard the way Walter used to for their girls. When her granddaughter went to school, it was as though Kate's entire life's purpose had been ripped out from under her – the same way it had, years earlier, when her own children started getting older. And over time, Kate slowly became invisible to her granddaughter. Which is why it seems impossible, now, that they are here in this car together. When did things change? Was it today? Yesterday? Or is Kate forgetting years of bonding, of shared secrets, of inside jokes that she should be laughing at?

Ahead, inexplicably, there is a stop light. Perhaps they are in a place where people live. Kate sees a place for cars on her right-hand side, where they sell the stuff that makes the car go. *Maybe we can just pull in for a moment*, she thinks, *until I can gather my thoughts*. But then she gets mixed up – the things at her feet, what are they, what do they do? And the girl is screaming and the car is speeding up and there are horns honking and people outside shouting and the sun is blinding through the windshield, the steering wheel unresponsive beneath her hands. Then they are bounding up over the place where the people walk and into a field of buttercups and thistle and Queen Anne's lace, coming to a stop among these silly flowers whose names are right there when Kate wants them when everything else is buried so deep she's not sure if she will ever be able to uncover it.

They sit in the car in silence. Kate is too embarrassed to speak because of what she's done and because she no longer has the ability to explain why she's done it. The girl is visibly shaken. "I'm driving," she says, opening the side door and stepping out of the car. On the left-hand side of the road, Lake Superior laps up against the land, sparkling like glitter beneath that same blinding sun. Had Kate's hand jerked to the left instead of the right, they would be underwater by now.

TWENTY-ONE

K atriina's phone rings.

It seems almost impossible that here, on her magic floating couch in the middle of an empty living room in the middle of an empty house, there is even such a thing as a phone. She has been lying here for hours, long enough for the blood to have dried on her legs and the initial exhilaration of the cutting to have faded into a dull, nauseating ache. Long enough for the regular sounds the house makes to transform into the voices of ghosts. At some point she must have passed out, sleeping fitfully, the rough corduroy chafing against her cheek, as she dreamed of her skin flaking off, peeling back in long, translucent sheets like an old sunburn, her entire body being stripped away layer by layer until she was nothing but a pile of skin on the ground.

She fumbles around on the couch, which is her whole world now, her up and her down, her heaven and her hell. Her black work pants are balled up at the other end of the couch by her feet; she can feel the box cutter digging into her back, an uncomfortable distraction as she tries to locate the source of the ringing. She finally finds the phone squished between two of the cushions, the sound vibrating up through the layers of material, demanding her attention like one of her children. A momentary panic as she remembers Tommy and Petey. Where are her boys? Her parents – they are with her parents. Relieved, she looks down at the screen of her phone, still ringing in her hand. Well, of course. She puts it on speakerphone and rests it on her chest. "Hello?"

"Katriina," Shawn says. "I need you."

She almost laughs. "No, you don't," she says, stretching her arms over her head and arching her back like a cat. Below her, her legs feel heavy, and she lets them rest there. She is lightheaded, almost giddy. Sparkles dance in front of her eyes. "You don't need me at all."

This was clearly not the response Shawn was expecting. "Are you drunk?" he asks.

She does *feel* drunk, likely due to blood loss. Now she wishes she was. "Maybe," she says. "Are you the only one who's allowed to get drunk to forget his problems?"

"Katriina, Mom's missing."

This time Katriina does laugh, waving her arms back and forth in the space over her head, trailing her fingers through the air. "She's in the Thunder Bay General Hospital. Room 8157. In a coma." It comes back to Katriina, the drop, bang, flip. What must it have felt like, those moments suspended in midair? The weightlessness. The deceptive feeling of freedom. The irresistible pull of gravity. Kate is likely the only person who will ever know. What would that be like, to be the only person in the world to ever experience a particular thing? Katriina is quite sure she will never find out.

"No. She isn't, Katriina."

With the phone still balanced on her chest, Katriina shimmies herself up against the arm of the couch, rests her head back, and looks up at the ceiling. Things have suddenly gone from sparkly to dark and cloudy as she tries to get her bearings in the conversation. "You say my name a lot," she says, stalling.

"I'm trying to get your attention, *Katriina*."

"Did you know that when I was a kid everyone at school called me Kat? They did. Right up until I started middle school." She watches the black cloud tracking across the ceiling, hovering just above her head. "I had this best friend in kindergarten, Sam something, and she thought that Katriina was too long. She wanted us to match, be Kat and Sam. You know, like best friends should."

"You've told me this before," Shawn says.

"Do you think that's why Finn started going by Finn?" she asks, the thought just occurring to her. "Because Nicki did it first, and she wanted them to match?"

"Actually, Finn did it first. When she was four. She couldn't make an R facing the right way to spell Serafina, so she just started calling herself Finn."

The black cloud descends, settling around Katriina's head. "Well, aren't you just a regular Finn encyclopedia." She laughs to herself. "A Finncyclopedia!"

Shawn sighs. "She's my sister. I know a lot of things about her. Just like you know lots of things about Hanna."

"You know what's really sad?" Katriina says, ignoring him. "I can't remember anything about Sam except this one story. I wonder what happened to her. I wonder if she grew up to be Samantha."

Katriina can hear Shawn sucking on his teeth the way he does when he doesn't know what to say. There is a long pause while she listens to it. Suck, suck, suck. "Where are you?" he asks finally. "Are you at the house? I think I should come get you."

"Why are you so upset, anyway?" Katriina asks, confused. "They probably just took her for some tests or something. She's in a coma, it's not like she can just get up and walk out of the room." It's a cold thing to say, but a few hours ago Shawn intimated that he wanted to end their marriage. He can't come crying to her now that he's sad because he can't see his mommy for five minutes.

"They didn't, Katriina, this is what I'm trying to tell you. They think she woke up. And now she's gone. And I need my wife to get her shit together and come here and help me look for her."

Katriina closes her eyes, feels her pulse fluttering in her eyelids. "Well, at least you still think of me as your wife." Silence on the other end of the phone. She opens her eyes again. "Did she really wake up?"

"They think so, yeah."

"Okay. Okay." Katriina props herself up on her elbows and then lowers one leg towards the floor. The pain doesn't hit her with its full force all at once; it's like an engine revving at the starting line, teasing her with a little taste of what's to come. When the starter's gun goes off it lurches forward like a jackrabbit and speeds away, the pain spiking inward towards the centre of her, so breathtaking that Katriina is unable to speak. She rolls over on her side, gasping, the phone falling to the floor.

"Katriina?" She hears Shawn's tinny voice through the speaker. "Are you still there? Katriina, what's going on? Where are you?"

"Shawn," she whispers and then passes out.

At first everything is dark and all she can feel is pain, bone-deep and nauseating. She is immediately hit with a sense of betrayal – pain has always been her calm centre, the one thing she could count on to keep her rooted firmly to the ground. Now she feels as though she is floating in outer space, inky black and oppressive, unable to get her bearings, unable to breathe. Then, slowly, a tiny pinprick of light appears, a speck so far off in the distance that she isn't sure if it is really there. But then the light grows brighter and she latches on to it, she clings to that light with everything she has, struggling towards it, taking long, ragged breaths of air. And then underneath the pain, something else starts to emerge, a sensation she can't quite name yet, her brain still foggy and fragile. As the world around her starts to come back into focus she realizes that she is back on the couch at the Paulsson house and someone else is there, someone is touching her. *Claudia*, she thinks. *You're here.*

"Babe," a voice says. It's Shawn, of course, not Claudia, sitting on the couch next to her, his hand resting against her cheek.

She makes her mouth move. "I'm sorry," she says.

He looks down at her legs, at the intricate spirals etched into her pale skin, with a mixture of fascination and worry. It feels like he is looking right into her, at a part of her that no one was ever meant to see. "Oh, Katriina," he says. He begins to trace the lines that she has carved there, still raw and glistening, the dried blood flaking away underneath his fingers. She can't tell from his face what he is thinking. Is he disgusted with her? Is he angry? Or is he laughing at her on the inside? What a stupid thing for her to do, how immature, how desperate. *Does he think I'm ugly now?*

The pain of his touch is nearly intolerable, his finger leaving a trail like a white-hot flame on her skin. But then there is also an unexpected pleasure, the touch of her husband's hand, the warm, rough edges of it, the delicacy with which he makes contact with her broken skin. It is like electricity running through her body, stunning her slightly, making her skin vibrate, her muscles twinge. The sensation is almost too much for her to handle. She wants to say something, to make him stop, but she doesn't want him to stop, and the whole thing is making her head spin – why is he here, why is this happening, why can't she figure out how to get back to who she was? Then Shawn's hand is gone and he is kissing her, gently, the way a mother might kiss her child's skinned knee, his lips moving along the same path as his fingers. She closes her eyes and her breath grows shallow as he makes his way across her mangled shin and up the side of her calf, the top of her kneecap, the delicate skin on the inside of her thigh.

"Don't stop," she whispers, and he doesn't, his mouth moves between her legs over newer, smoother, unmarked territory, his teeth gently nipping at the crotch of her underwear before he pushes it to one side with his tongue and buries his face into her. She comes almost instantly, her shoulders pressing violently back into the armrest of the couch, but he doesn't stop, and she is coming and coming and her legs are on fire and the sparkles are back, like constellations on the ceiling, bright and beckoning stars. "Fuck me," she says, but he seems unsure, his eyes travelling up and down her legs until she reaches forward and grabs at the waist of his jeans and starts to unbutton his fly, pulling him down on top of her. The corduroy feels strange against her bare skin as they move back and forth, and at one point he stops and pulls out the box cutter from beneath her back, letting it drop to the floor before leaning back over her, his breath hot against her neck.

Afterward, he goes to the bathroom and comes back with a wad of damp toilet paper. "I couldn't find anything else," he says apologetically. Part of her is grateful that he hasn't asked about what happened to her legs, but part of her wishes he had. If he really cared, wouldn't he press her? Or maybe this is just Shawn being Shawn – if they don't talk about it, then they don't have to acknowledge it is happening. She doesn't know anymore.

As he begins to clean her wounds, her skin feels tender, but it doesn't hurt nearly as much as it did before. She wonders if she is just numb from the sex, or if it really wasn't all that bad to begin with, if she was just being overly dramatic, a baby. Fainting like that, calling out for Shawn feebly over the phone. It all seems so ludicrous now, embarrassing. She grimaces, causing Shawn to stop.

"No, it's okay," she says. "Keep going."

Shawn bows his head back over her leg. "We should really get you some Polysporin or something."

"How did you find me, anyway?" she asks.

"It was the only place I could think you might be. It's like a rock you wear around your neck, this house. It's practically a part of you."

254

Katriina thinks about telling him that it is, in fact, quite a big part of her now. But she decides against it. "And your mom?"

Shawn clenches his jaw. "Still missing. When I left the hospital they were trying to pull the security tapes, see if they could tell where she went. I doubt she left the hospital, I mean, she just woke up from a coma. Plus she has all those injuries. She couldn't make it too far."

"I'm sure she didn't." Katriina moves her free leg back and forth, trying to replicate the earlier pain. But it's gone. If it was ever really there in the first place. She decides to just keep going, push her luck, with the leg and with Shawn. "And what about last night?"

A pause. "I went out for drinks with some of the kitchen guys."

Katriina considers playing along with him. But what would be the point? "I know. Hanna called me this morning. She told me you crashed at her place."

Shawn shakes his head. "I got too drunk. It was stupid."

"You should have called."

"Yeah."

"I was worried. I thought you were mad at me about the miscarriage."

Shawn stands up and wipes his damp hands on his jeans. He focuses on the floor, avoiding her eyes. "I'm going to look for some rubbing alcohol or something."

"No," says Katriina sharply, struggling to sit up. The adrenaline pumping through her body at the sound of the word coming out of her mouth, the feeling of it being expelled on air from her own lungs. "No," she says again. "You need to stay. Every time the conversation stops going your way, you leave the room. Every. Damn. Time."

Shawn stops in the doorway, but keeps his back to her. Katriina can see his shoulders rising and falling under the thin material of his T-shirt as he tries to get his breathing under control. "I'm trying to help you, Katriina."

"No, you're not. You just can't stand it when I confront you about anything. Everything always has to be on your terms." She can't believe she didn't see it before. It's like a light switch has turned on in her brain, illuminating all the dark corners where her bad thoughts about Shawn used to hide.

"*My* terms?" says Shawn, turning around. "You think these are *my terms*?" He sweeps his hand out in front of him, gesturing to the entire room, but Katriina knows he means her. His imperfect wife, who for one tiny second, when everything piled up too heavily on her shoulders, had the gall to break.

"Well, they're not my terms either." She crosses her arms defiantly, staring him down. "I didn't make this happen, you know. I didn't lose the baby on purpose."

Shawn doesn't say anything. *Oh my god*, Katriina thinks. *He thinks I lost the baby on purpose.*

"No," he says after a minute. "You just lied to me about it, and left me to look like an idiot in front of my entire family."

Katriina exhales. "I didn't lie about it. I was just waiting for the right time to tell you. I didn't think you were going to announce it like that, in front of everyone."

"Whatever." He walks away abruptly towards the kitchen.

"Please, Shawn. We need to talk about this." Slowly, Katriina pushes herself up to her feet, her legs wobbly and stiff. She starts hobbling forward, thinking about how unnatural it feels to be away from the couch. But there is no way she is going to let Shawn walk out on her this time, not a chance in hell.

She stops in the doorway to the kitchen and immediately loses her breath. Shawn has opened every cupboard door in the kitchen: ten of them, to be precise, upper and lower, cheap white pressboard with fake brass knobs, raised panels, unfinished edges. The shelves are empty, save for an open bag of plastic cups left over from her last open house and a balled-up rag she uses for wiping the dust from the counter. But plastered there on the insides of all the doors, covering them from top to bottom, are her Post-it notes. Hundreds of them, fluttering there in the breeze from the air vent, like some kind of repulsive sea creature from the deepest, darkest parts of the ocean waving its tentacles, all with the same two words written on them.

Be better.

Be better.

Be better.

"What the hell is this, Katriina?"

She doesn't know how to answer him. After the first one, she had just started writing, and with each new Post-it she started to feel happier. Lighter. But now she sees everything through Shawn's eyes: him innocently opening the first cupboard and finding the notes, and then opening another and another, each one bringing with it a new kind of sickening horror.

"I bought this house," she says. The words just come out.

"You . . . what?"

She walks over to one of the bottom cabinets and pulls off a Post-it. It's the first one she wrote, with the crossed-off "a." She flicks the edge with her finger, thinking about how there once was a time when she thought there were only certain aspects of herself that she had to fix, instead of her whole entire being. She hands the Post-it to Shawn, the adhesive making a snapping noise as he pulls it away from her fingers. She feels giving him this will explain it all, but almost as quickly understands that it won't. He is almost comically baffled, a cartoon character with little question marks circling his head.

"I bought this house," she says again.

He looks down at the Post-it note in his hand, and then back at her. "You bought this house," he echoes.

"I couldn't sell it, so I bought it." She runs her hands along the edge of the counter. It sounds simple enough, logical enough: She couldn't sell it, so she bought it. A good investment. A business decision.

Shawn's face is white with anger and so close now she can see the thin blue veins running along his temples. "How in the fucking world," he says, his voice calm, level, "could you buy a house and not tell me?"

"I don't know." Katriina averts her eyes, picking at a tear in the laminate. "How could you get a job offer in Ottawa and not tell me?"

Shawn slams his hand down on the counter, making Katriina jump. "I already told you, that wasn't a big deal!" he yells.

"If it wasn't a big deal, why did you tell Finn?" Katriina can barely hear herself through the pounding in her ears, the dull roar of blood rushing to her head.

"Who gives a shit what I told Finn?" Shawn grabs her by the shoulders, his fingers digging into her arms. *Dig harder*, she thinks, her head swimming. *Please*. "It's not like I went out and bought a house!"

"It was a *business decision*!" The roar in her ears grows into a wail, and all she can think is *Claudia, Claudia. Claudia has come to save me*. She looks to Shawn for confirmation, but she can already tell that he can't hear it. "Why can't you hear that?" she asks. "Why can't anyone hear that?"

"What about the miscarriage?" he says. "What about the fact that you lost our baby?"

Katriina wrenches free and pushes Shawn back. "I didn't lose her! Stop saying I lost her! Maybe she just decided she didn't want to be a part of this screwed-up family!"

For a moment, she is sure that Shawn is going to hit her. She braces herself, but instead he stalks across the kitchen, running his hands through his hair. The wailing reaches a crescendo.

"Shh, Claudia," Katriina says, her voice barely above a whisper. "It's going to be okay."

"Who the hell is Claudia?" Shawn yells. "What else are you keeping from me, Katriina? Huh? What else are you keeping from me while my family is in crisis?"

"*I'm* in crisis, Shawn!" she yells back. The noise suddenly stops. In the resulting silence, her voice echoes off the bare kitchen walls. "I am. Your wife." She spreads her arms wide. "Look at me. Look at this house. Look what happened to your own family while you were dealing with the fucking Parkers!"

Shawn stares at her, and she can see herself reflected in his eyes – standing there in her half-buttoned blouse and her underwear against a backdrop of Post-it notes, her legs sliced up, ranting about phantom noises, imaginary children.

"I can't handle this right now," he says. He raises his arms in defeat and walks out the door.

TWENTY-TWO

After Martha Jane left with Colin, Kate had a choice to make. She could stay in London alone, or she could sail home on the next Cunard steamer, another three-week journey back after a three-week journey there for five days in the U.K. It was a tempting thought: her cozy bed instead of the lumpy cot at Miss Featherton's, the safe streets of Fort William, her part-time job at the seamstress's. Maybe even Walter, if she hadn't already lost him for good. But she stayed on.

It felt different being in the city on her own, and she ventured away from the tourist attractions, taking photos of the double-decker buses, the sleek black cabs, the tall, narrow houses – so unlike the buses, cabs, and houses back home. Often she just sat and stared in awe at the beautiful girls of Kensington and Covent Garden, with their short skirts and shorter hair – they seemed so light, so free. London in 1969 had a terrifying, crazy spark to it, an electricity, and Kate could feel something reigniting in herself as well.

After three weeks in London alone, one evening she returned to her room to discover that Miss Featherton had accidentally given it to another guest. Kate can still remember walking in and finding Lydia sitting there on the bed in a diaphanous nightgown, brushing her long brown hair and smoking a cigarette. "I knew Miss Featherbrain gave me the wrong room, but I decided I just had to stay and meet the woman who wears this beautiful dress," she said, gesturing to a garment strewn over the foot of the bed.

"I sewed it myself," Kate said, feeling herself blush, although the world in which she sewed dresses seemed very far away.

But Lydia smiled, tossing aside her hairbrush and clapping her hands. "That's even better!" she said. "Please tell me you also like brandy because I just happen to have some stashed in my suitcase."

So they drank the brandy and sat up talking until dawn. Lydia was from Toronto, but she had been living in Spain for the previous four months. She was a poet and an artist, and had stories of travelling with street musicians, learning to dance flamenco, living in a tent in the Sierra Morena. And although next to all of Lydia's extraordinary experiences, Kate felt like her life had been as insubstantial as a dandelion pod on the wind, she told her own stories, and Lydia listened – her eyes bright, her hair falling in waves on either side of her face. Kate talked about the farm, about Walter, and, as the sun rose and her defences crumbled, about falling through the ice at Chippewa. She had never met anyone like Lydia, or someone who made her feel so completely like herself.

With the city waking up around them, Lydia stretched her long, brown legs across Kate's lap and crossed her ankles, arched her neck as she leaned back on arms as willowy as reeds on a riverbank. "Let's go to Brighton," she said.

"When?" asked Kate.

"Right now," said Lydia with a mischievous grin.

So they took the bus to Brighton and found a room above a pool hall, but they were hardly ever in it. They sunbathed on the beach and sat outside the Palace Pier, Lydia drawing portraits of strangers and trying to sell them for money. At night they danced on the sand to the music playing in the clubs along the boardwalk, and later, to the rhythm of the waves. Lydia taught her flamenco *floreos*, twisting her wrists in the air *adentro* and *afuera* – into her body, and out to the world – holding her back straight as a pin, her eyes shadowy and dark under the pale light of the moon.

When Lydia had made enough money from her sketches, she took Kate to the fortune teller's to have their palms read, in a booth set up beside the pier on the beach, festooned with gold bunting and closed off with thick purple velvet curtains. The fortune teller wore a cheap turban and smelled of garlic, and spoke with a thick Eastern European accent that Kate suspected was faked. She told Kate that she would live a long and happy life with a man with sandy-coloured hair, and Kate couldn't help but think about Walter, back home in Fort William – probably engaged to Frances Halliday by now and forgetting all about her. It gave her an ache in her chest when she thought about it, but the pain was distant and muted, more like the memory of pain than pain itself. After only a few weeks away, it already felt as though her entire life in Canada had been just a dream.

When it was Lydia's turn, the fortune teller glanced down at Lydia's palm and then abruptly sent her away, refusing to tell her anything or to take her money. The girls laughed about it, spilling out of the booth and onto the beach in a fit of giggles, but the botched reading did cast an ominous shadow over the rest of their time in Brighton, as though they both were half waiting for something terrible to happen.

"What happened, Nana?"

Kate shakes her head, trying to bring herself back to the present. *Car, road, trip, girl.* "I don't know, sweetheart," she says.

The girl is driving now, although she seems tense, her hands clutching the steering thing very close to the top, the way they teach you to do when you first learn how to drive. Does the girl even have a driver's licence? Kate suddenly feels very impotent and weak. She wraps her arms around herself, then gasps at the stabbing pain. She remembers now that her ribs are broken; how she broke them is quite hazy, although she knows she didn't just break them raking the yard or falling down a flight of stairs. Her broken ribs are somehow the source of this strange lightness in her body. If this were a movie, she would somehow be able to transmit this lightness to the girl, who looks like she might break down any minute and cry. *Where is her mother? Does she know where they are? Where* are *they?*

They stop to get gas. Neither of them knows where the lever is to open the tank. "Isn't this your car?" the girl asks, exasperated. Eventually they find it, where it has always been. The girl uses Kate's money card to fill up, then buys them licorice, Cokes, and gum in the store. *Don't I have to sign for this? Is she signing for me?* When Kate asks the girl, she just stares at her like she's stupid. "You have a PIN code, remember, Nana?" Kate is sure she does remember, but right now she has no idea what a PIN code is. She tells the girl she is all right to drive, and the girl seems relieved. Driving is one thing Kate can still do well, her earlier mishap notwithstanding. And it has always been her refuge. All those times during the early years of their marriage when everything seemed too much to handle, when it all felt so out of control, she would just get in her car and drive. To Geraldton, to Wawa, to Hearst, all those tiny outposts along deserted highways, or across the border into Manitoba, or Minnesota, or Wisconsin. Stopping to eat, sleeping in her car. Thinking, or not thinking, about anything but the road. Never planning to drive to any specific destination. Just driving.

Driving is all she has. If she can't drive, she might as well die.

Back on the highway, they pass a sign announcing they are in Lutsen, and Kate suddenly knows where they are. They used to take the girls skiing here when they were young, sometimes with their neighbours from Victor Street – March breaks and long weekends spent in cozy log cabins in front of crackling fireplaces, with hot chocolate for the kids and warm spiced wine for the grown-ups. The kids would fall asleep exhausted in their beds at night, all windburnt cheeks and aching muscles and quietly throbbing hearts. The year that they installed the outdoor hot tub, Kate remembers running with her daughters through the snow in their bathing suits before submerging themselves in the scalding-hot water, steam rising off their frozen skin as they dared each other to do it again. One year – the first year with the boy, when Walter refused to come with them – it was so warm out that they had a barbecue, the boy flipping steaks on the deck of their chalet in his shorts and clunky winter boots. Another year, they got snowed in for two days and all five of them played an ancient game of Trivial Pursuit that no one knew any of the answers to, until the girl's mother got fed up and threw the game board into the fire.

Sometimes Kate wonders, did these things really happen, or is she just imagining them? How can she be expected to trust her memories when they are as slippery as fish in her hands? Sometimes they seem too good to be true, too picture-perfect, all this beautiful familial bliss. She knows there must have been dark times, but they are harder to recall from beneath the debris of her ramshackle mind, so she usually gives up trying. Maybe everything she remembers is false, anyway. Maybe her memories have all been stolen and replaced with fake ones, and the ones that can't be replaced simply disappear.

◆ ◆ ◆

Kate had always assumed that after they left Brighton they would return to London and Miss Featherton's, but Lydia had other plans. "I've always wanted to see Paris in the spring," she said one rainy afternoon as they sat in the pool hall below their room, playing cards and drinking terrible coffee.

"It sounds wonderful," Kate said, her heart breaking into a thousand pieces, imagining trudging back through the streets of London by herself. "I'm sure you'll have a great time."

Lydia rolled her eyes. "Don't even pretend you're not coming with me," she said. "You're the only one who can understand my terrible French."

They hitchhiked from Brighton to Dover in the cab of a truck and then caught the ferry to Calais, where they met a young Frenchman named Luc with a speech impediment, a trust fund, and a car. He drove them to Paris and dropped them right beneath the Arc de Triomphe, where they sat for hours watching the traffic driving around Place Charles de Gaulle, Lydia using her actually quite-passable French to ask strangers if they wanted her to sketch their portrait. "I never imagined that I would ever be in Paris," Kate said that night as they wandered the narrow streets of the fourteenth arrondissement, past brightly lit cafés and secretive little alleyways, searching for a place to stay. "I always thought it was like Oz or Never Never Land. One of those places that doesn't really exist." She paused, watching a woman with flaming red hair speed by on an equally red moped. "A place that you could only visit if you had an imagination."

"It *is* a place you can only visit if you have an imagination," Lydia said, linking her arm with Kate's. "And surprise! You're here."

London. Of course. How ridiculous that it's while she's thinking of Paris that she remembers her granddaughter's name is London. It's a name that's been on Kate's lips for sixteen years. When Kate named her own daughters, she gave them the most extravagantly beautiful, elaborately luxurious names she could come up with – Veronica and Serafina. How could she have forgotten those, too? When she thinks of those names, Kate pictures angels. But then they had to go and shorten them, extracting syllables as though they could just mould better names from the pieces. Nicki and Finn. Kate is quite sure she never gave birth to a Nicki or a Finn.

"London," Kate says. "What's our plan?"

She says this because it might sound as though she knows what is going on – as if she knows their general mission, but not the specifics. It's funny how clever she is at hiding how dumb she has actually become.

"I don't know yet," London says. "I was hoping you could help me come up with one."

This is not the answer Kate was hoping for. Maybe London doesn't remember what they are doing either, and is trying to put the ball back into Kate's court, which is Kate's tactic: don't answer anything directly, just lob it back in the most ambiguous way possible so they can't tell that you don't know what they're talking about. It's a trick that Kate has mastered, although it's not exactly something she's proud of.

"Well," Kate says. "Let me see." She is stalling for time, pretending to think, but the way that London is watching her is distracting. It's as if she is expecting Kate to have all the answers. Kate is not sure what she's done to convince this girl that she knows what she is doing, or that she is her ally, or that she is in any way qualified to make plans about anything. But somehow she has, and London needs Kate to guide her. This much she can see.

"How do you think we're going to find him?" London asks, and now Kate is faced with an entirely new task, an entirely new puzzle to solve. Who is "him"? Why are they searching for him? She's trying to think of the answers, but she's also trying to keep her eye on the car path. If she ends up in a field again, she might as well call one of her daughters to come and take them home.

❖ ❖ ❖

In Paris, Lydia and Kate stayed at a guest house owned by a woman named Madame Clou, who might as well have been a French Miss Featherton. Again, they spent their days visiting the tourist sites – the Louvre, the Tuileries, the Eiffel Tower – but instead of going in, they sat outside and tried to sell Lydia's sketches. One even slower than typical day as they sat on a bench on the Champs-Élysées, Kate caught Lydia staring at her own reflection in the window of the boulangerie on the other side of the sidewalk. "I'm waiting for the day that I disappear," Lydia said, and Kate thought back to that day in Brighton, the flash of panic on Lydia's face when the fortune teller refused to tell her fortune. Kate knew nothing of palm reading, but she also instinctively knew there wasn't anything in those lines worth getting worked up over. She took Lydia's hand.

"She was frightened of you," she said, running her finger over the thick line bisecting Lydia's palm. "She could tell you have great powers of intuition and instinct, and she knew that if she tried to sell you a line about your fortune, you would call her out as the fraud that she is."

Lydia let her hand linger in Kate's as she mulled over her words. Then she smiled. "I think you're the one with the great power of intuition," she said. Kate's stomach tumbled over itself as she became aware of the weight of Lydia's hand in hers, the heat of her skin, the shape of her wrist as it curved delicately away from her palm.

"I'm hungry," says London.

Kate squints through the windshield, trying to orient herself, and a sign tells her they are now in Two Harbours. "We could stop at McDonald's," she suggests. "There's one right up here."

"Are you *kidding*?" London says. "McDonald's is, like, the worst place on the planet. Do you know how much environmental destruction they're basically *completely responsible* for? Anyone who eats at McDonald's should be, like, reincarnated as a cow or something, so they can know what it's like to be *slaughtered for meat*."

"Oh," says Kate. She has no idea what London is talking about. All she knows is that when London was small and her mother would leave her with Kate so she could party with her friends, the only thing that would keep London from screaming all night long was a Happy Meal. But Kate gives in and takes her instead to a café that sells ten-dollar sandwiches filled with ingredients she has never heard of, or if she has, she has forgotten what they are.

Food – what things are called, what they taste like – is something that Kate has lost touch with, to the point that she can only make maybe half a dozen simple meals. When she shops for food, she goes to the exact places in the store where she knows she can find the things she buys every week, and avoids the aisles that contain the multitudes of foods that she used to enjoy and now has no clue what they are. She covers this up by telling people that she can only eat certain things, that strange spices and sauces make her ill, that she will take everything plain. But she knows in the past she used to be an adventurous eater. Walter will tell her, "Oh, you used to love this," and she'll stare blankly into space, trying to picture what *this* is, what shape it takes on a plate, what sensations it produces on the tongue. But it is gone, all of it, and so she sticks to bread and cheese and butter, apples and potatoes and carrots, chicken and eggs and yogurt.

But now Kate is eating something called prosciutto sandwiched into something called a ciabatta and smothered in something called balsamic vinaigrette, which she can only remember by checking the receipt the woman behind the counter gave to London after she paid with Kate's credit card. The flavours are too salty, too tangy for her tongue. When London gets up to go to the washroom, Kate wraps up the rest of her sandwich in her napkin and tucks it into her purse. She can't bring herself to throw it away – it is, after all, a ten-dollar sandwich – but maybe where they are going she can find someone who is hungry who might want to take it. London's sandwich is supposedly roasted vegetables, although from where Kate is sitting she can't see one vegetable she recognizes. London has also ordered a drink called a chai latte. Kate sneaks a sip and the flavour is so strong she can't even swallow it. She is still holding it in her mouth when London comes back, so Kate makes a motion towards the door and runs for the bathroom, where she spits it out in the sink and then splashes cold water on her face as though that is going to make the taste go away. Back at the table London looks at her quizzically, but doesn't ask if she's okay – Kate suspects that the ins and outs of her grandmother's digestive issues are not something London is interested in discussing over a meal.

◆ ◆ ◆

One rainy afternoon when they were stuck inside their room at Madame Clou's with nothing to do but read the same books and listen to the same records, Lydia presented Kate with a book on palm reading she'd bought at a used bookstore. They spent the afternoon lounging on pillows on the floor, poring over the book, memorizing the diagrams, figuring out what the lines were called and what they signified. The most important thing, the book stressed, was to instill faith in your clients by using the right terminology, which was all the book could really teach you. After that, your success as a fortune teller hinged on your ability to read people, not palms.

Kate was surprised that a book that was supposed to teach her how to be a palm reader was actually confirming that the entire discipline was basically a sham. "It's an art, not a science," said Lydia, her head resting on Kate's stomach as she held the book open above her head. "And like with all art, there has to be talent. Either you have it or you don't."

Kate snatched the book from Lydia and slammed it shut. "That's not true," she said. Having been raised with a strict Protestant work ethic, Kate found it hard to fathom something that you could not work at to achieve. "All I need is practice."

Lydia turned her head to gaze at Kate's face, her cheekbone bumping against the bottom of Kate's rib cage, sending a pleasant vibration through her body. "So let's get you some practice," she said.

They dashed across the street to Café d'Esprit. The baker, Jules, had been very kind to them over the weeks, giving them day-old croissants and letting them occupy a table by the window for hours for the price of only one espresso. "Jules," Kate said breathlessly as they swept in from the street, closing the door on the rainstorm behind them. "Did you know that before I came here, I had never even tried espresso or croissants? And now I'm pretty sure I can't live without them."

"*Oui*, Katherine," said Jules wearily. "You tell me every time you come in."

"You saved my life with coffee and pastries, Jules," Kate said solemnly, taking his coarse, flour-dusted hand in her own. Behind her, she could hear Lydia snickering. "Please, let me repay you by reading your palm for you."

Kate sat Jules down at a table, and in her most authoritative fortune-teller voice, she tried to read him. She spoke of a long life line, broken by an illness later in life that would be fought and conquered. She told him his marriage line revealed a wife and two children, and his success line revealed financial hardship and then finally stability. She showed him the Ring of Solomon, and how its depth indicated that he was, at that very moment, hesitating at a very significant fork in the road, and that deep down he knew which path he should choose. She told him that the proximity of the ring to his heart line meant that if he followed his heart, the choice would be the right one. She said all this without looking once at Lydia, for she knew if she did she would burst out laughing.

When she finished, she was startled to discover that Jules was crying. With shaking hands, he lit a cigarette, and minutes went by before he was able to speak. When he did, it was in French, which he never spoke with Kate or Lydia – as though his emotions were too complex for him to express in such a prosaic language as English. Then he got up from the table, went to the kitchen, and brought out a whole cake – round and tall and covered with a cloud of pristine white frosting. That was when Kate realized that the future was something everyone was afraid of, even if they didn't feel, as she had ever since that day at Chippewa, as though they were living on borrowed time.

"I guess you have the gift," Lydia said as they dashed back to their room, giggling and holding on to each other to keep from slipping in their waterlogged shoes. They put on a Sly and the Family Stone record and danced around the room while the rain pelted the window, eating the cake with their hands and drinking from a cheap bottle of champagne that Lydia had bought when they first arrived in Paris.

Later, when the cake and champagne were finished, they lay next to each other on the bed they shared, their hands still sticky with icing as they held their palms side by side above their heads, comparing the lines. The room was dark, the lines barely visible, but as Kate looked from her palm to Lydia's, she suddenly realized what the fortune teller in Brighton had seen. "The future doesn't matter, anyway," she said, her heart pounding as she shifted onto her side to face Lydia.

Lydia rolled over, too. "You're right. The only thing that matters is now," she said, pressing her palm against Kate's. They fell asleep with their fingers intertwined, and when they woke the next morning, eyes fluttering open in the dusty haze of the breaking dawn filtering in through the window, their hands were fused together, bonded by icing and the heat of their own skin.

"You are so beautiful," Lydia whispered.

No one had ever said those words to Kate before, in that voice. Their faces were so close that she could see the fine spray of freckles across the tops of Lydia's cheeks, the delicate creases between her eyebrows above the bridge of her nose. Before she could stop herself, she leaned in and kissed Lydia. And Lydia, in all her infinite, indescribable radiance, kissed her back.

Kate felt so free in Paris. But maybe freedom is all relative. Right now, she feels free because she is driving, she is in a foreign country, and she has an inkling that no one knows where she and London are. She tries her memory exercises again. There are pieces that come to her. She was hurt somehow. Was London with her when she got hurt? No, that can't be right. She remembers a young man in a uniform, but she doesn't know what kind. She remembers falling, but that is nothing new. She dreams of falling every night, waking herself with a start, panting in her bed next to Walter as the breeze blows through the bedroom window. No, whether she fell or not will remain a mystery.

London is pressing buttons on her phone, and Kate wonders for a moment if she should tell her to call her mother, just to let her know where they are. But even Kate knows that to do that would be to break this tenuous bond between her and her granddaughter, a bond that is the only thing tethering her to reality at this moment. She doesn't want to lose London's trust. So she just continues to drive.

TWENTY-THREE

Looking back on her day, there are quite a few things that Finn would have done differently, if given the chance. Like not get out of bed. The sunroom might have been hot and stuffy, her eyes might continuously water from all the dust in the old duvet, her 70s-era hide-a-bed might have a metal rollbar that dug into her back, but at least it would have been peaceful. Calm. One hundred percent less of a clusterfuck than the rest of the day.

Even now, thinking about the hospital staff on the case of her missing mother – a crack team consisting of three nurses, two doctors, two security guards, several orderlies, and one very grumpy chief of staff – makes Finn want to punch a wall. They *assured* the Parker family that Kate must still be on the premises, that there was *no way* she would be able to leave without someone noticing, that her pain would be too great, that the staff were too engaged, that she didn't even have a car or a change of clothing, other than the pyjamas she was wearing. She had to be holed up in another room, or in a bathroom somewhere, an empty waiting room, the cafeteria. There were too many dark, unpopulated corners in the hospital on a quiet Sunday night – it would take some time to search all of them. They would call as soon as they found her, they *promised*. It was slick, smooth, well rehearsed – almost as though they lost coma patients all the time.

Even worse, Finn and Nicki and Shawn and Walter just accepted the idea that Kate was hiding out somewhere in the hospital. But they were tired, Finn tells herself. They were distracted. And in that moment, standing in the hospital room with one empty bed and the weight of the past three days pressing down on them from above, the four of them looked at each other, then down at the floor, and said, "Okay," and felt the relief of letting someone else take care of things for once.

There is nothing we can do anyway.

We might as well just go home and let the hospital staff do their jobs.

Kate is a grown woman, she can handle herself.

It's all probably a misunderstanding.

Everything is going to be okay.

They told themselves whatever it was they wanted to hear, they said whatever they could to absolve themselves of guilt. And then they left. They picked up their things, shuffled out of the hospital, past the cameras and reporters camped at the front entrance, and just left. Shawn took off in a cab without a word; Finn gave the keys to the truck back to her father and rode home with Nicki and Ross. In the car she sat in the passenger seat and watched Nicki while she drove, her hands resting on the steering wheel just like Finn's did, the expression of concentration on her face as she merged onto the highway the same one Finn makes. It occurred to her that she knew exactly what Nicki and Dallas looked like while they were fucking. Nicki and Dallas, fucking. Again. She didn't know if she wanted to throw up, punch someone, or burst out laughing. Instead, she just pressed her head against the window, watching the other cars on the highway fly by as they headed south, wishing she was in one of them instead, going somewhere else, back to another life.

It was just after eight when they got back to Victor Street, pulling into the driveway at the same time as Hamish, who was just arriving home from Terrace Bay.

"Who's with the girls?" Hamish asked as he hopped out of his truck.

Nicki and Finn turned to each other. In the quiet of the evening they could suddenly hear a burst of laughter, an underlying thump of bass. "Oh, Christ," said Nicki. "I'll fucking kill them."

They walked into what appeared to Finn to be the set of an over-the-top movie-of-the-week on the dangers of drinking: kids making out in corners, grinding on couches, and dancing on tables, music blasting, the ground carpeted with empty Gatorade bottles that most certainly had, at one point, contained a horrifying mixture of sports drink and whatever kind of liquor they could find. Meanwhile Tommy and Petey – where did they even come from? – had turned the kitchen into a battlefield, with a line of whipped cream sprayed as a boundary down the middle and a boy on either side flinging hamburger meat balled up into little pellets at the other. Ross took one look at the scene and ran upstairs to his room. Through the kitchen window Finn saw her father's truck pull into the driveway, and then back out again, peeling away up the street. Lucky bastard.

"Everyone get the fuck out!" Nicki roared.

Kids scattered, including Milan and Vienna, who Hamish stopped at the door. "Not you two, ya wee brats." He grabbed each girl by an arm and dragged them into the living room. While Nicki and Hamish did whatever it was that parents do to their kids when they get in trouble, Finn tried to deal with the boys in the kitchen, wiping up whipped cream with a roll of paper towels as they laughed and threw raw hamburger meat at her head.

"You know, people would like you more if you weren't such jerks," she said. This just made the boys laugh harder, although they moved on from the hamburger throwing to whipping each other with an old extension cord, reaffirming Finn's decision to never, ever have children.

Ross reappeared in the kitchen. "There's a girl asleep in my room," he said. Then he ran away again, narrowly missing the flick of an extension cord to the back of his legs.

Things can't possibly get any worse, Finn thought. But then she couldn't reach either Shawn or Katriina to tell them to come pick up the boys, and Hamish had a load of machine parts he bought in Terrace Bay tied down in a trailer attached to his truck that he needed to unload *right away*, he was *sure* it was going to rain tonight and he didn't want them to rust. And then the girl in Ross's room was awake and puking red Gatorade all over the floor and they certainly couldn't send her home in that state. And then Tommy and Petey locked Ross in the upstairs bathroom and he broke the handle off trying to get out and started screaming like it was the end of the world.

"Where's London?" Nicki asked.

"I think I saw her upstairs," said Finn, because she had seen the door to London's room open and then close again as she was trying to fix the handle on the bathroom door – although she was too distracted by Tommy and Ross setting up a battalion of green army men around her feet ten minutes later to notice Milan coming out of London's room wearing London's favourite hoodie, which she *never* let Milan borrow, even though she *promised* she wouldn't suck on the cuffs of the sleeves the way she did with every other sweater she owned. And when all the kids had been tucked up somewhere, including the inherited ones, Tommy and Petey and the passed-out girl – whose name was, ironically, Kate – and the mess was as cleaned up as it was going to get that night, and Hamish had unloaded all his parts and the bathroom door handle had been put back together with a combination of duct tape and sheer force of will, Finn collapsed back into her 70s-era hide-a-bed with the rollbar and the dusty duvet and closed her eyes.

"Fuck this day."

Upstairs, she can hear Nicki and Hamish talking in low voices in their room. Is Nicki telling him about Dallas? she wonders. But she immediately shuts that thought down. She doesn't want to think about Nicki and Dallas, sneaking around having sex with each other like hormonal teenagers. She doesn't want to think about Tanya, standing there doing nothing while Dallas ruins her life, or Hamish, whose life is probably already ruined. She doesn't want to think about Kate – Kate her mother, somewhere out there with two broken ribs, a fractured pelvis, two chipped front teeth, a ripped-off pinky nail, and a severe concussion, or Kate the passed-out girl, who most certainly has some level of alcohol poisoning. She doesn't want to think about anything to do with this family, with this house, with this fucking city. She just wants to go to sleep.

But of course she can't sleep because the sunroom is hot and stuffy, and her eyes are continuously watering from all the dust in the old duvet, and there is a metal rollbar digging into her back. She tosses and turns for another hour before giving up, pulling on a pair of shorts, and walking through the finally silent house and out onto the back deck.

Once she is outside, she tilts her head up to the sky, staring at the thick wash of stars. It's hard to believe that all these stars are always there, even when they're not visible. She can remember Walter trying to teach her about the constellations when she was a kid, Andromeda, Ursa Major, Perseus, and his favourite, Draco, the dragon who guards the pole star. Finn had tried to love the stars – she always thought it would make her father love her more. But no matter how hard she tried, she could never see the constellations. To her, they were just sets of stars grouped together by astronomers. Stars with nothing in common, likely not even close to each other in reality, travelling on their own separate orbits through the galaxy yet locked together for the entire span of their lives because someone thought that they formed the shape of a bear, or a spoon, or a guy with a bow.

Her father probably thought she was just being stubborn. But she remembers Kate telling her once that Walter couldn't see the shape of the Sleeping Giant, so you'd think he'd be a little more understanding. Maybe it's genetic, she thinks, this lack of ability to see the shape of things in other things: rock formations, constellations, even the shape their family took. If neither she nor her father could recognize its contours and edges, how could they be expected to fit themselves into it without changing its fundamental form? Without screwing it up? Maybe that's why she and her father are both outsiders. Why couldn't she see that before? *Oh. Right.*

"Hi, Finn." Startled, Finn turns towards the voice to find Shawn sitting on the steps, smoking a cigarette.

"Jeez, you scared the crap out of me," she says. "Wait, are you *smoking?*" Shawn tips his head back and breathes out a stream of smoke in response. She sits on the step next to him, clipping the cigarette from his fingers and taking a drag, until the smoke burns her lungs and she coughs. "Where were you tonight?" she asks, handing it back to him.

"Dealing with my wife," he says. "I think my marriage is over." He stubs the cigarette out against the railing and flicks the butt onto the lawn. His face is half-obscured by shadows, but she can tell that he has been crying. She's not sure if she has ever seen Shawn cry before, but then she has a sudden memory of being very young and coming in for dinner to find him in the kitchen cooking Hamburger Helper, his face red and puffy. It couldn't have been long after he moved in. She hadn't really paid much attention, but now she wonders, what would make a fifteen-year-old cry like that over a skillet full of beef and noodles?

"Do you want to talk about it?" she asks now, resting her head against the railing.

"She bought a house without telling me. And she's been cutting herself." He pulls out another cigarette and holds it between his fingers, unlit. "She also lost the baby."

"Oh, no." Once again, Finn finds herself searching for the right words. What would someone else's sister say in this situation? "Is there anything I can do?"

Even in the dark she can feel Shawn glaring at her. "Don't give me that canned sympathy bullshit," he says. "You're not my fucking *barber*."

"Sorry," she says. Somewhere beyond the river, she can hear the howl of a coyote. The workers out at the paper mill used to feed the coyotes, guys throwing their sandwich scraps and apple cores out onto the riverbank until the city made them stop. But by then it was too late: the coyotes had forgotten how to feed themselves. You'd find them rifling through your garbage on Monday nights, or hovering around the edges of the baseball diamonds on Sunday afternoons, waiting like begging dogs for a scrap from the dugout. Often, you would find them dead on the side of the road. Those mill guys thought they were doing something nice, feeding those coyotes. But what they really did was destroy them.

"You want kids?" Shawn asks suddenly.

Finn laughs. "I don't even have a boyfriend."

Shawn rubs his hands over his face. She has always known him to be clean-shaven, but now he has the beginnings of a beard growing in. She's not sure if this is something he's doing on purpose, or if it's a side effect of the past couple of days.

"I always thought I'd be a really shitty parent," he says. "I'm still worried my kids are going to grow up to be psychopaths."

Finn thinks about Petey swinging the extension cord over his head like a lasso while Tommy smeared raw hamburger onto his face like war paint. "They might," she says. Shawn kicks her, lightly. "Well, they *might*. But it won't be because you were a shitty parent. All parents are shitty parents, in some ways."

"Not all parents. Not Kate."

Finn rolls her eyes. "Stop getting all sentimental on me. Do you remember the time Mom left us at the mall? It was like she just forgot she had kids at all."

"I wasn't a kid," Shawn says. "I was fifteen."

"Whatever. You were as freaked out as we were. You thought we were going to have to hide in Sears and sleep in the mattress department."

"I was only freaked out 'cause you were there. I didn't know how I was going to support two spoiled brats on my lawn-mowing salary."

"I think you would have done okay." From where she is sitting, Finn can feel the force of his exhalation, and only then does she realize she has subconsciously timed her own breathing to his.

"Did you watch the video?" Shawn asks.

"Yeah," says Finn. "Did you?"

"Yeah." He rolls the cigarette between his finger and thumb, staring out into the night. "She looked . . . I don't know."

"Happy?"

"Not happy. Content, I guess. Like everything was working out exactly how she planned it." He doesn't say anything for a moment, then shakes it off, finally bringing the cigarette to his lips and lighting it. "How about you?" he asks. "How are you doing?" He looks at Finn and his eyes are dark, so much darker than Parker eyes. It reminds her that Shawn does not have the luxury of taking his family for granted. Just looking in the mirror is a reminder of where he stands in relation to everyone else in the family.

"You don't have to do that," she says.

"Do what?"

"Stay on top of everyone, all the time. Making sure we're all okay. You can loosen your grip a little. You're not going to lose us." She stares at the glowing end of the cigarette, leaving orange trails through the darkness as Shawn brings it to his lips. "You're more of a Parker than I am now."

"Oh, come on, Finn." He exhales slowly, the smoke curling away over his head. "If you want to be a part of this family, then just *be* a part of this family."

Finn shakes her head. "No one wants that."

"Clearly you do." He stubs out the cigarette in the same spot as the last one. Then he pulls the pack out of his pocket and hands it to her. "Take these away," he says. "I can't start this shit again."

She takes the pack and twirls it around in her hand. "I just don't want to be left out of everything."

"Finn, the only reason you've been left out is because you *left*."

"Because Mom wanted me to!" she says a little too loudly. She can hear her voice carry out across the river. "Because she always chose Nicki over me."

"She *protected* you from Nicki," says Shawn. "You just couldn't see it." He pauses. "But you know this isn't about Nicki. You think that Kate pushed you away. But did you ever think maybe she was trying to push you *towards* something instead?"

Finn pictures her mother, smiling in the kitchen window and waving as the school bus pulled up to the driveway. Had she just been playing the part of the happy housewife, when all along she was yearning to know what lay beyond the four walls of Victor Street and the limits of her life? Had she moved through her days with a hollow longing in the pit of her stomach for all the things she was told she shouldn't want? Had she felt the same restlessness that Finn did?

"No," says Finn. "That's stupid." Suddenly her body is shuddering with sobs, but once she's started, she can't stop. "That's the . . . stupidest thing I . . . ever heard."

Shawn puts his arm around her, and she leans against him and rests her head on his shoulder. The tears just keep coming, soaking through Shawn's T-shirt and making her already swollen nose feel like it's going to explode. *I should have stayed in bed*, she thinks. *No rollbar is as bad as this.*

After a while she asks, "Do you remember the day Mom fell off the roof?"

"You mean when Nicki and Dallas first slept together?"

Finn lifts her head. "You said *first*." Shawn doesn't say anything. She puts her head back down on his shoulder. "You know about Nicki and Dallas, don't you?"

"Yeah."

Neither of them says anything. Above them Finn can make out the Big Dipper hanging low over the river, still the only constellation she can pick out by sight. Just one more way she let her father down. "Everything changed that day." She means with her and Dallas, but she also means something else. Something shifted in their family, cracking the foundation, as if whatever tenuous structure that once held them all together had started to crumble. She knows Shawn feels it, too.

"Sure," he says. "But things are supposed to change *every* day, Finn. That's the way life goes. You move on. You don't get to live in one day for the rest of your life."

Finn wipes at her eyes, sitting up straight. "Everyone always says that, Shawn. But how do you do that? How do you move on, in real, practical terms? I don't know how to do that."

Shawn looks down at his hands. "Neither do I," he says.

alling. Falling. The word sticks in Kate's brain like a burr, like a snippet of a song that you can't shake loose. Falling inside darkness, how can that be possible? Falling and yet still safe inside. It must have been a dream, it must have. Through the glass in the front of the car Kate sees a deer standing on the side of the road, its ears back, as though sensing danger. Stay back, little deer, Kate says in her head, as she does whenever she passes a deer, willing it not to jump in front of her car in fear. As she passes it, their eyes meet through the glass and she is sure that she feels its confusion, this road appearing in the middle of its place with the trees, this strange hard surface, these swiftly moving masses of steel and rubber, suddenly people there when before there had been none.

London doesn't notice the deer. She is busy fiddling with the dial on the box that plays music. Kate wonders if she should say something, but then decides against it. The less she says these days, the better – there is less of a chance of getting something wrong, of giving something away. Soon they will reach Duluth, and then Kate will have to face the fact that she doesn't know where they are going. Because they are either going to Duluth or they are going somewhere south of Duluth. Those are the only two options.

"So?" she says to London. She had been hoping the words after "so" would come to her as she started talking, but they don't, and so it just hangs there, two little letters floating in the air between them.

"You're not tired, are you, Nana?" London asks.

"No," says Kate, and she's not. She feels as though she has been sleeping for a thousand years, as though she might never sleep again.

"You're okay to drive the rest of the way to Duluth?"

"Yes," Kate says, feeling triumphant. Duluth. They are going to Duluth.

"We'll stay at the Radisson, okay? I think that's where he's staying."

A night in a hotel room. Kate can't even remember the last time she spent a night in a hotel room, although this seems like something a person would remember, even a person who can only remember random snippets of their past. London seems confident about where they are going, as though she has been on this path before. Yes, that's right, Nicki used to bring the kids to the States all the time. Kate suddenly has a terrible taste in her mouth, so at the next traffic light she reaches into her purse for some gum and puts her hand directly into something soft and squishy.

"What on earth?" she says. She pulls out what appears to be the remnants of a sandwich, which has been stuffed into the main compartment of her purse without any sort of wrapper or container, save for some bits of soggy napkin clinging to one edge.

"Nana, that's your sandwich," London says.

"What sandwich?" Kate asks, wiping some sort of purplish goo off her hands and onto the steering wheel. She realizes as soon as she says it that it is the wrong thing to say, that she has given too much away. London just stares at her. Then she takes Kate's purse and peers inside, where the sandwich has deconstructed itself all over her belongings.

"How did it get in here, all unwrapped like that?" she asks. "What were you thinking?"

"I don't know," Kate says. She truly doesn't. She doesn't remember lunch, or a sandwich, or why on earth she would order something covered in all that purple goo. The road behind her has disappeared, and all she has left now is the road ahead, and she's racing to get to where she is going before the disappearing catches up to her and the road vanishes under her feet.

◆ ◆ ◆

Becoming Lydia's lover was a path that, a year earlier, Kate could never have possibly imagined taking. But with Lydia it seemed as natural and pure as the wind ruffling the leaves in the trees. Ever since she crawled out of a frozen Lake Superior, Kate had felt off-kilter, as though the pieces of the world didn't quite fit together properly. The moment she kissed Lydia, it was as if the world shifted slightly and those pieces all clicked into place. Being with her made life brighter, more vibrant, more defined. Suddenly, Kate's past didn't matter anymore, and she stopped worrying about the future. Nothing existed but the present: the smell of bread baking from the café across the street, the sound of a violin floating under the door, Lydia's hair rippling like cool, dark water across the pillow. Kate's heart, so restless in the past, was somehow stilled by Lydia.

As spring passed into summer they took up daily residency on the Left Bank, and although there were many other artists working there, Lydia always drew a crowd. Kate bought a beautiful purple blanket and matching purple pillows that she laid out on the ground, inviting people from Lydia's crowd to sit while she read their palms – for a small fee, of course. They lived on wine and bread, spent days on end speaking to each other only in their pathetic grade-school French, walked barefoot through rivers when it got too hot, and bought rusty second-hand bikes on which they raced each other around the city at night, the headlights from the cars reflecting off the gleaming chrome of their fenders.

One night, they snuck into the backyard garden of a wealthy French banker whose palm Kate had read earlier that day, and made love on Kate's purple blanket while the banker and his wife entertained friends inside the house. Afterward, they smoked cigarettes and looked up at the moon, as round and bright as a crystal ball in the dark night sky, breathing in the heady fragrance of evening primrose and listening to the sweet, melodic jazz floating down from the dinner party.

"If this were a movie, the credits would be rolling right now," Lydia said, resting her head against Kate's shoulder. Kate could almost see the words scrolling above their heads, the music swelling in its grand finale as the banker showed his guests to the door.

"Turn right here, Nana," London says, and Kate realizes they have arrived in Duluth, Thunder Bay's American twin tucked into the westernmost crook of Lake Superior, smaller and yet somehow seeming more like a big city.

When they check in at the Radisson, the teenaged male desk clerk eyes London with a look that Kate remembers, a look that fills her with a sort of quiet sadness for the past. Then they head up to their room with suitcases that London has produced from the trunk of the car. Kate doesn't remember packing one, but when she opens it up, there it all is: her toothbrush, her nightgown, even her bathing suit. "I guess I knew we would be staying somewhere with a pool."

London twists nervously at a piece of her hair. "Nana, this was just your stuff from the hospital," she says. "They had to change you out of the bathing suit."

"Oh," Kate says, for once so entirely confused that she's unable to hide it. "Well, then."

But London doesn't seem to notice. She stands awkwardly by the door for a few minutes, tracing her finger along the edge of the closet. Kate worries she's about to ask something about this mysterious hospital visit. "Would it be okay if I go and walk around a little?" London asks instead, shoving her hands into her pockets.

"Yes, of course," Kate says, because what else is she going to say? She is beginning to realize how little agency she has in this entire adventure, and she wonders if the Kate of a few hours ago knew that this was going to happen when she agreed to it.

After London leaves, Kate searches through her suitcase for clues to why she might have been in the hospital – although her body is already giving her clues of its own. She feels sore in places that she didn't even know could be sore, and the pain is getting worse. She finds a bottle of prescription painkillers, prescribed to Katherine Parker on July 20, 2012, by some doctor named Liston at the Thunder Bay General Hospital. July 20. Kate has no idea what the date is today, so she reaches into her pocket in search of receipts, finally finding one from the gas station in Grand Marais. July 22. She was in the hospital two days ago. No wonder she is still in pain.

She takes two of the painkillers, then she turns on the television. It takes her a few minutes to figure out how to change the channel, but she is sure this is normal. All old people have trouble using remote controls. She looks at the clock, determined to keep track of how long London has been gone. It's seven. Have they had dinner yet? She doesn't feel hungry, so perhaps they stopped somewhere when they arrived in Duluth. This reminds her of the sandwich that is still in her purse. The purple goo is oily and smells strongly of something that she can't quite put her finger on, but she can smell it on her breath, too. She flushes the remnants of the sandwich down the toilet and wipes down the things in her purse as best she can. By the time she's finished she's nauseated from the smell, but the painkillers have kicked in so at least she's not hurting like she was before. She checks the clock again: 7:23.

She thinks about calling Nicki, but something holds her back – no, she needs to see this journey through.

She lies back on the bed and flicks through the channels. She can't seem to find anything except for local news. They even get the feed from the local station in Thunder Bay. "The worst local television news of all time," she can remember her other daughter saying once. Kate has a vague notion that the other one is back in Thunder Bay, too – she can't picture her, but she can hear her voice. Did she come back because of something to do with her hospital stay? It seems rather arrogant to think so.

The other one. She's been reduced to calling her own daughter "the other one." It's not that she occupies any less space in Kate's heart, but she is not as present in her thoughts. Nicki is there, every day. Her sister is not, and that is her choice. Kate can't remember the last time the other one was home. It's hard for her to even remember the last time she called. Kate knows nothing about her life; she has never invited Kate to visit, and never provides many details. Kate doesn't even fully understand her job, although she is proud of her, no matter what she does. Of course she is proud of her. Of course.

Serafina. Her name is Serafina. Finn. How could she ever forget that?

From the time Finn was young, Kate saw so much of herself in her. She seemed so restless, so lost, so out of place in Thunder Bay, and in her own family. For a while Kate tried to be her ally, her co-conspirator, the one she could rely on to understand how she felt. On Saturday nights they would sit in the kitchen at Victor Street and play Scrabble, and Kate would play words that she knew wouldn't be in the dictionary – she knew Finn loved words, and Kate preferred to foster that love and her imagination, and build Finn's confidence, rather than win.

"Murple? Come on, Mom. That sounds like something from Dr. Seuss."

"It *did* originate with Dr. Seuss, but now it's a real word. The English language evolves, you know."

"It's not a real word just because you say it's a real word."

"Sure it is. I bet you even know what it means, if you think about it."

"A colour that's right on the edge between maroon and purple?"

"See? If my super-smart daughter knows what it means, it *must* be real."

They had so much fun. But Kate assumed that given the choice, her teenaged daughter would rather be out with friends or with a boy than at home with her mother. It was only natural. It was the way things should be. Then one Saturday night, right before they sat down to play, Finn got a phone call. She pulled the phone into the hall while Kate made tea, but her furtive whispering carried through the doorway.

"It sounds like fun," Kate could hear Finn say. "But I think I'm just going to stay in tonight." She paused. "Yes, *again*. I just don't want to go out, okay?"

Kate felt her heart sink. All this time, she had been hoping that she was providing a safe haven for Finn from an inhospitable world, a temporary shelter she could retreat to when things got rough. It never occurred to her that Finn would settle into that shelter and make herself at home there. When Finn came back in, Kate had put the Scrabble board away. "I don't really feel like Scrabble tonight," she said, concentrating on pouring her tea into the cup. "I think I'm just going to go to bed early and read my book."

Finn stared at her. "But we always play Scrabble."

"Sometimes it's good to do different things, Serafina." Kate went to the fridge and got out the milk. She didn't turn around until she knew that Finn was gone. They never played Scrabble again.

It was for her own good. Kate had wanted Finn to leave, it's true. But she never imagined that she would leave with such finality. She never imagined that she would leave for good.

So, Kate will not call either of them. Nor will she call her husband. She can't bear to see the disappointment in his eyes, the irritation that he tries to hide, the sadness at what his wife is becoming. Most of all, she can't bear the knowledge that she is the one causing him this pain. Nor will she call the boy – Shawn (she remembers, and lets herself revel momentarily in the small victory of the remembering) – who would surely drop everything to dash across the border and rescue her as if she were a damsel in distress. Who continued to carry the weight of the world on his shoulders long after he was in a position to put it down and rest. She is glad for the way that things turned out with Shawn – having him in her life was a reminder that she was still capable of taking risks, of reaching for a life less ordinary. Still, she can't bring him into this. He has done too much for her already, and more than she deserves.

No. She will stay here in her hotel room in Duluth and keep this vague promise that she has made to London (though now she's not even sure that she's actually made one in the first place, but just trusting her intuition). She is tired of doing the right thing all the time. She is tired of living a life without adventure. Perhaps she wouldn't feel this way if she had never known anything different, if she had lived the staid and quiet life in Thunder Bay the way she was supposed to, the way her family thinks she did. She doesn't know what they think of her now, but she does know that there are quite a few things they would be surprised to discover about her, things she keeps in her heart like a song that only she knows the words to, that she can hum to herself when things get difficult, when she can't remember someone's name or how to use the telephone, when she is feeling lost or hopeless or stupid. These are the memories that she is most terrified of losing. The memories she has no photos of, the memories that are her only connection to the brave and wonderful person she used to be – the person who sang onstage with the house band at a jazz club in Paris because their front woman was too drunk to perform, the person who climbed Mount McKay in a party dress, the person who jumped the fence at the airport to lie underneath a plane as it took off. If she loses them, there will be no one who can remind her of what she's lost, and that brave and wonderful person will be gone forever.

7:31. Has London been gone too long already? Should she go look for her? She changes the channel again, and something catches her eye. Video footage of a waterfall with something going over it. A barrel. A barrel going over Kakabeka Falls.

It comes back to her then. The water, clear and swirling and magical. Letting her hand drag through it, the feel of the pull on her fingers. She had never seen the river that close, at that distance from the beach, where the current picked up and the surface was scuffed with foam – how different its contours appeared now from moment to moment, its rhythm always in flux, its depth like infinite layers of something papery and transparent, like tissue wrapping a present. She watched leaves toss on its surface, tree branches, flower petals, what appeared to be the wrapper from someone's chocolate bar, and something else, a flash of silver, or grey, something alive being propelled to the edge – all of it moving with the water, helping define its shape. Everything looked so peaceful, submitting their will to the river before reaching the edge. Then: nothing. They were simply gone. Where did they go? What lay beyond the edge of that river? No one knows.

Except Kate. Kate knows.

Falling, falling. Kate smiles a little secret smile, in part because she's remembering what the falling felt like, and in part for remembering at all. Then she feels the painkillers kick in and push her over the edge to sleep.

TWENTY-FIVE

T wo nights ago, a woman came into the hotel bar and punched Adam Pelley in the arm. The worst part is it didn't even remotely faze him. It's as if he just expects strange women to punch him in the arm in bars now, even in a tiny buttfuck-nowheretown like Duluth, Minnesota.

"Adam fucking Pelley," she said. "That's for that show you did last year on shark finning. I cried for, like, three hours."

Her hair was wet and pulled into a bun, and she smelled vaguely of chlorine, probably from the hotel pool. She ordered a vodka and tonic and crossed and uncrossed her legs. Adam took her to his room before *The Daily Show* went to commercial, like he did with any other woman he'd met since his divorce, even though something about the encounter felt off. Normally, women are tripping over their panties once they find out he's on television, imagining Kardashian-packed parties and red carpets lit up with paparazzi flashbulbs. Not Yasmine. Yasmine wanted to fuck him and be done with it. Or maybe she wanted to fuck him and also cause him a little bodily harm, but that was it. Afterward, she drank his whisky and asked about the shark. That was the other thing. The other women, they cared about the television show, but not the sharks.

In retrospect, he should have known better, but at the time Adam was sure he was being paranoid, that there was nothing really different about her at all. In the few months since he and Jessica got divorced, he has slept with a lot of women, and not all of them were shallow gold diggers. Some of them he would classify more as groupies – eco-sluts, his *Marine Life* cameraman, Mark, calls them, although in reality they are usually just college girls looking for a certain whale-saving cachet. But the one thing they had in common was that none of them really cared about *why* Adam was on television, only that he *was* on television – even if *Marine Life* airs on a station that no one has ever heard of, shoe-horned in on Sunday mornings between a talk show about local politics and a show called *Nothing But Trailers* that actually shows nothing but movie trailers. Adam could have been a news anchor or a soap opera actor or a judge on a reality-TV show. He could have hosted the goddamned *Price Is Right*.

"But how did the shark get into the lake in the first place?" Yasmine kept asking, swirling the whisky in the little plastic hotel cup, her knees pulled up to her chest on the flower-patterned duvet.

"You'll just have to watch the show to find out," Adam said. He was trying to sound coy, but really he just wanted her to leave so he could take a shower.

"My boyfriend loves sharks," she said, settling back against the pillow. "Wait until I tell him." Burying her cherry-painted toes beneath the duvet, digging herself in.

Ever since his night with Yasmine, Adam has been sitting in this hotel bar. What he *should* be doing is going back to L.A. and doing research for the special they're pitching on manta ray rehab in Monterey for *Animal Planet*. He should just leave. Get away from the lake shark, Yasmine, everything. Get away from fucking Shark Week.

Shark Week: one of those necessary evils that feeds one part of Adam's career while completely cannibalizing the rest. Before Shark Week, if you had a nature show you were lucky if you got a time slot on some public-access channel. But then shark docs were in demand and you just couldn't pump them out fast enough. And that itself was the problem: suddenly everyone with a hand-held camera and a wetsuit started making shark docs and making them poorly, relying on bad science and shock value and calling them things like *Monster Sharks!* or *Killer Sharks!* or *Sharkageddon!* Of course ratings went through the roof; people would have Shark Week parties and invent drinking games and make brackets like it was some kind of sporting event. And now what Adam thought was the point of Shark Week was no longer the point of Shark Week. People weren't learning to love sharks. They were learning to see them as monster freaks of the week.

And still Mark and Adam were out there every year tracking down this shark or that shark, trying to make the hunt sound sensational while at the same time injecting some real science into their shows. But people didn't want real science. They wanted to see an animatronic shark take a bite out of a minivan, or a guy on a kneeboard trail behind a speedboat in chummed waters. They wanted prehistoric myths, they wanted death and destruction and mysterious circumstances. They wanted fucking lake sharks.

What Adam wants is another drink. But this bartender, she hates him. Her name is Lisa, and beautiful Lisa will not give him the time of day.

"Hey, Lisa," Adam says. "Any chance of a refill?"

"Any chance you're going to actually tip me?"

"Don't be mad. I'm donating your tips to starving children in Africa." Lisa just rolls her eyes, wings a pint of beer at him so the foam spills onto his pants.

"So what are you going to call your show?" Yasmine had asked him. "*Monsters in the Lake* or something?"

"*Monsters in the Lake,*" Adam repeated. "Has a nice ring to it, actually."

She shook her head. "A fucking lake shark. I can't even believe it."

The fucking lake shark. The reason he's here in this backwater town in this shitty landlocked state, no salt water for thousands of miles. A colleague of his in Canada had called him up saying he had been gathering reports of a bull shark that had somehow gotten off course and ended up in the Great Lakes, managing to adapt its saline secretions and reverse the effects of osmosis in order to stay alive. Adam did some research and found bull shark sightings all the way up the Mississippi River and into Lake Michigan, then right up to Duluth, where it appeared weak, likely exhausted, and on the verge of death. He got some footage and sent in a proposal to Discovery Channel for a live shark rescue during Shark Week, and they ate it up like a fat kid at a buffet. It was new, it was mysterious, it was emotional. It was going to make Adam a million dollars.

"Maybe I'll just call it *The Fucking Lake Shark,*" he said. "That's kind of edgy, right? People will love it."

Yasmine leaned forward so that her unbuttoned shirt fell open and he could see her entire left breast, in all its goddamn beautiful glory. "Well, you know," she said, "people love anything to do with fucking."

"Mmm-hmm," said Adam, sliding his hand under her shirt. But she pushed it away and took another sip of her whisky, glaring at him. Yasmine had turned out to be somewhat unpredictable.

Someone else who is proving to be unpredictable is Lisa. Adam can feel her eyes on him, which is strange because he doesn't think she has looked at him once in four days. He turns and sees her leaning against the wall by the cash register, watching him and filing her nails, which he's pretty sure has got to be a health violation.

"What's your deal, anyway?" she asks, blowing on the tip of her nail.

"My deal?"

Her tongue darts out and licks the edge of the file. "Where are you from?"

"Why are you suddenly so interested?"

"I don't know." She moves on to her thumbnail with the wet file. "I'm bored."

"No offence," Adam says, cringing at the sound of the file against her nail, "but it seems like you're always bored."

She shrugs. "It's Duluth. I mean, you're here, you know." She tucks the file away in her apron, then leans in towards him. Her face is very close to his; he can smell the cinnamon gum on her breath. "Why don't you buy me a drink and we can talk about it?"

"Oh, I get it. Now you want something."

"Fuck you," she says. She turns her back to him, pulls out a rag from the pocket of her apron that her nail file just disappeared into, and starts rubbing down the back bar. He can see her shoulder muscles working underneath the thin material of her blouse. He runs his finger over his wedding ring, which he still can't bring himself to take off.

"Are you here until close?" he asks.

She doesn't turn around. "Do you see anyone else here to relieve me?"

"Can I meet you after? There's something I want to show you."

She laughs. "Oh, I'm sure."

"No, seriously."

She doesn't say anything for a few minutes. Adam watches the Twins game on the screen behind him and finishes the last of his drink. He's thinking about ordering a whisky when she says, "I'll meet you in the lobby at ten after one."

"Great," Adam says, trying not to sound surprised. He drops a ten on the bar and leaves before she can change her mind. He is halfway across the lobby before he realizes he doesn't really have anywhere else to go.

At five to one, Adam goes back down to the lobby. The lights in the bar are already off, so he sits on a bench across from the front desk to wait for Lisa. At the other end of the lobby, a janitor pushes a floor polisher in a slow path in front of the elevators.

"Hey," a voice says. "Adam?"

He turns around, smiling, expecting Lisa. Instead, it is a young girl, fifteen or sixteen, with a *Teen Vogue* pout, rebel-pink streaks in her hair, and a clipboard under her arm, staring at him with an expression of earnest adoration. *Great, just great,* he thinks. He takes in a breath, composing himself. "Hi there," he says.

"I can't believe I'm really here!" The girl sits down next to him on the bench, her eyes wide and bright. "It was the craziest thing, I went to visit my grandmother this afternoon and she woke up right when I walked in, and I was like, okay, clearly this was meant to be, right? It was like, karma or something repaying me for everything I've been through, you know what I mean?"

"Well, that's good to hear," Adam says, cranking up the television charm. "Adam Pelley. Nice to meet you." He holds out his hand.

The girl's eyes transform from bright to baffled as she looks down at his hand. Maybe kids don't shake hands anymore, he thinks. Maybe a fist bump would have been more demographic-appropriate.

"I'm *London*," she says slowly, emphasizing her name, as if she is talking to someone who doesn't speak the language.

Wonderful, thinks Adam. *She sent a fan letter and got a publicity photo in return, and now she thinks we're best friends.* "Great," he says. "Always nice to meet a fan." He pulls out his phone, hoping she will take the hint and just go away.

"London *Parker-Stewart*." She gazes at him so hopefully that he begins to feel uncomfortable. "From Thunder Bay." Then, in a smaller, quieter voice, she says, "I'm Ponyo."

"Okay, then," Adam says, nodding. He gives her what he hopes is an end-of-conversation-type smile.

Her face collapses into an expression of such crushing disappointment that for a moment Adam wonders if her name really should mean something to him. He sees her lip start to wobble. *Oh great, she's going to cry.* He does a furtive sweep of the room to see if anyone is watching.

Then she takes in a deep breath and her face changes. "You're here for the shark rescue, right?" she says, crossing her arms over her chest. "I'd like to volunteer. I could help you with some of your equipment, or running tests, or something . . ."

Adam sighs inaudibly. She must have seen him on the news. He knew that news clip was a bad idea, but his publicist said that they needed to drum up some local support. "Actually, London, usually the volunteers just do onshore stuff. Getting coffee for the crew, that kind of thing."

"What kind of coffee do you like?" she asks. "I think there's probably a Starbucks around here somewhere, and I know there's a Caribou Coffee down in Canal Park. I've never had their coffee but I know their hot chocolate is really good. I can do anything. I'm just here with my grandmother, she won't mind." From the mouth of a more, well, *American* sixteen-year-old, her words might have come across as flirty, even sexual, but she seems so much younger than he remembers sixteen-year-olds being, so much more innocent.

"Actually, I don't think we'll be going out tomorrow," Adam says. "High winds."

"Oh." She uncrosses her arms and makes a little note on her clipboard. A fucking *clipboard*. Who, in the age of smartphones and tablets, laptops and iPods, who on earth carries a fucking *clipboard*?

But there it is, sturdy and utilitarian, with its rigid brown back, reams of three-hole-punched blue-lined paper clipped under the stiff, shiny metal clip. She even has a pen, a straight-up *pen*, tied with a piece of string and hanging from a hole in the top.

"What about the day after that?" she asks. "I'm really flexible."

I bet you are, thinks Adam before he mentally slaps himself. "Probably not, London."

"The wind's going down to ten knots tomorrow."

"Well, honey, there are these phenomena called seiches that happen after a high wind? It's kind of like when water sloshes back and forth in a bathtub but on a way bigger scale." He mimes a pendulum swing with his hands. "They're pretty complicated to explain. But they make it really dangerous for little boats like mine."

"Actually, seiches resulting from northwest winds on Lake Superior only last for around eight hours," says London. "If the wind dies down by morning, the water should have calmed enough to go out the next day."

What the hell. "How do you know that?"

She glares at him. "I'm not an idiot."

"Well, still," he says, watching as she makes another note on her clipboard. "What are you writing on there?" he asks, leaning over.

"Nothing," she says, moving her clipboard from his sightline.

"Stop writing things down." Adam doesn't know why, but suddenly this kid with a clipboard scares him more than any high-heeled executive with an artillery of technology tucked into her Chanel bag. This kid, she is *securing* things. None of her notes are going to blow away. Her pen will never get lost. She is going to change the world, one sheet of paper at a time.

"There must be something we can do while we wait. Some kind of research?"

"I don't think so." Adam is suddenly tired of this conversation. He checks the door to the bar, making sure Lisa isn't standing there watching him chat up a teenager. "All the research is done."

"What about publicity?"

"No."

"Do you need any kind of production help, with the cameras? For the show?"

"There's not going to *be* any *fucking* show," he says through gritted teeth. "Okay? Do you get it? No. Fucking. Show."

London looks so stunned that he has to avert his eyes to keep himself together.

"But what about the shark rescue?" she asks in a voice so small and sad it almost seems like a joke, a cruel joke that someone is playing to fuck with him even more. "What about counteracting all the shark fearmongering in the mainstream media?"

"No show, no shark rescue," he says. "Now leave me the fuck alone."

London stares at him, and in her eyes is pure, unadulterated disillusionment. Then she turns around and walks out of the lobby.

Never meet your heroes, kid, he thinks, leaning his head back against the wall.

"What was that all about?" Lisa asks, coming around a corner.

Adam jumps up. "Nothing," he says. "Let's go." He ushers Lisa out the side door, just praying that he is going in the opposite direction of London. As it is, he knows he is stuck with that look, that goddamn heartbreaker of a look, haunting his fucking dreams for the rest of his sorry, pathetic life.

◆ ◆ ◆

Adam's boat, the *Rum Runner*, is a two-level cabin cruiser with the cockpit on the lower level. He and the *Rum Runner* have been together so long, longer than any other relationship he's had in his life. She's like a younger sibling that you love all of the time and are annoyed with most of the time. She has never behaved properly for him, and she will probably go to her grave giving him grief.

But there's no other boat he would rather work on, no other thing he loves in this world. Stupid, he knows. A boat. He wonders if the boat is feeling the same way he is, a fish out of water, or a fish in the wrong kind of water.

"The *Rum Runner*," Lisa says. "Why?"

"I was eighteen when I bought her," he says. "I liked rum. I thought it was cool."

"It's kind of cool," she says. She reaches out and touches the side, then draws her hand back.

It's odd being out here at night, Adam thinks as he navigates out of the marina. He's not a stranger to night boating, but he is a stranger to this harbour and he's distracted by the fresh water lapping at the side of the boat. It might seem crazy, but fresh water just *sounds* different from salt water, although once they are out in the open waters of Lake Superior, they might as well be in the ocean.

The wind has picked up, and when Lisa eventually makes her way down to the cockpit, she is shivering. "I have some jackets inside," he says. "Hold this." He puts her hands on the wheel and heads into the cabin. When he comes back, he tries to pass her a jacket, but she doesn't move. She just stares at her hands on the wheel, her face tense, awestruck.

"You just left me with it," she says.

"Uh, yeah," he says, putting the jacket over her shoulders. "We're in the middle of the lake. You're not going to hit anything."

She stares at him, eyes wide, reminding him, like a punch in the gut, of that girl in the lobby. "But what if I did hit something and destroyed your boat and we both drowned?"

Oh great. Why is he only attracted to women who are afraid of drowning? "That wouldn't happen," he says. Gently, he peels her fingers back from the wheel and places her hands at her sides. She slips her arms into the sleeves of the jacket, which is a thousand times too big for her, her hands disappearing into the cuffs.

She moves closer to him, looking at the wheel with a mixture of desire and fear. He's got her now, the way a dealer has an addict. It's not why he brought her out here, but right now he'll take it. He steps aside and she reaches out. The *Rum Runner* responds with a shudder and a sigh, which is better than he'll ever get from either of them.

Later, on the upper deck, Adam gazes out over the water. What if there really *are* sharks out there? he thinks. What if there's a whole species of freshwater sharks that they just haven't discovered yet? If they were going to be anywhere, they'd be in Superior, this ten-thousand-year-old basin full of three quadrillion gallons of meltwater, likely swimming around Isle Royale, the Graveyard of the Great Lakes, feasting on the bodies of sailors who never made it to the surface. Superior is infamous for never giving up her dead. According to Wikipedia, that is.

He could find it. If it was out there, he could. What would Jessica think then, after all those things she said about integrity and trust, about Adam not being the man she thought he was? Maybe she would leave the family farm in southern Indiana and come back to the water with him. Her parents always thought she would drown, that was what they were worried about: not whether Adam would make her happy, but that by being around water all the time, she was increasing her odds of drowning. Her parents had never even seen the ocean. To them, it was just a big, salty death hole waiting to claim their first-born daughter. Which ended up being how they saw Adam, too.

There was a moment, back in the hotel room, when things with Yasmine changed. He had been avoiding her questions, trying to get her to fuck him again, when suddenly she said, "You made the whole thing up about the lake shark to get a show on Shark Week, didn't you?"

"That's ridiculous," Adam said. Outside the room, he could hear a woman arguing with a hotel employee about whether she had reserved a king or a queen bed. "Why would I reserve a queen-sized bed?" the woman was yelling. "I mean, look at us? Do you think we fit in a queen-sized bed?" Inside the room, the air became heavier. He swirled the whisky in his glass, focusing his eyes on the liquid. He didn't dare raise them in case the truth was written all over his face, which he was sure it was.

Of course there was no shark. There was no colleague in Canada, no research on bull shark sightings either. All it had taken was a few big words, a few fancy numbers, some made-up first-hand testimonials from people whose names he had gotten out of a phone book. Later, when the search came up empty, they could frame it as a mystery, add in some CGI re-enactments, a few dramatic shots of Adam forlornly staring out over the lake.

"What did you do, pay all those people on the news to say they had seen it?" Yasmine asked. "That must have been hard."

It had been pretty easy, actually. The first person only wanted a new windshield for his snowmobile. The second took four hundred in cash and a bottle of vodka. They were more excited about being on the news than anything else, saying things like, "We were out in our boat when we seen it. Grandpa thought it was some new kind of bass, but bass ain't got no head like that."

One of them must have talked. The only other people who knew were Mark and his publicist, and they wouldn't tell anyone, their careers were riding on it, too. It had been two years since Adam had had anything picked up by Shark Week, and people at the other stations were starting to forget he existed at all. At first he thought it was a good thing: it was time for him to spend more time on his research. But after a few months, something happened that he's sure, deep down, he always knew would happen if he quit television: he got fucking *bored*. All those years being so self-righteous, pretending he hated being on TV and how it was beneath him, and it turned out that it was the television part that got his fire going, it was the television part that he loved.

"You're crazy," he said to Yasmine.

"Am I? I talked to seven different marine biologists, and they all think your data is fraudulent."

"Fraudulent?" He was still staring at the swirling liquid, and he felt each syllable fall out of his mouth and sink to the bottom of the glass. "Wait, what?" he said suddenly, looking up at her. "How did you get my data?"

"I have my sources," she said. It was only then that Adam recognized her, from some weekly piece-of-trash news show on one of the 24-hour news stations. He felt sick, but he downed the rest of his whisky anyway. The trick is to remain calm in these sorts of situations. Not let on that you're dying a little inside.

"Get out," he said, his voice low and dark. So much for remaining calm. Yasmine smiled at him, a knowing smile, a cat with a fucking mouse in her mouth.

Lake Superior seems calm from a distance, but Adam knows that can be deceiving. Just like the surface can be deceiving, all 31,700 square miles of it. What Adam knows about Lake Superior: the Ojibwe call it *gichigami*, which means "big water," and there is enough water in it to cover the entire land mass of North and South America to a depth of one foot. It is the largest lake in the world by surface area, and is fed by over two hundred rivers. Its temperature below 110 fathoms is consistently 39 degrees. What Adam knows about Lake Superior is the same thing everyone else with an internet connection knows. Which is to say, statistics, factoids, trivia. He doesn't know the duration of a Lake Superior seiche after a northwesterly wind. He doesn't know Lake Superior. He probably never will.

Adam has spent his life surrounded by oceans, by tides and salt, the Gulf Stream and the Equatorial Countercurrent, trade winds and westerlies. Who knows what would happen if he suddenly submerged himself into a freshwater ecosystem? Maybe he would bloat up and die, the way a mackerel would, or a tuna. The way a shark would. Of course the way a shark would.

But still, if it was out there, he could find it. He is Adam fucking Pelley. He could adapt.

TWENTY-SIX

S hawn wakes up and he is alone.

He can't remember another time he was alone in his own home for an entire night. The room is bright and cold, the air conditioner cranked up and the blinds wide open. Katriina must close them every night before they go to bed. What else does she do that he doesn't notice? What other kind of household magic does she produce behind the scenes with a little smoke and mirrors? He had never thought of Katriina as a deceptive person until last night. Now, it's as if everything in their life has been operating on a frequency he can't quite tune to, as if even the simple act of opening and closing the blinds has become layered with meaning.

He opens his leg out across the divide between the two sides of their bed, feeling the coolness of the sheets on her side. Then he shifts himself until he is spread-eagle across the entire mattress, marvelling at how he ever slept any other way, how the bed could even fit two people without them accidentally smothering each other in their sleep. He listens for the sound of Petey, their earlier riser, tramping down the stairs. But Petey and his older brother are tucked away safely at Victor Street, where he dropped them off last night, far away from their parents, who, as far as Shawn is concerned, have absolutely no right to be parents at all.

Katriina didn't come home last night. Not that he thought she would. After he left Victor Street, he drove his rental car back to the Paulsson house and sat outside in the car, watching Katriina through the windows as she walked from room to room in her blouse and bare legs. He told himself that he was just making sure she didn't cut herself again, but deep down he knew he was spying on her. Hoping to see her do something – anything – that would give him a clue as to what the hell was going on in her head. When he first saw her cuts at the Paulsson house, he had been too shocked to ask her why she would do that to herself. He also couldn't bear to hear her say the words out loud; in that moment, anything she said would have felt like a betrayal. But after he left and the shock turned to anger, all the unanswered questions began to eat away at him, driving him crazy. Compelling him to come back and look for answers. But Katriina did nothing but curl up on the couch, staring into space, until Shawn finally gave up and drove away. While he drove, he wondered if she would call, ask him to come pick her up and take her home. He thought of what he would say: if she loved that house so much she should just stay there. That house where she hid all her craziness. That house where she spilled her own goddamn blood, the cupboards papered with evidence of her breakdown. He thinks now about all the strange "quirks" he'd dismissed: her manic mornings up at five to make casseroles for the week, the way she constantly recited mantras to herself under her breath, that stupid elastic around her wrist. When he had asked what other secrets she was keeping from him, he hadn't realized the biggest one had been staring him right in the face the whole time.

And for how long? He remembers an afternoon the previous summer, when they had taken Tommy and Petey to Hazelwood Lake for a picnic. The boys were in the water, and Katriina and

Shawn lay on a blanket on the grass, drinking beer from a cooler and snacking on kettle corn she had bought at the farmers' market. She was tucked under his arm with her head against his chest, one leg thrown casually across his shins, and they were talking about the weather, a movie they wanted to see, how Petey wanted them to get a dog – nothing about the restaurant, or houses, or the Parkers. They were just lying there talking about nothing. Shawn couldn't remember ever feeling more at peace. The warmth of the sun on his face. The feeling of his wife's soft hair on his chest, the scent of her shampoo like a forest after the rain. The laughter of his children as they splashed through the water, shooting each other with water guns, making happy childhood memories. The kind of perfect day that people like Shawn just weren't supposed to have.

Then Tommy and Petey snuck up and dumped a bucket of lake water on them. Katriina jumped up with a scream, then, after shaking herself off like a puppy, raised her arms high over her head and roared like a monster. "I'm coming to get you!" she growled, grabbing Tommy and carrying him over her shoulder while she chased Petey to the edge of the water. "I will sacrifice you both to the lake monster!" She tried to throw Tommy into the lake, but the momentum knocked her in, too, and as she fell she grabbed Petey's arm and they all toppled into the lake with a monumental splash.

The three of them emerged from the water laughing, Katriina's hair in wet strands around her face, mascara running down her cheeks. Shawn ran down to the shore and the boys started screaming, "Slay the lake monster! Slay the lake monster!" as they pulled him in, too, all of them splashing together in the water until the sun got low and their fingers started to prune. On the way home they stopped at Merla Mae for ice cream, and while the kids chased each other through the parking lot, Katriina and Shawn sat wrapped in a blanket in the open trunk of the SUV, Katriina trying to catch the drips from her chocolate dip before they fell to her lap. Shawn remembers her reaching up to wipe a drop of ice cream from the corner of his mouth, the touch of her hand making him shiver, the sparkle in her eyes reminding him of the Katriina he fell in love with, so self-possessed and beautiful and ready to take on the world with him.

Does he have to parse this memory for telltale signs now? Little indications that their happiness was all a facade? *What did I miss?* Were there red marks on her legs, or puffiness under her eyes, or a vacant stare when he turned his head? Some dark subtext in her musing on the shape of the clouds, in her indecision over what kind of ice cream to buy? This is what makes him angriest – she's made him second-guess all the good times, all his favourite memories.

She's made him feel like their life together has been a lie.

Shawn is downstairs in the kitchen having his morning coffee when Katriina finally comes home. Her hair is pulled back into a ponytail, and she is wearing the same clothes she had on the night before. Her face is bare of makeup. She looks tired, but also more relaxed than he has seen her in weeks.

"Are the boys still at my parents'?" she asks.

"They're at Victor Street."

"Oh. Okay."

Neither of them moves. He knows he should go over to her, put his arms around her, tell her everything is going to be okay. But it's as though the distance between them, the mere length of their kitchen, is impossible to bridge. Instead, he takes a sip of his coffee. It needs more sugar, but he drinks it anyway, not wanting to turn away from Katriina in case she disappears.

"I thought I should get some of my things," she says eventually.

"What things? Why?"

She reaches into her purse and pulls something out. "Here," she says, holding out her hand.

So she's making him go to her. He moves slowly around the garbage bag still in the middle of the floor. In her palm is an elastic band – the one she wears around her wrist, Shawn assumes. "Why are you giving this to me?" he asks, staring down at the elastic without making a move to take it from her hand.

"I thought you should have it."

"Katriina –"

"I want a divorce."

Shawn slowly raises his head. "You want a divorce?"

"Yes." She pauses. "Don't you?"

He collapses back against the kitchen table. *I think my marriage might be over*, he had told Finn last night. But now he realizes he didn't mean it. "No," he says. "Of course not."

Katriina narrows her eyes at him. "I just think it's for the best."

There is a sudden perceptible shift – inside him, inside Katriina, in the tension in the room. The balance is tipping. He can feel himself losing control. *Just pretend this isn't happening.*

"We should really get those cuts on your legs checked out," he says, his voice hoarse. "You don't want to get an infection."

"Please listen to me, Shawn."

He can't breathe. *Just pretend, and it will stop.* "I can take care of you," he says, touching her face.

She flinches away from his hand. "I don't need you to take care of me."

You can fix this. "We just need some Polysporin. Some rubbing alcohol. Everything will be just fine."

"Shawn, your wife just cut up her legs with a box cutter. Do you really think that everything is *just fine?*"

Shawn starts pacing around the kitchen, his hands clasped on the back of his neck. "No, I don't think everything is *just fine.*" He knows that getting angry is not the way to make things better, but he can't stop himself. It's like a freight train running straight through his heart. "I think things are actually really shitty right now. I think we have major problems with our marriage. I think you need to stop keeping things from me. And I think you need professional help for . . . whatever the fuck this is." He flings the elastic band on the table.

Katriina walks over and picks it up, holding it like a baby bird in the palm of her hand. "And what about you, Shawn?" she asks quietly, still focused on the elastic. "What do you think you need to do?"

"I . . . I don't know. Whatever you want me to do."

She is silent for a moment, rubbing the elastic between her fingers. Then she raises her eyes to meet his. "I want you to take that job in Ottawa."

Shawn's whole body jerks. "What?"

"I want you to take that job in Ottawa," Katriina repeats. "I want us to leave Thunder Bay. I want us to leave the Parkers."

Leave the Parkers. The words hit him like a shot to the stomach. He sits down at the table and drops his head into his hands. He remembers his first month at Victor Street, him with one foot out the door, listening to the call of the train running by the house. Playing Parker for a week, a month, six months. A year. Ten years. If he left now, wouldn't it all have been for nothing? Wouldn't he just have been playing Parker for twenty-five years? Sometimes he wonders when will he have done enough to feel like a real Parker. He has been there for the birth of four children. A wedding. A cancer scare. A difficult goodbye. An epic plunge over a waterfall. But is it the big moments that make up a family? Or is it the quiet conversations on the front porch over a hand of cards, playing Star Wars in the backyard, the mundane arguments, the shared meals and baseball games and cups of tea with a shot of whisky? He doesn't know, so he has to be there for all of them, collect them all and hope in the end they add up to something that feels like a real family.

He lifts his head and looks at Katriina. "I can't do that."

"I see," she says. She lets the elastic drop on the table. "You know, for someone who's so devoted to *family*, you seem awfully willing to let your own fall apart."

Shawn feels his anger return, bubbling up like acid in his throat. "Why does it have to be one or the other? Why can't we all just live our lives together?"

"Because we *can't*, Shawn. We've tried, and it isn't working."

"I actually thought it was working pretty well. Up until now." Shawn gets up from the table and slams his coffee mug into the sink. Then he picks up the carafe and dumps the rest of the coffee down the drain. "You know what it seems like to me? All this drama, the cutting, this stupid ultimatum? You're jealous. I've been busy focusing on the Parkers and you're just trying to get attention."

Katriina stares at him incredulously. "Do you think this all happened overnight?"

"It certainly seems that way." He turns back to the sink and fills the carafe with water and dish soap and begins scrubbing violently.

"That's because you haven't been paying attention!"

"You haven't let me!" He spins around to face her, the wet dishcloth in his hands. "You shut me out of everything, Katriina. How am I supposed to know what's going on with you?"

"You didn't want to know what was going on!" She breathes in and crosses the room to stand in front of him. Gently she takes the dishcloth from him and places it in the sink, then holds both his hands in hers. "You wanted everything to be *just fine*, Shawn. And so that's what I gave you."

It's true, he realizes, with a sickening moment of clarity. He loves Katriina because she is strong, stable, reliable, a counterpoint to the Parkers. But no one can be like that all the time. He had asked her to do the impossible. He had taken her strength for granted.

"Katriina." Something breaks inside of him, and he drops down to his knees, presses his head against her legs like a hysterical child. "Please."

She puts her hand on his head, strokes his hair.

Then Shawn feels his cell phone vibrate in his pocket. Katriina feels it, too. "Don't answer," she whispers. But he can't help it.

"Hey, Nicki," he says, peeling himself away from Katriina and standing up, turning his back to her so he doesn't have to see the look on her face.

"We found Mom," Nicki says. "She's with London. In Duluth."

Relief floods through his entire body. Kate, awake, alive, found. For a moment he forgets about everything else. "Thank god," he says, sinking back against the kitchen table. "Did you talk to her?"

"No. We still need to track them down." There is a pause. "I need you to come to Duluth with me," she says.

"Come to Duluth with you?"

"What are you, fucking deaf?"

"Nicki, I can't."

"Yes, you can. I'll pick you up in half an hour."

"Why doesn't Finn go with you?"

Laughter erupts from the phone. "Because Finn is a selfish, irresponsible brat who always fucks everything up? Because she doesn't really give a shit what happens to Mom, let alone to my daughter? Because the thought of spending three hours in a car with her makes me want to drive chopsticks through my eyeballs? I don't know, you pick a reason."

"You know none of that's true, Nick. I mean, except for the chopsticks part, maybe. You don't give her enough credit, you know. She cares about you."

Nicki sighs. "I don't care. I don't want Finn to come with me, I want *you*."

"You can't get everything you want all the time, Nicki."

"I never get anything I want," she says. "That is the great Parker myth. *Oh, Nicki always gets what she wants.* As if I ever wanted any of *this*!"

Shawn pictures her standing in the middle of the kitchen at Victor Street, sweeping her arm through the air. *This.* This house, this family, this life. It's true, she didn't choose it. *But I did,* Shawn wants to tell her. *And it's a pretty fucking good life when you consider the options.* "Just ask Finn," he says. "I promise it will all work out."

"I hate you," Nicki says and hangs up.

"I love you, too, Nicki," Shawn says to the silent phone. When he turns around to face the kitchen again, Katriina is gone. The garbage bag is still sitting in the middle of the floor, a rogue Cheerio lying defiantly next to it. *How is it that everything could fall apart all at once?*

Shawn pockets his phone and puts his hand on the back of his neck, trying to release some of the tension. *If this were a movie, I'd chase after her and win her back,* he thinks. But he has no energy left for that, so he starts to make a fresh pot of coffee instead.

TWENTY-SEVEN

F inn wakes up to a pillow being thrown in her face. "Get up!"
Nicki screams at her. "Where the fuck is my daughter?" Finn
barely has her eyes open when a second pillow slams into her gut.
"Where. The. Fuck. Is. London?"

Finn had been dreaming that she was back in her own house.
There was nothing more to the dream than that, just Finn, in her
house, sitting on her couch, breathing her air. Alone. Now, she
struggles to remember where she is, what is going on. She pushes
the pillow off her face and sits up. "In her room?"

"Nope," says Nicki, her eyes blazing. She is already dressed for
work, in tight black pants, a tight black scoop-neck shirt with a
shiny, bedazzled cross on the front, and black patent leather stilet-
tos. Just looking at her makes Finn sweat. "She's not in her room.
She is not anywhere in the whole house."

"Did you try texting her?" Finn asks, rubbing her eyes.

"Do you think I'm an idiot? Of course I texted her!" Nicki
shakes her phone in Finn's face. "Then I texted the twins, who said
they haven't seen her since yesterday. Not since *yesterday. When
you fucking told me my daughter was in her room!*"

"You didn't go in and check on her?" Finn asks, and then immediately regrets it as Nicki's whole body clenches with rage.

"No, Finn, I didn't go check on her, I was too busy cleaning up the mess that inevitably happened when you decided to go off god knows where and leave a bunch of kids in charge of the house!"

"Excuse me? This is my fault? Where the hell were you?" Finn watches Nicki's chest rise and fall, her face pink with rage. "What was that, Nicki? Where did you say you were? I didn't quite hear you."

"Fuck you, Finn."

Finn pushes back against the pillows, shifting so she is no longer sitting directly on the rollbar. "You know, you're so quick to blame everyone else for everything all the time," she says. "Why do you get a free pass?"

"Because I'm always here, Finn!" Nicki yells, slamming her fists against the bed. "While you're off doing whatever the hell it is you do all day in Mississauga, *I'm always here*! I'm dealing with Mom constantly forgetting where she is and Dad just ignoring everyone all the time. I have to deal with everyone's bullshit, and the second I want to do something for myself, everything falls apart."

"Do what, Nicki? What did you want to do for yourself? What was so important to you?" Finn covers Nicki's fist with the palm of her hand. "No, *really*, you can tell me," she says sweetly. "I'm your sister. I just want you to be *happy*. If you want something, I want it, too. Oh wait." She pulls her hand back. "I'm sorry, I forgot. It's the other way around."

"You're a fucking psychopath," Nicki says.

"At least I'm not a liar."

"No, you're just a backstabber."

"Look who's talking!"

They lock eyes. Then the phone starts ringing in the kitchen, and Nicki storms out of the room, her shoes clacking against the floor. Finn yanks off the covers and follows her into the kitchen, leaning against the counter in her T-shirt and underwear while Nicki listens on the phone. The rest of the house is quiet – Finn imagines the twins and pseudo-Kate upstairs sleeping off their bender, the boys, who Shawn left sleeping here last night, playing somewhere outside, Hamish in his shed playing with his new parts. Meanwhile Finn and Nicki stand with nothing but three feet of linoleum and a phone call keeping them from just going ahead and killing each other.

Nicki slams down the phone without saying a word to the person on the other end, then continues to stare at it, as though it might come to life and attack her. "That was the hospital," she says, still watching the phone warily. "The security footage they pulled from the loading bay shows Mom leaving the hospital yesterday with a teenaged girl at 4:37 p.m. They said it shows them driving away in a green Volvo."

"Wait, what?"

Nicki goes over to the kitchen window. Finn joins her, and together they do a mental check: Nicki's Civic. Shawn's Jeep, with a crushed right fender. Hamish's Chevy, with the trailer still attached. Walter's truck is with him, wherever the hell that is. Also gone: Kate's Volvo.

Finn puts her hand on Nicki's back. How is it that despite everything, she still feels the need to comfort her sister? "Hey," she says. "We'll find them. It'll be okay."

Nicki tightens up, shrugging Finn's hand off her back. "Don't fucking touch me," she says through gritted teeth.

Finn's jaw tightens. "You were just bitching that no one ever helps you," she says, through her own now gritted teeth. Nicki turns away from the window, starts gathering up her stuff – keys, wallet, lipstick – and shoving it in her purse. "Nicki, look at me," says Finn. Nicki ignores her, keeping her eyes stubbornly averted as she picks up her phone and begins scrolling through her contacts. Finally, Finn grabs her arm. "Nicki!"

Nicki wrenches her arm free. "You think you can just sweep in here like some kind of superhero and save us all? No one trusts you, Finn! When things get tough, you run."

Finn steps back, reeling. She takes a breath. "I'm not going anywhere, Nicki. I'm here, okay? I'm here until we get things back to normal."

Shaking her head, Nicki puts down her purse and sits at the kitchen table. "That's what you don't fucking get, Finn," she says. "This *is* normal." With a resigned sigh, she starts phoning her clients to cancel the day's appointments.

When they were kids, Finn used to imagine herself and Nicki as two halves of a whole, balancing each other out, like yin and yang, coming together to make one full person. As she got older, the image changed to a pair of magnetic poles, each constantly repelling the other. But now she thinks that maybe they are just two versions of the same person, and if circumstances were different – if she had been the one to get pregnant and stay in Thunder Bay and live with Kate and Walter all these years – she wonders if she would have turned out just like Nicki.

◆ ◆ ◆

The Thunder Bay Mall hasn't changed much in the years since Finn has been gone – it is still mostly teen moms with giant strollers, old men drinking Tim Hortons coffee, middle-aged women scouring the sale rack at Zellers for discount bras. Finding herself back here, with the same drab vinyl-tile floor and dusty fake trees that were here in the eighties, wearing the same *Superior Tours* T-shirt that she slept in and Kate's ugly ancient Birkenstocks after discovering her own flip-flops were covered in raw hamburger meat, she feels like an acne-scarred sixteen-year-old misfit again, hunched over and self-conscious, all too-long arms and legs, her eyebrows unplucked, her hair dull and lifeless.

Nicki had eventually conceded to let Finn help her search for London and Kate, sending Finn to the mall while she went down to the police station to file a missing person report and Hamish stayed home with the kids, including three very sorry-looking thirteen-year-old girls with wicked hangovers. When Finn left, he was cheerily forcing them to eat plates full of runny eggs and fatty bacon, saying, "It's gane be awright once the pain has gane away," which Finn translated into "I'm having a lot of fun torturing you little demonspawn." At least he has a sense of humour about it.

Nicki had said the mall was as good a place as any to start looking, but London's not here. There are just a bunch of girls with shiny hair and expertly shaped brows who Finn is guessing are the popular kids at her school and probably hate her because if memory serves, that's what popular girls do in high school: hate you. Finn knows teenaged girls don't come with any kind of warnings. But she was a teenaged girl once, and she knows she wanted to be sexy and she wanted people to like her, and she wanted to be smart, and she was never sure how to make all those things work at once, or in her favour. More than anything, though, what she wanted was to be smarter than her parents, and for a while she thought she was – after all, they were old and out of touch and dead inside. Like London, she thought that unless you grew up to be an artist or a humanitarian, you had sold out.

"Everyone just, like, buys into the *facade* of happiness that society is trying to sell them," she can remember London saying last night, before dinner. "Like, really, death is the only thing that can ever save them from their boring, pointless life of *drudgery*." The embarrassing thing is, at thirty-four, Finn can still relate to this. She watches the girls hanging out in the food court on a Monday morning in July texting their friends, drinking pop, flirting with boys, and waiting for something to happen, thinking their lives are going to be so much better when they are grown up because they are going to do it right, they are going to beat the odds and hold on to their ideals and not let themselves turn into boring, jaded adults. And she thinks, Yes! Yes, do that! For the love of god, please, somebody do that.

It's with this hope in her heart that Finn goes over to the nearest table of long legs and pink hoodies and, in what she hopes is her least creepy-old-person voice, says, "Hey, do any of you guys know London Parker-Stewart?"

Four blond-ponytailed heads turn towards her. "Who?" asks the ponytail closest to her, in a voice so withering she can almost feel her inner child curling up and dying.

"London Parker-Stewart," another girl says. "London Parker-Stewart. Doesn't she go to Westgate?"

"Isn't she some kind of eco-slut?" another girl asks.

"Doesn't she have, like, seventeen brothers and sisters, all with different dads?"

"Didn't her mother, like, die in a boat that went over the falls?"

Finn clenches her fists at her sides. "It was a barrel," she says. "And it wasn't her mother. And she didn't die." *And what the fuck is an eco-slut?*

Four blond ponytails whip away from her. "Um, touchy, much?" the first girl says. "By the way, nice *Birkenstocks*."

It's amazing how you can grow up and think you're self-assured and confident and then one biting comment from a bitchy teenaged girl can cut you into pieces. She looks down at her sad feet in her sadder shoes. She can still smell the coffee she spilled on herself in Hamish's truck on the way here, which is bigger than her father's and unwieldy and a bitch and a half to park with a Tim's cup in your hand. She doesn't understand why they haven't mentioned her swollen nose, or her three-days-unwashed hair, or that her shirt is on inside out, something she is just noticing now as she surveys her pathetic self. "So, what I'm getting from you is that you haven't seen London," she says, mostly to her feet.

323

"Check, like, the forest or something," the first girl says. "She's probably off hugging a tree."

"Or fucking a shark," another girl says.

At the next table, a girl Finn recognizes sits with three boys, watching something on an iPad. Could she be a friend of London's? Someone whose face she remembers from sleepovers at Victor Street? As she approaches their table, Finn realizes that whatever they are watching sounds familiar. The girl, who has been looking at her while the other three watch the screen, tilts her iPad sideways as Finn walks over, making sure she can see what it is.

Drop, bang, flip. *Shit.*

"The Conqueror of Kakabeka," the girl says, gesturing to the iPad. "What an adorable sobriquet. I know you. You're the other twin."

This is what you get for leaving, Finn thinks. *Forever known as the other twin.*

"I'm London's aunt," she says, feeling this is a more pertinent relationship to focus on. She shoves her hands into the pockets of her shorts, tries to appear casual. The video starts playing again – they obviously have it on some kind of loop. The girl places the iPad screen up on the table, volume at full. Drop, bang, flip.

"Ugh," she says, reaching her hand out across the table towards Finn. "I'm *so sorry*. I can't even *imagine* what your family must be going through right now."

The three boys laugh, although now that Finn is closer she's not sure if two of them are actually boys or not. "Uh, thanks," she says. "You guys are friends with London?"

"Oh *yeah*," the girl says. "We're *super* close."

"*Super* close," the one most likely to be a boy says, a big grin on his face.

The girl turns to him, eyes wide. "Andy, she must be *just devastated* about this."

"Well, actually," says Finn, "she, uh, she went missing last night."

The four of them glance at one another, and Finn could swear she sees something pass between them. "Oh, dear," the girl says. She pulls a long red Twizzler from a bag on the table and sticks one end in her mouth, and when she leans back in her chair Finn can see she is wearing a black-and-white-striped shift dress that barely skims her crotch. With her thick black bangs and red lips she looks like something out of a French New Wave film, and definitely not someone you would find in the food court of the Thunder Bay Mall. She seems like someone that London could be friends with, Finn thinks. So why does she suddenly feel like she's being duped?

"Do you have any idea where she may have gone?" Finn asks, deciding to forge ahead.

The girl sighs loudly, chewing on her Twizzler. "Unfortunately, I do," she says. She raises her eyebrows questioningly. "Should I tell her?" she asks the other three. "I feel kind of weird about it."

"Anastasia, you *can't*," one of the androgynous ones says. "You promised you'd keep her secret."

"I know," Anastasia says. "But I'm just so *worried* about her, Dylan. I have a totally bad feeling about this. I think it's time we got a responsible adult involved." She gazes up at Finn with black-lined eyes, her face plastered with a perfectly arranged expression of concern. "What would you do, Ms. Parker? If you had made a promise to someone, but keeping that promise might end up hurting them?"

Drop, bang, flip. Finn doesn't want to be talking to these four anymore. She is sure she has heard the name Anastasia before, from London or Kate or maybe one of the twins. She wishes she had paid more attention, had been a better aunt all these years, knew her niece better. This is all Nicki's fault, of course. If Nicki hadn't been such a miserable human being, Finn would have been able to spend more time with her children.

"I don't know, Anastasia," Finn says. "I think I would probably keep the secret, and then feel really shitty about it when something terrible ended up happening that I could have easily put a stop to just by telling someone. But that's just me. I do stupid stuff. I'm pretty sure you're smarter than that, though."

Anastasia smiles. "You're right, of course. I don't think you're stupid at all, Ms. Parker. Or do you go by your married name now?"

WARNING: ATTACKING TEENAGED GIRLS IN SHOPPING MALL FOOD COURTS IS NOT RECOMMENDED. "I didn't say *I* was stupid," Finn says, staring at her. "I said I do stupid stuff."

"Just tell her, Anastasia," Andy says. "Then we can get the fuck out of here."

"Andy! Don't be so callous." Anastasia bites her lip. "I heard she . . . met someone on the internet. A boy. Well, a *man*, actually." She rips off a piece of the Twizzler and begins to chew.

Finn feels her stomach drop to the floor. "A man? On the internet? Are you sure?"

With the licorice still in her mouth, Anastasia nods.

"Do you know his name?"

"No. I'm sorry, I wish I could tell you more. But London's been so secretive lately, hasn't she, Ms. Parker?" Anastasia folds her hands primly on the table in front of her. "Do you think she's going to be okay?"

"I don't know." Something is working in her brain, sifting through all the mush of yesterday's chaos. London, down at the dock, her glasses, her legs in the river, a video about . . . what was it? "Something to do with sharks?" Finn asks.

Anastasia smiles. The video starts up again. Drop, bang, flip.

Finn speed-walks through the mall as fast as her Birkenstocks can take her, dialling Nicki's cell on the way. She can't stop shaking. *I should have known*, she thinks, dodging an old man with a walker. *I should have figured it out. I should have done something. No wonder no one fucking trusts me.*

"I know where they are," she says as soon as Nicki picks up.

"You found them?"

"Well, not exactly." Finn tells her an abbreviated version of the story, leaving out the part about London asking her to drive her to Duluth.

"So they're heading for Duluth?" Nicki says. "Great. That's just great."

"At least we know where they're going. You can get the cops here to call the police in Duluth and put out an APB or whatever on the Volvo, track them down somehow."

"These stupid piece-of-shit cops aren't going to do anything," Nicki says. "She's with an adult family member, and she hasn't been missing for twenty-four hours. They told me to go home and calm the fuck down." Nicki's voice has turned shrill, bordering on unbearable. "Did you hear that, Finnie? They told me to *calm the fuck down.*"

"I heard you," Finn says, trying to remember the last time Nicki called her Finnie. She must really be scared. "Well, look, we can try to track that guy down, the shark guy. He has to be the person she's going to see. I can Google him –"

"Adam Pelley," Nicki says. "London's been obsessed with him for years. He's not just a shark guy, Finn, he's a TV celebrity. She's being fucking *scammed.* Some disgusting pedophile stalked her Facebook profile or something and convinced her he was Adam Pelley to lure her in." Nicki's breath comes in short bursts. She sounds like she might be running. "What the fuck, Finn. How can this be happening?"

"I don't know." Finn sprints across the parking lot and reaches Hamish's truck. Inside, it still smells like coffee. "Look, if she thinks this guy is Adam Pelley, she's going to go to Adam Pelley, right? He's definitely in Duluth, Nicki, I saw the news clip."

"You saw it?"

"Yeah. London showed it to me." So much for leaving out her own part in this. "Yesterday. She showed me this news clip about how he was in Duluth filming some kind of shark special. She wanted me to drive her down there."

She hears a banging noise on the other end of the phone, then a muffled scream. Finn starts up the truck and presses her head against the steering wheel, waiting for Nicki to finish her tantrum. When she finally comes back on the line, her voice is dangerously calm. "So. London asked you to drive her to Duluth, and you didn't think to tell me about it?"

"I'm sorry, Nicki, I had other things on my mind."

"Right. And even when she went missing, you didn't think to mention it?"

"I said I was sorry! Can we just move on and figure out a plan? We need to go to Duluth."

"*We* are not going anywhere," Nicki says, her voice like an ice pick. "*I'm* going to go to Duluth and try to stop my daughter from being kidnapped by some dirty criminal. *You* can go wherever the fuck you want." The line goes dead.

"Right," says Finn, slamming her phone down on the passenger seat. She should know better by now. No matter how many times she tries to do the right thing, it will never balance out the millions of times she has done the wrong thing. It's strange how, once she made the decision to come home, she thought it was her family who was going to have to fight to win her back. It never occurred to her that it would actually be the other way around.

TWENTY-EIGHT

Anastasia sits in her kitchen, watching the video of London's grandmother going over the falls in slow motion on her laptop. The video, the one that has been on everyone's feed since Friday, is of very poor quality, and was probably filmed by some skid named Terrance from Murillo on a cracked-screen iPhone 4. If it had been Anastasia's footage, she would have run it through some editing software, or at least applied an Instagram filter, added some background music, some swelling strings – Mozart, or maybe Lana Del Rey.

Terrance had been standing on the first platform on the eastern side of the Kam River, the one where everyone goes to have their pictures taken with the pretty view of the falls in the background when they can't be bothered to walk farther than twenty feet from their car. And janky-ass Terry, there with a woman who Anastasia can only assume is both his wife and also his sister, just happened to end up right in the optimum spot to watch Granny's big plunge. Had a current come along and pushed Granny over to the other side of the falls, Terrance would have been SOL, too far away from the action to get any kind of shot. But her man T has some kind of horseshoe up his ass. Granny's barrel stayed on course, and she plunged over the eastern flume towards her destiny of broken bones and internet fame. And T-Bone, the fortuitous hillbilly, the chosen one, got the ultimate money shot.

The drop. The bang. The flip.

"Holy shit," says Terrance, giving censors all around the world a heart attack. "That was a lady in a motherfucking barrel."

Anastasia replays the video. At first, as the barrel is floating down the river, London's grandmother is facing the other direction, and so all you can see is the blob of white that is the back of her head. But then, like some kind of miracle, God sent His angels down from heaven above to flap their ethereal wings and gently turn the barrel on the current so her face comes into view just moments before she plunges over the precipice. Anastasia pauses the video a split second before the drop, and then scrolls through it frame by frame, looking for some evidence, some tiny, minuscule trace of fear. But London's grandmother's expression is as blank as the slate cliffs around her. It's absolutely fucking outstanding.

Anastasia has watched the video at least two hundred times since she found out that the woman in the barrel was, in fact, London's grandmother. London's ever-loving batshit-crazy fucking grandmother. Anastasia has done everything she can to ensure that everyone in their high school also knows who the woman in the barrel is. It's not the kind of thing that anyone could legitimately expect her to keep to herself, that would just be ludicrous. Not to mention, it would be un-civic-minded. Her father has always taught her that her first duty is to her community because she is a natural-born leader and people are going to continually look to her for guidance, whether she wants them to or not. It is a heavy burden to carry, but when you are born with a gift, that is the price you have to pay. She *owed it* to people to let them know what had happened to one of their classmate's family. A tragedy of this magnitude needed to be openly shared with others so they could come together and heal as a community.

"Holy shit. That was a lady in a motherfucking barrel." Anastasia giggles. She can't help it, it gets her every time.

When she finally gets bored of the video, she opens a folder called AP and scrolls through the files, which are all saved IM histories, looking for the most recent one.

PONYO: You promise you won't tell anyone?
SHARKBOY: Of course not.
SHARKBOY: Besides, who would I tell?
PONYO: https://www.youtube.com/
    watch?v=HffbME_B7JGGHSTN
PONYO: Did you watch the video?
PONYO: Adam? Did you watch it?
PONYO: Adam, are you still there?
PONYO: Adam?
PONYO: . . .

Was it too abrupt? Anastasia wonders. She had known that her fun would be coming to an end sooner or later. As soon as she had seen online that Adam Pelley was going to be in Duluth, she suddenly understood the path she was meant to take, what her true mission was, what her endgame should be. Finding out about London's grandmother was a happy accident that just happened to have an immediate applicable use. There was no point in continuing – why expend energy on a project that had already produced better results than you had originally hoped for? But now she can't help thinking that she may have been too hasty, and in her impatience to move on actually done herself a disservice. London, for all her faults, is a smart girl, and has developed a shrewdness since her arrest that Anastasia would never have imagined. Had she figured it out?

No. That's crazy. Just because Adam Pelley had stopped communicating with London after she sent him the video did not mean that London had assumed he had stopped communicating with her forever. She is on her way down there to meet him, everything has played out according to plan. So why does Anastasia have this nagging feeling in the back of her mind that something has gone wrong?

She decides to forget about it. What's done is done, she thinks. She closes her laptop and goes to the fridge, pulling out four cans of coconut water. Then she pops them open and dumps out half of each, topping them off with the last of a bottle of Grey Goose. It's important, in this heat, to stay hydrated. She takes a sip of her drink and makes a face. Too much coconut water. She finishes it off, then, rummaging through a bag on the counter, she finds another bottle and opens it up. The bottle, like everything else in the bag, was something she and Andy had stolen from the mall that morning. It's easy to steal when you're well dressed, clever, and confident. Everyone else just assumes that they are the ones who have made the mistake.

It's not that she can't afford this stuff – it's just fun to see what they can get away with. People in this city are not exactly the big-picture types. They are short-term planners, paycheque-to-paycheque survivors; they fight and scrape for everything they have and wake each new day to a battlefield of obstacles to overcome before going to sleep and waking up to another battlefield. But Anastasia is a visionary. Every decision she makes is another nail, another screw, another beam in her dream house; every house a new development in her city, every city a new pinpoint on the map of her world. She is a builder's daughter – she doesn't just see materials; she sees what they can become. This, more than anything, is what separates her from the rest of the good, honest, hard-working down-home northern folk she has grown up with, who she goes to school with, and who will eventually work for her. She knows that being good and honest and hard-working is just running on a hamster wheel. She would prefer to expend her energy in more productive ways.

She pours more vodka into the remaining three cans, then heads outside to the pool, handing one to Andy and one to Ryan. "Sorry," she says to Dylan, taking a sip of the third. "There were only three left." Dylan glares at her but doesn't say anything.

"Were you watching that stupid video again?" asks Andy, climbing onto her chair and straddling her. Andy, he is not a visionary. But he is a useful sidekick. He is smart enough to know that is where his strengths lie. He also looks really good in a pair of swim trunks.

"I just find it so *fascinating*," she says. "Although I think it missed the mark a bit, cinematographically. It could have been so much more."

"Yeah, well, I doubt whoever filmed it was thinking about artistic camera angles."

She wraps her hand around the back of Andy's neck and pulls him down, kissing him hard, letting go when she's had enough. "You're right," she says, wiping her mouth. "It's all function over form. It's just kind of tragic to see all that missed potential." She wiggles her hips, signalling for Andy to get off her. He bounds over to the pool like a puppy and cannonballs past Ryan's head, spraying the pool deck with water.

"Speaking of missed potential," Ryan says, brushing the water off. "How come you didn't tell London's aunt about Adam Pelley?"

Anastasia rolls her eyes. "*Really*, Ryan? Didn't you feel like she would figure it out for herself?"

Ryan shrugs. "She wasn't exactly a rocket scientist."

"Yeah, but I don't *exactly* think that London has been discreet about everything." She pulls out her phone, reverses the camera, and begins to reapply her lipstick. "It's way more fun to see how things unravel, don't you think?"

Dylan giggles. "Imagine the look on London's face when she tracks him down in Duluth."

Anastasia shakes her head sadly. "I take no joy in this, Dylan. London used to be my friend. But she needs to understand the consequences of her actions." She finishes with her lipstick and snaps a quick selfie, for posterity. She considers texting it to London, along with a pertinent quote about karma from Deepak Chopra, or maybe Rihanna. But she decides against it. She is not a monster. She has her limits.

The thing she finds most strange about this whole situation is that London doesn't understand why Anastasia does the things she does to her. The day London was arrested, she looked at her with such an expression of betrayal on her face as the cops dragged her out of the school in handcuffs that Anastasia almost laughed. There are a lot of things you could call Anastasia, but *fake* is not one of them. *Duplicitous*, maybe. *Sneaky, conniving, unfeeling,* certainly. But she will never pretend to be someone she isn't. As one of her oldest friends, London had seen the things Anastasia had done to other people, and yet somehow she had expected to be exempt from all of that. She had expected Anastasia to care, and was shocked to discover that she didn't.

In the months following her arrest, London kept begging Anastasia for an explanation: What had she done to make Anastasia hate her? But Anastasia *didn't* hate her – not then, and not now. She actually thinks London is an interesting person, intelligent and sharp, although with an overinflated sense of moral superiority that often tends to flip over into righteous indignation, which Anastasia finds tedious. She believed London had potential until she saw the way she behaved after her arrest – claiming the drugs weren't hers, that Anastasia had been the one selling them, that she had planted them on London because she knew that the police were about to come down on her. Anastasia had been floored. Like, talk about betrayal! She had obviously seen something in London that wasn't there, a bond of loyalty that she assumed would never break, no matter what the circumstances.

Still, Anastasia forgave her. In fact, she feels she behaved quite magnanimously towards London after the whole debacle. It wasn't her fault that London continued to blame her for what had happened, or that she decided to launch a campaign of hatred against Anastasia in the following months – badmouthing her to everyone at school, ratting her out to their teachers every time she cheated, trying to derail her bake sale – starting a war that she had not the slightest chance in hell of winning.

Outside, they have now bypassed the coconut water and have moved on to straight Grey Goose, the bottle knotted into a pool noodle drifting back and forth between the four of them on their loungers. Anastasia has a nice buzz, and is thinking maybe it would be a good idea to call up some people and have a party. Her father and stepmother are at their camp in Lake of the Woods, and the housekeeper is off for two days – just enough time for a proper rager. But she finds she just doesn't have the energy. All the people she would have to talk to, all of them so officious, so grateful to her. Everyone wants to be invited to Anastasia's house, but not everybody can be. It's just the way the world works.

As if reading her thoughts, Andy says, "We should invite Julie and Dex over. They might have some E."

"I don't want to do E with a bunch of dirty hipster wannabes," she snaps. "And if you do, you probably should just go do that. Somewhere else."

Andy drops his hand in the water and stares at her. "Maybe I will," he says.

He tips himself out of the lounger and swims to the side of the pool. Anastasia watches him climb out, rivers of chlorinated water running down his swim trunks as he stalks off into the house. She knows he'll be back. She lets her hand drag through the water, the Grey Goose bottle now resting on her chest, and looks over at Ryan and Dylan, smiling.

"You should go, too," she says. "I'm sure it will be a blast."

Ryan and Dylan glance at each other. "Just give me that bottle," Ryan says. Anastasia hands it over. They're not going to go anywhere. None of them are. And they know it.

For some reason, Anastasia finds herself thinking about the last time London was at her house. It was a night a week or so before her arrest, and it was just the two of them, eating veggie wraps from Pita Pit and working on an assignment for English class where they had to write a modern-day adaptation of *Julius Caesar*. Anastasia hadn't wanted to do it – she had a great guy for English assignments – but London had said for research they could watch the *Romeo and Juliet* with Leonardo DiCaprio and maybe even *10 Things I Hate About You*. After the movie, London had gotten all weird and said she wanted to walk down to the lake.

When they got to the beach, London took her shoes off and waded into the water, although it was already October and Lake Superior is freezing cold even in the middle of the summer. "What are you doing?" Anastasia called from the shore. London was making her feel uncomfortable. She liked to be around calm, sane, rational people, not people who went barefoot into lakes in, like, zero degree weather.

"Are you in love with Andy?" London asked.

Anastasia sighed. Is that what this was about? "Come on, London. I expected more of you than that."

"What?" said London, without turning around. "You expected I didn't give a shit about being in love?"

"Yes," said Anastasia, crossing her arms over her chest. "Love just slows you down."

"Maybe I *want* to slow down," London said. She waded out a little farther, the inky-black water rippling out around her ankles.

Briefly, Anastasia thought about following her into the lake. What would happen if she did? Would the sky open up and rain fire? Would the water rise up over them, would their skin turn to stone? She pressed the toe of her left shoe against the heel of her right, about to apply the pressure needed to pull it off.

"Or maybe love slows *you* down," London added.

Anastasia planted her left foot firmly back into the sand. "That's ridiculous," she said. "Have you even *met* Andy?"

But London just raised her arms over her head and clasped her hands together. "Look at that moon," she said.

"Are you high or something?" Anastasia asked. "Because if you are, that would explain a lot." This angsty side of London's was getting pretty tiresome. Like, what was she going to do next, dye her hair blue and get a tattoo? Run away from home for the weekend to go to the Marianas Trench concert in Winnipeg? OD on oxy in their drug dealer's squat on Simpson Street and have to have her stomach pumped? She had thought that London had a little more originality than that.

"My grandfather knows everything about this lake, you know," London said. "Every rock under the surface, every place where a ship went down. Did you know that there have been forty-five shipwrecks in Lake Superior?"

"Are we going to work this into *Julius Caesar* somehow?"

London turned her gaze slowly towards her. "You know, you're remarkably short-sighted for someone who always talks about the big picture." She air-quoted "the big picture," as if it was something Anastasia just made up, and not something that was a true universal thing.

"I'll see you inside, if you ever get over yourself," Anastasia said. She started walking towards the house, and although she didn't want to look back, she couldn't help it. London had walked

337

farther out into the lake, and with the moon in her hair and the water around her feet she looked – well, she looked like she was the main character of the story, instead of just the sidekick. Anastasia watched her for another minute, but she didn't turn around, no matter how much Anastasia wanted her to.

Now, she thinks about that night and wants to vomit. She almost took her *shoes* off. In the *sand*. What was she even *thinking*? As if she could ever be the kind of person who would even stand barefoot next to a lake. Her father always says that dignity is the most important trait a leader can possess because if you don't have dignity, how can you expect people to respect you? If you lose respect, you lose everything. And for a moment of freedom at the edge of a lake? Her skin might as well turn to stone.

Anastasia leans back in her lounger and pulls her sunglasses down over her eyes. Keep moving forward, she thinks. It's the only thing you can do.

TWENTY-NINE

When Kate wakes up, it is light outside and her body feels tight and cramped, as though she has slept for a long time. She is in a hotel room. She checks the clock: 1:04 p.m. She knows she is supposed to be watching the clock but she can't remember *why* she is supposed to be watching the clock, or why she is in a hotel room, or even what city she is in. In the bathroom, she washes her face with the hotel soap and brushes her teeth with a tube of toothpaste and a toothbrush that she recognizes as her own, though she doesn't understand how they could have possibly gotten here. Then she fumbles around for the key card to the hotel room door and heads down to the lobby. She's not sure what she is looking for, but she's sure that she is here with someone important and that person is not supposed to be gone.

In the lobby, Kate begins to remember little snippets from the previous day. The girl. Yes, she is here with the girl. Sleep has always been the worst eraser, it's like the sleeping has wiped away everything that happened before the sleeping. There was a drive, the girl, something about a sandwich. A deer. The girl is searching for someone. The girl is her granddaughter. Her name is on the tip of Kate's tongue. They are in Duluth. They are staying at a hotel. Kate parked the Volvo somewhere. The girl is her granddaughter.

The girl, of course, is no longer a girl but a young woman, although it is easy for Kate to forget this. Her most vivid memories of her granddaughter are from when she was young. Kate would wait for her to get off the school bus at the end of their driveway. She was looking forward to school, at first. The summer before, when they would go to town for groceries, they would drive past the elementary school and she would say, "I'm going to go to the big school," and it was as though she thought she was going to Disney World. On her first day, Kate took a photo of her as she waited for the bus, her hair in braids and her jeans rolled up at her ankles, her Dora the Explorer backpack and her lunch bag packed with pudding cups and a juice box, her feet shaking in her shoes with the excitement of what the day would bring.

"I made an art with pipe cleaners," she announced as she got off the bus that first day. "And I met a friend named Emma!" The second day, it was, "I got picked last for gym class. But I got a goal in soccer and Ms. Smylie said I was really fast!" The third day, Kate could tell she had been crying. "Emma called me a dirty Indian. And when I told her I had a bath last night she just laughed at me." The fourth day, she didn't say anything at all about school – nor did she the next day, or the next week, or the next month, no matter how much Kate tried to get her to talk. By Christmas, she had built up a shell around her that no one could get through.

No person, anyway. The girl surrounded herself with pictures of horses – taped to her walls, adorning her scribblers, patched onto her backpack. She rescued squirrels from the backyard, half-dead things with mangy tails and rabid eyes; she started up a collection on Walter's boats to protect the snapping turtles that came up from the Kam onto Victor Street in the spring to lay their eggs on higher ground. When she was in second grade she made her mother drive her to the humane society every weekend so she could walk the unwanted dogs; it was on her innocent, wide-eyed insistence that they adopted poor three-legged Bruno. Still, she begged her mother to take in more. "We have to save them!" she would plead, and every time Kate would be overwhelmed with the desire to save *her* instead.

Everything will be okay, Kate tells herself as she looks around the lobby for the girl. She wonders again if she should call her mother, but at this point she thinks she would rather find the girl first, rather than tell her mother that she has lost her. At the front desk, she talks to a nice young man named Liam who tells her that he thinks her granddaughter is probably down by the pool.

Of course, Kate thinks. All young girls love the pool. But when she finally locates the aquatic centre, tracking its chlorine smell through the dingy halls of the basement, the pool is empty. She checks the change rooms, the sauna: nothing. Standing at the edge of the pool, she stares down at its still surface, silently begging it to tell her if the girl has been here, her body slicing through the blue water, pushing off from the tile walls, diving down to touch its bottom. She leans down and dips her hand in, as though she might be able to feel the girl's lingering presence beneath the surface. But the pool reveals nothing except Kate's own worried face.

Back in the lobby, Kate sits down in one of the chairs and stares at the bank of calling things along the opposite wall. How long does a person have to be gone before you can report them missing? Twenty-four hours? But how on earth is she going to fill out a missing person report for her granddaughter when she can't even remember her name?

London. How could she forget? The girl's name is London. But she remembered, that was the important thing. She remembered, so all hope is not lost.

The only logical thing to do is to call Nicki. But instead, Kate goes into the lobby bar and sits on a stool facing the bartender.

"Hi there," says the bartender, whose nametag reads Lisa. She slides a narrow drinks menu across the bar. "What can I get you?"

What does she usually order at a bar? Kate has no idea. "I think I'd like a glass of white wine," she says.

"We have a Pinot Grigio, a Chardonnay, a Riesling . . ."

None of these words means anything to Kate. "Just pour me a glass of whichever you like best."

Smiling, Lisa points to the top line on the menu. "I like the Chardonnay, myself."

"Chardonnay sounds good," says Kate. "You have a very beautiful smile," she adds as Lisa turns away to pour the wine. Even from behind she can tell that Lisa is blushing, a flush creeping up the back of her neck.

"Thanks," she says, without turning around. "So do you."

As Kate sips the wine, she watches the television behind the bar while keeping one eye on the lobby to see if the girl walks by. She's hoping the wine will relax her, help her remember what they are doing there, what great mission they are on. But the more she tries to remember, the more anxious she gets. By the time she finishes her drink, staring at her empty hands is the only thing she can do to keep herself from completely panicking.

◆ ◆ ◆

Kate spent that fall and winter palm reading on her purple blanket on the Left Bank, warming her hands with her breath before peeling off her customers' gloves, sharing a thermos of tea and whisky with Lydia to keep themselves warm. For months she thought about nothing but palms, until she could swear she had stopped thinking in words and phrases and instead thought in lines, mounts, skin patterns, fingerprints. She read so many palms that she became convinced that she had seen every possible permutation of converging lines that existed, that there was no version of the future that she had not already envisioned in someone's hand.

It started to depress her, the way life had become so predictable. You would die either young or old or somewhere in between; before that happened you may or may not fall in love, have a successful career, a healthy body. Your mind is on a spectrum somewhere in between very weak and very strong, your heart somewhere between loving and generous, and cold and unfeeling. And none of it mattered anyway because everyone's life line stopped eventually, and no matter what you did, you couldn't change that. You couldn't change any of it. It was all etched there, in your palm, from the very beginning. Of course, she still didn't believe any of it. And yet.

"Do you think people can change their destiny?" she asked Lydia one night, sharing a bottle of wine in their room at Madame Clou's.

"I do," Lydia said, taking her hand.

Kate flipped Lydia's hand over, caressing the lines there. She had read Lydia's palm many times before, but she kept going back to it, in the hope that maybe something had changed. But it never did.

"If that's really the case," Kate said, holding Lydia's palm up for her to see, "then this is a sham."

"My little con artist." Lydia curled her hand around Kate's wrist and pulled her close, kissing her softly.

Kate let herself briefly melt into the moment before pulling away, pressing her forehead against Lydia's. "I'm serious," she said. "Sometimes I don't know why I'm doing this."

"To make enough money to survive until you go back to Canada?"

Back to Canada. A wave of panic washed over her. Lydia had been saying those words more frequently lately, and it terrified her. She and Martha Jane had only planned to be gone a few months, but since she had met Lydia it was almost as though time had stopped moving forward. They rarely talked about their future together, at least not in any sort of concrete way. Deep down, Kate thought she understood why. In her wildest dreams she imagined that she and Lydia and all of Paris were actually caught in a time warp, never having to think about the future because the future would never come.

"Reading someone's palm is like sealing their destiny. It's as if knowing makes it real." She wished they could stay young and happy and in love in Paris forever. She wished they could make new lines, outwit fate. She wished, so much, that she didn't know. But it wasn't possible.

Lydia laughed, reaching for the bottle of wine. "They're just lines, Kate," she said. "They might tell you where you're going, but they don't tell you how you get there. The fun part is filling in the details."

"That's the part I hate the most," Kate said. "It's not fair to tell people what's going to happen to them without telling them how. You only find out the how when it's too late." She took the bottle from Lydia and held it by the neck, pressing her palms into the glass, needing to feel something solid, tangible, *real*. Something that would bring her back to the present, to that room at that moment – the smell of the musty drapes, the soft wool blanket they had wrapped themselves in to keep warm, the delicate snow falling silently outside the window, the squeal of the water pipes as Claude ran his bath next door. The curve of Lydia's ear, her hot breath on Kate's neck, her soft sighs.

A week later, Lydia was crossing the street to buy a loaf of bread from Jules when a car came speeding down the road. Kate saw it happen in horrifying slow motion from the window of their room, a seething eternity between the second she saw that car and the second it hit Lydia. "No!" she cried. She ran down the stairs as fast as she could, her feet barely touching the floor. *No, no, no.* Others had already made their way out to the street, and Kate had to fight her way through the crowd to the spot where Lydia's body had been thrown. *Not yet*, she kept thinking, over and over. *It can't be now. We haven't had enough time.*

She felt someone's hands on her, pulling her back, and she heard Jules's voice say *Ne regardez pas, ne regardez pas* as he shielded her from Lydia's broken body, holding her while she screamed and screamed. Only later did she realize her screams were only in her head, that standing there by the side of the road, in the middle of the crowd and the yelling and the sirens, she hadn't uttered a sound.

Later, Kate understood that she had been wrong. It was not finding out the *how* when it was too late that was unfair. What was unfair was that you never, ever got to find out the *why*.

Three nights after Lydia's death, Kate left for Canada. She sat on a plane, a hollowed-out version of herself, watching the clouds through the window, not even registering the fact that she was flying, actually flying. She was wearing the dress that Lydia had liked so much that first night they met. That dress had brought them together, and she couldn't stop touching it, couldn't stop thinking that there was some essence of Lydia there, some part of her that Kate had sewn into the fabric without even knowing. When she looked down at her shoes, somewhere over the North Atlantic, she saw they still had a dusting of flour on them from Jules holding her there on the street.

When she arrived back in Thunder Bay, she went straight from the airport to Walter's house, where his parents directed her to his new apartment in Port Arthur. On her way back to the car, she picked a wild rose from a bush in his parents' driveway and tucked it into her hair. Her own heart line showed one big love, but she couldn't let herself believe that. She couldn't let herself believe that her one big love had died on that street at the age of twenty-one. She couldn't let herself believe there was nothing more than this.

Now, she examines her palm, that same thick line bisecting her heart line. She has waited decades for that line to break up, to disentangle, to reveal itself as two. It never happened. Even though so much *did* happen. She married Walter, and had two beautiful, difficult, extraordinary daughters, one tenacious survivor of a son, six mysterious and lovely grandchildren. Their family, their house, their life together. None of this would have happened if Lydia had truly been able to outwit fate. How could she look back on her life and wish that things had been different? How could she reconcile her love for her family with her regret over losing Lydia?

"Would you like another glass of wine?"

Kate takes one last glance at her palm and then looks up at Lisa. "I don't think so," she says. As she brings a hand up to her face she realizes her cheeks are wet, even though she can't remember any tears falling. She wipes them away, hoping Lisa hasn't noticed. "But maybe you can help me with something. If you were a sixteen-year-old girl staying in this hotel, where would you go?"

"The roof," Lisa says without hesitation. She studies Kate's face. "Hey, aren't you the lady from that video? The Conqueror of Kakabeka?"

"I don't know what you're talking about," Kate says, but as she walks out of the bar, a smile spreads across her face. The Conqueror of Kakabeka. Nothing on her palm could ever have predicted that one.

◆ ◆ ◆

If Kate had read the hotel literature in her room, she would have known that the Radisson had a beautiful rooftop patio with breathtaking views of the city and the harbour. She finds London sitting in a chair facing eastward, towards the aerial lift bridge. When London was little, she used to love walking across that bridge – always giggly with fear that the bridge would begin to lift while she was on it, even though Kate assured her that it wouldn't.

"Hi, Nana. I'm sorry I was out so late last night."

"It's okay, dear," Kate says, relieved to hear that she had, in fact, come back to the room last night. "You should have woken me up this morning, though."

"I tried," London says, avoiding her eyes. "You were passed out cold. I was worried you were back in a coma and it was all my fault."

A coma. The word sounds familiar to Kate, but she can't remember what it means. It doesn't matter, she thinks. London is here and everything is okay. "I'm just glad I found you," she says. "What are you doing up here?"

"Just thinking." London finally turns to face her, and Kate sees that her eyes are red and puffy. "I messed up, Nana. We shouldn't have come here."

"Don't be silly," Kate says. "I'm having a lovely time." She sits down on the chair next to London's, suddenly feeling dizzy. Maybe having a glass of wine before breakfast was not exactly the best idea. "Do you want to go get lunch somewhere? If I remember correctly, there's a nice restaurant down in Canal Park, right on the water." The words come out of her mouth unforced, naturally, and she is surprised to find herself completely clear-headed. She can see Canal Park, see the restaurant, the streets, the bridge – and more importantly, she remembers the words *restaurant, street, bridge*. "We could walk across the lift bridge after, if you want," she says, smiling. *Bridge.* She wants to say it over and over before she loses it again, before this moment of clarity disappears. *Bridge. Bridge. Bridge.*

"Okay," says London. But she doesn't get up. Kate realizes that, in her relief over finally finding her granddaughter, she hasn't noticed the way she is sitting, with her shoulders slumped and her arms crossed over her chest. It reminds Kate of the way she looked getting off the school bus. Defeated.

"Are you okay, sweetheart?"

London is quiet for a moment. "I really wanted to save it," she says finally.

Save what? For the love of god, just say it! "Yes," says Kate, carefully. "Me, too."

"I mean, I also wanted other things. But it was the shark that was the most important thing, you know?"

With that word, *shark*, it all comes back to her like a sudden downpour – their conversation at the grocery store, the hospital, all of it. Kate wants to leap up and cheer for her own small victory, but one look at London and her triumph seems insignificant in the face of her granddaughter's obvious heartbreak. "I know how much it meant to you," she says. "What happened?"

"They cancelled the show, and Adam Pelley is leaving. It's over. The shark is going to die, and there's nothing I can do to change things."

Kate's breath catches in her throat. She presses her fingers against her palm, closing it off. *No, London*, she thinks. *You can't change destiny, no matter what you do.* In Paris she had believed that, so she hadn't tried. But when she came home, she *had* tried – and, well, that line never diverged into two, did it? It had been Kate's destiny to lose her true love, just as it had been Lydia's destiny to die young – their destinies had intertwined, the way their hands had refused to let go of each other that morning.

But what does she know, really? Her love line never diverged, no, but she *did* have two loves of her life. More. Her daughters, her son, her grandchildren. *They're just lines, Kate*, she hears Lydia say. Why should London let her destiny be tied to this Adam person, anyway? Let London be the one to break away from this legacy. Let her be the one to take action. Let her be the one to embrace her own free will.

Kate takes her hand. "We came here to save a shark. So let's save a shark!"

"We can't," London says, her eyes downcast. "It's over."

"It's not over. Do you know why? Because you're here. *You* can save it."

London gives a snort. But when she raises her eyes to meet Kate's, there is a light that hadn't been there before. "I know where we can find a boat," she says.

On the way down in the elevator, London turns to Kate. "Can I ask you something?"

"Of course, dear." The back and side walls of the elevator are mirrored, and Kate can see her granddaughter's and her own reflection from all angles. *Ask me anything*, she thinks. *I am ready.*

"Are you and Papa in love?"

Oh. Not that. "Yes, very much," she says.

"That's nice," London says. "Really nice." She takes off her glasses and rubs her eyes. "I don't think that anyone will ever love me."

That's ridiculous, Kate wants to say. *You're just a child, you don't even know what love is yet.* But she senses that this is the wrong answer. Instead, she takes London's hand and turns it over, muscle memory kicking in as she runs her fingers over the girl's palm. "Do you want to know what it says?" she asks. London nods. "It says that you will have many loves in your life. But only if you concentrate on finding someone who *you* love, instead of worrying about finding someone who will love you."

"Wow, Nana," London says after a minute, putting her glasses back on. "I didn't know you could read palms. That's really cool."

If London had her glasses on, she might have noticed that Kate didn't actually look at London's palm once. Some things, Kate thinks, are better left a mystery.

THIRTY

"Say cheese," says Walter, holding up a camera.

He is standing on the main viewing platform at Kakabeka Falls – the same platform where the video of Kate was taken – waiting for a family of four blond, tanned, athletic-looking Midwesterners to compose themselves in front of the wooden railing. He has been at the falls for three hours and has already taken twelve similar pictures of people with their own cameras – mostly families and young couples, dressed in their provincial park best, shorts and T-shirts and sun hats, toting expensive cameras with multiple lenses. Walter likes tourists, especially these cross-country camping types – he respects their stick-to-it-ness, their relentless joviality in the face of mosquitoes, endless meals of hotdogs and hamburgers, poorly maintained restroom facilities, day after day of close quarters with family members. Regardless of their weeks of poor diet and questionable sleeping arrangements, when faced with an important landmark they smooth down their hair, take a deep breath, hand their expensive digital camera over to a complete stranger, and smile.

For this family, however, pulling it together is taking more effort. "Kylie, get your ass over here," the father yells at the elder daughter, who has wandered off, her eyes glued to her phone.

"You shouldn't talk to her like that, Steve," the mother says. "She needs to be allowed to have some independence."

"Well, you shouldn't undermine me in front of the kids, Karen," Steve shoots back.

Walter waits them out, wondering what has happened to the probably thousands of photos like this he has taken over the years. How many of them actually made it off the memory card and onto a computer or were uploaded to a website? Or even, heaven forbid, printed and framed? Most of them probably just stay on that memory card forever. He imagines a giant collage of all the pictures he has taken of people on Superior Tours – the families, the birdwatchers, the researchers, the journalists, the adventure sportists. No matter what their reasons for visiting, when they finally come face to face with one of the great masterpieces of nature, all of them just want a picture of themselves standing in front of it. *I was here. I did this thing. I exist.*

Walter isn't judging; he has photos of himself in front of half the waterfalls in this region, most of the beaches, and the lake from all angles. He wants the world to know he exists, too.

Kylie has finally returned to the fold, reluctantly stuffing her phone into her pocket, when the younger boy starts crying. "Frank needs to be in the photo," he wails. "I want Frank in the photo!"

"I'm sorry, Jayden, Frank can't be in the photo," Karen says.

Steve looks at Walter apologetically. "Frank is his . . . you know." He gestures to his crotch. "He thinks it's his pet."

"Honey, stop," says Karen as Jayden starts to unzip his pants.

"*Gross*, Jayden," says Kylie.

Walter lowers the camera. Behind them, the falls thunder on, oblivious to the family drama unfolding in front of them. He has been here hundreds of times, but the falls never fail to take his breath away – those twin curtains on either side of the exposed

351

rock outcropping, spilling over the shale cliff and cascading down into the river in a cloud of mist. At the top, the river is traversed by a bridge, and the cliffs are built up with boardwalks and viewing platforms and informational signage, but Walter prefers to picture what the falls looked like back in the fur-trading days when they were discovered, wild and pristine. Untouched by man.

At the top of the staircase leading down to the falls is a brand-new sign saying that due to recent events, a security fence has been erected along the edge of the cliff, and any trespassers will be prosecuted. This makes little sense to Walter, considering that Kate accessed the river at the beach hundreds of yards upstream, but maybe the beach is closed off, too. Even though it's crazy, he feels as though people are staring at him, as though they know who he is, who he is married to. Standing here, he feels a little like a criminal returning to the scene of a crime.

So why is he here? When he pulled the truck into the driveway at Victor Street last night, he realized he just couldn't be there anymore. It had been hard, the night before, being alone in their bed without Kate for the first time in years, knowing that she was lying unconscious in a hospital room on the other side of town and he couldn't be with her. But knowing that she was now conscious and had gone somewhere other than back home to him, to their bed – well, that was just too much to take. Wherever Kate has gone, it is difficult for Walter to not feel that it is away from him.

So he drove away from the house, and he found himself following the same roads that Kate had taken on Friday morning, staring out the windshield of his truck the same way she had, passing the same houses, the same trees, the same street signs. When he got to the village of Kakabeka Falls he checked in at a motel and stared at the television without comprehending what he was seeing. Finally he went out and ate dinner at the Chinese buffet at the Kakabeka Curling Club, where there seemed to be no shortage of old men like himself eating alone.

After dinner, he drove back to the motel room, where he couldn't stand the thought of sitting back on the bed and watching more television as though nothing had happened. It just seemed disrespectful, somehow. So he sat in a chair in the dark and tried to think of places Kate might be. The hospital staff had seemed so convinced that she was still in the building, but he just couldn't picture her hiding out in a closet or under a bed. Walter had never known Kate to hide from anything. Maybe she had fallen asleep, but he somehow doubted that, too. If Kate had just woken up from a coma in the hospital, the last thing she would want to do would be to lie down again and sleep. Then again, Walter would have also said that the first thing she would want to do is see her family, and clearly he had been wrong about that. Still, it just didn't make sense for her to still be in the building. Kate hated hospitals. The only logical explanation was that she was gone.

But where?

Walter has asked himself that question so many times before, during the early years of their marriage when she used to disappear just like this. Maybe if he had pushed her then to tell him where she had gone, he would have some idea of where she might be now. As it is, he has only come up with completely ridiculous ideas, like Antarctica, a place that Kate had once called "the last place to be first at anything."

Of course, there is always Paris. Walter knows more about Kate than she remembers him knowing about her – a few details spilling out over a bottle of wine, a dreamy, faraway look in her eyes whenever a Sly and the Family Stone song comes on. He knows Kate fell in love in Paris, although he doesn't know with whom, or what happened. But whenever he brought up the idea of the two of them travelling there together, she completely shut down. If she *is* in Paris, she doesn't want Walter there with her.

"Okay," Steve says. "We're ready."

The family – minus Frank, thankfully – poses in front of the railing, smiling. Walter brings the camera up to his eye. When he peers through the viewfinder, for a second he sees his own family: Kate, coaxed out from behind the camera for once, standing next to him in the back, Nicki and Finn and Shawn in front, flicking each other, pulling on hair, giving each other wet willies while a stranger patiently waits for them to get it together. The girls are maybe twelve or thirteen; Shawn is just about to graduate from high school. This will be the only photo they have of the five of them together.

"On three," the stranger says.

They all freeze, smiling. And although Shawn has his shirt buttoned up wrong, and Nicki has her fingers in bunny ears over Finn's head, and Kate is distracted by something off to the left, Kate kept that picture in a frame on their living room wall for years. "It's the best I'm going to get out of the lot of you," she'd joke, but Walter knew there was a sobering truth to it. Sometimes it seemed as though that one moment as a family was all they were ever going to have.

"All right," Walter says, bringing himself back to the present. "On three. One, two, three!"

The family grins wider. Walter clicks the button and lowers the camera. As he does, he sees a man standing on the bridge, staring at him. He seems familiar, but Walter can't place him. "One more for safety," he says. When he lowers the camera again, the man is gone.

"Thanks so much." Steve takes the camera back from Walter. "Hey, maybe you can tell us. This is that place where the lady went over the falls in a barrel, right? Do you know which side she was on?"

Walter clenches his fists. "No, sorry."

"*I* want to go over the falls in a barrel," Jayden whines.

"I wish you would," says Kylie.

"You don't want to do that, honey," Karen says, ushering her children towards the boardwalk. "That lady was crazy. Only a terribly disturbed person would do something like that."

And that just about does it for Walter. He excuses himself and makes his way up the stairs, a great crushing feeling in his chest that causes his breath to come in sharp bursts. His heart is pounding and he is sweating profusely, but he keeps climbing, dodging the crowds, up to the nearly empty bridge near the top of the falls. It's not until he is about halfway across that his panic begins to subside. He leans his arms against the railing and lowers his head.

It occurs to him that likely every single person who has ever visited this place has imagined what it would be like to go over the falls. He can remember standing here many times, gazing down at the Kam and wondering himself. From this angle, the river is only a river – there is no dramatic veil, no cloud of mist, no whirlpool at the bottom, no photogenic view. Just a river, and then an end to the river. It's impossible to see what lies beyond the precipice, and from there it is easy to let your mind wander, to follow the current along to that point, and then perhaps speculate about a glorious free fall, wings sprouting from your back moments before you reach the bottom, or a thrill ride like a waterslide on an acute-angled descent, maybe some twists and turns, a loop-de-loop, spitting you out at the bottom, waterlogged and laughing, chanting "Again, again!" as you clap your hands like a child.

But from another angle, the one from the viewing platform, there is no mystery. There is only horrifying reality: millions of gallons of water surging over the edge and crashing into the whirlpool below, with a sound like a constant drum roll, a bleak warning of death. No one standing here has any illusions of wings or waterslides. You imagine going over the edge and you feel nothing but fear.

"Walter," a voice says.

Walter raises his head to find the man he spotted earlier standing next to him. The confusion must have shown on his face because the man says, "You don't remember me, do you?"

And suddenly Walter does. "Dallas." *Finn's ex-boyfriend*, he almost adds, until he realizes that he is, of course, also Ross's father. *Which one does he identify with more?* Walter wonders. *How would he have introduced himself if I hadn't remembered his name?* He never spent much time with Dallas when he was dating Finn – he just figured Dallas wouldn't be around long enough to bother getting attached. Eight years is longer than Walter expected, but in the end he was right – Dallas was gone from their lives for good, although not without leaving a little piece of himself behind. Or a big piece of himself. Looking at Dallas now, Walter realizes that Ross looks exactly like his father.

"I'm surprised to see you here," Dallas says.

"I could say the same thing," says Walter. "Didn't you move to B.C.?"

"I moved back here a couple of years ago."

"Oh." The two of them stand side by side in awkward silence. Walter feels he should say something, do something fatherly, stand up for his daughters in some way. But it was so long ago, and he is just too tired to care anymore.

"So, is Kate . . ." Dallas pauses. "Is she okay?"

"Yes," says Walter. He decides not to tell Dallas that Kate is awake. At this moment, he doesn't trust anyone – especially a stranger, which is essentially what Dallas is.

"I knew it was her, you know." Dallas drums his fingers against the railing. Walter suspects he might be stoned. His eyes keep darting away, flitting from face to face as people pass by them on the bridge, then back down to the water. "Before I even saw the video. I heard on the radio that a woman had gone over the falls and I thought, *That's gotta be Kate.*"

Walter feels his pulse pick up again. "Why did you think that?"

356

"Well, I mean, she was always talking about those Niagara daredevils, right? You know, Annie Taylor, Bobby Leach, Karel Soucek. How cool it would be if someone tried it at Kakabeka. When I heard that on the radio I was like, *Oh man, she actually did it.*" Dallas reaches in his pocket and pulls out a Kleenex, which he starts systematically shredding. "But I'm not telling you anything new. You must have known it was going to happen."

Walter thinks about that day, a week ago, when Kate said, "Let's go to Kakabeka." He had thought she was being nostalgic for those afternoons they spent as a family wandering along the cliffs, climbing down the Little Falls trail, stopping on the way home at the Big Scoop for ice cream. Now he realizes it was a reconnaissance mission. How was he to know?

He knows Kate, that's how. He knows her far better than this sorry excuse for a man standing next to him on the bridge. "People talk about stuff like that all the time," he says, trying to control the shaking in his voice. "It doesn't mean they're going to do it."

"Come on, man. This is *Kate* we're talking about. You know how she always used to say that thing, the quote from the side of Soucek's barrel or whatever? 'It's not whether you fail or triumph, it's that you try,' or something like that? The reporter said she'd look it up."

It takes all of Walter's willpower not to push Dallas over the edge of the bridge. "You talked to a reporter?"

"Oh, yeah. Cassandra something? She said she was tracking down members of the Parker family."

"You are not a Parker," Walter says quietly.

"No, I know, man, I just . . . well." He lets the shredded Kleenex go, and it drifts down to the river. "I didn't really have much to tell her anyway. I just gave her that picture I had. I figured Kate would have wanted them to use a nice one for her big moment of fame, you know?"

Walter watches the river carry the Kleenex to the brink, and then it is gone. "You shouldn't have done that," he says.

"I guess it wasn't the best idea. I just figured, why would you do something like that if you didn't want people to know it was you?" Dallas shoves his hands back into his pockets. "I always used to kind of imagine she was my mom, you know? You guys don't know how lucky you are."

He's right, Walter realizes. In all this time, it has never occurred to him that they were lucky – or how someone like Dallas might look at them and see not dysfunction but beautiful, crazy chaos. Why couldn't he see it before? It's as though all of them, the entire Parker family, are so short-sighted they can't even see what's right in front of them. Maybe they're born with the inability to make sense of the bigger picture. Maybe it's just in their genes.

You should come by sometime and see your son, he thinks, but he knows it is not his place to say this. So he leaves Dallas on the bridge, still watching the river.

Walter continues across the bridge and over to the portage trail, used by the voyageurs to navigate around the falls, the same route that he walked with Kate a week earlier. She had talked about mundane things then: getting the windshield wipers replaced on her Volvo, what she was going to buy Milan and Vienna for their birthday, how she was worried about Bruno's left eye. "There used to be *some* stuff in his eye in the morning, but now there's *lots* of stuff in it. Do you know what I mean, stuff? The stuff in your eye in the morning?" she asked.

"Yes, I know the stuff," Walter said.

"No, but what is it called?" Kate asked. "It's not *stuff*. I just can't think of the word."

"It's *stuff*," Walter said, feeling irritated. "People just call it stuff."

"But it must have a name," Kate insisted. "An actual name."

"Not really."

"Why won't you tell me?"

"I don't know, Katie. Mucus? That's the technical term, but most people call it other things, like sand or sleep or goop or, yes, stuff. So there are a lot of words people use. I'm not sure which one you're thinking of."

Kate's brow furrowed. "None of those words sound familiar," she said. "Are you sure those are the right ones?"

Walter said nothing. He didn't want to be like this. He wanted to be a good husband, to try to explain things to Kate in a kind and patient tone. *This is called a strawberry. You use this for grating cheese. Clouds are made of vapour. Vapour is made of water. I don't know how it gets in the sky, Kate, okay?* Question after question, until Walter either snapped or gave her an answer so complicated that he knew it would shut her up. He understood his frustration was a manifestation of his own fear, and not a reflection on her, or how he felt about her. Thankfully, she didn't seem to notice how upset he got with her when she couldn't remember things. None of this made him feel like any less of an ass.

They stopped at their favourite look-off point, the way they always did, reading the plaque there quoting American geologist William H. Keating's account of his expedition to the Great Lakes in 1825: *Directly opposite to the place from which we contemplated the fall, there is in the rock a cavity, which, in the superstitious legends of the Indians, is regarded as the residence of the evil spirit.* Just imagine, evil spirits haunting the holes left behind by ancient creatures trapped in the rock, exposed by the river slicing it open, all of this taking place over the course of 1.6 million years.

"Maybe the Ojibwe were right about this," Kate said. "The earth must have been quite a different place back then. Full of magic and mystery. There could have been evil spirits all over the place."

"I'm sure a lot of life has come to an end in this gorge," Walter agreed. "Prehistoric flies, Ojibwe princesses. Probably a voyageur or two. That's quite a legacy."

"A person could do a lot worse than become a part of that," Kate said, running her fingers over the railing as she stared out into the gorge.

How could he not have known?

Throughout their lives together, Walter has always thought of Kate as fearless. But he was wrong. She wasn't fearless; she was brave. You can't be brave if you don't feel fear. What makes you brave is that you feel the fear and do it anyway.

Kate faced that waterfall and felt no fear. She couldn't have, otherwise she would never have done what she did. Bravery does not take you over waterfalls. Bravery lets you jump across rivers, lets you stare into the abyss of a frozen lake and fight your way back to the surface. Bravery takes you to Europe and leaves you on your own for a year. Bravery opens your front door to a homeless boy and makes him your son. Bravery helps you face an illness that eventually takes everything away from you, including your bravery. But bravery does not take you over waterfalls.

So then. What does?

And – Walter thinks, as he pulls the parking ticket out from under his windshield wipers – if he can't figure that out, how is he supposed to keep her safe?

THIRTY-ONE

When Finn and Nicki were kids, their parents would take them to Duluth every year at the end of summer vacation to buy them new clothes and school supplies, just like every other family in Thunder Bay. They would stay at the hotel with the indoor waterslides, and in the evenings they would sometimes walk down to Canal Park to watch the lift bridge go up and down, eating ice cream sandwiches or drinking pop while sitting on the breakwater, feeling as though they were in the most exotic place on Earth even though they were less than three hours away from home. Finn loved those trips, but she hated the drive: three hours of trying not to get carsick on a curvy single-lane highway through tiny northern Minnesota towns, just trees and lake and more trees. If only she had remembered this before following Nicki out to the driveway in her bare feet, stepping lightly across the gravel.

"Come on, Nicki. You probably don't even have any music! What are you going to do, listen to NPR the entire way to Duluth?" Nicki got into the car, ignoring her. Finn jumped into the passenger seat next to her, pulling her phone out of her pocket. "I have eight hours of songs on here," she said.

Nicki raised two fingers to her temple and pretended to pull the trigger. "You better at least have some classic rock."

They have been on the road for an hour now, listening to nothing but Guns N' Roses while Finn, shoeless and hungry and regretting all her life decisions, counts the number of near accidents they've had as Nicki almost rear-ends an RV towing a boat slowing down to pull into Judge Magney State Park. Finn just stares out the window and tries not to get sick, watching the trees fly by and wondering if she will ever see her house again, or if she will die here on Highway 61 before she even has a chance to get some lunch.

Despite Nicki's threatening to call the police, Adam Pelley's publicist refused to tell them where he is staying in Duluth. None of the hotels they called will tell them anything either. So Nicki has decided that their best course of action is to go down to the Canal Park and start checking the hotels on the waterfront. "We might even be able to spot the Volvo parked somewhere," she says, reaching for the volume on the stereo as "Welcome to the Jungle" comes on for the second time. Finn wonders if Nicki has ever listened to any music that came out after 1995. At least she's in a better mood – Nicki needs to have a purpose, to have something to focus on. For her part, despite her best intentions to keep her mind on the task at hand, Finn has mostly been thinking about food.

"Maybe we could stop at Culver's?" Finn says.

"We're not stopping. I just passed like five transports. I don't want to have to pass them again."

Of course she won't stop. Nicki is so like their father – single-minded, practical, unable to detour from a plan. She talks to Finn the way that Walter would sometimes talk to Kate: "No, we can't stop to go tubing in Stanley, I need to get the boat ready for tomorrow." "No, we can't build a dance floor in the basement, we need the space for storage." "No, the girls can't have cake at midnight, they've already brushed their teeth." For the first time, Finn feels some small degree of solidarity with her mother.

"Fine." Finn crosses her arms, acutely aware that she sounds like a five-year-old on the verge of a tantrum. "But I'm going to get something to eat as soon as we get to Duluth."

"Do what you want," says Nicki. "This isn't your problem anyway."

"You keep saying that. But I'm here, aren't I?"

"You're *not* here," says Nicki, speeding up to a minivan towing a boat. "You're just *vacationing*. You're on the full Parker Immersion Tour, and in a few days you're going to go back home and everything will just be a beautiful fucking memory." She pulls out into the oncoming lane, then swerves back as another SUV towing a boat whizzes past in the other direction, narrowly missing them. "How can we be the only ones on this highway not towing a fucking boat?" Nicki yells out the window to no one in particular.

"Oh yeah, this is going to be a really beautiful memory," says Finn, bracing herself against her seat.

"Face it, Finn. This is no longer your life. Stop trying to convince us you wish it still was."

Everything Nicki is saying, she has already thought herself, in her darker moments. Still, it makes her angry. "I just don't get it," she says. "In other places, it is a normal, functional thing for children to grow up and move away. But everyone in Thunder Bay just *stays*. Nothing ever changes, but still everyone stays. Everyone is so afraid of going off on their own, of doing something outside their comfort zone. They just want everything to be familiar and easy. That's not how life works! Life is not about what is familiar. It's about . . . something else. It has to be. It *has* to be."

"Some of us like it here, you know." Nicki's voice is level, but her knuckles are white on the steering wheel. "You don't get to just judge people like that."

WARNING: PROCEEDING WITH THIS CONVERSATION MAY RESULT IN FORCIBLE EJECTION FROM A MOVING VEHICLE. Screw it. If this is how she's going to die, then at least she'll die having said what she needs to say. "Come on, Nicki. You were going to travel. You were going to go see Europe. You didn't stay in Thunder Bay because you liked it, you stayed because you got knocked up."

"Yeah. It's called fucking taking *responsibility*, Finn."

"You call living at home with Mom and Dad being responsible?"

"So you have your own house. That doesn't make you better than me."

"Why does everyone assume I think I'm better than everyone else? My life is actually pretty shitty. I live alone in a crappy suburb, I have a boring job, I haven't dated anyone since Dallas. I don't even have my own dog, I have to borrow my neighbour's."

Nicki laughs. "Wow. You're really selling me on this whole leaving thing."

"I . . . that's not what I meant."

"No, no, I get it. Basically what you're telling me is that even your boring, shitty life is better than life with us."

Finn closes her eyes, leaning her head back against the seat. *Her boring, shitty life.* She had so many plans when she moved to Toronto. Start another master's. Go to cooking school. Volunteer at the art gallery. Call that Jennifer Hardy chick she went to Lakehead with who worked at MuchMusic and go out for drinks at a bar so underground it didn't even have a name, where the DJ played music so new no one had ever heard it before. She would meet interesting people, get offered a job in social media, go to Fashion Week. She would be a Torontonian, which, in her mind, was exactly the opposite of being a Thunder Bayer.

She had hinged all her hopes for a new life on Jennifer Hardy, who, as it turned out, had quit her job at MuchMusic to teach yoga in Scarborough and would only meet Finn for lunch because she didn't like to come downtown after dark. It only took a few months for Finn to realize that her day-to-day life in Toronto would not be the triumphant exile she had imagined during all those lonely high school lunch periods sitting alone in the cafeteria. She was soon doing the same things there that she had done in Japan – hiding in her apartment, reading books she had brought from home, eating at McDonald's because it was the only place she could understand the menu. In a place where she had explicitly gone to find something new and exciting, she had actively sought out the easy and comfortable. The familiar.

So maybe she was a bit of a hypocrite. But at least she had tried something. Even if she was failing, at least she hadn't just given up before she started.

"My life might be boring and shitty, but at least it's mine," she whispers out the window.

By the time they get to Duluth, it is after three. They drive straight to Canal Park and Nicki pulls in behind the Dairy Queen so that they can start their search on foot.

"So many tourists," she says as she starts speed-walking through the crowds towards Minnesota Avenue, Finn running to catch up. "I'm never going to find them."

"I'm pretty sure we'll be able to pick out an old woman with a broken pelvis and a teenager on a mission to save the planet," says Finn.

"What's this *we* business? I thought you were dying of starvation or something."

"Like I'm going to give you the chance to leave me stranded in Duluth."

Nicki shakes her head but doesn't argue. They make their way towards the lift bridge, past all the tourist shops and bars and restaurants with their faux northern outdoorsy wholesomeness, window displays of trees and bears, pictures of fishermen in red plaid, airbrushed photos of wolves on T-shirts, while the restaurants advertise walleye as "the catch of the day," as if it were ever anything different. But whether they come up from the Twin Cities or down from Thunder Bay, the tourists love it, and they buy into it all.

"All these people," Finn says to herself. "Just out together, being normal."

"What people? What are you talking about?" Nicki peers into the doorway of an old-timey toy store with model trains and creepy dolls set up in the windows.

Finn points at a family just inside the door, a mother and father and two kids playing with some puppets stuck on a wooden stand. The father sticks his hand in a green frog puppet and starts singing "The Rainbow Connection" in a pretty convincing Kermit the Frog voice as the kids collapse into giggles. "Like them," she says. "Normal. Having fun."

Nicki shakes her head. "It's all a lie," she says. "The kids are assholes. The parents probably haven't had sex in five years."

"Okay, fine," says Finn, turning to look at two twenty-something girls next door, both blond and robust and Nordic, reading the menu for Little Angie's Cantina. "What about them?"

"Oh, they post really bitchy comments on each other's Instagram photos. Now can we please fucking focus?" She walks away without checking to see if Finn is following her.

Finn continues to watch the two girls, mesmerized.

"I don't see anything on here that's gluten-free," one girl says. "Let's go to the Korean place inside."

"I can't do Korean," the second girl says. "They have nothing vegan."

"You're not vegan," Gluten-Free says. "You're just trying to impress that TV guy."

"Whatever," the second girl says. "I've been vegan for, like, two months now."

"I guess the milk in those twenty White Russians you drank the other night was *vegan* milk then, was it?" Gluten-Free says, poking her in the arm. "All-natural vegan milk at the Radisson hotel bar."

"You're just jealous because Adam didn't invite *you* to come out on his boat."

Adam. "Excuse me," Finn says. "Are you guys talking about Adam Pelley? The television host?"

Pseudo-Vegan looks at her scathingly. "He's a *marine biologist,*" she says. "He only does the TV stuff because he *has* to. For educational purposes."

"Of course," says Finn. "I'm sure he's very altruistic."

"That sounded sarcastic," Gluten-Free says.

"Why are you talking to us, anyway?" Pseudo-Vegan says.

"And where are your shoes?"

Finn curls her bare toes against the pavement. "I'm just trying to find Adam Pelley," she says.

"I bet," says Gluten-Free. She turns to the other one. "I totally feel like I saw her the other night at the Radisson, staking out the place."

"Well, sure, I was there," says Finn. "He and I are actually friends. We went to, uh, marine biology school together."

The girls glance at each other, trying to figure out whether to believe her. In the end Finn supposes they don't see why she would have any reason to lie. "That's cool," Gluten-Free says. "He's a super-awesome guy."

"Are you going to be in the documentary?" Pseudo-Vegan asks.

"I was going to be," Finn says, "but I lost the directions to where they're shooting." She tries to make her best "oh well" face, dropping her gaze, scuffing her toe against the ground.

"Well, the *Rum Runner*'s right over there, at Bayside Marina," Pseudo-Vegan says. "Just on the other side of the lift bridge." When Finn raises her eyebrow, Pseudo-Vegan shakes her head in disbelief. "Uh, his *boat?*"

Nicki has already made it to the breakwater by the time Finn catches up with her. "Nicki," she says, out of breath and sweating, the bottoms of her feet scorched and buzzing. "Adam's filming his documentary at the marina on the other side of the bridge." They both stare at the lift bridge, which is on its way up. Just beyond, they can see a line of slips dotted with boats.

"They're over there?" Nicki asks. "How did you find out?" The wind has picked up, and her hair, usually shellacked into place, has come loose, strawberry-blond tendrils dancing in the wind around her head. Finn knows that later, Nicki's hair will be so tangled that she won't be able to get a brush through the end without using some leave-in conditioner and serious upper body strength. Finn knows this because her hair is exactly the same.

"Those two girls who hate each other are apparently Adam Pelley groupies."

"Right," Nicki says. "We'll just base our entire search on the word of random skanks."

"They weren't skanks, they were just regular girls. And they knew where Adam is, which is also where we'll probably find London and Mom, too."

"*Probably?*" Nicki shakes her head. "So you don't actually know where they are. You just want to be right about something, as usual."

"I don't care about being right!" Finn yells. "I just want to find Mom and London!"

"Why?" asks Nicki. "Why do you suddenly care now? I just don't understand, Finn. I just don't get it. This bullshit has been going on for *years*, and you've never wanted anything to do with your crazy mother and your criminal niece before."

"Who, London?" Finn laughs. "London's not a criminal."

"Oh my god, Finn! Did you know that she was *arrested* for drug possession? Fucking *arrested*. Dragged out of her school in handcuffs, in front of all her classmates. The only way she could get out of it was ratting out her suppliers, and all her friends ditched her because of it. Did you know your niece is basically a teenaged pariah?"

"Of course I knew," says Finn. She can remember some snippets of conversations with Shawn while she was half-distracted by dinner on the stove or Max in the yard, emails from her mother that were poorly punctuated and full of statements of questionable accuracy. She *must* have known.

"So you knew, but you didn't do anything about it? I feel *so much better* knowing that."

"Come on, Nicki, that's not fair."

"Fair? You want to talk about fair?" Nicki's voice grows louder, shriller.

An elderly couple holding hands stares at them as they walk past. "Shh," Finn whispers.

"Don't fucking shush me, Finn! Do you have any idea what it's like to have to get up every morning and wonder what messed-up thing Mom is going to do today? To wonder if I'm going to have to go down to Safeway and explain to the security guard that she just forgot that she had to pay for that watermelon? Or if I'm going to come home from work to discover that she's ripped her entire bedroom apart looking for a pair of boots that she hasn't had since 1972? If I'm going to have to do all of that and then come home and make supper for my kids and my husband and just pretend that everything is all right? Do you know what that feels like, Finn? Do you know *anything* about us? Anything at all?"

Finn stares at her. "I know you're cheating on Hamish." She doesn't say "Dallas." She doesn't have to. His name has been hanging unsaid in the space between her and Nicki for years.

"Yeah, well," says Nicki, her gaze narrowing. "Guess I won the goddamn jackpot on that one."

"Don't do that! Don't make it seem like you didn't choose this, Nicki, like you're a fucking martyr. You slept with my *boyfriend*. Why does everyone keep forgetting that!"

"He shouldn't have been your boyfriend!"

Finn laughs again. "Oh, right, because he should have been *your* boyfriend, is that it?"

"No!" yells Nicki. "Because you fucking deserved better!"

"I . . . what?"

Nicki takes a deep breath, and Finn can feel her own diaphragm contracting, her own lungs expanding, air travelling down her bronchial tubes and filling her alveoli, oxygen dispersing through her capillaries. "You were going to get out," Nicki says. "If any of us were going to get out, it was you." She rests her elbows on the breakwater wall. "He wasn't going anywhere. But you, you could. And you did."

Finn thinks of Nicki's map of the world, her little pins. "You could have, too," she says.

"No," says Nicki, shaking her head. She traces a pattern on the cement wall with one ragged fingernail, head bent low. "I was never going anywhere."

They both look out over the water. Finn suddenly finds herself thinking about the night that Dallas got Nicki pregnant. Finn had been at their apartment, in that old run-down house behind that church in Current River, sulking. He had wanted Finn to come out with him that night. "You never come out anymore," he said. "The guys are all starting to think you don't actually exist."

The guys. That nebulous group of guys – and a few girls – who Dallas spent most of his time with at various bars, or house parties, or camps. Finn just couldn't stomach one more night with them, drinking and smoking weed and playing the same five or six songs on the guitar. "Why can't we just spend the night in for once?" she asked. "Maybe try to save some money?"

"Save money for what?"

"I don't know, to get out of here!" This was the same fight they had, night after night, so familiar it was almost boring. "I just wish you would do something real. Why can't we just fucking *do something real*?"

"What does that even mean? This is life, babe. This *is* real."

She didn't have an answer for him. She didn't know what she wanted. All she knew was it wasn't this.

The next morning, she woke up to Walter calling her from the hospital to tell her Kate had fallen off the roof, that he didn't know where Nicki was, that she didn't come home the night before. Something started ticking inside Finn then, so softly that she barely noticed it save for the slightly sick feeling it gave her – the gentle momentum propelling her towards a foregone conclusion she should have seen coming, but that still somehow totally blindsided her. She called Nicki's cell phone, the ringing in sync with the ticking, her heart speeding up to meet the rhythm. The ticking was a warning she ignored.

"Finn? Hey, baby," Dallas said. "I had a rough night out with the guys."

The ticking stopped. But there was no explosion, nothing. It was like someone had cut the live wire. Everything became calm, still, eerily silent. She can remember stopping at Tim Hortons on her way to the hospital and getting a blueberry bagel with cream cheese, smiling at the woman at the drive-thru, leaving her a loonie as a tip. She sang along with the radio, a Stones song, something she didn't even realize she knew the words to. She parked her car and ran with her hood pulled up against the rain to the emergency room doors, still humming the melody under her breath.

But when she got to the hospital and saw Nicki getting out of Dallas's car, wearing Dallas's shirt, and smiling at Finn as she walked through the doors like she was fucking royalty, the ticking started up again. It has been ticking ever since.

Now, the ticking finally stops. Something clicks in her brain, something that has been working its way into her consciousness since her run-in with Tanya. All these years she has blamed her inability to be in a relationship, her inability to move forward, on the scars Dallas left behind.

But this wasn't about Dallas anymore. Maybe it never had been.

"What do you mean, you were never going anywhere?" Finn asks.

"You said it yourself." Nicki pulls her hair back from her face, wrapping it with an elastic from her wrist. "I got knocked up."

"You got pregnant on purpose." It's suddenly so clear to Finn. Nicki had never been stupid, even back then, back when Finn felt she needed to warn her about the risks of everything from smoking weed in the parking lot before school to driving home drunk from parties, from getting that fake ID so she could sneak into that Helix show to telling everyone those stories about what she may or may not have done with the drummer backstage afterward. Of course she knew about birth control. There was no reason she should have gotten pregnant unless she had planned it.

Nicki shrugged. "It wasn't on purpose. I just didn't care one way or the other."

"But why?"

"Because *Finn's the smart one*," Nicki says in a high-pitched, mocking voice. "*Finn's the brave one. Finn's the adventurous one. Finn's the one who is going to make something of herself.*" She keeps her gaze fixed out over the water. "I might as well have gotten pregnant, right? Dumb, trashy Nicki."

"It didn't have to be that way. You could have still gone somewhere, done something."

"But I didn't want to! Don't you get it? That stupid map, those pins, the trip to Europe? I just thought it would maybe make her . . ." Suddenly she turns to Finn, her eyes hard. "And then what happened? After all that? You met Dallas. And you *fucking stayed*."

It hits her then, how she's always taken for granted that they had the same thoughts, when really she's never known what Nicki was thinking at all. The realization hollows Finn out with such a deep, visceral grief that she is momentarily winded. She and

Nicki stand next to each other on the breakwater and watch the bridge clang and wheeze to the top of its trajectory, allowing an expensive-looking cabin cruiser to glide underneath. In the cockpit, two figures are standing with their backs angled towards the shore, focused on the lake ahead of them. Even without being able to see their faces, Finn knows. It seems impossible, but she knows. London and Kate are on that boat.

She turns to Nicki, ready for something shrill, for Nicki to scream out at them, call them back to shore. But Nicki hasn't seen the boat. She has her head down on the breakwater wall, resting on her arms, and she is crying.

"I think Mom and London stole Adam Pelley's boat," Finn says.

"That sounds about right," Nicki mumbles into the wall.

Finn wants to wrap her arms around her sister, but something is holding her back. Instead, she reaches out and places her hand on Nicki's shoulder. This time, Nicki doesn't shrug her off, so Finn stands there beside her, feeling the rise and fall of Nicki's breath and watching the boat motor away from them, out into the lake. Coming to the realization that what a few minutes ago might have seemed like the end was really only the beginning.

THIRTY-TWO

K atriina had thought it would be easier. But telling Shawn she wanted a divorce had turned out to be the easy part. She had been in the moment, full of adrenaline, inspired by her own goddamn brave and beautiful heart. But once that moment was over, the anger dissipated and she suddenly felt paralyzed. She walked out of the house and sat in her car, her breath coming in short gasps. The thought of going back in, pulling out a suitcase, packing her clothes, deciding what to take and what to leave behind, of abandoning her life, starting from scratch in an empty house, facing an unknown future – it was impossible. And what about Tommy and Petey? What would happen to them? What scars would this leave behind on her beautiful boys? It was impossible. How did people find the strength to leave, with so many reasons to stay?

And what would she even want to take with her, anyway? Everything had too much history attached to it. She thought about their bedroom, realizing she was able to remember the exact moment she had acquired everything in it. The duvet, a Christmas present from her mother five years ago. The curtains, an impulse buy during a family trip to Minneapolis. The lamp a find at a vintage store on Court Street while out for coffee with Hanna. It's funny, now that she thinks about it. It's as if she was convinced there was this perfect combination of things that would line up like numbers in a code unlocking a happy life. If she made all the right choices, bought all the right things, said all the right words, her family would be happy. And when they weren't, well, it was clearly her fault. She hadn't been good enough.

Back at the Paulsson house, she peels the Post-it notes down one by one, carefully, as though she is performing some kind of ritual. She counts the Post-its as she goes, and by the time she is finished there are three hundred of them. She fumbles around in the kitchen drawers until she finds a set of matches, and then strikes one, staring at it as it burns in her fingers. Then she sweeps the pieces of paper into the sink and lights them on fire, watching them curl into black ash against the stainless steel. Once they are gone, she runs the faucet, dousing the remnants and washing them down the drain. The kitchen is now full of smoke, but she doesn't care. What does it matter? This is her house. Hers. Not her father's, not her husband's. Hers. She can fill it with smoke if she wants to. She can do anything.

She would have gone to Ottawa with Shawn. She would have left her parents and Hanna, she would have moved to an apartment if she had to. She would have tamed her wild northern boys into city kids, with bus passes and a taste for sushi – tamed them into skating in a straight line down the Rideau Canal, into living the alternate future she had envisioned for them. Shawn would wear a suit instead of an apron, she would learn how to sell houses in a different market. Maybe it was a lot to ask for – a whole new life – but she is starting to learn that sometimes it is necessary to ask for a lot.

Her ultimatum to Shawn, that had been her Margaret Paulsson moment. It had been her hand on the bedroom doorknob, her life split in two, unravelling. Pieces of the old Katriina slowly crumbling away with every agonizing heartbeat in the terrible, breathless eternity between saying the words and understanding they would not be leaving. It was over.

She finds herself thinking back to high school, a Canada Day spent watching the fireworks from Hillcrest Park, the entire city gathered on a humid summer night with their kids and their dogs and their blankets and their picnic baskets, and Katriina and Shawn sitting under a tree, passing back and forth a bottle of Old English in a paper bag. She was wearing a sundress she had bought at Eaton's with her own money earned babysitting the girl next door. Shawn had been working for a landscaping company, and he always smelled like cut grass, his arms and legs tanned to a deep brown. It wasn't even their first date, or the first time they had sex, or the first time he told her he loved her. It was just a random night, malt liquor on their breath, the warm summer air on their bare skin, their entire lives in front of them, achingly promising. It just might have been the best moment of their relationship. If Katriina had known that then, she would have left him under that tree and never looked back.

As she opens the kitchen window to let out the smoke, she hears a squeaking noise behind her. But it is just a cabinet door she has left open, creaking to a close on a rusty hinge. The ghosts have gone, she knows, and it is a good thing, the right thing, the *sane* thing. And yet, she can't help but feel a tiny twinge of regret.

"I'm still here, Claudia," she whispers. Just in case.

Later, Katriina drives to Victor Street to pick up Tommy and Petey. She's not sure yet where she's going to put them, but she has decided that they shouldn't stay there, not after everything that has happened. They all need a break from the Parkers, including her children. On the drive over, she tries to figure out what she is going to tell the boys – about Shawn, about the house, about how they are not, in fact, going to have a little brother or sister. By the time she arrives, she has decided she will not tell them anything. Not yet.

There is an unfamiliar car in the driveway. *One of the girls' friends*, she thinks, anticipating a flurry of activity as soon as she steps through the door. But the house is quiet, quieter than she has ever known it. She can hear the soft rumble of the television in the living room, but not much else. There is a stack of dirty dishes in the kitchen sink, but otherwise the room is spotless. Even the floor looks freshly mopped. There is no sign of any kids. There is no sign of anyone.

This is a good house. Certainly worth much, much more than Walter would have paid for it in 1973. The property itself is a gold mine, backing onto the river the way it does. And while most of the neighbours had long ago torn down the original wooden houses in order to build enormous new brick ones, the original Parker house still stood, proud and wooden and flawed and beautiful, against that growing backdrop of McMansions. Much like the Parkers themselves, Katriina allows. It has become easier to love her extended family, to see the charm in their boisterousness, in their eccentricity, now that she knows she will no longer have to deal with them.

She walks from the kitchen to the living room, expecting to see a herd of children parked in front of the television, but the room is empty and the back door is wide open. The kids must be out in the yard. A minor league baseball game is playing on the local channel. As she sits down on the couch, she wonders if she will ever come back to this house, if she will ever sit here again.

"Katriina?"

She turns to the open door and finds Shawn standing there, a beer in his hand. "What are you doing here?" he asks.

Her breath catches in her throat. "I came to get Tommy and Petey."

"They're outside with Hamish and Ross and the girls. They're building some kind of waterslide using garbage bags."

"Oh." They are both quiet. It has only been a few hours since she last saw him, but it might as well have been years. Everything feels strange, awkward. "I thought you were going to Duluth," she says finally.

"You heard that, huh." He leans against the doorway and tilts the beer bottle back and forth, watching the liquid move up one side, then the other. "I told Nicki I couldn't go."

"Why?" Katriina asks, surprised.

Shawn shrugs, still focused on the bottle. "There was stuff I needed to take care of here."

"Oh," she says again. *It's too late, though, Shawn*, she thinks. *It's too late, it's too late.* She folds her hands in her lap, resisting the urge to scratch at her arms. She wasn't prepared for this – she just needs to get her thoughts under control. On the television screen the pitcher stands at the mound, warming up, and she wishes that something would happen, that someone would make a big play, that there was something there to distract her other than just a man swinging his arm around.

Eventually Shawn says, "I can go get the boys, if you want to take them to your place."

The words *your place* sound like another language coming from his mouth. Katriina nods, unable to speak. Those words are like a hairline fracture in a load-bearing wall, spidering through her, branching into multiple fissures until she knows that one small tap, one tiny breath of wind will cause her to crumble.

Shawn walks out the door, but then turns around and walks back in. "I just need to know one thing," he says. "Why, Katriina? Why would you hurt yourself like that?"

Katriina feels the world fall out from under her, and for a moment she is floating, untethered, in a vast, unknown galaxy. Then just as quickly she tumbles unceremoniously back down to

Earth. She opens her mouth to speak, but no words come out. *I don't know*, she means to say. But instead, she says, "I don't know how else to get it all out."

Shawn nods, his eyes red. "I know what you mean," he says. "I sometimes feel like that, too." He flicks his finger against the label of the beer bottle. "Like now. With losing . . . with losing the baby and everything. I can't . . ." The label tears off in his fingers, and he stares at it uncomprehendingly, as though he's just carelessly ripped a wing from a butterfly.

Before Katriina can help herself, she is sobbing, her whole body shaking, and Shawn sits down next to her and puts his arms around her and he is crying, too, and all she can think is, *I can't do this, I have to stop this*, even though she already knows they can't stop, they are past the point of no return, they might just end up crying forever.

She squeezes her eyes tight and then opens them again. "Shawn, we can't do this. The boys are right outside." But his face is in her hair and she can feel his pain radiating from every pore in his body, so she takes a shuddering breath and pulls him closer, just for a minute. Just for one more minute. Over his shoulder she stares at the television screen, and through the blur of her tears she sees the pitcher is about to throw the ball. He is staring down the hitter, he is adjusting his cap, he is winding up, he is pitching.

And then he is gone.

In his place, a photo of Kate appears on the screen. *No, no, this can't be happening.* Katriina fights the urge to scream. *This isn't fair.* She has managed to avoid the video for this long, she can't watch it now. And yet she can't bring herself to look away. What new things could they possibly be saying about the Conqueror of Kakabeka? What great insights could they have had in the last twenty-four hours? Then she realizes they are not talking about the video at all.

"Shawn," she whispers as the image changes. "Shawn, look."

He pulls away from her, his face red and puffy. "What is it?"

She points to the screen, which is showing aerial footage of a boat – by the looks of it, an expensive and well-equipped boat – skimming across the surface of a body of water. She can't hear the voiceover, but she doesn't have to. The caption at the bottom of the screen says it all.

Breaking: Woman from Viral "Conqueror of Kakabeka" Video Steals Boat Belonging to Well-Known Marine Researcher Adam Pelley.

"What the hell." Shawn reaches for the remote and turns up the volume, a familiar voice gradually becoming discernible.

". . . for the last twenty minutes, according to local officials here in Duluth," says the unmistakable voice of Cassandra Coelho. "All attempts to hail the boat by radio have been unsuccessful."

"What's going on?"

Katriina and Shawn both turn to find Walter standing in the doorway to the living room, a glass of orange juice in his hand. His expression is so quizzical and innocent that she has the urge to throw her body between him and the television, shielding him from what he is about to see. "Are you two okay?"

The television cuts to a shot of Cassandra Coelho standing in front of what appears to be a marina. "Katherine Parker, also known as the Conqueror of Kakabeka, was in a coma up until yesterday afternoon, when this reporter saw her leaving the Thunder Bay General Hospital along with a teenaged girl, and followed her here to Duluth. Reports from local officials have not confirmed whether this unnamed young woman is with Parker on the stolen boat, although the boat's owner, noted marine biologist and TV host Adam Pelley, asserts that it is unlikely Parker would be able to operate the boat on her own."

The channel cuts to commercial, and the three of them stare dumbly at the television as an attractive young woman tells them about the importance of life insurance. Katriina can feel her heartbeat in every wound she has made on her body, a low hum of pain spreading across her skin. *Someone say something,* she thinks. *Someone say something before I explode.*

"Well," says Shawn after a minute. "It looks like they found Kate."

Walter continues to watch the insurance ad. "She's okay."

"*Okay?*" Shawn stares at him incredulously. "Walter, she stole a boat!"

"Yes, she did," says Walter. He puts down his glass of orange juice and heads out the back door.

Shawn and Katriina turn to each other, and she gets a little jolt, remembering that she has been crying. Her hands fly up to her face and she rubs at her eyes, hoping that it's not obvious, that Walter couldn't tell. Then she realizes how ridiculous that is – worrying about how she looks when there is so much else going on. Still, she starts to rub harder. Shawn grabs her gently by the wrists, pulling her hands away.

"You'll hurt yourself."

"Shawn . . ."

"You can leave," he says, his voice soft. "This isn't your problem anymore."

Behind him, the television is showing footage from the helicopter again, the boat a tiny dot crawling across a span of blue. Somewhere in that tiny dot is Kate. The woman who saved Shawn. Who raised him to be the man he is.

"Of course it is," she says.

By the time they catch up to Walter, he is already on the *Veronica,* with the engine running. "What are you doing?" Shawn asks as they step out onto the dock.

"I know where she's going," Walter says, starting to untie the ropes. "I'm going to go get her."

"I'm coming with you." Shawn climbs up onto the boat before Walter can stop him. Walter watches him silently for a moment and then goes back to the rope.

Katriina stands at the end of the dock. The *Veronica*'s engine is sputtering, kicking up a small wake that rocks her gently back and forth. The bumpers are up, the lines are untied, and Katriina has only a split second to make her decision. A split second, and then everything changes. So many moments that cleave our lives in two.

"I'm coming, too."

THIRTY-THREE

One Saturday morning in October, almost nine years ago, Walter woke up to find Kate and the *Miss Penelope* gone. It was the fourth time he almost lost Kate, if anyone was counting. He still isn't quite convinced he didn't lose her that day.

He waited for an hour for her to come back, pacing across the dock, feeling powerless. The *Serafina* and *Veronica* were already in dry dock for the winter, and without a boat he felt stranded. Nicki's girls were still asleep, though Nicki herself was nowhere to be found. But Walter didn't want Finn or Shawn to know what had happened, so he woke a neighbour and asked her to stay with the children. Then he called his old friend Harry Hatt, who he had worked with at the Ministry of Natural Resources, and asked if he could borrow his boat. When Harry got the whole story out of him, he told Walter he would take him out himself.

Harry picked him up and they sped back down the Kam to the mouth of the river and out into Lake Superior. Walter tried several times to hail Kate on the radio, but no one was answering. He was pretty sure she wouldn't know how to use the radio, but he figured it was worth a shot – he hadn't thought she would have known how to steal a boat either, and yet here they were. She hadn't been on the lake since she fell through the ice. Forty years of avoiding Lake Superior, of watching it warily from afar while her family swam, boated, and fished in it. What had happened?

"Which way do you think she would have gone?" asked Harry as they peered out at the vast lake, and Walter was suddenly confronted with the enormous futility of his task: 82,103 square kilometres, to be precise. Walter always went east, but he imagined Kate would turn the other way, towards the border, so that's the way they went. At the very least, Walter thought, there was less water to cover that way – if they didn't find her before the crossing at Pigeon River, they knew she had to be in the other direction. Unless, of course, she had just gone straight out into the lake, in which case they were really in trouble.

They were just past Thompson Island when the Coast Guard boats came flying up behind them, sirens blaring. Walter felt a hard knot of worry form in his chest. Harry looked at him, one eyebrow raised. "Might as well follow them," Walter said, leaning against the gunwale, resigned. They motored through the Coast Guard wake past Spar Island and Victoria Island, then veered suddenly and swiftly away from the shoreline towards Isle Royale, across the border in Michigan.

"Oh," said Walter softly, suddenly making the connection.

A few weeks earlier, Kate had come to him with a map. According to a book she had read, there was a tiny island outcrop off the coast of Isle Royale that used to house a lighthouse. Back in the 1920s, the lighthouse keeper had apparently been a fugitive from the law, something that wasn't discovered until after his death. He had stolen thousands of dollars during a bank robbery in Eau Claire and hidden the cash on the island. It was blocked off from public access, and the lighthouse had subsequently fallen into disrepair, but Kate was sure the treasure, as she called it, must still be there. Walter had laughed at her, told her it was just a legend, a fairy tale. He had heard the story before. One of many myths around Lake Superior.

"You don't know that for sure," she said. "We should go. It will be like an adventure."

"A highly illegal and completely pointless adventure," Walter replied.

Kate pouted. "You're no fun at all. What's the point of even having a boat if you don't get to take it to remote islands to search for buried treasure?" But she had dropped the idea. Or so Walter had thought. Now, he realized that the idea had been festering in her mind since then. He should have known. Kate was never one for dropping things.

The Coast Guard had already found her by the time Walter and Harry tracked them down to a tiny outcropping no more than half a kilometre wide, edged with steep rock faces. Through a small cut in the rock Walter could see the *Miss Penelope* tied loosely to a piece of deadwood, rocking perilously close to the cliff face with each incoming wave. For one brief moment he imagined that the boat had been hijacked by some thieving relative of the fugitive lighthouse keeper come to claim his rightful inheritance, and that Kate was just off at the grocery store or the doctor's office. But then he saw Kate's slender outline, her hair blowing behind her in the wind as she carefully picked her way along the cliff face towards the lighthouse, and he knew that had just been wishful thinking.

The Coast Guard had surrounded the outcropping and were trying to hail her with a bullhorn. Walter was surprised to see that the lighthouse even existed, crumbling and neglected on a bare slab of rock surrounded by a stand of scrubby Jack pines. "Hey!" an officer yelled as Harry pulled the boat up alongside them. "This is a security matter."

"That's his wife!" Harry yelled back, and the officer motioned for Walter to board.

"We've been trying to hail her on the radio, but she hasn't been answering," said the officer, who introduced himself as Briggs. He was tall and burly and distinctly American. That's when Walter realized that this had become an international incident. Not only were the rock outcropping and lighthouse protected territory, but they had been breached by someone who had technically illegally crossed the border. His head began to pound.

"She doesn't know how to use the radio," Walter said.

Briggs stared at him with what Walter recognized as barely disguised pity. "Do you think you can get her to come down?"

Walter nodded, although he wasn't sure. He took the bull-horn from Briggs and switched it back on. "Katie," he said, his voice echoing out across the water at an alarming volume. "Please come down. They're not going to arrest you." He looked sideways at Briggs as he said it, hoping it was true. "But you're not allowed to be here. I need you to come down."

He saw her stop and then turn. The knot of worry tightened. She was scanning the horizon, trying to see where the sound was coming from. Then her direction changed. *She's coming back down*, he thought. *She's actually listening.* But she was descending too quickly. She wasn't coming down, she was falling. She had turned towards the sound of his voice and she had let go and now her body was disappearing between the rocks. *No*, thought Walter. *Get up, get up, get up. You can do it, Katie, get up.* He stared at the spot on the rugged coastline where she had fallen, willing her head to appear over the rock. *Come on, Katie, come on.* Next to him, he could feel Harry and Briggs both holding their breaths. Once again, he had blinked and Kate was gone. Forty years had passed and nothing had changed. He was still Waiting Walter, standing there watching Kate slip away from him.

When they found her, floating in the water at the base of the cliff, she had a severely broken leg and a possible concussion from hitting the rocks below. The Coast Guard base in Houghton wanted her brought back there, but Briggs, suddenly tender-hearted in the face of Walter's misery, persuaded them to airlift her back to Thunder Bay instead. Walter rode back in the boat with Harry – he couldn't just abandon him, after everything he had done. When he got back to Victor Street, the kids were awake and watching television. He asked the neighbour to stay a little longer, and then he called Shawn and Finn.

"I don't know where your sister is," he told Finn on the phone. "But your mother's in the hospital, and I've got the girls here."

"The hospital?" Finn sounded as though she had just woken up even though it was almost eleven in the morning. *I should make her come out on the coffee cruise tomorrow*, Walter thought. "What happened?"

"She fell off the roof," he said before he could think it through.

"I think Dallas is out with the car, but I'll come as soon as I can," Finn said, although Walter had a feeling it wouldn't be soon at all. "And I'll try Nicki's cell."

He got to the hospital before anyone else and found her lying on a bed behind a curtain in the emergency room. They didn't even have a proper room for her. Her leg was in traction, her arms were covered in scrapes, and she had an angry red welt on her fore-head that was growing into a goose egg. He sat down on the one chair next to the bed. He tried to meet her eyes, but they darted around the makeshift room, resting on a crack in the curtain.

"I told the kids you fell off the roof," he said.

"Why?"

"I didn't want them to know you were causing an international incident."

"Fine," said Kate.

Those were the last words they spoke to each other for the rest of the day. The kids came. There seemed to be some kind of tension between Finn and Nicki, but Walter didn't pay attention at the time, and didn't find out until weeks later that Nicki had spent the night with Finn's boyfriend. All he could think about was Kate disappearing between those rocks, and how part of him wished she had never been recovered, that the Coast Guard had just said, "Oh well" and headed back to Houghton. He wished he had jumped off Harry's boat and swum to shore. He wished he had pulled Kate out from between those rocks and carried her over his shoulder to the crumbling lighthouse and just stayed there, forever. But it was such a small part of him. He was angry at Kate for wanting something more than she wanted to be a part of this family. But he was also angry at himself for not wanting the same things that she did.

"As far as I know, you guys never found out that Kate didn't actually fall off the roof," Walter says now to Shawn and Katriina, who have been sitting silently in the cockpit of the *Veronica*, listening to him tell his story. "The Coast Guard impounded the *Miss Penelope* for three weeks, while the charges against Kate were pending. Eventually the Americans dropped all the charges except for trespassing, and Kate was fined fifty-five hundred dollars in an out-of-court settlement." He pauses. "They also ordered a psychological exam." How long would they have gone on without knowing, Walter wonders, if she hadn't been evaluated? Would they have just continued on, oblivious to the changes happening gradually, unobserved, Kate just slowly fading away to a shadow of her former self? At what point would they have rung the bell, called the game, admitted there was something wrong? Knowing the Parkers, Walter thinks, probably never.

"What was the diagnosis?" Katriina asks quietly.

"Frontotemporal dementia," says Walter, checking the depth finder as the GPS warns they are approaching a shoal. "Symptoms include loss of semantic understanding, social awareness, and executive function." He still has the pamphlet they gave him at the hospital, stuffed into the glove compartment of his truck – he didn't read it, but he remembers those words. *Semantic understanding, social awareness, executive function.* Things that make a human being a human being. "It won't affect her long-term memories," the neurologist had told him. "Just her ability to understand them." Walter still isn't sure he has heard of anything sadder.

Katriina pulls her legs up and wraps her arms around them. As her pants ride up over her ankles, Walter can see a trickle of blood dripping from a cut on her leg. *Oh, Katriina,* he thinks. *Why do you do this to yourself?* Shawn has moved over by the railing, gazing out over the lake, and so Walter pulls open the console beneath the dash and rummages through a first aid kit, searching for a bandage. He tucks one into his palm and passes it covertly to Katriina. She looks at him, surprised. He motions to her leg, and her face turns red. She mouths *Thank you* as she quietly removes the wrapper and covers the wound.

Shawn still hasn't said a word. Looking at the two of them, the pain on their faces, Walter suddenly wishes he hadn't said anything. He supposes somewhere deep down, he thought they already knew. But they were not prepared for this. And they are dealing with so much already, and not just in the past few days, with losing the baby and everything to do with Kate. For the first time, Walter can see how much they've been struggling, and for how long. He wants to tell them that they can make it through, that the pain will go away, that life will get easier. But he knows it wouldn't matter. These are things that you have to discover for yourself.

"So what does that mean?" Katriina asks. "For the future?" She is speaking to Walter, but her eyes are on Shawn's back as he hunches over the railing.

"It means that, eventually, she is going to forget everything," Walter says. He turns the wheel eastward, towards Isle Royale. "Including how to keep herself alive."

When Shawn finally speaks, his voice is hoarse. "Is that why she's been doing . . . what she's been doing?"

"No. It's actually the opposite. It's like . . ." Walter struggles to find the words, clenching and unclenching his hands on the wheel. "It's like she's scared of losing a part of herself. But it's a part of herself she doesn't understand anymore, so she's holding on all wrong." It's only as he says it out loud that he realizes this is what has been happening. "Don't tell your sisters yet, okay?"

Shawn nods.

In the distance, Walter can see a fleet of Coast Guard boats and a helicopter converging on an island. It's strange, he thinks. This part of herself that Kate is scared of losing, the part he always found hard to love, is now the one true part of her that remains. And as terrified as he is, as long as she is stealing boats and going over waterfalls, there is still a chance he hasn't lost her yet.

THIRTY-FOUR

Dear Mrs. Pelley,

My name is London Parker-Stewart, from Thunder Bay, Ontario, and for the tiniest millisecond of time in relation to the entire great history of our world, I dreamed I was in your shoes. Even though I'm sure your shoes, which are likely very expensive and hard to walk in, wouldn't really fit me. I'm sorry. That was a bad metaphor.

Let me start again.

I drove to Duluth from Thunder Bay with my grandmother so I could meet up with your husband and help him with his mission to save the world's sharks. Before I go any further, I just want you to know that while it might seem like I was more interested in the former than the latter, in all actuality the sharks are my main focus in life, and saving all animals in general. I believe that we as a society will ultimately be judged by how we treat those who are more helpless and voiceless than us, and that we have a responsibility to stand up for and protect those whose habitats and ways of life we have damaged with our own selfish ambition and consumerism and general antipathy towards our planet. But I'm sure I don't have to explain this to you, Mrs. Pelley, as you are married to one of the most dedicated and respected champions of animals that the world has ever seen.

I am writing this letter in the cabin of your husband's boat while my grandmother pilots. She also believes in the mission, and she believes in me. You may recognize my grandmother from the recent viral video of an old lady going over Kakabeka Falls in a whisky barrel. It has had over 10 million views on YouTube, and was featured on several news programs and talk shows, and was even the focus of a pretty lame skit on Saturday Night Live. *I am telling you this because I want you to know that I come from a family of brave and relentless women, Mrs. Pelley, women who long to defy the odds, not only to dream impossible dreams but to turn around and make them possible. My grandmother has the magic heart of a dragon, and I can only hope that some of that has been passed down to me.*

London puts down her pen and gazes out the cabin window. Outside in the cockpit, her grandmother stands at the wheel of the *Rum Runner*, her gaze fixed on some destination off in the distance. They have been taking turns watching for the shark, but London has a suspicion that her Nana is focused on something else, that she has set her own secret plan in motion. Or maybe London is just deluding herself. Her grandmother isn't capable of making secret plans anymore.

No one in the family ever talks about what's wrong with Nana. They won't even give it a name. Sometimes London wonders if they are scared of the word, or if they just don't think she will understand it, which makes her want to grab them and scream, "Dementia! She has dementia!" London is not stupid, she knows how to Google a few symptoms. But still, people treat her like she is just a baby who can't handle the truth.

But maybe it's not her they're keeping the truth from. Maybe they are so *blinded* by their own *hubris*, they can't even see what is going on in their own family. But London sees everything. Like how her sisters and brother hide from Nana when they are home because they are scared of what weird thing she is going to say to them. How her mom thinks that no one notices when she has to take the TV remote out of the freezer every morning on the sly and put it back on the coffee table. The way she pretends she is going to pick up some hair-colouring supplies when Nana can't find her own way home. The way she lies to Papa when he gets home and tells him everything is fine, and the way he lies and tells her he believes her.

And yes, maybe she did take advantage of the situation yesterday afternoon when she went to visit Nana at the hospital, expecting her to still be in that coma but instead finding her awake and wandering around her room, looking for her shoes.

"Nana," London said, putting her hand on her grandmother's shoulder. "Are you okay?"

"I'm fine, dear," Nana said. "I'd just like to get out of here. If I could just find something to put on my feet."

It was pretty clear to London that her grandmother had no idea what had happened to her. But London didn't try to explain it. "I think your Birkenstocks are in your suitcase," she said and pulled it out of the closet. Inside, she found a pair of what looked like aqua shoes that must have been the ones Nana wore while going over the falls.

While Nana pulled the aqua shoes on her feet, she eyed the suitcase. "Are we going on a trip?" she asked.

London took a deep breath. She thought about Adam Pelley, and his important mission to save the lake shark, and his beautiful eyes, the colour of the ocean on a calm, sunny day.

"Yes," she said. "We are."

I don't want to hurt you, Mrs. Pelley, that was not my intention in writing this letter, but I have to tell you this: your husband and I had a relationship. He told me he loved me. He told me he wanted me to be with him, to help him on his mission to save the planet. I am sorry if it hurts you to hear this, but I think it's best that you do, for your own sake. I imagine you are close in age to Adam, so you are not too old to start again, if you wanted to. You also probably have a successful career. I bet you're like a journalist or something, like one of those reporters on CNN who goes to war-torn areas and has to live in a tent and wear camo so you don't get shot, or maybe a lawyer who goes to work in a high-rise every day and wears business suits with little skirts instead of pants and very tall heels that you never fall over in. I also picture you with red hair, for some reason, and kind of looking like Scarlett Johansson. When I put all that together in my head, it makes you seem very intimidating, and I will never be as good as you in a million years. There is no reason at all why Adam would choose me over you, and at times I'm not sure why I don't just jump off this boat right now and drown myself in the lake.

Suffice it to say, I did not know that Adam was married. The entire time we were together I had no idea of your existence, and even now I don't know what your first name is. If I had known, it probably wouldn't have changed anything about the way I behaved, which is, I have to say, one hard truth about myself that this entire situation has revealed to me. It's like I looked into a mirror and I saw my soul, Mrs. Pelley, and I didn't really like what I saw there at all.

And when I went over to Adam sitting in the hotel lobby and I smiled and introduced myself, he looked right through me as if he didn't know me. And at first I was confused because of all the intimate things we had shared over the months – I just couldn't understand how he could dismiss me so easily, after telling me how much he wanted to be with me. But then he held out his hand for me to shake, and I saw the ring glinting there, and I thought, Ahh, now I understand. I don't know what made him change his mind, but I like to think it was a moment of conscience. That he had decided, even though he and I are basically soul mates who see the world through the same pair of eyes, that it was more important for him to honour his commitment to you.

Except, that wasn't true either. There was the other woman. Tall, blond, perfect in her dumb little skinny jeans and cable-knit sweater, walking across the lobby towards Adam like she was queen of the fucking world. London stood outside, her entire body filling with rage, using every ounce of her willpower to keep herself from smashing through the hotel window and throwing that stupid ugly skank up against the wall, pulling out chunks of her silky blond hair, breaking her cute little button nose with the heel of her palm. *Who does she think she is? Does she even know that Adam used to make cheese and jelly sandwiches for his little brother when his mom was at work? Does she even know that Adam cried during* Finding Nemo? Then another thought occurred to London: Did *she* really know those things? Had any of those things actually been true? Or had Adam been lying to her this whole time? He lied about being married. He lied about wanting London to be with him. He could have lied about everything.

She followed them, Adam and the girl, as they left the hotel and crossed the bridge to the marina, trying to keep herself together, to keep from screaming or crying or throwing herself off the bridge and into the cold, black waters of Duluth Harbour and, like, letting her eyes be eaten out by pickerel or something. When they got to the marina, Adam took the girl's hand and led her up onto the deck of the *Rum Runner* as if she were completely helpless, a delicate fucking princess who couldn't do anything on her own. Why would Adam want to be with someone who couldn't even climb up onto a boat by herself? What could he possibly see in her?

London sat on a bench by the main building and watched as the *Rum Runner* motored out into the calm waters of Lake Superior. *So much for high winds*, she thought. She sat there for two hours, waiting for them to come back. She had a vague idea that when they got back she was going to confront Adam for being a lying, cheating scumbag, but she fell asleep before she could come up with any sort of plan. When she woke up, the sun was just breaking over the horizon. The *Rum Runner* was back at its berth, and Adam and the girl were nowhere to be seen.

London wandered out onto the dock, towards the *Rum Runner*, and that's when she saw him. Adam, alone, standing at the very end of the dock, gazing out over the lake. Searching for the lake shark. In spite of herself, she felt sorry for him. She was sure it wasn't his choice to cancel the show. And no matter what a liar he was, he had still done so much good. How hard must it be to know that you can change the world, but some insurmountable obstacle is standing in your way?

London could still help him. She could still prove herself to him. If she brought the shark back then he would have to save it, no matter what "the man" told him he could or couldn't do.

While Adam stood watching the lake, London slipped onto the *Rum Runner*. She stood in the cockpit, holding her breath, looking at all the knobs and buttons and levers. *This is crazy*, she thought. *What am I going to do, motor off while he's just standing there?* Adam would be back any minute. In a moment of panic, she snatched the keys out of the ignition and jumped lightly back onto the dock, running as fast as she could all the way back to the hotel.

◆ ◆ ◆

*But I digress. This is not the real reason I am writing you,
Mrs. Pelley. I realize that I am a teenaged girl and we are
notoriously self-absorbed, so I can understand why you
might think this letter was simply a way for me to vent my
anger at being spurned by your husband, or a way to get
back at him for hurting me. But this is not about me. This is
about a shark, Mrs. Pelley. A sad, lonely, lost shark who is
slowly dying in an inhospitable habitat – "weak, confused,
and mercilessly hunted by locals who don't understand not
only the magnificence of this creature, but also the important scientific discoveries that could be made by studying its physiology," according to your husband's website.
I was moved by your husband's words, Mrs. Pelley. After
all, it was his dedication to the cause that made me fall
in love with him in the first place. And even if we couldn't
be together, I still felt I had a responsibility to try to help.
I could go home and curl up with my broken heart, or I
could do what I came here to do, and maybe in the process,
become a woman who your husband would be proud of.*

"Honey, are you okay in there?" London's grandmother sticks
her head in the cabin door.

"Yup. I'll be right out." London folds up the piece of paper
she is writing on and stuffs it in the back pocket of her jeans. *It's
stupid anyway*, she thinks. *As if I'm going to send a real, actual letter
to someone.*

In the cockpit, she sits on the bench next to her grandmother.
Nana looks so comfortable at the wheel, so natural, in the too-
large windbreaker they found in the cabin, the wind tossing her
grey curls around her head. "How do you know how to drive a
boat, Nana?"

Nana takes her hands off the wheel and looks at them, as though the answer is etched there somewhere in the lines on her palm. "I don't know, dear," she says. She lowers her hands. "Who does this boat belong to?"

"I told you, it's my friend Adam's." She had told Nana this an hour ago, but it's like her grandmother's brain is a sieve, and her words are like water flowing through the little holes. In fact, she probably wouldn't remember anything London told her right now. "Actually, Adam's not really my friend," London says slowly. "I thought he was my boyfriend, but I was wrong."

"Oh, well." Nana pauses. "You're too young to have a boyfriend anyway."

London pulls the sleeves of her sweater down over her hands. "I'm so stupid," she says, blinking back tears. "How could I actually believe that someone like Adam Pelley could be in love with me?"

"I believe it," says Nana. "A boy would have to be crazy to *not* be in love with you."

A confession starts bubbling up inside London, and she struggles to keep it in but it bursts out through her seams. "Sometimes I think it could all just be a lie, you know? And maybe when he didn't recognize me, he wasn't really pretending at all," she says. "But I mean, what else am I supposed to believe? That someone I once considered my friend pretended to be the person I admire most in the world to trick me into telling secrets about myself? That she thought it would be hilarious to make me believe that I was special enough to be loved by Adam Pelley?"

"My darling," Nana says gravely. "You are the most special person in the world. Look at what you're doing." She waves her arm out towards the lake.

London shakes her head. "All I did was steal a boat."

"You took a chance." Nana smiles. "You're going to change the world, my sweet Serafina."

"I'm not –" London stops. What does it matter? So what if

Nana wants to believe that she is Aunt F? Or if London wants to believe she was really talking to Adam Pelley all that time? They are speeding across Lake Superior in a stolen boat looking for a shark in the middle of the world's largest lake. Reality is basically, like, *completely fluid* at this point. They should both be allowed to live in their ridiculous delusions for a little while longer.

"Oh my," says Nana. "What's that over there?"

London stands up, peering out into the lake. "Is that . . . a fin?"

And suddenly, there it is, coming towards them. A dorsal fin, slicing through the surface of the water at breakneck speed, heading straight for their boat. Nana cuts the engine and they both run to the railing, watching as the fin submerges and a long, grey body glides beneath the boat.

"It's the shark," London breathes. A bull shark, named for his stocky shape, broad, flat snout, and aggressive behaviour, with a bite force of up to thirteen hundred pounds. Found in warm, shallow waters along coasts and in rivers, and known to survive in brackish and even fresh water. Sighted only as far north as the Mississippi River in Illinois.

Until now.

London and her grandmother race to the other side of the boat, staring incredulously as the fin resurfaces and swims away. "He's beautiful, isn't he?" Nana says eventually.

"Yes," London whispers.

She tries to remember now how she imagined she was going to save him. Had she planned on jumping into the lake and wrestling him into the boat? Was she going to tie him up with a rope and tow him back to shore? She had pictured him weak and disoriented, near death, maybe even somehow understanding that she was rescuing him and submitting to her. But the more she watches the shark, the more she realizes he isn't weak and disoriented, he isn't near death, he isn't sad or lonely, and he certainly isn't about to let a bunch of northern Minnesotan redneck fishermen take him down. He is just a shark out having an adventure, doing something that he was probably told all his life that sharks weren't supposed to do, but he did it anyway because he is his own shark and he doesn't have to abide by, like, *society's rules* or whatever. He probably didn't fit in at home in the Gulf of Mexico, and he was sure there was a whole incredible world out there, just waiting to be explored.

This shark has the magic heart of a dragon.

They watch the shark for a few more minutes, the boat rocking silently in the breeze, until the fin disappears under the surface of the lake and doesn't reappear. Behind them, London can hear the distant wail of a siren. She knows they don't have much time left. "They're coming for us," she says.

"That's okay," Nana says, hands on the rail, gazing out across the lake to the horizon. "We're almost there."

Sure we are, thinks London. She takes the piece of paper out of her back pocket and begins to write.

Mrs. Pelley, this letter is an apology, but also a request. Tell Adam not to worry about the shark. The shark is doing just fine without him.

THIRTY-FIVE

From high atop a cliff on a rocky outcropping just west of Isle Royale, Kate watches a boat approach from the north. Even before she can make out the shape of it, she knows it is one of Walter's. Had she known all along that if she came to this spot he would find her? But how could she possibly know that? She remembers being here before, though. Something about the way the cliff feels under her hands when she climbs it, the way the rough rock scrapes against her palms. It's familiar, giving her a feeling somewhere in her brain like the hairs on her arm standing on end. She has done this before.

Kate doesn't remember how she got here, but there is another boat floating placidly in the small cove below and she has a vague idea that her granddaughter is down there, too. Her name escapes Kate now, but it will come back – it always does. Until, she supposes, the one time that it doesn't. That's when she will know it's all over. If she is still able to know things at all. She peels back layers in her mind: the lake, the marina, a boat, her granddaughter handing her a key, a hotel, a long drive, a sandwich, a hospital, a waterfall. That was what started this whole thing: the waterfall. At least the waterfall is still there, for now. She circles it cautiously, sneaking glances at it, praying it doesn't disappear, too. The layers peel back somewhat easily now, but even as she thinks these words she can feel them slipping away from her. What came after the boat – the drive, the hospital? Gone – the way a star disappears when you try to look right at it. The past few days are now only something that she can glimpse out of the corner of her eye.

She watches as Walter pulls his boat up along the other boat and ties them up together. There are two others with him, the boy and his wife, who climb from one boat to the other as Walter picks his way over the rocks in his workboots and jeans, carefully, precisely, never losing his balance. He pulls himself up over the last section of cliff and comes to a rest by sitting next to her.

"Hi, Katie," he says.

"Hi, Walter."

Below them, the boats rustle against each other as the lake laps up against the edge of the rocks. Kate can see her granddaughter inside the cabin, talking to the boy and his wife. She wonders if she will ever find out what this trip has been about, or if she has known all along and just forgotten. Just like almost everything else – she only has frustratingly random snippets, images, out-of-context moments that bring her no clarity, no cohesiveness, no narrative of what the past few days have been about.

"I wonder if there's treasure here," Kate says. "It seems like the kind of place that would have treasure."

Walter turns his head towards her. His legs are drawn up, his arms resting on his knees, workboots planted against the rock. "You're right," he says. "It does." He narrows his eyes. "Do you remember this place, Kate?"

"I . . ." She searches her mind for a way to stall, to play it coy, all the tricks she uses to make it through conversations. But her tricks have always been useless on Walter. "I keep thinking I might. But I don't. Not really."

Walter nods. "You've been here before. Nine years ago. You fell off the cliff into the water and broke your leg."

"Oh dear," says Kate. "What does *cliff* mean again? It sounds so familiar."

"It's not important."

But it *is* important. It's important to her. She tries to focus, running through her word associations. *Fall. Water.* Is this that place? It can't be that place. "The waterfall?" she asks tentatively. She turns to look behind her, but everything is all wrong. No river. No bridge. No people. Just the remains of the house with the lights that guides boats, crumbling back into the earth.

"It was before the waterfall. You were out on the lake for a while. And then you came here."

"Oh." There is something there, something she can almost catch on to, streaking through her mind and then disappearing. *Lake, lake.* "When I fell through the ice," she says, uncertainty in her voice. That doesn't seem right either.

Walter's shoulders tense up, and she knows she is wrong again. "That was when we were kids, Katie. At Chippewa."

Chippewa. The word means nothing to her. But in her mind she sees a watery darkness, her path to the light above obscured by something solid, impenetrable. The image scares her, and she picks up a rock and turns it over and over in her hand, its cool, smooth surface against her skin bringing her back to the present.

Holding the stone in her palm, she gazes out over the lake. Not the waterfall, not the ice. The water, here. "I fall into water a lot," she says.

A beat, and then Walter bursts into laughter. And it is so unexpected and beautiful that she laughs, too, even though she doesn't know why they are laughing. It feels good. He has been so angry with her lately that it seems like years since she has heard him laugh. *But I made him do this,* she thinks. *I'm making him laugh like this.*

"Yes, you did," Walter says. "And you do fall in the water a lot. I never even realized." He pauses. "You did other things, too, you know."

"I wish I could remember."

He studies her face, as though trying to decide whether he should actually say out loud what he is thinking. "You snuck onto McConnell's farm to ride their horse every night for three straight weeks. You and London tobogganed off the roof that year the snowbanks were so high. You taught Serafina how to ride a bike with no hands. You won an MGB off of Peter Soloway in a drag race. You went to Paris," he adds, leaning over to adjust the lace of his boot.

"Paris," she says. The word floats in front of her, just beyond her grasp, as do all the others. She can see Walter's body rocking back and forth with the rhythm of his breath. What must it be like, she wonders, to have to hold all these memories for both of them? How will he manage? Where will he put them all?

She folds the stone into her palm, squeezing. "I'm scared," she says quietly, the words wringing out of her as she squeezes the stone tighter. "Soon it will all be gone."

"*I* won't," says Walter. He pries her fingers away from the stone and takes it from her, slipping it into his breast pocket. "I'm not going anywhere, okay, Katie?"

Those words fill her with relief, although she doesn't know why. On the horizon, she can see boats approaching, flashing lights and sirens, and this, too, seems familiar. "What happens now?"

"We'll figure it out," says Walter. "I'm ready. I'm not waiting anymore."

His eyes are full of meaning that Kate can't understand, but she knows what he has just said is important, so she reaches out and takes his hand. It feels strong, familiar. It occurs to her that she has never read Walter's palm; she has never so much as looked at it, all those pathways, the map of his life. She wonders what she would see there. If this were the movies, she would look at Walter's palm now and see one strong, thick, steadfast love line, matching her own. And she would suddenly realize, after all this time, that he had, in fact, been the one great love of her life. It would be a poignant closing chapter to their lives together, one last beautiful moment before she descends into the deepening darkness of her memory.

But this is not the movies. And so instead she just holds his hand in hers, hoping that this moment is one of the ones she will remember.

"What was going through your mind that morning?"
"Which morning are you talking about, dear?"
"She means the morning you went over the falls, Mom."
"Oh, well. I suppose I was thinking about what a beautiful day it was. The sun was shining, and there wasn't a cloud in the sky."

◆ ◆ ◆

Three months after what the Parkers now refer to as "the incident," Finn is back in Thunder Bay to join the rest of her family for a taping of the first episode of Cassandra Coelho's new talk show, *Northwest Now*, featuring an interview with none other than the Conqueror of Kakabeka herself. Finn had thought they could do better – *The Ellen Show*, maybe, or at least a national program, *Canada AM* or something – but it is astonishing how quickly people forget about internet celebrities these days. The only person who still cares about the Conqueror of Kakabeka is Cassandra Coelho, whose career has been made (if a regional morning talk show could be considered "made") by her coverage of the drop, the bang, the flip, and the subsequent boat chase across Lake Superior, which ended up trending on social media for about thirty seconds before another celebrity decided to have an affair with a nanny.

They're now all gathered at the television studio before the taping, stuffed into a room they were told was the "green room," but which Finn is sure is actually just a broom closet – Walter and Kate, Shawn and Katriina, Nicki and Hamish, and Finn. Good old seventh-wheel Finn, although somehow the thought doesn't bother her as much anymore.

Fifteen minutes before the show is scheduled to go live, Shawn pulls Finn out of the green room and into the hallway. "You need to go on stage with her," he tells her.

A flutter of panic skitters through her veins. "Um, no," she replies.

"Someone has to do it," Shawn says. "She can't go on by herself. We all decided it should be you."

The flutter grows into a pounding. The prospect of having to wrangle Kate on live television – even if it is only a local news show – is enough to send her screaming back to Mississauga for good. "Why can't one of you do it?"

Shawn sighs. "We all *live* here, Finn," he says. "You don't. It doesn't matter if you humiliate yourself."

"You don't get to play that particular card for much longer."

"I know." Whenever Shawn talks about his family's impending move to Ottawa, his voice is tinged with sadness, although Finn knows he is ready. She has been trying to be supportive, unlike Nicki, who swore she would never speak to him again. Kate just stared, blinking rapidly, until Finn explained that, yes, Ottawa was, in fact, a city. "I know the timing is terrible," Shawn had said when he told them. "I don't know if I can do this." But Kate just touched his face, smiling up at him brightly. "You can do anything, Shawny," she said.

"It's going to be fine, Shawn," Finn reassures him now.

"I hope so. I'm ready for what comes next. We're all ready." He breathes out in a long, steady exhale. "It's just turning out to be a lot harder than I thought it would be."

"Look, if anyone knows how hard it is to leave the Parkers, it's me. But I also know that unlike me, you'll do it the right way."

"What, you mean like actually telling people I'm leaving instead of sneaking off in the middle of the night like a criminal?"

"Thanks a lot, jerkface." She pauses. "And okay. Fine, I will go on the stupid show because – see? – I'm still paying for doing it the wrong way."

Shawn grins. "Also because you love us and want to be there for Mom."

"Yeah, sure, that, too."

Back in the green room, Kate is sitting at a small vanity, gazing at herself serenely in the mirror, while Katriina stands behind her, fixing her hair. Walter sits next to her in a suit and tie, holding her hand, his leg bouncing up and down. Sitting still was never one of Walter's fortes, and it had gotten worse since he handed over the day-to-day operations of Superior Tours to Nicki and Hamish.

"Why in the hell would you do that?" Finn had said when her father told her his plan. Old habits die hard.

"You know why. I need to be here for your mother. Besides, Nicki and Hamish both know how to run a business."

"Hamish is a *bootlegger*!"

"Well, yes, but he's a *successful* bootlegger."

And despite Finn's warnings that Nicki and Hamish were sure to turn Walter's boats into a Mexican drug-smuggling fleet, it actually hasn't been a total disaster. Even now, Nicki is coaching Kate on ways to work a Superior Tours plug into her interview. "If Cassandra asks if going over the falls was fun, you should say, 'Not as fun as one of our new Friday-night booze cruises,'" Nicki instructs her, holding up a flyer. "We have discounts for groups over twenty."

Walter frowns. "The *Miss Penelope* only has seating capacity for twenty."

Nicki waves him off. "They never all show up anyway."

A production assistant with a headset and a clipboard comes to the door. "It's time," she says.

Kate doesn't respond. She simply pats her hair in the mirror, humming under her breath.

"Mom?" Finn tries to catch Kate's eye in the mirror. "It's time."

"Of course," says Kate, standing up. "It's time." It's obvious she has no idea what it is time for, but it doesn't matter. Together, they will get her through it.

◆ ◆ ◆

"But there must have been something that happened that spurred you to take that barrel over the falls. Were you trying to kill yourself?"

"Of course not, dear. Why on earth would I want to do that? Life is too short as it is."

◆ ◆ ◆

After the taping, the production assistant asks if Walter, Nicki, and Shawn will join Kate and Finn on stage for a photo. "We'd like to have a picture on the website, for promo," she says.

As the five of them gather on the set, the assistant enters from backstage, followed by two crew members wheeling something on a dolly.

"Oh, *hell* no," says Nicki, inhaling sharply.

A wave of nausea washes over Finn as soon as she recognizes what it is. The barrel. They are wheeling in the fucking barrel.

"Isn't this great?" asks the production assistant. "It will really get people excited about the show."

"Are you kidding me?" says Shawn.

"Where did you even get that?" asks Finn. What she wants to ask is, *Who could have possibly thought, in the midst of everything, "I bet that crazy woman in a coma will want her whisky barrel back, I'd better go grab it."*

"We don't know where it came from," the production assistant replies, shrugging. "It just showed up at the studio one day."

"This is fucked up," says Nicki. Her mouth is pinched in a hard line, but there is a hint of something other than anger in her eyes, a vulnerability Nicki has never let Finn see before.

"Let's just get it over with," Walter hisses through gritted teeth.

They position themselves awkwardly around the barrel, which appears disturbingly unscathed by its trip over the falls. Finn can't help touching it. The wood is rough under her hand, and the cold steel rings bite into her flesh. She glances over at her mother to see if she recognizes the barrel. But if she does, she isn't letting on.

"Say *Kakabeka*," the production assistant says, holding up a camera. No one does. Finn forces her mouth into a fake smile, and from the tension around her, she can tell everyone else is doing the same.

Everyone except Kate. Her smile is genuine. "I knew I could get a better photo out of all of you," she says. Everyone whips their heads around to look at her. The flash goes off.

Later, as they are gathering their things and preparing to leave, Nicki grabs Finn's arm. "Come with me," she says. "I need your help with something."

Finn raises her eyebrows. All she wants is a cold beer and the couch. "Can't Hamish help you?"

"I need *you* for this."

Finn follows her out to the parking lot, where a cold October breeze blows from the west, whipping dead leaves around in a vortex. Finn zips her jacket up higher. As they approach Hamish's

410

truck, Finn can distinctly see the top of the barrel sticking out of the flatbed. "What . . . how did you get that?"

"I stole it, okay?" Nicki turns to look behind her, checking furtively to see if anyone is watching them as she bounces from foot to foot. "I just can't stand the thought of it being here." Her eyes widen with that same bewildering expression, and that's when Finn realizes it's fear.

Out of everyone in the family, Finn had assumed Nicki would have been the one least surprised by Kate's diagnosis – after all, she had been dealing with Kate's lapses every day for years. But when Walter finally sat them down and explained those two words, *frontotemporal dementia*, Nicki lost it, cancelling all her appointments and wandering around the house in her bathrobe for days, scaring Finn so much that she stayed an extra week just to make sure Nicki didn't drown herself in the Kam or something. But now, watching her sister stare at that barrel as if it were full of poisonous snakes, it occurs to her that for Nicki, knowing what is going to happen to their mother only makes it worse. So far, she has been able to deal with her lapses. The diagnosis means that one day she won't.

"Then let's get rid of it," Finn says.

With the whisky barrel clattering and banging in the bed of the truck, they drive back towards Victor Street. When they get to the corner of Broadway and Victor, Nicki pulls the truck over to the side of the road, by the mailboxes on the shoulder next to the vacant lot, where a house and its foundations had tumbled over the bank into the river years before Nicki and Finn were even born. Nicki pulls down the gate and together they haul the barrel off the truck. It is heavier than Finn expected.

"How the hell was Mom able to carry this?" Finn groans as they each grab an end and lug it over the guardrail.

"She's a lot stronger than she looks," says Nicki. "Must be all those steroids."

411

They stumble through the overgrown grass across the lot to the edge of the cliff a hundred feet above the Kam – just a few miles downstream from where their mother went over the falls – where the ground has crumbled away, leaving a few twisted roots and gnarled tree trunks protruding from the eroding earth. Below them, the riverbank is thick with saplings and underbrush, tangled vines and deadwood. But the view is spectacular: the sparkling river beneath them, snaking towards the mill; the Nor'Wester Mountains erupting against the southeastern skyline, flecked with the last remnants of autumn's orange and red; the wide, manicured lawns of Riverdale rolling across the low southern riverbank.

"Okay," says Finn. "Let's do it."

A curious crow watches them from its perch on top of a huge red pine as they swing the barrel back and forth, back and forth, until Nicki nods and they let it go. About halfway down, the barrel bounces into the edge of the cliff and gets caught in the branches of a tree, swaying precariously as the tree tries to balance its weight. Finn holds her breath. *Come on*, she thinks.

"Come on," she hears Nicki say softly beside her. "Come on, come on."

The crow caws loudly, taking off from the pine, startling them. Then a branch snaps and the barrel falls free, tumbling the rest of the way down the cliff into the river. They watch in silence as it disappears under the water for a moment before bobbing to the surface and floating serenely downriver towards the lake and whatever lies beyond. Finn doesn't care where it ends up. Just let it be gone.

"I ended things with Dallas," Nicki says, her eyes still focused on the barrel.

Finn stares at her, unsure how to respond. Nicki's back is straight, her chin tilted upward slightly, as though she is daring the world to throw something else at her. Nicki has always faced the world as if bracing for impact, and she's clearly expecting resistance from Finn now – a rant about how stupid she is, a withering *I-told-you-so*, a punch in the face.

There are many things Finn wants to say, and she knows that, eventually, they will have to talk – about Dallas and Ross, about their mother, about the future. About everything. But for now, she takes Nicki's hand. Her fingers are ice-cold, but Finn doesn't let go.

◆ ◆ ◆

"But why, Mrs. Parker? Why did you do it?"

"Everyone keeps asking me that. Why? It's as if you don't already know the answer."

"Well, Mrs. Parker, I don't think we do."

"Everyone wants to be remembered for something. That's the only reason for doing anything in life – to be remembered, and to be worth remembering. For people to know you were here, you existed. Something like this . . . well. People will remember it. Even if I don't."

◆ ◆ ◆

"*Hexad*. Double word score." Finn lays her tiles down carefully, lining the edges up perfectly with the square outlines on the board. "Forty points."

"That's not a real word," says Kate, frowning.

"Yes, it is. It means a group of six."

Kate fiddles with her tiles. "You know so many words. And I only know a few." She looks up, her face brightening. "I know a hexad!"

"I'm sure you know more than a hexad, Mom." Finn gets up to make some tea. "Take your time," she calls over her shoulder. "I've got nothing else to do tonight."

Finn had, in fact, made plans to go visit Alyssa and her baby girl that evening. When Kate first suggested they play Scrabble, Finn hadn't taken her seriously.

"You don't really want to do that, do you?" she asked. What she really meant, of course, was, *You're not capable of doing that anymore.* Finn didn't want to hurt her mother, but she didn't want to humiliate her either.

But Kate insisted. "It's something we used to do, right?" she'd asked, her eyes wide and guileless, and Finn realized the window of time for playing Scrabble with her mother was rapidly closing.

"Yes, Mom, you're right."

And so they pulled out the old board and set it up in the kitchen, the way they used to. They counted out the tiles.

Finn started off with *frog*. Kate stared at her tiles, then stared at the board, then stared at her tiles again. While Finn waited, she wondered if Kate would remember how she used to make up words: *daker, farden, pizzi. Sluba.* If she plays a nonsense word now, will it be on purpose? Probably not.

"Aha!" said Kate finally. She put down her tiles: *frog*.

Finn gave a short laugh. "Good word, Mom," she said.

Now, Finn pours water into the kettle, pulls a tea bag out of the canister on the counter, and drops it in the brown Betty – the same pot that her mother has used for as long as Finn can remember. She never even washed it, just rinsed it out. "There's residue in there from a thousand cups of tea and a thousand conversations," she would always say. Long before her mother started losing her memory, she was already obsessed with holding on to the past.

As Finn is pulling down two teacups from the cupboard, London comes into the kitchen. "Hey, Aunt F," she whispers. "Can I talk to you?"

"Sure," says Finn. They both glance over at Kate, who is still engrossed with her tiles.

"I just . . ." London leans against the counter. She pulls on a lock of her hair, wrapping it around and around her finger. There are more colours in her hair now, blue and purple as well as the pink. "I feel like . . ." The lock of hair goes in her mouth.

Finn reaches up and brushes it away. "Say what you have to say, honey."

London glances towards Kate. "She's worse, isn't she?"

Finn considers lying. It would be the kind thing. But she doesn't want to keep things from London anymore. "Yes. She is worse."

Her hair now off limits, London starts chewing on her nail. "Is it because . . . of the Duluth thing?" She pauses. "Is she worse because of me? Did I do this to her?"

"Oh my god, no," says Finn, feeling her heart break a little at the worried expression on London's face. How long has she been carrying this particular guilt? Finn takes London's shoulders by the hand and looks her straight in her Parker-grey eyes. "London, this has nothing to do with anything that you did, okay? This is just the way the disease works. It gets worse."

London blinks away tears. "Are you sure?"

"Positive." The kettle reaches a scream, and Finn turns back to the counter, pouring the boiling water into the brown Betty. She's not sure London is entirely convinced, but at least her niece is confiding in her again.

"Actually, I think that trip with you was the most fun she's had in years."

London smiles reluctantly. "It had its moments," she admits.

"Maybe we can all go to Duluth together sometime," Finn says. "You, me, your mom –"

"Oh god, no," London says, smiling for real this time. "Not Mom. Besides, in case you've forgotten, I'm grounded for basically the rest of eternity."

"I'm sure we can work something out," says Finn.

"Okay!" Kate sings, clapping her hands together. "I did it!"

Finn and London return to the table, where Kate has played the word *destin*. Finn shakes her head. "You need a 'y' for that, Mom. It's 'destiny.'"

"No, it's 'destin.'" She pronounces it "desTAN."

"That's French," says London, sitting down in a chair next to Kate. "French for 'destiny.'" She puts her hand on Kate's arm. "Did Lydia teach you that?"

Kate blinks. "Who's Lydia?" she asks.

"Yeah, who's Lydia?" Finn asks, too. She carries the tea tray over the table and sets it near the board, raising an eyebrow at London. Someone they met on the road, perhaps? Maybe one of London's old French teachers? Why would she expect Kate to know who she was?

But London is staring at Kate, and there is a look on her face that Finn can't quite describe – as though she is overcome with an emotion she is too young to understand. "You don't remember?" London asks finally, squeezing Kate's arm. "Are you sure?"

"I'm quite sure, dear," says Kate. She picks up a tile and moves it next to a different tile, humming under her breath.

London sits back in her chair, and Finn is surprised to see there are tears in her eyes. "It's okay," London says. "I do." She puts her head on Kate's shoulder as the tears slide down her cheeks. Kate tilts her head, resting it contentedly on top of London's.

This family, Finn thinks, watching the way their bodies fit together to form the shape of something entirely new. *Even if I had spent every day of my life in this house, it would still be full of mysteries.* She sits back down at the table and begins to pour the tea.

◆ ◆ ◆

"One last question, Mrs. Parker. Knowing how it all turned out, would you do it again?"

"That question makes no sense, dear. We never know how things will turn out before we act. We can imagine all the different permutations of our possible futures, but we can't choose the one we like the best. We just have to live our lives and trust that where we end up is where we are meant to be."

"So you don't believe we can choose to change our destiny? . . . Mrs. Parker?"

"Mom?"

"I'm sorry, what's 'destiny' again? It sounds so familiar. But I'm afraid I don't know what it means."

ACKNOWLEDGEMENTS

Thanks to my amazing editor, Anita Chong, and everyone at McClelland & Stewart; my superhero agent, Chris Bucci; Michael Christie, Kris Bertin, Naben Ruthnum, Matthew J. Trafford, Taslim Alani, Shantah Kanhai-Evans, Peter and Natalie Smyk, and Valerie Uusitalo, for reading, listening, pushing me, and making me leave the house; Andrea Novoa, Samantha Mendendorp, and the rest of my dance family at World Dance Centre for keeping me sane; the Bean Fiend for having plug-ins at every booth; the Canada Council for the Arts and the Ontario Arts Council for the ongoing support; and Darren and Michelle McChristie and all my colleagues at *The Walleye – Thunder Bay's Arts and Culture Magazine* for your vision, your commitment to the Thunder Bay arts community, and your unwavering belief in the vast potential of our city.

Special thanks to my family: Richard Jones, Bonita Jones, Erin Jones, Shelagh Hagen, and Elving and Sandra Josephson. You can all stop asking when the book is coming out now.

And, as always, to Cory and Morgan, for letting me live with you.

The title of Tanya's thesis, "Constraints on the formation of depositional placer accumulations in coarse alluvial braided river systems," is borrowed from the title of an MSc thesis by John Peter Burton of Lakehead University (Ontario Geological Survey, 1991), which is excellent reading for anyone interested in geology.

DISCUSSION QUESTIONS FOR
WE'RE ALL IN THIS TOGETHER BY AMY JONES

1. Amy Jones tells the story of the Parker family from the perspectives of multiple characters. Why do you think that is? Discuss what you learned about the characters in their own chapters versus what other characters tell you about them. Did anything surprise you in this respect? Why are parts of the story told from Tanya's, Adam's, and Anastasia's perspectives?

2. In different ways, members of the Parker family feel outside of or apart from the family, even in one another's presence. Why do you think that is? Discuss what it means to be a Parker. Is there any Parker who feels a sense of belonging? Does anything about the Parker family remind you of your own family?

3. How do themes of familial bonds and broken loyalty manifest in *We're All in This Together*? How do members of the Parker family deal with betrayal? Is there anything a character does in this book that, if it were your relative, you wouldn't be able to forgive?

4. Family systems theory posits that families are an emotional unit comprised of individuals who do not operate in isolation from the family system. Each person has a role to play. What is the emotional quality of the Parker family? What roles in the family do various characters play? Explore how these roles shift throughout the course of the novel.

5. Though Finn is isolated and does not seem to like her life in Toronto, before she leaves for Thunder Bay she worries if she will be able to return to her life there. Do you think she wants to go back to Toronto after visiting her family, or does she really hope something will keep her in Thunder Bay? What does she need from the people in her hometown?

6. When Finn sees Nicki's children for the first time in three years, she feels jealous of the twins' closeness and regrets having left London behind when she left Thunder Bay. Finn's response to Ross is more complicated. What do her reactions to Nicki's children tell you about Finn?

7. Describe Walter and Kate's relationship. Why did Kate ask Walter to marry her? Was she happy in their marriage? Walter fell in love with Lake Superior when Kate was in Europe and it became  an almost deific force in his life: "He was certain that he was meant to make serving Lake Superior his life's goal. To thank it for giving Kate back" (91). What does the lake offer Walter that Kate does not?

8. Shawn's closeness to Finn bothers Katriina. Are her fears valid and/or validated? When Shawn wakes up at Hanna's house, he says he's "frequently disturbed by how much she looks like Katriina – a younger, blonder, hippie-chick Katriina – but right now he finds it comforting. It's like being with his wife without having to actually be with his wife" (151). Why doesn't Shawn respond compassionately to Katriina when she tells him she's lost the baby?

9.   Katriina finds a kind of solace in the Paulsson house, though it is the site of both crisis and catharsis for her. Explore Katriina's purchase of the Paulsson house and why she needs it. Why is Katriina fixated on Claudia? In the end, do you think that Shawn and Katriina should stay together?

10.   What is the significance of London's obsession with sharks? Discuss the connection between the prospect of a salt-water shark in Lake Superior and London's experience in her family and in her community. What characteristics does London share with Finn and with Nicki? Who is she more like?

11.   Tanya says that she punched Finn because "She got angry, thinking about how much time she spent thinking about Dallas, and how little time he spent thinking about her. And so she hit the woman. It wasn't fair" (209). Is this the full truth? For what other reasons might Tanya have hit Finn?

12.   Discuss the character of Nicki. Is she a sympathetic character or someone you can identify with even though she is frequently belligerent? Is Finn fair in her assessments of her twin sister? What redeeming qualities does Nicki have that Finn fails to see?

13.   Why does Nicki sleep with Dallas in 2003? How do her reasons for involving herself with him change over time? Why, ultimately, does Finn forgive Nicki for sleeping with Dallas?

14.   Describe how each member of the family reacts to Kate's plunge over the falls. What are the shared sentiments? Is it curious or significant that the Parkers spend little time together at Kate's bedside? Has Kate's illness had an effect on how the family responds to her hospitalization?

15. Kate's condition is something the whole family is tacitly aware of but that none of the adults want to face. What effects of Kate's memory loss ripple through the lives of the characters in the book? Would anything have been different if the family had been able to face her illness together?

16. Was Kate lucid when she planned to go over the falls? What about when she didn't acknowledge Finn's pain after the fight at Nicki's wedding? (22). When she convinces London that together they will save the shark? (248). All of these actions have significant ramifications for the Parker family. Discuss whether or not Kate's cognitive function is relevant in regards to the outcome of her actions.

17. Prior to European settlement, the Ojibwe (Chippewa) people inhabited the land that is now Thunder Bay. Today the Fort William Reserve is located adjacent to the city. In 1970, the twin cities Fort William and Port Arthur amalgamated to form the city of Thunder Bay. Were you familiar with Thunder Bay before you read this novel? What did you learn about the city and the region from reading this book?

18. In what ways do Lake Superior, the Kaministiquia River, and the city of Thunder Bay compel and repel various characters? What elements of the geography depicted in the book are integral to the story? Could the story be set anywhere else? Describe what the book reveals about Canadian identification with and connection to the land.

19. *"If this were a movie,* Kate would always say, and then instead of being sad about life not being a movie, she would just go ahead and make it like one" (154). Is this an accurate interpretation of Kate? "If this were a movie . . . " is an expression other Parkers use, too. What does the use of this expression suggest about how things are passed through families and down generations?

20. We later learn that in Paris, Lydia said to Kate, "'If this were a movie, the credits would be rolling right now . . . '" (286) and we can surmise that Kate inherited the turn of phrase from her. What else have the Parkers inherited as a result of Kate's relationship with Lydia? Are there things in your life you've inherited as a result of events in the lives of your parents, grandparents, and other ancestors?

21. The concept of destiny suggests there's a force shaping events of the future. Do you believe in destiny? How does destiny affect the Parkers? As a result of Kate's going over the falls in a barrel, will anything be different for London and her generation of Parkers than it was for Kate and Walter or Finn, Nicki, and Shawn? Will anything be different for the Parker family unit?

© Spun Creative

AMY JONES's first novel, *We're All in This Together*, was a national bestseller, won the Northern Lit Award, and was a finalist for the Stephen Leacock Medal for Humour. Her debut collection of stories, *What Boys Like*, won the Metcalf-Rooke Award and was a finalist for the ReLit Award. She won the 2006 CBC Literary Prize for Short Fiction, was a finalist for the 2005 Bronwen Wallace Award, and is a graduate of the Optional Residency MFA Program in Creative Writing at the University of British Columbia. Her fiction has appeared in *Best Canadian Stories* and *The Journey Prize Stories*. Originally from Halifax, she lived in Thunder Bay for many years before moving to Toronto, where she is at work on her second novel, *Every Little Piece of Me*. Follow her on Twitter @AmyLauraJones.